# TALES OF THE UNCANNY AND SUPERNATURAL

# TALES OF THE UNCANNY AND SUPERNATURAL

*by*

ALGERNON BLACKWOOD

SPRING BOOKS

LONDON · NEW YORK · SYDNEY · TORONTO

THE HAMLYN PUBLISHING GROUP LTD
LONDON • NEW YORK • SYDNEY • TORONTO
HAMLYN HOUSE, FELTHAM, MIDDLESEX, ENGLAND

This edition first published 1962
Eighth impression 1969
Printed in Czechoslovakia by PZ, Bratislava
SBN 600 038505

# CONTENTS

*The Terror of the Twins* and *The Lost Valley* are included by kind permission of Messrs. Grayson and Grayson

## THE DOLL

Some nights are merely dark, others are dark in a suggestive way as though something ominous, mysterious, is going to happen. In certain remote outlying suburbs, at any rate, this seems true, where great spaces between the lamps go dead at night, where little happens, where a ring at the door is a summons almost, and people cry 'Let's go to town!' In the villa gardens the mangy cedars sigh in the wind, but the hedges stiffen, there is a muffling of spontaneous activity.

On this particular November night a moist breeze barely stirred the silver pine in the narrow drive leading to the 'Laurels' where Colonel Masters lived, Colonel Hymber Masters, late of an Indian regiment, with many distinguished letters after his name. The housemaid in the limited staff being out, it was the cook who answered the bell when it rang with a sudden, sharp clang soon after ten o'clock—and gave an audible gasp half of surprise, half of fear. The bell's sudden clangour was an unpleasant and unwelcome sound. Monica, the Colonel's adored yet rather neglected child, was asleep upstairs, but the cook was not frightened lest Monica be disturbed, nor because it seemed a bit late for the bell to ring so violently; she was frightened because when she opened the door to let the fine rain drive in she saw a black man standing on the steps. There, in the wind and the rain, stood a tall, slim nigger holding a parcel.

Dark-skinned, at any rate, he was, she reflected afterwards, whether negro, Hindu or Arab; the word 'nigger' describing any man not really white. Wearing a stained yellow mackintosh and dirty slouch hat, and 'looking like a devil, so help me, God', he shoved the little parcel at her out of the gloom, the light from the hall flaring red into his gleaming eyes. 'For Colonel Masters,' he whispered rapidly, 'and very special into his own personal touch and no one else.' And he melted away into the night with his 'strange foreign accent, his eyes of fire, and his nasty hissing voice'.

He was gone, swallowed up in the wind and rain.

'But I saw his eyes,' swore the cook the next morning to the housemaid, 'his fiery eyes, and his nasty look, and his black hands and long thin fingers, and his nails all shiny pink, and he looked to me—if you know wot I mean—he looked like—death...'

Thus the cook, so far as she was intelligently articulate next day, but standing now against the closed door with the small brown paper parcel in her hands, impressed by the orders that it was to be given into his personal touch, she was relieved by the fact that Colonel Masters never returned till after midnight and that she need not act at once. The reflection brought a certain comfort that restored her equanimity a little, though she still stood there, holding the parcel gingerly in her grimy hands, reluctant, hesitating, uneasy. A parcel, even brought by a mysterious dark stranger, was not in itself frightening, yet frightened she certainly felt. Instinct and superstition worked perhaps; the wind, the rain, the fact of being alone in the house, the unexpected black man, these also contributed to her discomfort. A vague sense of horror touched her, her Irish blood stirred ancient dreams, so that she began to shake a little, as though the parcel contained something alive, explosive, poisonous, unholy almost, as though it moved, and, her fingers loosening their hold, the parcel—dropped. It fell on the tiled floor with a queer, sharp clack, but it lay motionless. She eyed it closely, cautiously, but, thank God, it did not move, an inert, brown-paper parcel. Brought by an errand boy in daylight, it might have been groceries, tobacco, even a mended shirt. She peeped and tinkered, that sharp clack puzzled her. Then, after a few minutes, remembering her duty, she picked it up gingerly even while she shivered. It was to be handed into the Colonel's 'personal touch'. She compromised, deciding to place it on his desk and to tell him about it in the morning; only Colonel Masters, with those mysterious years in the East behind him, his temper and his tyrannical orders, was not easy of direct approach at the best of times, in the morning least of all.

The cook left it at that—that is, she left it on the desk in his study, but left out all explanations about its arrival. She had decided to be vague about such unimportant details, for Mrs. O'Reilly was afraid of Colonel Masters, and only his professed love of Monica made her believe that he was quite human. He paid her well, oh yes, and sometimes he smiled, and he was a handsome man, if a bit too dark for her fancy, yet he also paid her an occasional compliment about her curry, and that soothed her for the moment. They suited one another, at any rate, and she stayed, robbing him comfortably, if cautiously.

'It ain't no good,' she assured the housemaid next day, 'wot with that "personal touch into his hands, and no one else", and that black man's eyes and that clack when it came away in my hands and fell on the floor. It ain't no good, not to us nor anybody. No man as black as he was means lucky stars to anybody. A parcel indeed—with those devil's eyes—'

'What did you do with it?' enquired the housemaid.

The cook looked her up and down 'Put it in the fire o'course,' she replied. 'On the stove if you want to know exact.'

It was the housemaid's turn to look the cook up and down. 'I don't think,' she remarked.

The cook reflected, probably because she found no immediate answer.

'Well,' she puffed out presently, 'D' you know wot *I* think? You don't. So I'll tell you. It was something the master's afraid of, that's wot it was. He's afraid of something—ever since I been here I've known that. And that's wot it was. He done somebody wrong in India long ago and that lanky nigger brought wot's coming to him, and that's why I say I put it on the stove—see?' She dropped her voice. 'It was a bloody idol,' she whispered, 'that's wot it was, that parcel, and he—why, he's a bloody secret worshipper.' And she crossed herself. 'That's why I said I put it on the stove—see?'

The housemaid stared and gasped.

'And you mark my words, young Jane!' added the cook, turning to her dough.

And there the matter rested for a period, for the cook, being Irish, had more laughter in her than tears, and beyond admitting to the scared housemaid that she had not really burnt the parcel but had left it on the study table, she almost forgot the incident. It was not her job, in any case, to answer the front door. She had 'delivered' the parcel. Her conscience was quite clear.

Thus, nobody 'marked her words' apparently, for nothing untoward happened, as the way is in remote Suburbia, and Monica in her lonely play was happy, and Colonel Masters as tyrannical and grim as ever. The moist wintry wind blew through the silver pine, the rain beat against the bow window and no one called. For a week this lasted, a longish time in uneventful Suburbia.

But suddenly one morning Colonel Masters rang his study bell and, the housemaid being upstairs, it was the cook who answered. He held a brown paper parcel in his hands, half opened, the string dangling.

'I found this on my desk. I haven't been in my room for a week. Who brought it? And when did it come?' His face, yellow as usual, held a fiery tinge.

Mrs. O'Reilly replied, post-dating the arrival vaguely.

'I asked *who* brought it?' he insisted sharply.

'A stranger,' she fumbled. 'Not any one,' she added nervously, 'from hereabouts. No one I ever seen before. It was a man.'

'What did he look like?' The question came like a bullet.

Mrs. O'Reilly was rather taken by surprise. 'D-darkish,' she stumbled. 'Very darkish,' she added, 'if I saw him right. Only he came and went so quick I didn't get his face proper like, and...'

'Any message?' the Colonel cut her short.

She hesitated. 'There was no answer,' she began, remember ing former occasions.

'Any *message,* I asked you?' he thundered.

'No message, sir, none at all. And he was gone before I could get his name and address, sir, but I think it was a sort of black man, or it may have been the darkness of the night—I couldn't reely say, sir...'

In another minute she would have burst into tears or dropped to the floor in a faint, such was her terror of her employer especially when she was lying blind. The Colonel, however, saved her both disasters by abruptly holding out the half opened parcel towards her. He neither cross-examined nor cursed her as she had expected. He spoke with the curtness that betrayed anger and anxiety, almost, it occurred to her, distress.

'Take it away and burn it,' he ordered in his army voice, passing it into her outstretched hands. 'Burn it,' he repeated it, 'or chuck the damned thing away.' He almost flung it at her as though he did not want to touch it. 'If the man comes back,' he ordered in a voice of steel, 'tell him it's been destroyed—and say it *didn't reach me,*' laying tremendous emphasis on the final words. 'You understand?' He almost chucked it at her.

'Yes, sir. Exactly, sir,' and she turned and stumbled out, holding the parcel gingerly in her arms rather than in her hands and fingers, as though it contained something that might bite or sting.

Yet her fear had somehow lessened, for if he, Colonel Masters, could treat the parcel so contemptuously, why should she feel afraid of it. And, once alone in her kitchen among her household gods, she opened it. Turning back the thick paper wrappings, she started, and to her rather disappointed amazement, she found herself staring at nothing but a fair, waxen faced doll that could be bought in any toy-shop for one shilling and sixpence. A commonplace little cheap doll! Its face was pallid, white, expressionless, its flaxen hair was dirty, its tiny ill-shaped hands and fingers lay motionless by its side, its mouth was closed, though somehow grinning, no teeth visible, its eyelashes ridiculously like a worn tooth brush, its entire presentment in its flimsy skirt, contemptible, harmless, even ugly.

A doll! She giggled to herself, all fear evaporated.

'Gawd!' she thought. 'The master must have a conscience like the floor of a parrot's cage! And worse than that!' She was too afraid of him to despise him, her feeling was probably more like pity. 'At any rate,' she reflected, 'he had the wind up pretty bad. It was something else he expected—not a two penny halfpenny doll!' Her warm heart felt almost sorry for him.

Instead of 'chucking the damned thing away or burning it', however,—for it was quite a nice looking doll, she presented it to Monica, and Monica, having few new toys, instantly adored it, promising faithfully, as gravely warned by Mrs. O'Reilly, that she would never *never* let her father know she had it.

Her father, Colonel Hymber Masters, was, it seems, what's called a 'disappointed' man, a man whose fate forced him to live in surroundings he detested, disappointed in his career probably, possibly in love as well, Monica a love-child doubtless, and limited by his pension to face daily conditions that he loathed.

He was a silent, bitter sort of fellow, no more than that, and not so much disliked in the neighbourhood, as misunderstood. A sombre man they reckoned him, with his dark, furrowed face and silent ways. Yet 'dark' in the suburbs meant mysterious, and 'silent' invited female fantasy to fill the vacuum. It's the frank, corn-haired man who invites sympathy and generous comment. He enjoyed his Bridge, however, and was accepted as a first-class player. Thus, he went out nightly, and rarely came back before midnight. He was welcome among the gamblers evidently, while the fact that he had an adored child at home softened the picture of this 'mysterious' man. Monica, though rarely seen, appealed to the women of the neighbourhood, and 'whatever her origin' said the gossips, 'he loves her'.

To Monica, meanwhile, in her rather play-less, toy-less life, the doll, her new treasure, was a spot of gold. The fact that it was a 'secret' present from her father, added to its value. Many other presents had come to her like that; she thought nothing of it; only, he had never given her a doll before, and it spelt rapture.

Never, never, would she betray her pleasure and delight; it should remain her secret and his; and that made her love it all the more. She loved her father too, his taciturn silence was something she vaguely respected and adored. 'That's just like father,' she always said, when a strange new present came, and she knew instinctively that she must never say *Thank you* for it, for that was part of the lovely game between them. But this doll was exceptionally marvellous.

'It's much more real and alive than my Teddy bears,' she told the cook, after examining it critically. 'What ever made him think of it? Why, it even talks to me!' and she cuddled and fondled the half misshapened toy. 'It's my baby,' she cried, taking it against her cheek.

For no Teddy bear could really be a child; cuddly bears were not offspring, whereas a doll was a potential baby. It brought sweetness, as both cook and governess realised, into a rather grim house, hope and tenderness, a maternal flavour almost, something anyhow that no young bear could possibly bring. A child, a human baby! And yet both cook and governess—for both were present at the actual delivery—recalled later that Monica opened the parcel and recognised the doll with a yell of wild delight that seemed almost a scream of pain. There was this too high note of delirious exultation as though some instinctive horror of revulsion were instantly smothered and obliterated in a whirl of overmastering joy. It was Madame Jodzka who recalled—long afterwards—this singular contradiction.

'I did think she shrieked at it a bit, now you ask me,' admitted Mrs. O'Reilly later, though at the actual moment all she said was 'Oh, lovely, darling, ain't it a pet!' While all Madame Jodzka said was a cautionary 'If you squash its mouth like that, Monica, it won't be able to breathe!'

While Monica, paying no attention to either of them, fell to cuddling the doll with ecstasy.

A cheap little flaxen-haired, waxen-faced doll.

That so strange a case should come to us at second hand is, admittedly, a pity; that so much of the information should reach us largely through a cook and housemaid and through a foreigner of questionable validity, is equally unfortunate. Where precisely the reported facts creep across the feathery frontier into the incredible and thence into the fantastic would need the spider's thread of the big telescopes to define. With the eye to the telescope, the thread of that New Zealand spider seems thick as a rope; but with the eye examining second-hand reports the thread becomes elusive gossamer.

The Polish governess, Madame Jodzka, left the house rather abruptly. Though adored by Monica and accepted by Colonel Masters, she left not long after the arrival of the doll. She was a comely, youngish widow of birth and breeding, tactful, discreet, understanding. She adored Monica, and Monica was happy with her; she feared her employer, yet perhaps secretly admired him as the strong, silent, dominating Englishman. He gave her great freedom, she never took liberties, everything went smoothly. The pay was good and she needed it. Then, suddenly she left. In the suddenness of her departure, as in the odd reason she gave for leaving, lie doubtless the first hints of this remarkable affair, creeping across that 'feathery frontier' into the incredible and fantastic. An understandable reason she gave for leaving was that she was too frightened to stay in the house another night. She left at twenty-four hours' notice. Her reason was absurd, even if understandable, because any woman might find herself so frightened in a certain building that it has become intolerable to her nerves. Foolish or otherwise, this is understandable. An *idée fixe*, an obsession, once lodged in the mind of a superstitious, therefore hysterically-favoured woman, cannot be dislodged by argument. It may be absurd, yet it is 'understandable'.

The story behind the reason for Madame Jodzka's sudden terror is another matter, and it is best given quite simply. It relates to the doll. She swears by all her gods that she saw the doll 'walking by itself'. It was walking in a disjointed, hoppity, hideous fashion across the bed in which Monica lay sleeping.

In the gleam of the night-light, Madame Jodzka swears she saw this happen. She was half inside the opened door, peeping in, as her habit, and duty decreed, to see if all was well with the child before going up to bed herself. The light, if faint, was clear. A jerky movement on the counterpane first caught her attention, for a smallish object seemed blundering awkwardly across its slippery silken surface. Something rolling, possibly, some object Monica had left outside on falling asleep rolling mechanically as the child shifted or turned over.

After staring for some seconds, she then saw that it was not merely an 'object', since it had a living outline, nor was it rolling mechanically, or sliding, as she had first imagined. It was horribly taking steps, small but quite deliberate steps as though alive. It had a tiny, dreadful face, it had an expressionless tiny face, and the face had eyes—small, brightly shining eyes, and the eyes looked straight at Madame Jodzka.

She watched for a few seconds thunderstruck, and she suddenly realised with a shock of utter horror that this small, purposive monster was the doll, Monica's doll! And this doll was moving towards her across the tumbled surface of the counterpane. It was coming in her direction—straight at her.

Madame Jodzka gripped herself, physically and mentally, making a great effort, it seems, to deny the abnormal, the incredible. She denied the ice in her veins and down her spine. She prayed. She thought frantically of her priest in Warsaw. Making no audible sound, she screamed in her mind. But the doll, quickening its pace, came hobbling straight towards her, its glassy eyes fixed hard upon her own.

Then Madame Jodzka fainted.

That she was, in some ways, a remarkable woman, with a sense of values, is clear from the fact that she realised this story 'wouldn't wash', for she confided it only to the cook in cautious whispers, while giving her employer some more 'washable' tale about a family death that obliged her to hurry home to Warsaw. Nor was there the slightest attempt at embroidery, for on recovering consciousness she had recovered her courage, too—and done a remarkable thing: she had compelled herself to investigate. Aided and fortified by her religion, she compelled herself to make an examination. She had tiptoed further into the room, had made sure that Monica was sleeping peacefully, and that the doll lay—motionless—half way down the counterpane. She gave it a long, concentrated look. Its lidless eyes, fringed by hideously ridiculous black lashes, were fixed on space. Its expression was not so much innocent, as blankly stupid, idiotic, a mask of death that aped cheaply a pretence of life, where life could never be. Not ugly merely, it was revolting.

Madame Jodzka, however, did more than study this visage with concentration, for with admirable pluck she forced herself to touch the little horror. She actually picked it up. Her faith, her deep religious conviction, denied the former evidence of her senses. She had *not* seen movement. It was incredible, impossible. The fault lay somewhere in herself. This persuasion, at any rate, lasted long enough to enable her to touch the repulsive little toy, to pick it up, to lift it. She placed it steadily on the table near the bed between the bowl of flowers and the night-light, where it lay on its back helpless, innocent, yet horrible, and only then on shaking legs did she leave the room and go up to her own bed. That her fingers remained ice-cold until eventually she fell asleep can be explained, of course, too easily and naturally to claim examination.

Whether imagined or actual, it must have been, none the less, a horrifying spectacle—a mechanical outline from a commercial factory walking like a living thing with a purpose. It holds the nightmare touch. To Madame Jodzka, protected since youth within cast-iron tenets, it came as a shock. And a shock dislocates. The sight smashed everything she knew as possible and real. The flow of her blood was interrupted, it froze, there came icy terror into her heart, her normal mechanism failed for a moment, she fainted. And fainting seemed a natural result. Yet it was the shock of the incredible masquerade that gave her

the courage to act. She loved Monica, apart from any consideration of paid duty. The sight of this tiny monstrosity strutting across the counterpane not far from the child's sleeping face and folded hands—it was this that enabled her to pick it up with naked fingers and set it out of reach...

For hours, before falling asleep, she reviewed the incredibl thing, alternately denying the facts, then accepting them, yet tak ing into sleep finally the assured conviction that her senses ha not deceived her. There seems little, indeed, that in a court c law could have been advanced against her character for reli bility, for sincerity, for the logic of her detailed account.

'I'm sorry,' said Colonel Masters quietly, referring to her b reavement. He looked searchingly at her. 'And Monica w miss you,' he added with one of his rare smiles. 'She nee you.' Then just as she turned away, he suddenly extended hand. 'If perhaps later you can come back—do let me kn Your influence is—so helpful—and good.'

She mumbled some phrase with a promise in it, yet she with a queer, deep impression that it was not merely, not chi perhaps, Monica who needed her. She wished he had not quite those words. A sense of shame lay in her, almost as tho she were running away from duty, or at least from a ch to help that God had put in her way. 'Your influence is—so g

Already in the train and on the boat conscience attacke biting, scratching, gnawing. She had deserted a child she l a child who needed her, because she was scared out of he No, that was a one-sided statement. She had left a house b the Devil had come into it. No, that was only partiall When a hysterical temperament, engrained since early chil in fixed dogmas, begins to sift facts and analyse reaction and common sense themselves become confused. Thou one way, emotion another, and no honest conclusion dav her mind.

She hurried on to Warsaw, to a stepfather, a retired whose gay life had no place for her and who would

come her return. It was a derogatory prospect for this youngish widow who had taken a job in order to escape from his vulgar activities to return now empty-handed. Yet it was easier, perhaps, to face a step-father's selfish anger than to go and tell Colonel Masters her real reason for leaving his service. Her conscience, too, troubled her on another score as thoughts and memories travelled backwards and half-forgotten details emerged.

Those spots of blood, for instance, mentioned by Mrs. O'Reilly, the superstitious Irish cook. She had made it a rule to ignore Mrs. O'Reilly's silly fairy tales, yet now she recalled suddenly those ridiculous discussions about the laundry list and the foolish remarks that the cook and housemaid had let fall.

'But there ain't no paint in a doll, I tell you. It's all sawdust and wax and muck,' from the housemaid. 'I know red paint when I see it, and that ain't paint, it's blood.' And from Mrs. O'Reilly later: 'Mother o'God! Another red blob! She's biting her finger-nails—and that's not *my* job...!'

The red stains on sheets and pillow cases were puzzling certainly, but Madame Jodzka, hearing these remarks by chance as it were, had paid no particular attention to them at the moment. The laundry lists were hardly her affair. These ridiculous servants anyhow...! And yet, now in the train, those spots of red, be they paint or blood, crept back to trouble her.

Another thing, oddly enough, also troubled her—the ill-defined feeling that she was deserting a man who needed help, help that she could give. It was too vague to put into words. Was it based on his remark that her influence was 'good' perhaps? She could not say. It was an intuition, and few intuitions bear analysis. Supporting it, however, was a conviction she had felt since first she entered the service of Colonel Masters, the conviction, namely, that he had a past that frightened him. There was something he had done, something he regretted and was probably ashamed of, something at any rate, for which he feared retribution. A retribution, moreover, he expected; a punishment that would come like a thief in the night and seize him by the throat.

It was against this dreaded vengeance that her influence was 'good', a protective influence possibly that her religion supplied, something on the side of the angels, in any case, that her personality provided.

Her mind worked thus, it seems; and whether a concealed admiration for this sombre and mysterious man, an admiration and protective instinct never admitted even to her inmost self, existed below the surface, hidden yet urgent, remains the secret of her own heart.

It was naturally and according to human nature, at any rate, that after a few weeks of her stepfather's outrageous behaviour in the house, his cruelty too, she decided to return. She prayed to her gods incessantly, also she found oppressive her sense of neglected duty and failure of self-respect. She returned to the soulless suburban villa. It was understandable; the welcome from Monica was also understandable, the relief and pleasure of Colonel Masters still more so. It was expressed, this latter, in a courteous message only, tactfully worded, as though she had merely left for brief necessity, for it was some days before she actually saw him to speak to. From cook and housemaid the welcome was voluble and—disquieting. There were no more inexplicable 'spots of red', but there were other unaccountable happenings even more distressing.

'She's missed you something terrible,' said Mrs. O'Reilly, 'though she's found something else to keep her quiet—if you like to put it that way.' And she made the sign of the cross.

'The doll?' asked Madame Jodzka with a start of shocked horror, forcing herself to come straight to the point and forcing herself also to speak lightly, casually.

'That's it, Madame. The bleeding doll.'

The governess had heard the strange adjective many times already, but did not know whether to take it figuratively or not. She chose the latter.

'Blood?' she asked in a lowered voice.

The cook's body gave an odd jerk. 'Well,' she explained. 'I

meant more the way it goes on. Like a thing of flesh and blood, if you get me. And the way *she* treats it and plays with it,' and her voice, while loud, had a hush of fear in it somewhere. She held her arms before her in a protective, shielding way, as though to ward off aggression.

'Scratches ain't proof of nothing,' interjected the housemaid scornfully.

'You mean,' asked Madame Jodzka gravely, 'there's a question of—of injury—to someone?' She suppressed an involuntary gasp, but paid no attention to the maid's interruption otherwise.

Mrs. O'Reilly seemed to mismanage her breath for a moment.

'It ain't Miss Monica it's after,' she announced in a defiant whisper as soon as she recovered herself, 'it's someone else. *That's* what I mean. And no man as black as *he* was,' she let herself go, 'ever brought no good into a house, not since I was born.'

'Someone else—?' repeated Madame Jodzka almost to herself, seizing the vital words.

'You and yer black man!' interjected the housemaid. 'Get along with yer! Thank God I ain't a Christian or anything like that! But I did 'ear them sort of jerky shuffling footseps one night, I admit, and the doll did look bigger—swollen like—when I peeked in and looked—'

'Stop it!' cried Mrs. O'Reilly, 'for you ain't saying what's true or what you reely know.'

She turned to the governess.

'There's more talk what means nothing about this doll,' she said by way of apology, 'than all the fairy tales I was brought up with as a child in Mayo, and I—I wouldn't be believing anything of it.'

Turning her back contemptuously on the chattering housemaid, she came close to Madame Jodzka.

'There's no harm coming to Miss Monica, Madame,' she whispered vehemently, 'you can be quite sure about *her*. Any trouble there may be is for someone else.' And again she crossed herself.

Madame Jodzka, in the privacy of her room, reflected between her prayers. She felt a deep, a dreadful uneasiness.

A doll! A cheap, tawdry little toy made in factories by the hundred, by the thousand, a manufactured article of commerce for children to play with... But...

'The way she treats it and plays with it...' rang on in her disturbed mind.

A doll! But for the maternal suggestion, a doll was a pathetic, even horrible plaything, yet to watch a child busy with it involved deep reflections, since here the future mother prophesied. The child fondles and caresses her doll with passionate love, cares for it, seeks its welfare, yet stuffs it down into the perambulator, its head and neck twisted, its limbs broken and contorted, leaving it atrociously upside down so that blood and breathing cannot possibly function, while she runs to the window to see if the rain has stopped or the sun has come out. A blind and hideous automatism dictated by the race, provided nothing of more immediate interest interferes, yet a herd-instinct that overcomes all obstacles, its vitality insuperable. The maternity instinct defies, even denies death. The doll, whether left upside down on the floor with broken teeth and ruined eyes, or lovingly arranged to be overlaid in the night, squashed, tortured, mutilated, survives all cruelties and disasters, and asserts finally its immortal qualities. It is unkillable. It is beyond death.

A child with her doll, reflected Madame Jodzka, is an epitome of nature's remorseless and unconquerable passion, of her dominant purpose—the survival of the race. ...

Such thoughts, influenced perhaps by her bitter subconscious grievance against nature for depriving her of a child of her own, were unable to hold that level for long; they soon dropped back to the concrete case that perplexed and frightened her—Monica and her flaxen-haired, sightless, idiotic doll. In the middle of her prayers, falling asleep incontinently, she did not even dream of it, and she woke refreshed and vigorous, facing the fact that sooner or later, sooner probably, she would have to speak to her employer.

She watched and listened. She watched Monica; she watched the doll. All seemed as normal as in a thousand other homes. Her mind reviewed the position, and where mind and superstition clashed, the former held its own easily. During her evening off she enjoyed the local cinema, leaving the heated building with the conviction that coloured fantasy benumbed the faculties, and that ordinary life was in itself prosaic. Yet before she had covered the half-mile to the house, her deep, unaccountable uneasiness returned with overmastering power.

Mrs. O'Reilly had seen Monica to bed for her, and it was Mrs. O'Reilly who let her in. Her face was like the dead.

'It's been talking,' whispered the cook, even before she closed the door. She was white about the gills.

'Talking! *Who*'s been talking? What do you mean?'

Mrs. O'Reilly closed the door softly. 'Both,' she stated with dramatic emphasis, then sat down and wiped her face. She looked distraught with fear.

Madame took command, if only a command based on dreadful insecurity.

'Both?' she repeated, in a voice deliberately loud so as to counteract the other's whisper. 'What are you talking about?'

'They've *both* been talking—talking together,' stated the cook.

The governess kept silent for a moment, fighting to deny a shrinking heart.

'You've heard them talking together, you mean?' she asked presently in a shaking voice that tried to be ordinary.

Mrs. O'Reilly nodded, looking over her shoulder as she did so. Her nerves were, obviously, in rags. 'I thought you'd *never* come back,' she whimpered. 'I could hardly stay in the house.'

Madame looked intently into her frightened eyes.

'You *heard*...?' she asked quietly.

'I listened at the door. There were two voices. Different voices.'

Madame Jodzka did not insist or cross-examine, as though acute fear helped her to a greater wisdom.

'You mean, Mrs. O'Reilly,' she said in flat, quiet tones, 'that you heard Miss Monica talking to her doll as she always does, and herself inventing the doll's answers in a changed voice? Isn't that what you mean you heard?'

But Mrs. O'Reilly was not to be shaken. By way of answer she crossed herself and shook her head.

She spoke in a low whisper. 'Come up now and listen with me, Madame, and judge for yourself.'

Thus, soon after midnight, and Monica long since asleep, these two, the cook and governess in a suburban villa, took up their places in the dark corridor outside a child's bedroom door. It was a quiet windless night; Colonel Masters, whom they both feared, doubtless long since gone to his room in another corner of the ungainly villa. It must have been a long dreary wait before sounds in the child's bedroom first became audible—the low quiet sound of voices talking audibly—two voices. A hushed, secretive, unpleasant sound in the room where Monica slept peacefully with her beloved doll beside her. Yet two voices assuredly, it was.

Both women sat erect, both crossed themselves involuntarily, exchanging glances. Both were bewildered, terrified. Both sat aghast.

What lay in Mrs. O'Reilly's superstitious mind, only the gods of 'ould Oireland' can tell, but what the Polish woman's contained was clear as a bell; it was not two voices talking, it was only one. Her ear was pressed against the crack in the door. She listened intently; shaking to the bone, she listened. Voices in sleep-talking, she remembered, changed oddly.

'The child's talking to herself in sleep,' she whispered firmly, 'and that's all it is, Mrs. O'Reilly. She's just talking in her sleep,' she repeated with emphasis to the woman crowding against her shoulder as though in need of support. 'Can't you hear it,' she added loudly, half angrily, 'isn't it the same voice always? Listen carefully and you'll see I'm right.'

She listened herself more closely than before.

'Listen! Hark...!' she repeated in a breathless whisper, concentrating her mind upon the curious sound, 'isn't that the same voice—answering itself?'

Yet, as she listened, another sound disturbed her concentration, and this time it seemed a sound behind her—a faint, rustling, shuffling sound rather like footsteps hurrying away on tiptoe. She turned her head sharply and found that she had been whispering to no one. There was no one beside her. She was alone in the darkened corridor. Mrs. O'Reilly was gone. From the well of the house below a voice came up in a smothered cry beneath the darkened stairs: 'Mother o'God and all the Saints...' and more besides.

A gasp of surprise and alarm escaped her, doubtless at finding herself deserted and alone but in the same instant, exactly as in the story books, came another sound that caught her breath still more aghast—the rattle of a key in the front door below. Colonel Masters, after all, had not yet come in and gone to bed as expected: he was coming in now. Would Mrs. O'Reilly have time to slip across the hall before he caught her? More—and worse—would he come up and peep into Monica's bedroom on his way up to bed, as he rarely did? Madame Jodzka listened, her nerves in rags. She heard him fling down his coat. He was a man quick in such actions. The stick or umbrella was banged down noisily, hastily. The same instant his step sounded on the stairs. He was coming up. Another minute and he would start into the passage where she crouched against Monica's door.

He was mounting rapidly, two stairs at a time.

She, too, was quick in action and decision. She thought in a flash. To be caught crouching outside the door was ludicrous, but to be caught inside the door would be natural and explicable. She acted at once.

With a palpitating heart, she opened the bedroom door and stepped inside. A second later she heard Colonel Masters' tread, as he stumped along the corridor up to bed. He passed the door. He went on. She heard this with intense relief.

Now, inside the room, the door closed behind her, she saw the picture clearly.

Monica, sound asleep, was playing with her beloved doll, but in her sleep. She was indubitably in deep slumber. Her fingers, however, were roughing the doll this way and that, as though some dream perplexed her. The child was mumbling in her sleep, though no words were distinguishable. Muffled sighs and groans issued from her lips. Yet another sound there certainly was, though it could not have issued from the child's mouth. Whence, then, did it come?

Madame Jodzka paused, holding her breath, her heart panting. She watched and listened intently. She heard squeaks and grunts, but a moment's examination convinced her whence these noises came. They did not come from Monica's lips. They issued indubitably from the doll she clutched and twisted in her dream. The joints, as Monica twisted them emitted these odd sounds, as though the sawdust in knees and elbows wheezed and squeaked against the unnatural rubbing. Monica obviously was wholly unconscious of these noises. At the doll's neck screwed round, the material—wax, thread, sawdust—produced this curious grating sound that was almost like syllables of a word or words.

Madame Jodzka stared and listened. She felt icy cold. Seeking for a natural explanation she found none. Prayer and terror raced in her helter-skelter. Her skin began to sweat.

Then, suddenly Monica, her expression peaceful and composed, turned over in her sleep, and the dreadful doll, released from the dream-clutch, fell to one side on the bed and lay apparently lifeless and inert. In which moment, to Madame Jodzka's unbelieving yet horrified ears, it continued to squeak and utter. It went on mouthing by itself. Worse than that, the next instant it stood abruptly upright, rising on its twisted legs. It started moving. It began to move, walking crookedly, across the counterpane. Its glassy, sightless eyes, seemed to look straight at her. It presented an inhuman and appalling picture, a picture of the utterly incredible. With a queer, hoppity motion of its broken legs and joints, it came fumbling and tumbling across the rough unevenness of the slippery counterpane towards her. Its appearance was deliberate and aggressive. The sounds, as of syllables, came with it—strange, meaningless syllables that yet yet managed to convey anger. It stumbled towards her like a living thing. Its whole presentment conveyed attack.

Once again, this effect of a mere child's toy, aping the life of some awful monstrosity with purpose and passion in its hideous tiny outline, brought collapse to the plucky Polish governess. The rush of blood without control drained her heart, and a moment of unconsciousness supervened so that everything, as it were, turned black.

This time, however, the moment of dark unconsciousness passed instantly: it came and went, almost like a moment of forgetfulness in passion. Passionate it certainly was, for the reaction came upon her like a storm. With recovered consciousness a sudden rage rushed into her woman's heart—perhaps a coward's rage, an exaggerated fury against her own weakness? It rushed, in any case, to help her. She staggered, caught her breath, clutched violently at the cupboard next her, and—recovered her self-control. A fury of resentment blazed through her, fury against this utterly incredible exhibition of a wax doll walking and squawking as though it were something intelligently alive that could utter syllables. Syllables, she felt convinced, in a language she did not know.

If the monstrous can paralyse, it also can affront. The sight and sound of this cheap factory toy behaving with a will and heart of its own stung her into an act of violence that became imperative. For it was more than she could stand. Irresistibly, she rushed forward. She hurled herself against it, her only available weapon the high-heeled shoe her foot kicked loose on the instant, determined to smash down the frightful apparition into fragments and annihilate it. Hysterical, no doubt, she was at the moment, and yet logical: the godless horror must be blotted out of visible existence. This one thing obsessed her—to destroy beyond all possibility of survival. It must be smashed into fragments, into dust.

They stood close, face to face, the glassy eyes staring into her own, her hand held high for the destruction she craved—but the hand did not fall. A stinging pain, sharp as a serpent's bite, darted suddenly through her fingers, wrist and arm, her grip was broken, the shoe spun sideways across the room, and in the flickering light of the candle, it seemed to her, the whole room quivered. Paralysed and helpless, she stood utterly aghast. What gods or saints could come to aid her? None. Her own will alone could help her. Some effort, at any rate, she made, trembling, on the edge of collapse: 'My God!' she heard her half whispering, strangled voice cry out. 'It is not true! You are a lie! My God denies you! I call upon my God...!'

Whereupon, to her added horror, the dreadful little doll, waving a broken arm, squawked back at her, as though in definite answer, the strange disjointed syllables she could not understand, syllables as though in another tongue. The same instant it collapsed abruptly on the counterpane like a toy balloon that had been pricked. It shrank down in a mutilated mess before her eyes, while Monica—added touch of horror—stirred uneasily in her sleep, turning over and stretching out her hands as though feeling blindly for something that she missed. And this sight of the innocently sleeping child fumbling instinctively towards an incomprehensibly evil and dangerous something that attracted her proved again too strong for the Polish woman to control.

The blackness intervened a second time.

It was undoubtedly a blur in memory that followed, emotion and superstition proving too much for common-sense to deal with. She just remembers violent, unreasoned action on her part before she came back to clearer consciousness in her own room, praying volubly on her knees against her own bed. The interval of transit down the corridor and upstairs remained a blank. Yet her shoe was with her, clutched tightly in her hand. And she remembered also having clutched an inert, waxen doll with frantic fingers, clutched and crushed and crumpled its awful little frame till the sawdust came spurting from its broken joints and its tiny body was mutilated beyond recognition, if not annihilated... then stuffing it down ruthlessly on a table far out of Monica's reach—Monica lying peacefully in deepest sleep.

She remembered that. She also saw the clear picture of the small monster lying upside down, grossly untidy, an obscene attitude in the disorder of its flimsy dress and exposed limbs, lying motionless, its eyes crookedly aglint, motionless, yet alive still, alive moreover with intense and malignant purpose.

No duration or intensity of prayer could obliterate the picture.

She knew now that a plain, face to face talk with her employer was essential; her conscience, her peace of mind, her sanity, her sense of duty all demanded this. Deliberately, and she was sure, rightly, she had never once risked a word with the child herself. Danger lay that way, the danger of emphasising something in the child's mind that was best left ignored. But with Colonel Masters, who paid her for her services, believed in her integrity, trusted her, with him there must be an immediate explanation.

An interview was absurdly difficult; in the first place because he loathed and avoided such occasions; secondly because he was so exceedingly impervious to approach, being so rarely even visible at all. At night he came home late, in the mornings no one dared go near him. He expected the little household, its routine once established, to run itself. The only inmate who dared beard him was Mrs. O'Reilly, who periodically, once every six months, walked straight into his study, gave notice, received an addition to her wages, and then left him alone for another six months.

Madame Jodzka, knowing his habits, waylaid him in the hall next morning while Monica was lying down before lunch, as usual. He was on his way out and she had been watching from the upper landing. She had hardly set eyes on him since her return from Warsaw. His lean, upright figure, his dark, emotionless face, she thought magnificent. He was the perfect expression of the soldier. Her heart fluttered as she raced downstairs. Her carefully prepared sentences, however, evaporated when he stopped and looked at her, a jumble of wild words pouring from her in confused English instead. He cut her rigmarole short, though he listened politely enough at first.

'I'm so glad you were able to come back to us, as I told you. Monica missed you very much—'

'She has something now she plays with—'

'The very thing,' he interrupted. 'No doubt the kind of toy she needs... Your excellent judgment... Please tell me if there's anything else you think...' and he half turned as though to move away.

'But I didn't get it. It's a horrible—*horrible*—'

Colonel Masters uttered one of his rare laughs. 'Of course, all children's toys are horrible, but if she's pleased with it... I haven't seen it, I'm no judge... If you can buy something better—' and he shrugged his shoulders.

'I didn't buy it,' she cried desperately. 'It was brought. It makes sounds by itself—syllables. I've seen it move—move by itself. It's a doll.'

He turned from the front door which he had just reached as though he had been shot; the skin held a sudden pallor beneath the flush and something contradicted the blazing eyes, something that seemed to shrink.

'A doll,' he repeated in a very quiet voice. 'You said—a doll?'

But his eyes and face disconcerted her, so that she merely gave a fumbling account of a parcel that had been brought. His question about a parcel he had ordered strictly to be destroyed added to her confusion.

'Wasn't it?' he asked in a rasping whisper, as though a disobeyed order seemed incredible.

'It was thrown away, I believe,' she prevaricated, unable to meet his eyes, anxious to protect the cook as well. 'I think Monica—perhaps found it.' She despised her lack of courage, but his intensity scattered her wits; she was conscious, moreover, of a strange desire not to give him pain, as though his safety and happiness, not Monica's, were at stake. 'It—talks!—as well as *moves*,' she cried desperately, forcing herself at last to look at him.

Colonel Masters seemed to stiffen; his breath caught oddly. 'You say Monica has it? Plays with it? You've seen movement and heard sounds like syllables?' He asked the questions in a low voice, almost as though talking to himself. 'You've—listened?' he whispered.

Unable to find convincing words, she bowed her head, while some terror in him came across to her like a blast of icy wind. The man was afraid in his heart. Instead, however, of some explosive reply by way of blame or criticism, he spoke quietly, even calmly: 'You did right to come and tell me this—quite right,' adding then in so low a tone that she barely caught the ominous words, 'for I have been expecting something of the sort... sooner or later... it was bound to come...' the voice dying away into the handkerchief he put to his face.

And abruptly then, as though aware of an appeal for sympathy, an emotional reaction swept her fear away. Stepping closer, she looked her employer straight in the eyes.

'See the child for yourself,' she said with sudden firmness. 'Come and listen with me. Come into the bedroom.'

She saw him stagger. For a moment he said nothing.

'Who,' he then asked, the low voice unsteady, 'who brought that parcel?'

'A man, I believe.'

There was a pause that seemed like minutes before his next question.

'White,' he asked, 'or—black?'

'Dark,' she told him, 'very dark.'

He was shaking like a leaf, the skin of his face blanched; he leaned against the door, wilted, limp; unless she somehow took command there threatened a collapse she did not wish to witness.

'You shall come with me tonight,' she said firmly, 'and we shall listen together. Wait till I return now. I go for brandy,' and a minute later as she came back breathless and watched him gulp down half a tumbler full, she knew that she had done right in telling him. His obedience proved it, though it seemed strange that cowardice should borrow from its like to produce courage.

'Tonight,' she repeated, 'tonight after your Bridge. We meet in the corridor outside the bedroom. At half-past twelve.'

He pulled himself into an upright position, staring at her fixedly, making a movement of his head, half bow, half nod.

'Twelve thirty,' he muttered, 'in the passage outside the bedroom door,' and using his stick rather heavily, he opened the door and passed out into the drive. She watched him go, aware that her fear had changed to pity, aware also that she watched the stumbling gait of a man too conscience-stricken to know a moment's peace, too frightened even to think of God.

Madame Jodzka kept the appointment; she had eaten no supper, but had stayed in her room—praying. She had first put Monica to bed.

'My doll,' the child pleaded, good as gold, after being tucked up. 'I must have my doll or else I'll never get to sleep,' and Madame Jodzka had brought it with reluctant fingers, placing it on the night-table beside the bed.

'She'll sleep quite comfortably here, Monica, darling. Why not leave her outside the sheets?' It had been carefully mended, she noticed, patched together with pins and stitches.

The child grabbed at it. 'I want her in bed beside me, close against me,' she said with a happy smile. 'We tell each other stories. If she's too far away I can't hear what she says.' And she seized it with a cuddling pleasure that made the woman's heart turn cold.

'Of course, darling—if it helps you to fall asleep quickly, you shall have it,' and Monica did not see the trembling fingers, nor notice the horror in the face and voice. Indeed, hardly was the doll against her cheek on the pillow, her fingers half stroking the flaxen hair and pink wax cheeks, than her eyes closed, a sigh of deep content breathed out, and Monica was asleep.

Madame Jodzka, fearful of looking behind her, tiptoed to the door, and left the room. In the passage she wiped a cold sweat from her forehead. 'God bless her and protect her,' her heart murmured, 'and may God forgive me if I've sinned.'

She kept the appointment; she knew Colonel Masters would keep it, too.

It had been a long wait from eight o'clock till after midnight.

With great determination she had kept away from the bedroom door, fearful lest she might hear a sound that would necessitate action on her part: she went to her room and stayed there. But praying exhausted itself, for it both excited and betrayed her. If her God could help, a brief request alone was needed. To go on praying for help hour by hour was not only an insult to her deity, but it also wore her out physically. She stopped, therefore, and read some pages of a Polish saint which she did not understand. Later she fell into a state of horrified nervous drowse. In due course, she slept...

A noise awoke her—steps going softly past her door. A glance at her watch showed eleven o'clock. The steps, though stealthy, were familiar. Mrs. O'Reilly was waddling up to bed. The sounds died away. Madame Jodzka, a trifle ashamed, though she hardly knew why, returned to her Polish saint, yet determined to keep her ears open. Then slept again...

What woke her a second time she could not tell. She was startled. She listened. The night was unpleasantly still, the house quiet as the grave. No casual traffic passed. No wind stirred the gloomy evergreens in the drive. The world outside was silent. And then, as she saw by her watch that it was some minutes after midnight, a sharp click became audible that acted like a pistol shot to her keyed-up nerves. It was the front door closing softly. Steps followed across the hall below, then up the stairs, unsteadily a little. Colonel Masters had come in. He was coming up slowly, unwillingly she felt, to keep the appointment. Madame Jodzka started from her chair, looked in the glass, mumbled a quick confused prayer, and opened her door into the dark passage.

She stiffened, physically and mentally. 'Now, he'll hear and perhaps see—for himself,' she thought. 'And God help him!'

She marched along the passage and reached the door of Monica's bedroom, listening with such intentness that she seemed to hear only the confused running murmur of her own blood. Having reached the appointed spot, she stood stock still and waited while his steps approached. A moment later his bulk blocked the passage, shown up as a dark shadow by the light in the hall below. This bulk came nearer, came right up to her. She believed she said 'Good evening', and that he mumbled something about 'I said I'd come... damned nonsense...' or words to that effect, whereupon the couple stood side by side in the darkened silence of the corridor, remote from the rest of the house, and waited without further words. They stood shoulder to shoulder outside the door of Monica's bedroom. Her heart was knocking against her side.

She heard his breathing, there came a whiff of spirits, of stale tobacco smoke, his outline seemed to shift against the wall unsteadily, he moved his feet; and a sudden, extraordinary wave of emotion swept over her, half of protective maternal yearning, half almost of sexual desire, so that for a passing instant she burned to take him in her arms and kiss him savagely, and at the same time shield him from some appalling danger his blunt ignorance laid him open to. With revulsion, pity, and a sense of sin and passion, she acknowledged this odd sudden weakness in herself, but the face of the Warsaw priest flashed across her fuddled mind the next instant. There was evil in the air. This meant the Devil. She felt herself trembling dreadfully, shaking in her shoes, losing her balance, her whole body leaning over, but leaning in his direction. A moment more and she must have fallen towards him, dropped into his arms.

A sound broke the silence, and she drew up just in time. It came from beyond the door, from inside the bedroom.

'Hark!' she whispered, her hand upon his arm, and while he made no movement, spoke no word, she saw his head and shoulders bend down toward the panel of the closed door. There was a noise, upon the other side, there were noises, Monica's voice distinctly recognisable, another slighter, shriller sound accompanying it, breaking in upon it, answering it. Two voices.

'Listen,' she repeated in a whisper scarcely audible, and felt his warm hand grip her own so fiercely that it hurt her.

No words were distinguishable at first, just these odd broken sounds of two separate voices in that dark corridor of the silent house—the voice of a child, and the other a strange, faint, hardly human sound, while yet a voice.

'*Que le bon Dieu—*' she began, then faltered, breath failing her, for she saw Colonel Masters stoop down suddenly and do the last thing that would have occurred to her as likely: he put his eye to the key-hole and kept it there steadily, for the best part of a minute, his hand still gripping her own firmly. He knelt on one knee to keep his balance.

The sounds had ceased, no movement now stirred inside the room. The night-light, she knew, would show him clearly the pillows of the bed, Monica's head, the doll in her arms. Colonel Masters must see clearly anything there was to see, and he yet gave no sign that he saw anything. She experienced a queer sensation for a few seconds—almost as though she had perhaps imagined everything and proved herself a consummate, idiotic, hysterical fool. For a few seconds this ghastly thought flashed over her, the odd silence emphasising it. Had she been, after all, just a crazy lunatic? Had her senses all deceived her? Why should he see nothing, make no sign? Why had the voice, the voices, ceased? Not a murmur of any sort was audible in the room.

Then Colonel Masters, suddenly releasing his grip of her hand, shuffled on to both feet and stood up straight, while in the same instant she herself stiffened, trying to prepare for the angry scorn, the contemptuous abuse he was about to pour upon her. Protecting herself against this attack, expecting it, she was the more amazed at what she did hear:

'I saw it,' came in a strangled whisper. 'I saw it walk!'

She stood paralysed.

'It's watching me,' he added, scarcely audible. '*Me!*'

The revulsion of feeling at first left her speechless; it was the sheer terror in his strangled whisper that restored a measure of self possession to her. Yet it was he who found words first, awful whispered words, words spoken to himself, it seemed, more than to her.

'It's what I've always feared—I knew it must come some day—yet not like this. Not this way.'

Then immediately the voice in the room became audible, and it was a sweet and gentle voice, sincere and natural, with feeling in it—Monica's childish voice, pleading:

'Don't go, don't leave me! Come back into bed—please.'

An incomprehensible sound followed, as though by way of answer. There were syllables in that faint, creaky tone Madame Jodzka recognised, but syllables she could not comprehend. They seemed to enter her like points of ice. She froze. And facing her stood the motionless, inanimate bulk of him, his outline, then leaned over towards her, his lips so close to her own face that, as he spoke, she felt the breath upon her cheek.

'*Buth laga*...' she heard him repeat the syllables to himself again and again. '*Revenge*... in Hindustani...!' He drew a long, anguished breath. The sounds sank into her like drops of poison, the syllables she had heard several times already but had not understood. At last she understood their meaning. Revenge!

'I must go in, go in,' he was mumbling to himself. 'I must go in and face it.' Her intuition was justified: the danger was not for Monica but for himself. Her sudden protective maternal instinct found its explanation too. The lethal power concentrated in that hideous puppet was aimed at *him*. He began to edge impetuously past her.

'No!' she cried. 'I'll go! Let me go in!' pushing him aside with all her strength. But his hand was already on the knob and the next instant the door was open and he was inside the room. On the threshold they stood still a second, side by side, though she was slightly behind, struggling to shove past him and stand protectively in front.

She stared across his shoulder, her eyes so wide open that the intense strain to note everything at once threatened to defeat its own end. Sight, none the less, worked normally; she saw all there was to see, and that was—nothing; nothing unusual that is, nothing abnormal, nothing terrifying, so that this second time the threat of anti-climax rose to her mind. Had she worked herself up to this peak of horror merely to behold Monica lying sound asleep in a safe and quiet room? The flickering night-light revealed no more than a child in natural slumber without a toy of any sort against her pillow. There stood the glass of water beside the flowers in their saucer, the picture-book on the sill of the window within reach, the window opened a little at the bottom, and there also lay the calm face of Monica with eyes tight shut upon the pillow. Her breathing was deep and regular, no sign of disquiet anywhere, no hint of disturbance that might have accompanied that pleading sentence of two minutes ago, except that the bedclothes were perhaps somewhat tumbled. The counterpane humped itself in folds towards the foot of the bed, she noticed, as though Monica, finding it too warm, had tossed it away in sleep. No more than that.

In that first moment Colonel Masters and the governess took in this whole pretty picture complete. The room was so still that the child's breathing was distinctly audible. Their eyes roved all over. Nothing was anywhere in movement. Yet the same instant Madane Jodzka became aware that there *was* movement. Something stirred. The report came, perhaps, through her skin, for no sense announced it. It was undeniable; in that still, silent room there was movement somewhere, and with that unreported movement there was danger.

Certain, rightly or wrongly, that she herself was safe, also that the quietly sleeping child was safe, she was equally certain that Colonel Masters was the one in danger. She knew that in her very bones.

'Wait here by the door,' she said almost peremptorily, as she felt him pushing past her further into the quiet room. 'You saw it watching you. It's somewhere!—Take care!'

She clutched at him, but he was already beyond her.

'Damned nonsense,' he muttered and strode forward.

Never before in her whole life had she admired a man more than in this instant when she saw him moving towards what she knew to be physical and spiritual danger—never before, and never again, was such a hideous and dreadful sight to be repeatable in a woman's life. Pity and horror drowned her in a sea of passionate, futile longing. A man going to meet his fate, it flashed over her, was something none, without power to help, should witness. No human power can stay the course of the stars.

Her eye rested, as it were by chance, on the crumpled ridges and hollows of the discarded counterpane. These lay by the foot of the bed in shadow, confused a little in their contours and their masses. Had Monica not moved, they must have lain thus till morning. But Monica did move. At this particular moment she turned over in her sleep. She stretched her little legs before settling down in the new position, and this stretching squeezed and twisted the contours of the heavy counterpane at the foot of the bed. The tiny landscape altered thus a fraction, its immediate detail shifted. And an outline—a very small outline—emerged. Hitherto, it had lain concealed among the shadows. It emerged now with disconcerting rapidity, as though a spring released it. Out of its nest of darkness it seemed almost to leap forward. Fast it came, supernaturally fast, its velocity actually shocking, for a shock came with it. It was exceedingly small, it was exceedingly dreadful, its head erect and venomous and the movement of its legs and arms, as of its bitter, glittering eyes, aping humanity. Malignant evil, personified and aggressive, shaped itself in this otherwise ridiculous outline.

It was the doll.

Racing with incredible security across the slippery surface of the crumpled silk counterpane, it dived and climbed and shot forward with an appearance of complete control and deliberate purpose. That it had a definite aim was overwhelmingly obvious. Its fixed, glassy eyes were concentrated upon a point beyond and behind the terrified governess, the point precisely where Colonel Masters, her employer, stood against her shoulder.

A frantic, half protective movement on her part, seemed lost in the air...

She turned instinctively, putting an arm about his shoulders, which he instantly flung off.

'Let the bloody thing come,' he cried. 'I'll deal with it...!' He thrust her violently aside.

The doll came at him. The hinges of its diminutive broken arms and its jointed legs emitted a thin, creaking sound as it came darting—the syllables Madame Jodzka had already heard more than once. Syllables she had heard without understanding—'*buth laga*'—but syllables now packed with awful meaning: *Revenge*.

The sounds hissed and squeaked, yet clear as a bell as the beast advanced at this miraculous speed.

Before Colonel Masters could move an inch backwards or forwards in self protection, before he could command himself to any sort of action, or contrive the smallest measure of self defence, it was off the bed and at him. It settled. Savagely, its little jaws of tiny make-believe were bitten deep into Colonel Masters' throat, fastened tightly.

In a flash this happened, in a flash it was over. In Madame Jodzka's memory it remained like the impression of a lightning flash, simultaneously etched in black and white. It had happened in the present as though it had no past. It came and was gone again. Her faculties, as after a vivid lightning, were momentarily paralysed, without past or present. She had witnessed these awful things, but had not realised them. It was this lack or realisation that struck her motionless and dumb.

Colonel Masters, on the other hand, stood beside her quietly as though nothing unusual had happened, wholly master of himself, calm, collected. At the moment of attack no sound had left his lips, there had been no gesture even of defence. Whatever had come, he had apparently accepted. The words that now fell from his lips were, thus, all the more dreadful in their appalling common-placeness.

'Hadn't you better put that counterpane straight a bit... perhaps?'

Common sense, as always, enables the gas of hysteria to escape.

Madame Jodzka gasped, but she obeyed. Automatically she moved across to do his bidding, yet aware, even as she thus moved, that he flicked something from his neck, as though a wasp, a mosquito, or some poisonous insect, had tried to sting him. She remembered no more than that, for he, in his calmness, had contributed nothing else.

Fumbling with the folds of slippery counterpane she tried to straighten out, she was startled to find that Monica was sitting up in bed, awake.

'Oh, Doska—you here!' the child exclaimed innocently, straight out of sleep and using the affectionate nickname. 'And Daddy too! Oh, my goodness...!'

'Sm-moothing your bed, darling,' she stammered, hardly aware of what she said. 'You ought to be asleep. I just looked in to see...' She mumbled a few other automatic words.

'And Daddy with you!' repeated the child excitedly, sleep still about her, wondering what it all meant. 'Ooh! Ooh!' holding out her arms.

This brief exchange of spoken words, though it takes a minute to describe, occurred simultaneously with the action—perhaps ten seconds all told, for while the governess fumbled with the counterpane, Colonel Masters was in the act of brushing something from his neck. Nothing else was audible, nothing but his quick gasp and sudden intake of breath: but something else—she swears it on her Warsaw priest—was visible. Madame Jodzka maintains by all her gods she saw this other thing.

In moments of paralysing stress it is not the senses that act less speedily nor with less precision; their action, on the contrary, is intensified and speeded up: what takes longer is the registration of their reports. The numbed brain causes the apparent delay; realisation is slowed down.

Madame Jodzka thus only realised a fraction of a second later what her eyes had indubitably witnessed; a dark-skinned arm slanting in through the open window by the bed and snatching at a small object that lay on the floor after dropping from Colonel

Masters' throat, then withdrawing again at lightning speed into the darkness of the night outside.

No one but herself, apparently, had seen this—it was almost supernaturally swift.

'And now you'll be asleep again in two minutes, lucky Monica,' Colonel Masters was whispering over by the bed. 'I just peeped in to see that you were all right...' His voice was thin, dreadfully soundless.

Madame Jodzka, against the door, frozen, terrified, looked on and listened. 'Are you quite well, Daddy? Sure? I had a dream, but it's gone now.'

'Splendid. Never better in my life. But better still if I saw you sound asleep. Come now, I'll blow out this silly night-light, for that's what woke you up, I'll be bound.'

He blew it out, he and the child blew it out together, the latter with sleepy laughter that then hushed. And Colonel Masters tiptoed to join Madame Jodzka at the door. 'A lot of damned fuss about nothing,' she heard him muttering in that same thin dreadful voice, and then, as they closed the door and stood a moment in the darkened passage, he did suddenly an unexpected thing. He took the Polish woman in his arms, held her fiercely to him for a second, kissed her vehemently, and flung her away.

'Bless you and thank you,' he said in a low, angry voice. 'You did your best. You made a great fight. But I got what I deserved. I've been waiting years for it.' And he was off down the stairs to his own quarters. Half way down he stopped and looked up to where she stood against the rails. 'Tell the doctor,' he whispered hoarsely, 'that I took a sleeping draught—an overdose.' And he was gone.

And this was, roughly, what she did tell the doctor next morning when a hurried telephone summons brought him to the bed whereon a dead man lay with a swollen, blackened tongue. She told the same tale at the inquest too and an emptied bottle of a powerful sleeping-draught supported her...

And Monica, too young to realise grief beyond its trumpery meaning of a selfishly felt loss, never once—oddly enough—referred to the absence of the lovely doll that had comforted so many hours, proved such an intimate companion day and night in a life that held no other playmates. It seemed forgotten, expunged utterly from her memory, as though it had never existed at all. She stared blankly, stupidly, when a doll was mentioned: she preferred her worn-out Teddy bears. The slate of memory, in this particular, was wiped clean.

'They're so warm and comfy,' she described her bears, 'and they cuddle without tickling. Besides,' she added innocently, 'they don't squeak and try to slip away...'

Thus in the suburbs, where great spaces between the lamps go dead at night, where the moist wind comes whispering through the mournful branches of the silver-pines, where nothing happens and people cry 'Let's go to town!' there are occasional stirrings among the dead dry bones that hide behind respectable villa walls...

## RUNNING WOLF

The man who enjoys an adventure outside the general experience of the race, and imparts it to others, must not be surprised if he is taken for either a liar or a fool, as Malcolm Hyde, hotel clerk on a holiday, discovered in due course. Nor is 'enjoy' the right word to use in describing his emotions; the word he chose was probably 'survive'.

When he first set eyes on Medicine Lake he was struck by its still, sparkling beauty, lying there in the vast Canadian backwoods; next, by its extreme loneliness; and, lastly—a good deal later, this—by its combination of beauty, loneliness, and singular atmosphere, due to the fact that it was the scene of his adventure.

'It's fairly stiff with big fish,' said Morton of the Montreal Sporting Club. 'Spend your holidays there—up Mattawa way, some fifteen miles west of Stony Creek. You'll have it all to yourself except for an old Indian who's got a shack there. Camp on the east side—if you'll take a tip from me.' He then talked for half an hour about the wonderful sport; yet he was not otherwise very communicative, and did not suffer questions gladly, Hyde noticed. Nor had he stayed there very long himself. If it was such a paradise as Morton, its discoverer and the most experienced rod in the province, claimed, why had he himself spent only three days there?

'Ran short of grub,' was the explanation offered; but to another friend he had mentioned briefly, 'flies' and to a third, so Hyde learned later, he gave the excuse that his half-breed 'took sick', necessitating a quick return to civilisation.

Hyde, however, cared little for the explanations; his interest in these came later. 'Stiff with fish' was the phrase he liked. He took the Canadian Pacific train to Mattawa, laid in his outfit at Stony Creek, and set off thence for the fifteen-mile canoe-trip without a care in the world.

Travelling light, the portages did not trouble him; the water was swift and easy, the rapids negotiable; everything came his way, as the saying is. Occasionally he saw big fish making for the deeper pools, and was sorely tempted to stop; but he resisted. He pushed on between the immense world of forests that stretched for hundreds of miles, known to deer, bear, moose, and wolf, but strange to any echo of human tread, a deserted and primeval wilderness. The autumn day was calm, the water sang and sparkled, the blue sky hung cloudless over all, ablaze with light. Toward evening he passed an old beaver-dam, rounded a little point, and had his first sight of Medicine Lake. He lifted his dripping paddle; the canoe shot with silent glide into calm water. He gave an exclamation of delight, for the loveliness caught his breath away.

Though primarily a sportsman, he was not insensible to beauty. The lake formed a crescent, perhaps four miles long, its width between a mile and half a mile. The slanting gold of sunset flooded it. No wind stirred its crystal surface. Here it had lain since the redskins' god first made it; here it would lie until he dried it up again. Towering spruce and hemlock trooped to its very edge, majestic cedars leaned down as if to drink, crimson sumachs shone in fiery patches, and maples gleamed orange and red beyond belief. The air was like wine, with the silence of a dream.

It was here the red men formerly 'made medicine', with all the wild ritual and tribal ceremony of an ancient day. But it was of Morton, rather than of Indians, that Hyde thought. If this lonely, hidden paradise was really stiff with big fish, he owed a lot to Morton for the information. Peace invaded him, but the excitement of the hunter lay below.

He looked about him with quick, practised eye for a camping-place before the sun sank below the forests and the half-lights came. The Indian's shack, lying in full sunshine on the eastern shore, he found at once; but the trees lay too thick about it for comfort, nor did he wish to be so close to its inhabitant. Upon the opposite side, however, an ideal clearing offered. This lay already in shadow, the huge forest darkening it toward evening; but the open space attracted. He paddled over quickly and examined it. The ground was hard and dry, he found, and a little brook ran tinkling down one side of it into the lake. This outfall, too, would be a good fishing spot. Also it was sheltered. A few low willows marked the mouth.

An experienced camper soon makes up his mind. It was a perfect site, and some charred logs, with traces of former fires, proved that he was not the first to think so. Hyde was delighted. Then, suddenly, disappointment came to tinge his pleasure. His kit was landed, and preparations for putting up the tent were begun, when he recalled a detail that excitement had so far kept in the background of his mind—Morton's advice. But not Morton's only, for the storekeeper at Stony Creek had reinforced it. The big fellow with straggling moustache and stooping shoulders, dressed in shirt and trousers, had handed him out a final sentence with the bacon, flour, condensed milk, and sugar. He had repeated Morton's half-forgotten words:

'Put yer tent on the east shore, I should,' he had said at parting.

He remembered Morton, too, apparently. 'A shortish fellow, brown as an Indian and fairly smelling of the woods. Travelling with Jake, the half-breed.' That assuredly was Morton. 'Didn't stay long, now, did he,' he added to himself in a reflective tone.

'Going Windy Lake way, are yer? Or Ten Mile Water, maybe?' he had first inquired of Hyde.

'Medicine Lake.'

'Is that so?' the man said, as though he doubted it for some obscure reason. He pulled at his ragged moustache a moment. 'Is that so, now?' he repeated. And the final words followed him down-stream after a considerable pause—the advice about the best shore on which to put his tent.

All this now suddenly flashed back upon Hyde's mind with a tinge of disappointment and annoyance, for when two experienced men agreed, their opinion was not to be lightly disregarded. He wished he had asked the storekeeper for more details. He looked about him, he reflected, he hesitated. His ideal camping-ground lay certainly on the forbidden shore. What in the world, he wondered, could be the objection to it?

But the light was fading; he must decide quickly one way or the other. After staring at his unpacked dunnage, and the tent, already half erected, he made up his mind with a muttered expression that consigned both Morton and the storekeeper to less pleasant places. 'They must have *some* reason,' he growled to himself; 'fellows like that usually know what they're talking about. I guess I'd better shift over to the other side—for to-night, at any rate.'

He glanced across the water before actually reloading. No smoke rose from the Indian's shack. He had seen no sign of a canoe. The man, he decided, was away. Reluctantly, then, he left the good camping-ground and paddled across the lake, and half an hour later his tent was up, firewood collected, and two small trout were already caught for supper. But the bigger fish, he knew, lay waiting for him on the other side by the little outfall, and he fell asleep at length on his bed of balsam boughs, annoyed and disappointed, yet wondering how a mere sentence could have persuaded him so easily against his own better judgment. He slept like the dead; the sun was well up before he stirred.

But his morning mood was a very different one. The brilliant light, the peace, the intoxicating air, all this was too exhilarating for the mind to harbour foolish fancies, and he marvelled that he could have been so weak the night before. No hesitation lay in him anywhere. He struck camp immediately after breakfast, paddled back across the strip of shining water, and quickly settled in upon the forbidden shore, as he now called it, with a contemptuous grin. And the more he saw of the spot, the better he liked it. Therc was plenty of wood, running water to drink, an open space about the tent, and there were no flies. The fishing, moreover, was magnificent. Morton's description was fully justified, and 'stiff with big fish' for once was not an exaggeration.

The useless hours of the early afternoon he passed dozing in the sun, or wandering through the underbrush beyond the camp. He found no sign of anything unusual. He bathed in a cool, deep pool; he revelled in the lonely little paradise. Lonely it certainly was, but the loneliness was part of its charm; the stillness, the peace, the isolation of this beautiful backwoods lake delighted him. The silence was divine. He was entirely satisfied.

After a brew of tea, he strolled toward evening along the shore, looking for the first sign of a rising fish. A faint ripple on the water, with the lengthening shadows, made good conditions. *Plop* followed *plop*, as the big fellows rose, snatched at their food, and vanished into the depths. He hurried back. Ten minutes later he had taken his rods and was gliding cautiously in the canoe through the quiet water.

So good was the sport, indeed, and so quickly did the big trout pile up in the bottom of the canoe, that despite the growing lateness, he found it hard to tear himself away. 'One more,' he said, 'and then I really will go.' He landed that 'one more', and was in the act of taking off the hook, when the deep silence of the evening was curiously disturbed. He became abruptly aware that some one watched him. A pair of eyes, it seemed, were fixed upon him from some point in the surrounding shadows.

Thus, at least, he interpreted the odd disturbance in his happy mood; for thus he felt it. The feeling stole over him without the slightest warning. He was not alone. The slippery big trout dropped from his fingers. He sat motionless, and stared about him.

Nothing stirred; the ripple on the lake had died away; there was no wind; the forest lay a single purple mass of shadow; the yellow sky, fast fading, threw reflections that troubled the eye and made distances uncertain. But there was no sound, no movement; he saw no figure anywhere. Yet he knew that some one watched him, and a wave of quite unreasoning terror gripped him. The nose of the canoe was against the bank. In a moment, and instinctively, he shoved it off and paddled into deeper water. The watcher, it came to him also instinctively, was quite close to him upon that bank. But where? And who? Was it the Indian?

Here, in deeper water, and some twenty yards from the shore, he paused and strained both sight and hearing to find some possible clue. He felt half ashamed, now that the first strange feeling passed a little. But the certainty remained. Absurd as it was, he felt positive that some one watched him with concentrated and intent regard. Every fibre in his being told him so; and though he could discover no figure, no new outline on the shore, he could even have sworn in which clump of willow bushes the hidden person crouched and stared. His attention seemed drawn to that particular clump.

The water dripped slowly from his paddle, now lying across the thwarts. There was no other sound. The canvas of his tent gleamed dimly. A star or two were out. He waited. Nothing happened.

Then, as suddenly as it had come, the feeling passed, and he knew that the person who had been watching him intently had gone. It was as if a current had been turned off; the normal world flowed back; the landscape emptied as if some one had left a room. The disagreeable feeling left him at the same time, so that he instantly turned the canoe in to the shore again, landed, and, paddle in hand, went over to examine the clump of willows he had singled out as the place of concealment. There was no one there, of course, nor any trace of recent human occupancy. No leaves, no branches stirred, nor was a single twig displaced; his keen and practised sight detected no sign of tracks upon the ground. Yet, for all that, he felt positive that a little time ago some one had crouched among these very leaves and watched him. He remained absolutely convinced of it. The watcher, whether Indian hunter, stray lumberman, or wandering half-breed, had now withdrawn, a search was useless, and dusk was falling. He returned to his little camp, more disturbed perhaps than he cared to acknowledge. He cooked his supper, hung up his catch on a string, so that no prowling animal could get at it during the night, and prepared to make himself comfortable until bedtime. Unconsciously, he built a bigger fire than usual, and found himself peering over his pipe into the deep shadows beyond the firelight, straining his ears to catch the slightest sound. He remained generally on the alert in a way that was new to him.

A man under such conditions and in such a place need not know discomfort until the sense of loneliness strikes him as too vivid a reality. Loneliness in a backwoods camp brings charm, pleasure, and a happy sense of calm until, and unless, it comes too near. It should remain an ingredient only among other conditions; it should not be directly, vividly noticed. Once it has crept within short range, however, it may easily cross the narrow line between comfort and discomfort, and darkness is an undesirable time for the transition. A curious dread may easily follow—the dread lest the loneliness suddenly be disturbed, and the solitary human feel himself open to attack.

For Hyde, now, this transition had been already accomplished; the too intimate sense of his loneliness had shifted abruptly into the worst condition of no longer being quite alone. It was an awkward moment, and the hotel clerk realised his position exactly. He did not quite like it. He sat there, with his back to the blazing logs, a very visible object in the light, while all about him the darkness of the forest lay like an impenetrable wall. He could not see a yard beyond the small circle of his camp-fire; the silence about him was like the silence of the dead. No leaf rustled, no wave lapped; he himself sat motionless as a log.

Then again he became suddenly aware that the person who watched him had returned, and that same intent and concentrated gaze as before was fixed upon him where he lay. There was no warning; he heard no stealthy tread or snapping of dry twigs, yet the owner of those steady eyes was very close to him, probably not a dozen feet away. This sense of proximity was overwhelming.

It is unquestionable that a shiver ran down his spine. This

time, moreover, he felt positive that the man crouched just beyond the firelight, the distance he himself could see being nicely calculated, and straight in front of him. For some minutes he sat without stirring a single muscle, yet with each muscle ready and alert, straining his eyes in vain to pierce the darkness, but only succeeding in dazzling his sight with the reflected light. Then, as he shifted his position slowly, cautiously, to obtain another angle of vision, his heart gave two big thumps against his ribs and the hair seemed to rise on his scalp with the sense of cold that gave him goose-flesh. In the darkness facing him he saw two small and greenish circles that were certainly a pair of eyes, yet not the eyes of Indian hunter, or of any human being. It was a pair of animal eyes that stared so fixedly at him out of the night. And this certainty had an immediate and natural effect upon him.

For, at the menace of those eyes, the fears of millions of long dead hunters since the dawn of time woke in him. Hotel clerk though he was, heredity surged through him in an automatic wave of instinct. His hand groped for a weapon. His fingers fell on the iron head of his small camp axe, and at once he was himself again. Confidence returned; the vague, superstitious dread was gone. This was a bear or wolf that smelt his catch and came to steal it. With beings of that sort he knew instinctively how to deal, yet admitting, by this very instinct, that his original dread had been of quite another kind.

'I'll damned quick find out what it is,' he exclaimed aloud, and snatching a burning brand from the fire, he hurled it with good aim straight at the eyes of the beast before him.

The bit of pitch-pine fell in a shower of sparks that lit the dry grass this side of the animal, flared up a moment, then died quickly down again. But in that instant of bright illumination he saw clearly what his unwelcome visitor was. A big timber wolf sat on its hindquarters, staring steadily at him through the firelight. He saw its legs and shoulders, he saw its hair, he saw also the big hemlock trunks lit up behind it, and the willow scrub on each side. It formed a vivid, clear-cut picture shown in clear detail by the momentary blaze. To his amazement, however, the wolf did not turn and bolt away from the burning log, but withdrew a few yards only, and sat there again on its haunches, staring, staring as before. Heavens, how it stared! He 'shoo-ed' it, but without effect; it did not budge. He did not waste another good log on it, for his fear was dissipated now; a timber wolf was a timber wolf, and it might sit there as long as it pleased, provided it did not try to steal his catch. No alarm was in him any more. He knew that wolves were harmless in the summer and autumn, and even when 'packed' in the winter, they would attack a man only when suffering desperate hunger. So he lay and watched the beast, threw bits of stick in its direction, even talked to it, wondering only that it never moved. 'You can stay there for ever, if you like,' he remarked to it aloud, 'for you cannot get at my fish, and the rest of the grub I shall take into the tent with me!'

The creature blinked its bright green eyes, but made no move.

Why, then, if his fear was gone, did he think of certain things as he rolled himself in the Hudson Bay blankets before going to sleep? The immobility of the animal was strange, its refusal to turn and bolt was still stranger. Never before had he known a wild creature that was not afraid of fire. Why did it sit and watch him, as with purpose in its gleaming eyes? How had he felt its presence earlier and instantly? A timber wolf, especially a solitary wolf, was a timid thing, yet this one feared neither man nor fire. Now, as he lay there wrapped in his blankets inside the cosy tent, it sat outside beneath the stars, beside the fading embers, the wind chilly in its fur, the ground cooling beneath its planted paws, watching him, steadily watching him, perhaps until the dawn.

It was unusual, it was strange. Having neither imagination nor tradition, he called upon no store of racial visions. Matter of fact, a hotel clerk on a fishing holiday, he lay there in his blankets, merely wondering and puzzled. A timber wolf was a timber wolf and nothing more. Yet this timber wolf—the idea haunted him—was different. In a word, the deeper part of his original uneasiness remained. He tossed about, he shivered sometimes in his broken sleep; he did not go out to see, but he woke early and unrefreshed.

Again with the sunshine and the morning wind, however, the incident of the night before was forgotten, almost unreal. His hunting zeal was uppermost. The tea and fish were delicious, his pipe had never tasted so good, the glory of this lonely lake amid primeval forests went to his head a little; he was a hunter before the Lord, and nothing else. He tried the edge of the lake, and in the excitement of playing a big fish, knew suddenly that *it,* the wolf, was there. He paused with the rod, exactly as if struck. He looked about him, he looked in a definite direction. The brilliant sunshine made every smallest detail clear and sharp—boulders of granite, burned stems, crimson sumach, pebbles along the shore in neat, separate detail—without revealing where the watcher hid. Then, his sight wandering farther inshore among the tangled undergrowth, he suddenly picked up the familiar, half-expected outline. The wolf was lying behind a granite boulder, so that only the head, the muzzle, and the eyes were visible. It merged in its background. Had he not known it was a wolf, he could never have separated it from the landscape. The eyes shone in the sunlight.

There it lay. He looked straight at it. Their eyes, in fact, actually met full and square. 'Great Scott!' he exclaimed aloud, 'why, it's like looking at a human being!'

From that moment, unwittingly, he established a singular personal relation with the beast. And what followed confirmed this undesirable impression, for the animal rose instantly and came down in leisurely fashion to the shore, where it stood looking back at him. It stood and stared into his eyes like some great wild dog, so that he was aware of a new and almost incredible sensation—that it courted recognition.

'Well! Well!' he exclaimed again, relieving his feelings by addressing it aloud, 'if this doesn't beat everything I ever saw! What d'you want, anyway?'

He examined it now more carefully. He had never seen a

wolf so big before; it was a tremendous beast, a nasty customer to tackle, he reflected, if it ever came to that. It stood there absolutely fearless, and full of confidence. In the clear sunlight he took in every detail of it—a huge, shaggy, lean-flanked timber wolf, its wicked eyes staring straight into his own, almost with a kind of purpose in them. He saw its great jaws, its teeth, and its tongue hung out, dropping saliva a little. And yet the idea of its savagery, its fierceness, was very little in him.

He was amazed and puzzled beyond belief. He wished the Indian would come back. He did not understand this strange behaviour in an animal. Its eyes, the odd expression in them, gave him a queer, unusual, difficult feeling. Had his nerves gone wrong, he almost wondered.

The beast stood on the shore and looked at him. He wished for the first time that he had brought a rifle. With a resounding smack he brought his paddle down flat upon the water, using all his strength, till the echoes rang as from a pistol-shot that was audible from one end of the lake to the other. The wolf never stirred. He shouted, but the beast remained unmoved. He blinked his eyes, speaking as to a dog, a domestic animal, a creature accustomed to human ways. It blinked its eyes in return.

At length, increasing his distance from the shore, he continued fishing, and the excitement of the marvellous sport held his attention—his surface attention, at any rate. At times he almost forgot the attendant beast; yet whenever he looked up, he saw it there. And worse; when he slowly paddled home again, he observed it trotting along the shore as though to keep him company. Crossing a little bay, he spurted, hoping to reach the other point before his undesired and undesirable attendant. Instantly the brute broke into that rapid, tireless lope that, except on ice, can run down anything on four legs in the woods. When he reached the distant point, the wolf was waiting for him. He raised his paddle from the water, pausing a moment for reflection; for his very close attention—there were dusk and night yet to come—he certainly did not relish. His camp was near; he had to land; he felt uncomfortable even in the sunshine of broad day, when, to his keen relief, about half a mile from the tent, he saw the creature suddenly stop and sit down in the open. He waited a moment, then paddled on. It did not follow. There was no attempt to move; it merely sat and watched him. After a few hundred yards, he looked back. It was still sitting where he left it. And the absurd, yet significant, feeling came to him that the beast divined his thought, his anxiety, his dread, and was now showing him, as well as it could, that it entertained no hostile feeling and did not meditate attack.

He turned the canoe toward the shore; he landed; he cooked his supper in the dusk; the animal made no sign. Not far away it certainly lay and watched, but it did not advance. And to Hyde, observant now in a new way, came one sharp, vivid reminder of the strange atmosphere into which his commonplace personality had strayed: he suddenly recalled that his relations with the beast, already established, had progressed distinctly a stage further. This startled him, yet without the accompanying alarm he must certainly have felt twenty-four hours before. He had an understanding with the wolf. He was aware of friendly thoughts toward it. He even went so far as to set out a few big fish on the spot where he had first seen it sitting the previous night. 'If he comes,' he thought, 'he is welcome to them, I've got plenty, anyway.' He thought of it now as 'he'.

Yet the wolf made no appearance until he was in the act of entering his tent a good deal later. It was close on ten o'clock, whereas nine was his hour, and late at that, for turning in. He had, therefore, unconsciously been waiting for him. Then, as he was closing the flap, he saw the eyes close to where he had placed the fish. He waited, hiding himself, and expecting to hear sounds of munching jaws; but all was silence. Only the eyes glowed steadily out of the background of pitch darkness. He closed the flap. He had no slightest fear. In ten minutes he was sound asleep.

He could not have slept very long, for when he woke up he could see the shine of a faint red light through the canvas, and the fire had not died down completely. He rose and cautiously peeped out. The air was very cold, he saw his breath. But he also saw the wolf, for it had come in, and was sitting by the dying embers, not two yards away from where he crouched behind the flap. And this time, at these very close quarters, there was something in the attitude of the big wild thing that caught his attention with a vivid thrill of startled surprise and a sudden shock of cold that held him spellbound. He stared, unable to believe his eyes; for the wolf's attitude conveyed to him something familiar that at first he was unable to explain. Its pose reached him in the terms of another thing with which he was entirely at home. What was it? Did his senses betray him? Was he still asleep and dreaming?

Then, suddenly, with a start of uncanny recognition, he knew. Its attitude was that of a dog. Having found the clue, his mind then made an awful leap. For it was, after all, no dog its appearance aped, but something nearer to himself, and more familiar still. Good heavens! It sat there with the pose, the attitude, the gesture in repose of something almost human. And then, with a second shock of biting wonder, it came to him like a revelation. The wolf sat beside that camp-fire as a man might sit.

Before he could weigh his extraordinary discovery, before he could examine it in detail or with care, the animal, sitting in this ghastly fashion, seemed to feel his eyes fixed on it. It slowly turned and looked him in the face, and for the first time Hyde felt a fullblooded superstitious fear flood through his entire being. He seemed transfixed with that nameless terror that is said to attack human beings who suddenly face the dead, finding themselves bereft of speech and movement. This moment of paralysis certainly occurred. Its passing, however, was as singular as its advent. For almost at once he was aware of something beyond and above this mockery of human attitude and pose, something that ran along unaccustomed nerves and reached his feeling, even perhaps his heart. The revulsion was extraordinary, its result still more extraordinary and unexpected. Yet the fact remains. He was aware of another thing that had the effect of stilling his terror as soon as it was born. He was aware of appeal, silent, half expressed, yet vastly pathetic. He saw in the savage eyes a beseeching, even a yearning, expression that changed his mood as by magic from dread to natural sympathy. The great grey brute, symbol of cruel ferocity, sat there beside his dying fire and appealed for help.

The gulf betwixt animal and human seemed in that instant bridged. It was, of course, incredible. Hyde, sleep still possibly clinging to his inner being with the shades and half shapes of dream yet about his soul, acknowledged, how he knew not, the amazing fact. He found himself nodding to the brute in half consent, and instantly, without more ado, the lean grey shape rose like a wraith and trotted off swiftly, but with stealthy tread, into the background of the night.

When Hyde woke in the morning his first impression was that he must have dreamed the entire incident. His practical nature asserted itself. There was a bite in the fresh autumn air; the bright sun allowed no half lights anywhere; he felt brisk in mind and body. Reviewing what had happened, he came to the conclusion that it was utterly vain to speculate; no possible explanation of the animal's behaviour occurred to him: he was dealing with something entirely outside his experience. His fear, however, had completely left him. The odd sense of friendliness remained. The beast had a definite purpose, and he himself was included in that purpose. His sympathy held good.

But with the sympathy there was also an intense curiosity. 'If it shows itself again,' he told himself, 'I'll go up close and find out what it wants.' The fish laid out the night before had not been touched.

It must have been a full hour after breakfast when he next saw the brute; it was standing on the edge of the clearing, looking at him in the way now become familiar. Hyde immediately picked up his axe and advanced toward it boldly, keeping his eyes fixed straight upon its own. There was nervousness in him, but kept well under; nothing betrayed it; step by step he drew nearer until some ten yards separated them. The wolf had not stirred a muscle as yet. Its jaws hung open, its eyes observed him intently; it allowed him to approach without a sign of what its mood might be. Then, with these ten yards between them, it turned abruptly and moved slowly off, looking back first over one shoulder and then over the other, exactly as a dog might do, to see if he was following.

A singular journey it was they then made together, animal and man. The trees surrounded them at once, for they left the lake behind them, entering the tangled bush beyond. The beast, Hyde noticed, obviously picked the easiest track for him to follow; for obstacles that meant nothing to the four-legged expert, yet were difficult for a man, were carefully avoided with an almost uncanny skill, while yet the general direction was accurately kept. Occasionally there were windfalls to be surmounted; but though the wolf bounded over these with ease, it was always waiting for the man on the other side after he had laboriously climbed over. Deeper and deeper into the heart of the lonely forest they penetrated in this singular fashion, cutting across the arc of the lake's crescent, it seemed to Hyde; for after two miles or so, he recognised the big rocky bluff that overhung the water at its northern end. This outstanding bluff he had seen from his camp, one side of it falling sheer into the water; it was probably the spot, he imagined, where the Indians held their medicine-making ceremonies, for it stood out in isolated fashion, and its top formed a private plateau not easy of access. And it was here, close to a big spruce at the foot of the bluff upon the forest side, that the wolf stopped suddenly and for the first time since its appearance gave audible expression to its feelings. It sat down on its haunches, lifted its muzzle with open jaws, and gave vent to a subdued and long-drawn howl that was more like the wail of a dog than the fierce barking cry associated with a wolf.

By this time Hyde had lost not only fear, but caution too; nor, oddly enough, did this warning howl, revive a sign of unwelcome emotion in him. In that curious sound he detected the same message that the eyes conveyed—appeal for help. He paused, nevertheless, a little startled, and while the wolf sat waiting for him, he looked about him quickly. There was young timber here; it had once been a small clearing, evidently. Axe and fire had done their work, but there was evidence to an experienced eye that it was Indians and not white men who had once been busy here. Some part of the medicine ritual, doubtless, took place in the little clearing, thought the man, as he advanced again towards his patient leader. The end of their queer journey, he felt, was close at hand.

He had not taken two steps before the animal got up and moved very slowly in the direction of some low bushes that formed a clump just beyond. It entered these, first looking back to make sure that its companion watched. The bushes hid it; a moment later it emerged again. Twice it performed this pantomime, each time, as it reappeared, standing still and staring at the man with as distinct an expression of appeal in the eyes as an animal may compass, probably. Its excitement, meanwhile, certainly increased, and this excitement was, with equal certainty, communicated to the man. Hyde made up his mind quickly. Gripping his axe tightly, and ready to use it at the first hint of malice, he moved slowly nearer to the bushes, wondering with something of a tremor what would happen.

If he expected to be startled, his expectation was at once fulfilled; but it was the behaviour of the beast that made him jump. It positively frisked about him like a happy dog. It frisked for joy. Its excitement was intense, yet from its open mouth no sound was audible. With a sudden leap, then, it bounded past him into the clump of bushes, against whose very edge he stood, and began scraping vigorously at the ground. Hyde stood and stared, amazement and interest now banishing all his nervousness, even when the beast, in its violent scraping, actually touched his body with its own. He had, perhaps, the feeling that he was in a dream, one of those fantastic dreams in which things may happen without involving an adequate surprise; for otherwise the manner of scraping and scratching at the ground must have seemed an impossible phenomenon. No wolf, no dog certainly, used its paws in the way those paws were working. Hyde had the odd, distressing sensation that it was hands, not paws, he watched. And yet, somehow, the natural, adequate surprise he should have felt was absent. The strange action seemed not entirely unnatural. In his heart some deep hidden spring of sympathy and pity stirred instead. He was aware of pathos.

The wolf stopped in its task and looked up into his face. Hyde acted without hesitation then. Afterwards he was wholly at a loss to explain his own conduct. It seemed he knew what to do, divined what was asked, expected of him. Between his mind and the dumb desire yearning through the savage animal there was intelligent and intelligible communication. He cut a stake and sharpened it, for the stones would blunt his axe-edge. He entered the clump of bushes to complete the digging his four-legged companion had begun. And while he worked, though he did not forget the close proximity of the wolf, he paid no attention to it; often his back was turned as he stooped over the laborious clearing away of the hard earth; no uneasiness or sense of danger was in him any more. The wolf sat outside the clump and watched the operations. Its concentrated attention, its patience, its intense eagerness, the gentleness and docility of the grey, fierce, and probably hungry brute, its obvious pleasure and satisfaction, too, at having won the human to its mysterious purpose—these were colours in the strange picture that Hyde thought of later when dealing with the human herd in his hotel again. At the moment he was aware chiefly of pathos and affection. The whole business was, of course, not to be believed, but that discovery came later, too, when telling it to others.

The digging continued for fully half an hour before his labour was rewarded by the discovery of a small whitish object. He picked it up and examined it—the finger-bone of a man. Other discoveries then followed quickly and in quantity. The *cache* was laid bare. He collected nearly the complete skeleton. The skull however, he found last, and might not have found at all but for the guidance of his strangely alert companion. It lay some few yards away from the central hole now dug, and the wolf stood nuzzling the ground with its nose before Hyde understood that he was meant to dig exactly in that spot for it. Between the beast's very paws his stake struck hard upon it. He scraped the earth from the bone and examined it carefully. It was perfect, save for the fact that some wild animal had gnawed it, the teeth-marks being still plainly visible. Close beside it lay the rusty iron head of a tomahawk. This and the smallness of the bones confirmed him in his judgment that it was the skeleton not of a white man, but of an Indian.

During the excitement of the discovery of the bones one by one, and finally of the skull, but, more especially, during the period of intense interest while Hyde was examining them, he had paid little if any attention to the wolf. He was aware that it sat and watched him, never moving its keen eyes for a single moment from the actual operations, but sign or movement it made none at all. He knew that it was pleased and satisfied, he knew also that he had now fulfilled its purpose in a great measure. The further intuition that now came to him, derived, he felt positive, from his companion's dumb desire, was perhaps the cream of the entire experience to him. Gathering the bones together in his coat, he carried them, together with the tomahawk, to the foot of the big spruce where the animal had first stopped. His leg actually touched the creature's muzzle as he passed. It turned its head to watch, but did not follow, nor did it move a muscle while he prepared the platform of boughs upon which he then laid the poor worn bones of an Indian who had been killed, doubtless, in sudden attack or ambush, and to whose remains had been denied the last grace of proper tribal burial. He wrapped the bones in bark; he laid the tomahawk beside the skull; he lit the circular fire round the pyre, and the blue smoke rose upward into the clear bright sunshine of the Canadian autumn morning till it was lost among the mighty trees far overhead.

In the moment before actually lighting the little fire he had turned to note what his companion did. It sat five yards away, he saw, gazing intently, and one of its front paws was raised a little from the ground. It made no sign of any kind. He finished the work, becoming so absorbed in it that he had eyes for nothing but the tending and guarding of his careful ceremonial fire. It was only when the platform of boughs collapsed, laying their charred burden gently on the fragrant earth among the soft wood ashes, that he turned again, as though to show the wolf what he had done, and seek, perhaps, some look of satisfaction in its curiously expressive eyes. But the place he searched was empty. The wolf had gone.

He did not see it again; it gave no sign of its presence anywhere; he was not watched. He fished as before, wandered through the bush about his camp, sat smoking round his fire after dark, and slept peacefully in his cosy little tent. He was not disturbed. No howl was ever audible in the distant forest, no twig snapped beneath a stealthy tread, he saw no eyes. The wolf that behaved like a man had gone for ever.

It was the day before he left that Hyde, noticing smoke rising from the shack across the lake, paddled over to exchange a word or two with the Indian, who had evidently now returned. The Redskin came down to meet him as he landed, but it was soon plain that he spoke very little English. He emitted the familiar grunts at first; then bit by bit Hyde stirred his limited vocabulary into action. The net result, however, was slight enough, though it was certainly direct:

'You camp there?' the man asked, pointing to the other side.

'Yes.'

'Wolf come?'

'Yes.'

'You see wolf?'

'Yes.'

The Indian stared at him fixedly a moment, a keen, wondering look upon his coppery, creased face.

'You 'fraid wolf?' he asked after a moment's pause.

'No,' replied Hyde, truthfully. He knew it was useless to ask questions of his own, though he was eager for information. The other would have told him nothing. It was sheer luck that the man had touched on the subject at all, and Hyde realised that his own best role was merely to answer, but to ask no questions. Then, suddenly, the Indian became comparatively voluble. There was awe in his voice and manner.

'Him no wolf. Him big medicine wolf. Him spirit wolf.'

Whereupon he drank the tea the other had brewed for him, closed his lips tightly, and said no more. His outline was discernible on the shore, rigid and motionless, an hour later, when Hyde's canoe turned the corner of the lake three miles away, and landed to make the portages up the first rapid of his homeward stream.

It was Morton who, after some persuasion, supplied further details of what he called the legend. Some hundred years before, the tribe that lived in the territory beyond the lake began their annual medicine-making ceremonies on the big rocky bluff at the northern end; but no medicine could be made. The spirits, declared the chief medicine man, would not answer. They were offended. An investigation followed. It was discovered that a young brave had recently killed a wolf, a thing strictly forbidden, since the wolf was the totem animal of the tribe. To make matters worse, the name of the guilty man was Running Wolf. The offence being unpardonable, the man was cursed and driven from the tribe:

'Go out. Wander alone among the woods, and if we see you we slay you. Your bones shall be scattered in the forest, and your spirit shall not enter the Happy Hunting Grounds till one of another race shall find and bury them.'

'Which meant,' explained Morton laconically, his only comment on the story, 'probably for ever.'

## THE LITTLE BEGGAR

He was on his way from his bachelor flat to the club, a man of middle age with a slight stoop, and an expression of face firm yet gentle, the blue eyes with light and courage in them, and a faint hint of melancholy—or was it resignation?—about the strong mouth. It was early in April, a slight drizzle of warm rain falling through the coming dusk; but spring was in the air, a bird sang rapturously on a pavement tree. And the man's heart wakened at the sound, for it was the lift of the year, and low in the western sky above the London roofs there was a band of tender colour.

His way led him past one of the great terminal stations that open the gates of London seawards; the birds, the coloured clouds, and the thought of a sunny coast-line worked simultaneously in his heart. These messages of spring woke music in him. The music, however, found no expression, beyond a quiet sigh, so quiet that not even a child, had he carried one in his big arms, need have noticed it. His pace quickened, his figure straightened up, he lifted his eyes and there was a new light in them. Upon the wet pavement, where the street lamps already laid their network of faint gold, he saw, perhaps a dozen yards in front of him, the figure of a little boy.

The boy, for some reason, caught his attention and his interest vividly. He was dressed in Etons, the broad white collar badly rumpled, the pointed coat hitched grotesquely sideways, while, from beneath the rather grimy straw hat, his thick light hair escaped at various angles. This general air of effort and distress was due to the fact that the little fellow was struggling with a bag packed evidently to bursting point, too big and heavy for him to manage for more than ten yards at a time. He changed it from one hand to the other, resting it in the intervals upon the ground, each effort making it rub against his leg so that the trousers were hoisted considerably above the boot. He was a pathetic figure.

'I must help him,' said the man. 'He'll never get there at this rate. He'll miss his train to the sea.' For his destination was obvious, since a pair of wooden spades was tied clumsily and insecurely to the straps of the bursting bag.

Occasionally, too, the lad, who seemed about ten years old, looked about him to right and left, questionably, anxiously, as though he expected someone—someone to help, or perhaps to meet him. His behaviour even gave the impression that he was not quite sure of his way. The man hurried to overtake him.

'I really must give the little beggar a hand,' he repeated to himself, as he went. He smiled. The fatherly, protective side of him, naturally strong, was touched—touched a little more, perhaps, than the occasion seemed to warrant. The smile broadened into a jolly laugh, as he came up against the great stuffed bag, now resting on the pavement, its owner panting beside it, still looking to right and left alternately. At which instant, exactly, the boy, hearing his step, turned round, and for the first time looked him full in the face with a pair of big blue eyes that held unabashed and happy welcome in them.

'Oh, I say, sir, it's most awfully ripping of you,' he said in a confiding voice, before the man had time to speak. 'I hunted everywhere; but I never thought of looking *behind* me.'

But the man, standing dumb and astonished for a few seconds beside the little fellow, missed the latter sentence altogether, for there was in the clear blue eyes an expression so trustful, so frankly affectionate almost, and in the voice music of so natural a kind, that all the tenderness in him rose; like a sudden tide, and he yearned towards the boy as though he were his little son. Thought, born of some sudden revival of emotion, flashed back swiftly across a stretch of twelve blank years... and for an instant the lines of the mouth grew deeper, though in the eyes the light turned softer, brighter...

'It's too big for you, my boy,' he said, recovering himself with a jolly laugh; 'or, rather, you're not big enough—yet—for it—eh! Where to, now? Ah! the station, I suppose?' And he stooped to grasp the handles of the bulging bag, first poking the spades more securely in beneath the straps; but in doing so became aware that something the boy had said had given him pain. What was it? Why was it? This stray little stranger, met upon the London pavements! Yet so swift is thought that, even while he stooped and before his fingers actually touched the leather, he had found what hurt him—and smiled a little at himself. It was the mode of address the boy made use of, contradicting faintly the affectionate expression in the eyes. It was the word 'sir' that made him feel like a schoolmaster or a tutor; it made him feel old. It was not the word he needed, and—yes—had longed for, somehow almost expected. And there was such strange trouble in his mind and heart that, as he grasped the bag, he did not catch the boy's rejoinder to his question. But, of course, it must be the railway station; he was going to the seaside for Easter; his people would be at the ticket-office waiting for him. Bracing himself a little for the effort, he seized the leather handles and lifted the bag from the ground.

'Oh, thanks awfully, sir!' repeated the boy. He watched him with a true schoolboy grin of gratitude, as though it were great fun, yet also with a true urchin's sense that the proper thing had happened, since such jobs, of course, were for grown-up men. And this time, though he used the objectionable word again, the voice betrayed recognition of the fact that he somehow had a right to look to this particular man for help, and that this particular man only did the right and natural thing in giving help.

But the man, swaying sideways, nearly lost his balance. He had calculated automatically the probable energy necessary to lift the weight; he had put this energy forth. He received a shock as though he had been struck, for the bag had no weight at all; it was as light as a feather. It might have been of tissue-paper, a phantom bag. And the shock was mental as well as physical. His mind swayed with his body.

'By jove!' cried the boy, strutting merrily beside him, hands in his pockets. 'Thanks most awfully. This *is* jolly!'

The objectionable word was omitted, but the man scarcely heard the words at all. For a mist swam before his eyes, the street lamps grew blurred and distant, the drizzle thickened in the air. He still heard the wild, sweet song of the bird, still knew the west had gold upon its lips. It was the rest of the world about him that grew dim. Strange thoughts rose in a cloud. Reality and dream played games, the games of childhood, through his heart. Memories, robed flamingly, trooped past his inner sight, radiant, swift and as of yesterday, closing his eyelids for a moment to the outer world. Rossetti came to him, singing too sweetly a hidden pain in perfect words across those twelve blank years: 'The Hour that might have been, yet might not be, which man's and woman's heart conceived and bore, yet whereof time was barren...' In a second's flash the entire sonnet, 'Stillborn Love', passed on this inner screen 'with eyes where burning memory lights love home...'

Mingled with these—all in an instant of time—came practical thoughts as well. This boy! The ridiculous effort he made to carry this ridiculously light bag! The poignant tenderness, the awakened yearning! Was it a girl dressed up? The happy face, the innocent, confiding smile, the music in the voice, the dear soft blue eyes, and yet, at the same time, something that was *not* there—some indescribable, incalculable element that was lacking. He felt acutely this curious lack. What was it? Who was this merry youngster? He glanced down cautiously as they moved side by side. He felt shy, hopeful, marvellously tender. His heart yearned inexpressibly; the boy, looking elsewhere, did not notice the examination, did not notice, of course, that his companion caught his breath and walked uncertainly.

But the man was troubled. The face reminded him, as he gazed, of many children, of children he had loved and played with, both boys and girls, his Substitute Children, as he had always called them in his heart... Then, suddenly, the boy came closer and took his arm. They were close upon the station now. The sweet human perfume of a small, deeply loved, helpless and dependent little life rose past his face,

He suddenly blurted out: 'But, I say, this bag of yours—it weighs simply nothing!'

The boy laughed—a ring of true careless joy was in the sound. He looked up.

'Do you know what's in it? Shall I tell you?' He added in a whisper: 'I will, if you like.'

But the man was suddenly afraid and dared not ask.

'Brown paper probably,' he evaded laughingly; 'or birds' eggs. You've been up to some wicked lark or other.'

The little chap clasped both hands upon the supporting arm. He took a quick, dancing step or two, then stopped dead, and made the man stop with him. He stood on tiptoe to reach the distant ear. His face wore a lovely smile of truth and trust and delight.

'My future,' he whispered. And the man turned into ice.

They entered the great station. The last of the daylight was shut out. They reached the ticket-office. The crowds of hurrying people surged about them. The man set down the bag. For a moment or two the boy looked quickly about him to right and left, searching, then turned his big blue eyes upon the other with his radiant smile:

'She's in the waiting-room as usual,' he said. 'I'll go and fetch her—though she *ought* to know you're here.' He stood on tiptoe, his hands upon the other's shoulders, his face thrust close. 'Kiss me, father. I shan't be a second.'

'You little beggar!' said the man, in a voice he could not control; then, opening his big arms wide, saw only an empty space before him.

He turned and walked slowly back to his flat instead of to the club; and when he got home he read over for the thousandth time the letter—its ink a little faded during the twelve intervening years—in which she had accepted his love two short weeks before death took her.

## THE OCCUPANT OF THE ROOM

He arrived late at night by the yellow *diligence,* stiff and cramped after the toilsome ascent of three slow hours. The village, a single mass of shadow, was already asleep. Only in front of the little hotel was there noise and light and bustle—for a moment. The horses, with tired, slouching gait, crossed the road and disappeared into the stable of their own accord, their harness trailing in the dust; and the lumbering *diligence* stood for the night where they had dragged it—the body of a great yellow-sided beetle with broken legs.

In spite of his physical weariness, the schoolmaster, revelling in the first hours of his ten-guinea holiday, felt exhilarated. For the high Alpine valley was marvellously still; stars twinkled over the torn ridges of the Dent du Midi where spectral snows gleamed against rocks that looked like ebony; and the keen air smelt of pine forests, dew-soaked pastures, and freshly sawn wood. He took it all in with a kind of bewildered delight for a few minutes, while the other three passengers gave directions about their luggage and went to their rooms. Then he turned and walked over the coarse matting into the glare of the hall, only just able to resist stopping to examine the big mountain map that hung upon the wall by the door.

And, with a sudden disagreeable shock, he came down from the ideal to the actual. For at the inn—the only inn—there was no vacant room. Even the available sofas were occupied...

How stupid he had been not to write! Yet it had been impossible, he remembered, for he had come to the decision suddenly that morning in Geneva, enticed by the brilliance of the weather after a week of rain.

They talked endlessly, this gold-braided porter and the hard-faced old woman—her face was hard, he noticed—gesticulating all the time, and pointing all about the village with suggestions that he ill understood, for his French was limited and their *patois* was fearful.

'*There!*'—he might find a room, 'or *there*! But we are, *hélas,* full—more full than we care about. To-morrow, perhaps—if So-and-So give up their rooms——!' And then, with much shrugging of shoulders, the hard-faced old woman stared at the gold-braided porter, and the porter stared sleepily at the schoolmaster.

At length, however, by some process of hope he did not himself understand, and following directions given by the old woman that were utterly unintelligible, he went out into the street and walked towards a dark group of houses she had pointed out to him. He only knew that he meant to thunder at a door and ask for a room. He was too weary to think out details. The porter half made to go with him, but turned back at the last moment to speak with the old woman. The houses sketched themselves dimly in the general blackness. The air was cold. The whole valley was filled with the rush and thunder of falling water. He was thinking vaguely that the dawn could not be very far away, and that he might even spend the night wandering in the woods, when there was a sharp noise behind him and he turned to see a figure hurrying after him. It was the porter—running.

And in the little hall of the inn there began again a confused three-cornered conversation, with frequent muttered colloquy and whispered asides in *patois* between the woman and the porter—the net result of which was that, 'If Monsieur did not object—there *was* a room, after all, on the first floor—only it was in a sense "engaged". That is to say——'

But the schoolmaster took the room without inquiring too closely into the puzzle that had somehow provided it so suddenly. The ethics of hotel-keeping had nothing to do with him. If the woman offered him quarters it was not for him to argue with her whether the said quarters were legitimately hers to offer.

But the porter, evidently a little thrilled, accompanied the guest up to the room and supplied in a mixture of French and English details omitted by the landlady—and Minturn, the schoolmaster, soon shared the thrill with him, and found himself in the atmosphere of a possible tragedy.

All who know the peculiar excitement that belongs to lofty mountain valleys where dangerous climbing is a chief feature of the attractions, will understand a certain faint element of high alarm that goes with the picture. One looks up at the desolate, soaring ridges and thinks involuntarily of the men who find their pleasure for days and nights together scaling perilous summits among the clouds, and conquering inch by inch the icy peaks that for ever shake their dark terror in the sky. The atmosphere of adventure, spiced with the possible horror of a very grim order of tragedy, is inseparable from any imaginative contemplation of the scene: and the idea Minturn gleaned from the half-frightened porter lost nothing by his ignorance of the language. This Englishwoman, the real occupant of the room, had insisted on going without a guide. She had left just before daybreak two days before—the porter had seen her start—and ... she had not returned! The route was difficult and dangerous, yet not impossible for a skilled climber, even a solitary one. And the Englishwoman was an experienced mountaineer. Also, she was self-willed, careless of advice, bored by warnings, self-confident to a degree. Queer, moreover; for she kept entirely to herself, and sometimes remained in her room with locked doors, admitting no one, for days together; a 'crank', evidently, of the first water.

This much Minturn gathered clearly enough from the porter's talk while his luggage was brought in and the room set to rights; further, too, that the search party had gone out and *might*, of course, return at any moment. In which case——. Thus the room was empty, yet still hers. 'If Monsieur did not object—if the risk he ran of having to turn out suddenly in the night——' It was the loquacious porter who furnished the details that made the transaction questionable; and Minturn dismissed the loquacious porter as soon as possible, and prepared to get into the hastily arranged bed and snatch all the hours of sleep he could before he was turned out.

At first, it must be admitted, he felt uncomfortable—distinctly uncomfortable. He was in some one else's room. He had really no right to be there. It was in the nature of an unwarrantable intrusion; and while he unpacked he kept looking over his shoulder as though some one were watching him from the corners. Any moment, it seemed, he would hear a step in the passage, a knock would come at the door, the door would open, and there he would see this vigorous Englishwoman looking him up and down with anger. Worse still—he would hear her voice asking him what he was doing in her room—her bedroom. Of course, he had an adequate explanation, but still——!

Then, reflecting that he was already half undressed, the humour of it flashed for a second across his mind, and he laughed—*quietly*. And at once, after that laughter, under his breath, came the sudden sense of tragedy he had felt before. Perhaps, even while he smiled, her body lay broken and cold upon those awful heights, the wind of snow playing over her hair, her glazed eyes staring sightless up to the stars... It made him shudder. The sense of this woman whom he had never seen, whose name even he did not know, became extraordinarily real. Almost he could imagine that she was somewhere in the room with him, hidden, observing all he did.

He opened the door softly to put his boots outside, and when he closed it again he turned the key. Then he finished unpacking and distributed his few things about the room. It was soon done; for, in the first place, he had only a small Gladstone and a knapsack, and secondly, the only place where he could spread his clothes was the sofa. There was no chest of drawers, and the cupboard, an unusually large and solid one, was locked. The Englishwoman's things had evidently been hastily put away in it. The only sign of her recent presence was a bunch of faded *Alpenrosen* standing in a glass jar upon the washhand stand. This, and a certain faint perfume, were all that remained. In spite, however, of these very slight evidences, the whole room was pervaded with a curious sense of occupancy that he found exceedingly distasteful. One moment the atmosphere seemed subtly charged with a 'just left' feeling; the next it was a queer awareness of 'still here' that made him turn and look hurriedly behind him.

Altogether, the room inspired him with a singular aversion, and the strength of this aversion seemed the only excuse for his tossing the faded flowers out of the window, and then hanging his mackintosh upon the cupboard door in such a way as to screen it as much as possible from view. For the sight of that big, ugly cupboard, filled with the clothing of a woman who might then be beyond any further need of covering—thus his imagination insisted on picturing it—touched in him a startled sense of the incongruous that did not stop there, but crept through his mind gradually till it merged somehow into a sense of a rather grotesque horror. At any rate, the sight of that cupboard was offensive, and he covered it almost instinctively. Then, turning out the electric light, he got into bed.

But the instant the room was dark he realised that it was more than he could stand, for, with the blackness, there came a sudden rush of cold that he found it hard to explain. And the odd thing was that, when he lit the candle beside his bed, he noticed that his hand trembled.

This, of course, was too much. His imagination was taking liberties and must be called to heel. Yet the way he called it to order was significant, and its very deliberateness betrayed a mind that has already admitted fear. And fear, once in, is difficult to dislodge. He lay there upon his elbow in bed and carefully took note of all the objects in the room—with the intention, as it were, of taking an inventory of everything his senses perceived, then drawing a line, adding them up finally, and saying with decision, 'That's all the room contains! I've counted every single thing. There is nothing more. *Now*—I may sleep in peace!'

And it was during this absurd process of enumerating the furniture of the room that the dreadful sense of distressing lassitude came over him that made it difficult even to finish counting. It came swiftly, yet with an amazing kind of violence that overwhelmed him softly and easily with a sensation of enervating weariness hard to describe. And its first effect was to banish fear. He no longer possessed enough energy to feel really afraid or nervous. The cold remained, but the alarm vanished. And into every corner of his usually vigorous personality crept the insidious poison of a *muscular* fatigue—at first—that in a few seconds, it seemed, translated itself into *spiritual* inertia. A sudden consciousness of the foolishness, the crass futility of life, of effort, of fighting—of all that makes life worth living, oozed into every fibre of his being, and left him utterly weak. A spirit of black pessimism, that was not even vigorous enough to assert itself, invaded the secret chambers of his heart...

Every picture that presented itself to his mind came dressed in grey shadows; those bored and sweating horses toiling up the ascent to—nothing! That hard-faced landlady taking so much trouble to let her desire for gain conquer her sense of morality—for a few francs! That gold-braided porter, so talkative, fussy energetic, and so anxious to tell all he knew! What was the use of them all? And for himself, what in the world was the good of all the labour and drudgery he went through in that preparatory school where he was junior master? What could it lead to? Wherein lay the value of so much uncertain toil, when the ultimate secrets of life were hidden and no one knew the final goal? How foolish was effort, discipline, work! How vain was pleasure! How trivial the noblest life!...

With a jump that nearly upset the candle Minturn challenged this weak mood. Such vicious thoughts were usually so remote from his normal character that the sudden vile invasion produced a swift reaction. Yet, only for a moment. Instantly, again, the depression descended upon him like a wave. His work—it could lead to nothing but the dreary labour of a small headmastership after all—seemed as vain and foolish as his holiday in the Alps. What an idiot he had been, to be sure, to come out with a knapsack merely to work himself into a state of exhaustion climbing over toilsome mountains that led to nowhere—resulted in nothing. A dreariness of the grave possessed him. Life was a ghastly fraud! Religion a childish humbug! Everything was merely a trap—a trap of death; a coloured toy that Nature used as a decoy! But a decoy for what? For nothing! There was no meaning in anything. The only *real* thing was—DEATH. And the happiest people were those who found it soonest.

*Then why wait for it to come?*

He sprang out of bed, thoroughly frightened. This was horrible. Surely mere physical fatigue could not produce a world so black, an outlook so dismal, a cowardice that struck with such sudden hopelessness at the very roots of life? For, normally, he was cheerful and strong, full of the tides of healthy living; and this appalling lassitude swept the very basis of his personality into nothingness and the desire for death. It was like the development of a Secondary Personality. He had read, of course, how certain persons who suffered shocks developed thereafter entirely different characteristics, memory, tastes, and so forth. It had all rather frightened him. Though scientific men vouched for it, it was hardly to be believed. Yet here was a similar thing taking place in his own consciousness. He was, beyond question, experiencing all the mental variations of—*someone else*! It was un-moral. It was awful. It was—well, after all, at the same time, it was uncommonly interesting.

And this interest he began to feel was the first sign of his returned normal Self. For to feel interest is to live, and to love life.

He sprang into the middle of the room—then switched on the electric light. And the first thing that struck his eye was—the big cupboard.

'Hallo! There's that—beastly cupboard!' he exclaimed to himself, involuntarily, yet aloud. It held all the clothes, the swinging skirts and coats and summer blouses of the dead woman. For he knew now—somehow or other—that she *was* dead...

At that moment, through the open windows, rushed the sound

of falling water, bringing with it a vivid realisation of the desolate, snow-swept heights. He saw her—positively *saw* her!—lying where she had fallen, the frost upon her cheeks, the snow-dust eddying about her hair and eyes, her broken limbs pushing against the lumps of ice. For a moment the sense of spiritual lassitude—of the emptiness of life—vanished before this picture of broken effort—of a small human force battling pluckily, yet in vain, against the impersonal and pitiless potencies of inanimate nature—and he found himself again his normal self. Then instantly, returned again that terrible sense of cold, nothingness, emptiness...

And he found himself standing opposite the big cupboard where her clothes were. He suddenly wanted to see those clothes—things she had used and worn. Quite close he stood, almost touching it. The next second he had touched it. His knuckles struck upon the wood.

Why he knocked is hard to say. It was an instinctive movement probably. Something in his deepest self dictated it—ordered it. He knocked at the door. And the dull sound upon the wood into the stillness of that room brought—horror. Why it should have done so he found it as hard to explain to himself as why he should have felt impelled to knock. The fact remains that when he heard the faint reverberation inside the cupboard, it brought with it so vivid a realisation of the woman's presence that he stood there shivering upon the floor with a dreadful sense of anticipation; he almost expected to hear an answering knock from within—the rustling of the hanging skirts perhaps—or, worse still, to see the locked door slowly open towards him.

And from that moment, he declares that in some way or other he must have partially lost control of himself, or at least of his better judgment; for he became possessed by such an overmastering desire to tear open that cupboard door and see the clothes within, that he tried every key in the room in the vain effort to unlock it, and then, finally, before he quite realised what he was doing—rang the bell!

But, having rung the bell for no obvious or intelligent reason at two o'clock in the morning, he then stood waiting in the middle of the floor for the servant to come, conscious for the first time that something outside his ordinary self had pushed him towards the act. It was almost like an internal voice that directed him... and thus, when at last steps came down the passage and he faced the cross and sleepy chambermaid, amazed at being summoned at such an hour, he found no difficulty in the matter of what he should say. For the same power that insisted he should open the cupboard door also impelled him to utter words over which he apparently had no control.

'It's not *you* I rang for!' he said with decision and impatience. 'I want a man. Wake the porter and send him up to me at once—hurry! I tell you, hurry——!'

And when the girl had gone, frightened at his earnestness, Minturn realised that the words surprised himself as much as they surprised her. Until they were out of his mouth he had not known what exactly he was saying. But now he understood that some force, foreign to his own personality, was using his mind and organs. The black depression that had possessed him a few moments before was also part of it. The poweful mood of this vanished woman had somehow momentarily taken possession of him—communicated, possibly, by the atmosphere of things in the room still belonging to her. But even now, when the porter, without coat or collar, stood beside him in the room, he did not understand why he insisted, with a positive fury admitting no denial, that the key of that cupboard must be found and the door instantly opened.

The scene was a curious one. After some perplexed whispering with the chambermaid at the end of the passage, the porter managed to find and produce the key in question. Neither he nor the girl knew clearly what this excited Englishman was up to, or why he was so passionately intent upon opening the cupboard at two o'clock in the morning. They watched him with an air of wondering what was going to happen next. But something of his curious earnestness, even of his late fear, communicated itself to them, and the sound of the key grating in the lock made them both jump.

They held their breath as the creaking door swung slowly open. All heard the clatter of that other key as it fell against the wooden floor—within. The cupboard had been locked *from the inside.* But it was the scared housemaid, from her position in the corridor, who first saw—and with a wild scream fell crashing against the banisters.

The porter made no attempt to save her. The schoolmaster and himself made a simultaneous rush towards the door, now wide open. They, too, had seen.

There were no clothes, skirts or blouses on the pegs, but they saw the body of the Englishwoman suspended in mid-air, the head bent forward. Jarred by the movement of unlocking, the body swung slowly round to face them... Pinned upon the inside of the door was a hotel envelope with the following words pencilled in straggling writing:

'Tired—unhappy—hopelessly depressed... I cannot face life any longer... All is black. I must put an end to it.... I meant to do it on the mountains, but was afraid. I slipped back to my room unobserved. This way is easiest and best. ...'

# THE MAN WHOM THE TREES LOVED

## I

He painted trees as by some special divining instinct of their essential qualities. He understood them. He knew why in an oak forest, for instance, each individual was utterly distinct from its fellows, and why no two beeches in the whole world were alike. People asked him down to paint a favourite lime or silver birch, for he caught the individuality of a tree as some catch the individuality of a horse. How he managed it was something of a puzzle, for he never had painting lessons, his drawing was often wildly inaccurate, and, while his perception of a Tree Personality was true and vivid, his rendering of it might almost approach the ludicrous. Yet the character and personality of that particular tree stood there alive beneath his brush—shining, frowning, dreaming, as the case might be, friendly or hostile, good or evil. It emerged.

There was nothing else in the wide world that he could paint; flowers and landscapes he only muddled away into a smudge; with people he was helpless and hopeless; also with animals. Skies he could sometimes manage, or effects of wind in foliage, but as a rule he left these all severely alone. He kept to trees, wisely following an instinct that was guided by love. It was quite arresting, this way he had of making a tree look almost like a being—alive. It approached the uncanny.

'Yes, Sanderson knows what he's doing when he paints a tree!' thought old David Bittacy, C. B., late of the Woods and Forests. 'Why, you can almost hear it rustle. You can smell the thing. You can hear the rain drip through its leaves. You can almost see the branches move. It grows.' For in this way somewhat he expressed his satisfaction, half to persuade himself that the twenty guineas were well spent (since his wife thought otherwise), and half to explain this uncanny reality of life that lay in the fine old cedar framed above his study table.

Yet in the general view the mind of Mr. Bittacy was held to be austere, not to say morose. Few divined in him the secretly tenacious love of nature that had been fostered by years spent in the forests and jungles of the eastern world. It was odd for an Englishman, due possibly to that Eurasian ancestor. Surreptitiously, as though half ashamed of it, he had kept alive a sense of beauty that hardly belonged to his type, and was unusual for its vitality. Trees, in particular, nourished it. He, also, understood trees, felt a subtle sense of communion with them, born perhaps of those years he had lived in caring for them, guarding, protecting, nursing, years of solitude among their great shadowy presences. He kept it largely to himself, of course, because he knew the world he lived in. He also kept it from his wife—to some extent. He knew it came between them, knew that she feared it, was opposed. But what he did not know, or realise at any rate, was the extent to which she grasped the power which they wielded over his life. Her fear, he judged, was simply due to those years in India, when for weeks at a time his calling took him away from her into the jungle forests, while she remained at home dreading all manner of evils that might befall him. This, of course, explained her instinctive opposition to the passion for woods that still influenced and clung to him. It was a natural survival of those anxious days of waiting in solitude for his safe return.

For Mrs. Bittacy, daughter of an evangelical clergyman, was a self-sacrificing woman, who in most things found a happy duty in sharing her husband's joys and sorrows to the point of self-obliteration. Only in this matter of the trees she was less successful than in others. It remained a problem difficult of compromise.

He knew, for instance, that what she objected to in this portrait of the cedar on their lawn was really not the price he had given for it, but the unpleasant way in which the transaction emphasised this breach between their common interests—the only one they had, but deep.

Sanderson, the artist, earned little enough money by his strange talent; such cheques were few and far between. The owners of fine or interesting trees who cared to have them painted singly were rare indeed; and the 'studies' that he made for his own delight he also kept for his own delight. Even were there buyers, he would not sell them. Only a few, and these peculiarly intimate friends, might even see them, for he disliked to hear the undiscerning criticism of those who did not understand. Not that he minded laughter at his craftmanship—he admitted it with scorn—but that remarks about the personality of the tree itself could easily wound or anger him. He resented slighting observations concerning them, as though insults offered to personal friends who could not answer for themselves. He was instantly up in arms.

'It really *is* extraordinary,' said a Woman who Understood, 'that you can make that cypress seem an individual, when in reality all cypresses are so *exactly* alike.'

And though the bit of calculated flattery had come so near to saying the right, true thing, Sanderson flushed as though she had slighted a friend beneath his very nose. Abruptly he passed in front of her and turned the picture to the wall.

'Almost as queer,' he answered rudely, copying her silly emphasis, 'as that *you* should have imagined individuality in your husband, Madame, when in reality all men are so *exactly* alike!'

Since the only thing that differentiated her husband from the mob was the money for which she had married him, Sanderson's relations with that particular family terminated on the spot, chance of prospective 'orders' with it. His sensitiveness, perhaps, was morbid. At any rate the way to reach his heart lay through his trees. He might be said to love trees. He certainly drew a splendid inspiration from them, and the source of a man's inspiration, be it music, religion, or a woman, is never a safe thing to criticise.

'I do think, perhaps, it was just a little extravagant, dear,' said

Mrs. Bittacy, referring to the cedar cheque, 'when we want a lawn-mower so badly too. But, as it gives you such pleasure—'

'It reminds me of a certain day, Sophia,' replied the old gentleman, looking first proudly at herself, then fondly at the picture, 'now long gone by. It reminds me of another tree—that Kentish lawn in the spring, birds singing in the lilacs, and someone in a muslin frock waiting patiently beneath a certain cedar—not the one in the picture, I know, but——'

'I was not waiting,' she said indignantly, 'I was picking fir-cones for the schoolroom fire——'

'Fir-cones, my dear, do not grow on cedars, and schoolroom fires were not made in June in my young days.'

'And anyhow it isn't the same cedar.'

'It has made me fond of all cedars for its sake,' he answered, 'and it reminds me that you are the same young girl still——'

She crossed the room to his side, and together they looked out of the window where, upon the lawn of their Hampshire cottage, a ragged Lebanon stood in solitary state.

'You're as full of dreams as ever,' she said gently, 'and I don't regret the cheque a bit—really. Only it would have been more real if it had been the original tree, wouldn't it?'

'That was blown down long ago. I passed the place last year, and there's not a sign of it left,' he replied tenderly. And presently, when he released her from his side, she went up to the wall and carefully dusted the picture Sanderson had made of the cedar on their present lawn. She went all round the frame with her tiny handkerchief, standing on tiptoe to reach the top rim.

'What I like about it,' said the old fellow to himself when his wife had left the room, 'is the way he has made it live. All trees have it, of course, but a cedar taught it to me first—the 'something' trees possess that make them know I'm there when I stand close and watch. I suppose I felt it then because I was in love, and love reveals life everywhere.' He glanced a moment at the Lebanon looming gaunt and sombre through the gathering dusk. A curious wistful expression danced a moment through his eyes. 'Yes, Sanderson has seen it as it is,' he murmured, 'solemnly dreaming there, its dim hidden life against the Forest edge, and as different from that other tree in Kent as I am from—from the vicar, say. It's quite a stranger, too. I don't know anything about it really. That other cedar I loved; this old fellow I respect. Friendly though—yes, on the whole quite friendly. He's painted the friendliness right enough. He saw that. I'd like to know that man better,' he added. 'I'd like to ask him how he saw so clearly that it stands there between this cottage and the Forest—yet somehow more in sympathy with us than with the mass of woods behind—a sort of go-between. *That* I never noticed before. I see it now—through his eyes. It stands there like a sentinel—protective rather.'

He turned away abruptly to look through the window. He saw the great encircling mass of gloom that was the Forest, fringing their little lawn. It pressed up closer in the darkness. The prim garden with its formal beds of flowers seemed an impertinence almost—some little coloured insect that sought to settle on a sleeping monster—some gaudy fly that danced impudently down the edge of a great river that could engulf it with a toss of its smallest wave. That Forest with its thousand years of growth and its deep spreading being was some such slumbering monster, yes. Their cottage and garden stood too near its running lip. When the winds were strong and lifted its shadowy skirts of black and purple.... He loved this feeling of the Forest Personality; he had always loved it.

'Queer,' he reflected, 'awfully queer, that trees should bring me such a sense of dim, vast living! I used to feel it particularly, I remember, in India; in Canadian woods as well; but never in little English woods till here. And Sanderson's the only man I ever knew who felt it too. He's never said so, but there's the proof,' and he turned again to the picture that he loved. A thrill of unaccustomed life ran through him as he looked. 'I wonder, by Jove, I wonder,' his thoughts ran on, 'whether a tree—er—in any lawful meaning of the term can be—alive. I remember some writing fellow telling me long ago that trees had once been moving things, animal organisms of some sort, that had stood so long feeding, sleeping, dreaming, or something, in the same place, that they had lost the power to get away... !'

Fancies flew pell-mell about his mind, and, lighting a cheroot, he dropped into an armchair beside the open window and let them play. Outside the blackbirds whistled in the shrubberies across the lawn. He smelt the earth and trees and flowers, the perfume of mown grass, and the bits of open heath-land far away in the heart of the woods. The summer wind stirred very faintly through the leaves. But the great New Forest hardly raised her sweeping skirts of black and purple shadow.

Mr. Bittacy, however, knew intimately every detail of that wilderness of trees within. He knew all the purple coombs splashed with yellow waves of gorse; sweet with juniper and myrtle, and gleaming with clear and dark-eyed pools that watched the sky. There hawks hovered, circling hour by hour, and the flicker of the peewit's flight, its melancholy, petulant cry, deepened the sense of stillness. He knew the solitary pines, dwarfed, tufted, vigorous, that sang to every lost wind, travellers like the gipsies who pitched their bush-like tents beneath them; he knew the shaggy ponies, with foals like baby centaurs; the chattering jays, the milky call of cuckoos in the spring, and the boom of the bittern from the lonely marches. The undergrowth of watching hollies, he knew too, strange and mysterious, with their dark, suggestive beauty, and the yellow shimmer of their pale dropped leaves.

Here all the Forest lived and breathed in safety, secure from mutilation. No terror of the axe could haunt the peace of its vast subconscious life, no terror of devastating Man afflict it with the dread of premature death. It knew itself supreme; it spread and preened itself without concealment. It set no spires to carry warnings, for no wind brought messages of alarm as it bulged outwards to the sun and stars.

But, once its leafy portals left behind, the trees of the countryside were otherwise. The houses threatened then; they knew themselves in danger. The roads were no longer glades of silent turf, but noisy, cruel ways by which men came to attack them. They were civilised, cared for—but cared for in order that some day they might be put to death. Even in the villages, where the solemn and immemorial repose of giant chestnuts aped security, the tossing of a silver birch against their mass, impatient in the littlest wind, brought warning. Dust clogged their leaves. The inner humming of their quiet life became inaudible beneath the scream and shriek of clattering traffic. They longed and prayed to enter the great Peace of the Forest yonder, but they could not move. They knew, moreover, that the Forest with its august, deep splendour, despised and pitied them. They were a thing of artificial gardens, and belonged to beds of flowers all forced to grow one way....

'I'd like to know that artist fellow better,' was the thought upon which he returned at length to the things of practical life. 'I wonder if Sophia would mind him here for a bit—?' He rose with the sound of the gong, brushing the ashes from his speckled waistcoat. He pulled the waistcoat down. He was slim and spare in figure, active in his movements. In the dim light, but for that silvery moustache, he might easily have passed for a man of forty.

'I'll suggest it to her anyhow,' he decided on his way upstairs to dress. His thought really was that Sanderson could probably explain this world of things he had always felt about—trees. A man who could paint the soul of a cedar in that way must know it all.

'Why not?' she gave her verdict later over the bread-and-butter puddings; 'unless you think he'd find it dull without companions.'

'He would paint all day in the Forest, dear. I'd like to pick his brains a bit, too, if I could manage it.'

'You can manage anything, David,' was what she answered, for this elderly childless couple used an affectionate politeness long since deemed old-fashioned. The remark, however, displeased her, making her feel uneasy, and she did not notice his rejoinder, smiling his pleasure and content—'Except yourself and our bank account, my dear.' This passion of his for trees was of old a bone of contention, though very mild contention. It frightened her. That was the truth. The Bible, her Baedeker for earth and heaven, did not mention it. Her husband, while humouring her, could never alter that instinctive dread she had. He soothed, but never changed her. She liked the woods, perhaps as spots for shade and picnics, but she could not, as he did, love them.

And after dinner, with a lamp beside the open window, he read aloud from *The Times* the evening post had brought, such fragments as he thought might interest her. The custom was invariable, except on Sundays, when, to please his wife, he dozed over Tennyson or Farrar as their mood might be. She knitted while he read, asked gentle questions, told him his voice was a 'lovely reading voice', and enjoyed the little discussions that occasions prompted because he always let her win them with 'Ah, Sophia, I had never thought of it quite in *that* way before; but now you mention it I must say I think there's something in it....'

For David Bittacy was wise. It was long after marriage, during his months of loneliness spent with trees and forests in India, his wife waiting at home in the Bungalow, that his other, deeper side had developed the strange passion that she could not understand. And after one or two serious attempts to let her share it with him, he had given up and learned to hide it from her. He learned, that is, to speak of it only casually; for since she knew it was there, to keep silence altogether would only increase her pain. So from time to time he skimmed the surface just to let her show him where he was wrong and think she won the day. It remained a debatable land of compromise. He listened with patience to her criticism, her excursions and alarms, knowing that while it gave her satisfaction, it could not change himself. The thing lay in him too deep and true for change. But, for peace's sake, some meeting-place was desirable, and he found it thus.

It was her one fault in his eyes, this religious mania carried over from her up-bringing, and it did no serious harm. Great emotion could shake it sometimes out of her. She clung to it because her father taught it her and not because she had thought it out for herself. Indeed, like many women, she never really *thought* at all, but merely reflected the images of others' thinking which she had learned to see. So, wise in his knowledge of human nature, old David Bittacy accepted the pain of being obliged to keep a portion of his inner life shut off from the woman he deeply loved. He regarded her little biblical phrases as oddities that still clung to a rather fine, big soul—like horns and little useless things some animals have not yet lost in the course of evolution while they have outgrown their use.

'My dear, what is it? You frightened me!' She asked it suddenly, sitting up so abruptly that her cap dropped sideways almost to her ear. For David Bittacy behind his crackling paper had uttered a sharp exclamation of surprise. He had lowered the sheet and was staring at her over the tops of his gold glasses.

'Listen to this, if you please,' he said, a note of eagerness in his voice, 'listen to this, my dear Sophia. It's from an address by Francis Darwin before the Royal Society. He is president, you know, and son of the great Darwin. Listen carefully, I beg you. It is *most* significant.'

'I *am* listening, David,' she said with some astonishment, looking up. She stopped her knitting. For a second she glanced behind her. Something had suddenly changed in the room, and it made her feel wide awake, though before she had been almost dozing. Her husband's voice and manner had introduced this new thing. Her instincts rose in warning. '*Do* read it, dear.' He took a deep breath, looking first again over the rims of his glasses to make quite sure of her attention. He had evidently come across something of genuine interest, although herself she often found the passages from these 'Addresses' somewhat heavy.

In a deep, emphatic voice he read aloud:

'It is impossible to know whether or not plants are conscious; but it is consistent with the doctrine of continuity that in all living things there is something psychic, and if we accept this point of view——'

'*If*,' she interrupted, scenting danger.

He ignored the interruption as a thing of slight value he was accustomed to.

'If we accept this point of view,' he continued, 'we must believe that in plants there exists a faint copy of ***what we know as consciousness in ourselves.***'

He laid the paper down and steadily stared at her. Their eyes met. He had italicised the last phrase.

For a minute or two his wife made no reply or comment. They stared at one another in silence. He waited for the meaning of the words to reach her understanding with full import. Then he turned and read them again in part, while she, released from that curious driving look in his eyes, instinctively again glanced over her shoulder round the room. It was almost as if she felt some one had come in to them unnoticed.

'We must believe that in plants there exists a faint copy of what we know as consciousness in ourselves.'

'*If*,' she repeated lamely, feeling before the stare of those questioning eyes she must say something, but not yet having gathered her wits together quite.

'*Consciousness*,' he rejoined. And then he added gravely: 'That, my dear, is the statement of a scientific man of the Twentieth Century.'

Mrs. Bittacy sat forward in her chair so that her silk flounces crackled louder than the newspaper. She made a characteristic little sound between sniffing and snorting. She put her shoes closely together, with her hands upon her knees.

'David,' she said quietly, 'I think these scientific men are simply losing their heads. There is nothing in the Bible that I can remember about any such thing whatsoever.'

'Nothing, Sophia, that I can remember either,' he answered patiently. Then, after a pause, he added, half to himself perhaps more than to her: 'And, now that I come to think about it, it seems that Sanderson once said something to me that was similar.'

'Then Mr. Sanderson is a wise and thoughtful man, and a safe man,' she quickly took him up, 'if he said that.'

For she thought her husband referred to her remark about the Bible, and not to her judgment of the scientific men. And he did not correct her mistake.

'And plants, you see, dear, are not the same thing as trees,' she drove her advantage home, 'not quite, that is.'

'I agree,' said David quietly; 'but both belong to the great vegetable kingdom.'

There was a moment's pause before she answered.

'Pah! the vegetable kingdom, indeed!' She tossed her pretty old head. And into the words she put a degree of contempt that, could the vegetable kingdom have heard it, might have made it feel ashamed for covering a third of the world with its wonderful tangled network of roots and branches, delicate shaking leaves, and its millions of spires that caught the sun and wind and rain. Its very right to existence seemed in question.

## II

Sanderson accordingly came down, and on the whole his short visit was a success. Why he came at all was a mystery to those who heard of it, for he never paid visits and was certainly not the kind of man to court a customer. There must have been something in Bittacy he liked.

Mrs. Bittacy was glad when he left. He brought no dress-suit for one thing, not even a dinner-jacket, and he wore very low collars with big balloon ties like a Frenchman, and let his hair grow longer than was nice, she felt. Not that these things were important, but that she considered them symptoms of something a little disordered. The ties were unnecessarily flowing.

For all that he was an interesting man, and, in spite of his eccentricities of dress and so forth, a gentleman. 'Perhaps,' she reflected in her genuinely charitable heart, 'he had other uses for the twenty guineas, an invalid sister or an old mother to support! She had no notion of the cost of brushes, frames, paints and canvases. Also she forgave him much for the sake of his beautiful eyes and his eager enthusiasm of manner. So many men of thirty were already blasé.

Still, when the visit was over, she felt relieved. She said nothing about his coming a second time, and her husband, she was glad to notice, had likewise made no suggestion. For, truth to tell, the way the younger man engrossed the older, keeping him out for hours in the Forest, talking on the lawn in the blazing sun, and in the evenings when the damp of dusk came creeping out from the surrounding woods, all regardless of his age and usual habits, was not quite to her taste. Of course, Mr. Sanderson did not know how easily those attacks of Indian fever came back, but David surely might have told him.

They talked trees from morning till night. It stirred in her the old subconscious trail of dread, a trail that led ever into the darkness of big woods; and such feelings, as her early evangelical training taught her, were tempting. To regard them in any other ways was to play with danger.

Her mind, as she watched these two, was charged with curious thoughts of dread she could not understand, yet feared the more on that account. The way they studied that old mangy cedar was a trifle unnecessary, unwise, she felt. It was disregarding the sense of proportion which deity had set upon the world for men's safe guidance.

Even after dinner they smoked their cigars upon the low branches that swept down and touched the lawn, until at length she insisted on their coming in. Cedars, she had somewhere heard, were not safe after sundown; it was not wholesome to be too near them; to sleep beneath them was even dangerous, though what the precise danger was she had forgotten. The upas was the tree she really meant.

At any rate she summoned David in, and Sanderson came presently after him.

For a long time, before deciding on this peremptory step, she had watched them surreptitiously from the drawing-room window—her husband and her guest. The dusk enveloped them with its damp veil of gauze. She saw the glowing tips of their cigars, and heard the drone of voices. Bats flitted overhead, and big, silent moths whirred softly over the rhododendron blossoms. And it came suddenly to her, while she watched, that her husband had somehow altered these last few days—since Mr. Sanderson's arrival in fact. A change had come over him, though what it was she could not say. She hesitated, indeed, to search. That was the instinctive dread operating in her. Provided it passed she would rather not know. Small things, of course, she noticed; small outward sings. He had neglected *The Times* for one thing, left off his speckled waistcoats for another. He was absent-minded sometimes; showed vagueness in practical details where hitherto he showed decision. And—he had begun to talk in his sleep again.

These and a dozen other small peculiarities came suddenly upon her with the rush of a combined attack. They brought with them a faint distress that made her shiver. Momentarily her mind was startled, then confused, as her eyes picked out the shadowy figures in the dusk, the cedar covering them, the Forest close at their backs. And then, before she could think, or seek internal guidance as her habit was, this whisper, muffled and very hurried, ran across her brain: 'It's Mr. Sanderson. Call David in at once!'

And she had done so. Her shrill voice crossed the lawn and died away into the Forest, quickly smothered. No echo followed it. The sound fell dead against the rampart of a thousand listening trees.

'The damp is so very penetrating, even in summer,' she murmured when they came obediently. She was half surprised at her own audacity, half repentant. They came so meekly at her call. 'And my husband is sensitive to fever from the East. No, *please* do not throw away your cigars. We can sit by the open window and enjoy the evening while you smoke.'

She was very talkative for a moment; subconscious excitement was the cause.

'It is so still—so wonderfully still,' she went on, as no one spoke, 'so peaceful, and the air so very sweet... and God is always near to those who need His aid.' The words slipped out before she realised quite what she was saying, yet fortunately, in time to lower her voice, for no one heard them. They were, perhaps, an instinctive expression of relief. It flustered her that she could have said the thing at all.

Sanderson brought her shawl and helped to arrange the chairs; she thanked him in her old-fashioned, gentle way, declining the lamps which he had offered to light. 'They attract the moths and insects so, I think!'

The three of them sat there in the gloaming, Mr. Bittacy's white moustache and his wife's yellow shawl gleaming at their end of the little horseshoe, Sanderson with his wild black hair and shining eyes midway between them. The painter went on talking softly, continuing evidently the conversation begun with his host beneath the cedar. Mrs. Bittacy, on her guard, listened—uneasily.

'For trees, you see, rather conceal themselves in daylight. They reveal themselves fully only after sunset. I never *knew* a tree,' he bowed here slightly towards the lady as though to apologise for something he felt she would not quite understand or like, 'until I've seen it in the night. Your cedar, for instance,' looking towards her husband again so that Mrs. Bittacy caught the gleaming of his turned eyes. 'I failed with badly at first, because I did it in the morning. You shall see to-morrow what I mean—that first sketch is upstairs in my portfolio; it's quite another tree to the one you bought. That view'—he leaned forward, lowering his voice—'I caught one morning about two o'clock in very faint moonlight and the stars. I saw the naked being of the thing——'

'You mean that you went out, Mr. Sanderson, at that hour?' the old lady asked with astonishment and mild rebuke. She did not care particularly for his choice of adjectives either.

'I fear it was rather a liberty to take in another's house, perhaps,' he answered courteously. 'But, having chanced to wake,

I saw the tree from my window, and made my way downstairs.'

'It's a wonder Boxer didn't bite you; he sleeps loose in the hall,' she said.

'On the contrary. The dog came out with me. I hope,' he added, 'the noise didn't disturb you, though it's rather late to say so. I feel quite guilty.' His white teeth showed in the dusk as he smiled. A smell of earth and flowers stole in through the window on a breath of wandering air.

Mrs. Bittacy said nothing at the moment. 'We both sleep like tops,' put in her husband, laughing. 'You're a courageous man, though, Sanderson; and, by Jove, the picture justifies you. Few artists would have taken so much trouble, though I read once that Holman Hunt, Rossetti, or some one of that lot, painted all night in his orchard to get an effect of moonlight that he wanted.'

He chattered on. His wife was glad to hear his voice; it made her feel more easy in her mind. But presently the other held the floor again, and her thoughts grew darkened and afraid. Instinctively she feared the influence on her husband. The mystery and wonder that lie in woods, in forests, in great gatherings of trees everywhere, seemed so real and present while he talked.

'The Night transfigures all things in a way,' he was saying; 'but nothing so searchingly as trees. From behind a veil that sunlight hangs before them in the day they emerge and show themselves. Even buildings do that—in a measure—but trees particularly. In the daytime they sleep; at night they wake, they manifest, turn active—live. You remember,' turning politely again in the direction of his hostess, 'how clearly Henley understood that?'

'That socialist person, you mean?' asked the lady. Her tone and accent made the substantive sound criminal. It almost hissed, the way she uttered it.

'The poet, yes,' replied the artist tactfully, 'the friend of Stevenson, you remember, Stevenson who wrote those charming children's verses.'

He quoted in a low voice the lines he meant. It was, for once, the time, the place, and the setting all together. The words floated out across the lawn towards the wall of blue darkness where the big Forest swept the little garden with its league-long curve that was like the shore-line of a sea. A wave of distant sound that was like surf accompanied his voice, as though the wind was fain to listen too:

> Not to the staring Day,
> For all the importunate questionings he pursues
> In his big, violent voice,
> Shall those mild things of bulk and multitude,
> The trees—God's sentinels...
> Yield of their huge, unutterable selves.
>
> . . . . . . . .
>
> But at the word
> Of the ancient, sacerdotal Night,
> Night of the many secrets, whose effect—
> Transfiguring, hierophantic, dread—
> Themselves alone may fully apprehend,
> They tremble and are changed:
> In each the uncouth, individual soul
> Looms forth and glooms
> Essential, and, their bodily presences
> Touched with inordinate significance,
> Wearing the darkness like a livery
> Of some mysterious and tremendous guild,
> They brood—they menace—they appal.

The voice of Mrs. Bittacy presently broke the silence that followed.

'I like that part about God's sentinels,' she murmured. There was no sharpness in her tone; it was hushed and quiet. The truth, so musically uttered, muted her shrill objections though it had not lessened her alarm. Her husband made no comment; his cigar, she noticed, had gone out.

'And old trees in particular,' continued the artist, as though to himself, 'have very definite personalities. You can offend, wound, please them; the moment you stand within their shade you feel whether they come out to you, or whether they withdraw.' He turned abruptly towards his host. 'You know that singular essay of Prentice Mulford's no doubt 'God in the Trees'

—extravagant perhaps, but yet with a fine true beauty in it? You've never read it, no?' he asked.

But it was Mrs. Bittacy who answered; her husband keeping his curious deep silence.

'I never did!' It fell like a drip of cold water from the face muffled in the yellow shawl; even a child could have supplied the remainder of the unspoken thought.

'Ah,' said Sanderson gently, 'but there *is* 'God' in the trees, God in a very subtle aspect and sometimes—I have known the trees express it too—that which is *not* God—dark and terrible. Have you ever noticed, too, how clearly trees show what they want—choose their companions, at least? How beeches, for instance, allow no life too near them—birds or squirrels in their boughs, nor any growth beneath? The silence in the beech wood is quite terrifying often! And how pines like bilberry bushes at their feet and sometimes little oaks—all trees making a clear, deliberate choice, and holding firmly to it? Some trees obviously—it's very strange and marked—seem to prefer the human.'

The old lady sat up crackling, for this was more than she could permit. Her stiff silk dress emitted little sharp reports.

'We know,' she answered, 'that He was said to have walked in the garden in the cool of the evening'—the gulp betrayed the effort that it cost her—'but we are nowhere told that He hid in the trees, or anything like that. Trees, after all, we must remember, are only large vegetables.'

'True,' was the soft answer, 'but in everything that grows, has life, that is, there's mystery past all finding out. The wonder that lies hidden in our own souls lies also hidden, I venture to assert, in the stupidity and silence of a mere potato.'

The observation was not meant to be amusing. It was *not* amusing. No one laughed. On the contrary, the words conveyed in too literal a sense the feeling that haunted all that conversation. Each one in his own way realised—with beauty, with wonder, with alarm—that the talk had somehow brought the whole vegetable kingdom nearer to that of man. Some link had been established between the two. It was not wise, with that great Forest listening at their very doors, to speak so plainly. The Forest edged up closer while they did so.

And Mrs. Bittacy, anxious to interrupt the horrid spell, broke suddenly in upon it with a matter-of-fact suggestion. She did not like her husband's prolonged silence, stillness. He seemed so negative—so changed.

'David,' she said, raising her voice, 'I think you're feeling the dampness. It's grown chilly. The fever comes so suddenly, you know, and it might be wise to take the tincture. I'll go and get it, dear, at once. It's better.' And before he could object she had left the room to bring the homoeopathic dose that she believed in, and that, to please her, he swallowed by the tumbler-full from week to week.

And the moment the door closed behind her, Sanderson began again, though now in quite a different tone. Mr. Bittacy sat up in his chair. The two men obviously resumed the conversation—the real conversation interrupted beneath the cedar—and left aside the sham one which was so much dust merely thrown in the old lady's eyes.

'Trees love you, that's the fact,' he said earnestly. 'Your service to them all these years abroad has made them know you.'

'Know me?'

'Made them, yes,'—he paused a moment, then added,—'made them *aware of your presence*; aware of a force outside themselves that deliberately seeks their welfare, don't you see?'

'By Jove, Sanderson—!' This put into plain language actual sensations he had felt, yet had never dared to phrase in words before. 'They get into touch with me, as it were?' he ventured, laughing at his own sentence, yet laughing only with his lips.

'Exactly,' was the quick, emphatic reply. 'They seek to blend with something they feel instinctively to be good for them, helpful to their essential beings, encouraging to their best expression—their life.'

'Good Lord, Sir!' Bittacy heard himself saying, 'but you're

putting my own thoughts into words. D'you know, I've felt something like that for years. As though—' he looked round to make sure his wife was not there, then finished the sentence—'as though the trees were after me!'

'"Amalgamate" seems the best word, perhaps,' said Sanderson slowly. 'They would draw you to themselves. Good forces, you see, always seek to merge; evil to separate; that's why Good in the end must always win the day—everywhere. The accumulation in the long run becomes overwhelming. Evil tends to separation, dissolution, death. The comradeship of trees, their instinct to run together, is a vital symbol. Trees in a mass are good; alone, you may take it generally, are—well, dangerous. Look at a monkey-puzzler, or better still a holly. Look at it, watch it, understand it. Did you ever see more plainly an evil thought made visible? They're wicked. Beautiful too, oh yes! There's a strange, miscalculated beauty often in evil——'

'That cedar, then——?'

'Not evil, no; but alien, rather. Cedars grow in forests all-together. The poor thing has drifted, that is all.'

They were getting rather deep. Sanderson, talking against time, spoke so fast. It was too condensed. Bittacy hardly followed that last bit. His mind floundered among his own less definite, less sorted thoughts, till presently another sentence from the artist startled him into attention again.

'That cedar will protect you here, though, because you both have humanised it by your thinking so lovingly of its presence. The others can't get past it, as it were.'

'Protect me!' he exclaimed. 'Protect me from their love?'

Sanderson laughed. 'We're getting rather mixed,' he said; 'we're talking of one thing in the terms of another really. But what I mean is—you see—that their love for you, their "awareness" of your personality and presence involves the idea of winning you—across the border—into themselves—into their world of living. It means, in a way, taking you over.'

The ideas the artist started in his mind ran furious wild races to and fro. It was like a maze sprung suddenly into movement. The whirling of the intricate lines bewildered him. They went so fast, leaving but half an explanation of their goal. He followed first one, then another, but a new one always dashed across to intercept before he could get anywhere.

'But India,' he said, presently in a lower voice, 'India is so far away—from this little English forest. The trees, too, are utterly different for one thing.'

The rustle of skirts warned of Mrs. Bittacy's approach. This was a sentence he could turn round another way in case she came up and pressed for explanation.

'There is communion among trees all the world over,' was the strange quick reply. 'They always know.'

'They always know! You think then——?'

'The winds, you see—the great, swift carriers! They have their ancient rights of way about the world. An easterly wind, for instance, carrying on stage by stage as it were—linking dropped messages and meanings from land to land like the birds—an easterly wind——'

Mrs. Bittacy swept in upon them with the tumbler—

'There, David,' she said, 'that will ward off any beginnings of attack. Just a spoonful, dear. Oh, oh! not *all*!' for he had swallowed half the contents at a single gulp as usual; 'another dose before you go to bed, and the balance in the morning, first thing when you wake.'

She turned to her guest, who put the tumbler down for her upon a table at his elbow. She had heard them speak of the east wind. She emphasised the warning she had misinterpreted. The private part of the conversation came to an abrupt end.

'It is the one thing that upsets him more than any other—an east wind,' she said, 'and I am glad, Mr. Sanderson, to hear you think so too.'

## III

A deep hush followed, in the middle of which an owl was heard calling its muffled note in the forest. A big moth whirred with a soft collision against one of the windows. Mrs. Bittacy started slightly, but no one spoke. Above the trees the stars were faintly visible. From the distance came the barking of a dog.

Bittacy, relighting his cigar, broke the little spell of silence that had caught all three.

'It's rather a comforting thought,' he said, throwing the match out of the window, 'that life is about us everywhere, and that there is really no dividing line between what we call organic and inorganic.'

'The universe, yes,' said Sanderson, 'is all one, really. We're puzzled by the gaps we cannot see across, but as a fact, I suppose, there are no gaps at all.'

Mrs. Bittacy rustled ominously, holding her peace meanwhile. She feared long words she did not understand. Beelzebub lay hid among too many syllables.

'In trees and plants especially, there dreams an exquisite life that no one yet has proved unconscious.'

'Or conscious either, Mr. Sanderson,' she neatly interjected. 'It's only man that was made after His image, not shrubberies and things...'

Her husband interposed without delay.

'It is not necessary,' he explained suavely, 'to say that they're alive in the sense that we are alive. At the same time,' with an eye to his wife, 'I see no harm in holding, dear, that all created things contain some measure of His life Who made them. It's only beautiful to hold that He created nothing dead. We are not pantheists for all that!' he added soothingly.

'Oh, no! Not that, I hope!' The word alarmed her. It was worse than hope. Through her puzzled mind stole a stealthy, dangerous thing... like a panther.

'I like to think that even in decay there's life,' the painter murmured. 'The falling apart of rotten wood breeds sentiency; there's force and motion in the falling of a dying leaf, in the breaking up and crumbling of everything indeed. And take an inert stone: it's crammed with heat and weight and potencies of all sorts. What holds its particles together indeed? We understand it as little as gravity or why a needle always turns to the "North". Both things may be a mode of life...'

'You think a compass has a soul, Mr. Sanderson?' exclaimed the lady with a crackling of her silk flounces that conveyed a sense of outrage even more plainly than her tone. The artist smiled to himself in the darkness, but it was Bittacy who hastened to reply.

'Our friend merely suggests that these mysterious agencies,' he said quietly, 'may be due to some kind of life we cannot understand. Why should water only run downhill? Why should trees grow at right angles to the surface of the ground, and towards the sun? Why should the worlds spin for ever on their axes? Why should fire change the form of everything it touches without really destroying them? To say these things follow the law of their being explains nothing. Mr. Sanderson merely suggests—poetically, my dear, of course—that these may be manifestations of life, though life at a different stage to ours.'

'The "*breath* of life," we read, "He breathed into them". These things do not breathe.' She said it with triumph.

Then Sanderson put in a word. But he spoke rather to himself or to his host than by way of serious rejoinder to the ruffled lady.

'But plants do breathe too, you know,' he said. 'They breathe, they eat, they digest, they move about, and they adapt themselves to their environment as men and animals do. They have a nervous system too... at least a complex system of nuclei which have some of the qualities of nerve cells. They may have memory too. Certainly, they know definite action in response to stimulus. And though this may be physiological, no one has proved that it is only that, and not—psychological.'

He did not notice, apparently, the little gasp that was audible behind the yellow shawl. Bittacy cleared his throat, threw his extinguished cigar upon the lawn, crossed and recrossed his legs.

'And in trees,' continued the other, 'behind a great forest, for instance,' pointing towards the woods, 'may stand a rather splendid Entity that manifests through all the thousand individual trees—some huge collective life, quite as minutely and delicately organised as our own. It might merge and blend with ours under certain conditions, so that we could understand it by *being* it, for a time at least. It might even engulf human vitality into the immense whirlpool of its own vast dreaming life. The pull of a big forest on a man can be tremendous and utterly overwhelming.'

The mouth of Mrs. Bittacy was heard to close with a snap. Her shawl, and particularly her crackling dress, exhaled the protest that burned within her like a pain. She was too distressed to be overawed, but at the same time too confused 'mid the litter of words and meanings half understood, to find immediate phrases she could use. Whatever the actual meaning of his language might be, however, and whatever subtle dangers lay concealed behind them meanwhile, they certainly wove a kind of gentle spell with the glimmering darkness that held all three delicately enmeshed there by that open window. The odours of dewy lawn, flowers, trees, and earth formed part of it.

'The moods,' he continued, 'that people waken in us are due to their hidden life affecting our own. Deep calls to deep. A person, for instance, joins you in an empty room: you both instantly change. The new arrival, though in silence, has caused a change of mood. May not the moods of Nature touch and stir us in virtue of a similar prerogative? The sea, the hills, the desert, wake passion, joy, terror, as the case may be; for a few, perhaps, he glanced significantly at his host so that Mrs. Bittacy again caught the turning of his eyes, 'emotions of a curious, flaming splendour that are quite nameless. Well... whence come these powers? Surely from nothing that is... dead! Does not the influence of a forest, its sway and strange ascendancy over certain minds, betray a direct manifestation of life? It lies otherwise beyond all explanation, this mysterious emanation of big woods. Some natures, of course, deliberately invite it. The authority of a host of trees,'—his voice grew almost solemn as he said the words 'is something not to be denied. One feels it here, I think, particularly.'

There was considerable tension in the air as he ceased speaking. Mr. Bittacy had not intended that the talk should go so far. They had drifted. He did not wish to see his wife unhappy or afraid, and he was aware—acutely so—that her feelings were stirred to a point he did not care about. Something in her, as he put it, was 'working up' towards explosion.

He sought to generalise the conversation, diluting this accumulated emotion by spreading it.

'The sea is His and He made it, he suggested vaguely, hoping Sanderson would take the hint, 'and with the trees it is the same...'

'The whole gigantic vegetable kingdom, yes,' the artist took him up, 'all at the service of man, for food, for shelter and for a thousand purposes of his daily life. Is it not striking what a lot of the globe they cover... exquisitely organised life, yet stationary, always ready to our hand when we want them, never running away? But the taking them, for all that, not so easy. One man shrinks from picking flowers, another from cutting down trees. And, it's curious that most of the forest tales and legends are dark, mysterious, and somewhat ill-omened. The forest-beings are rarely gay and harmless. The forest life was felt as terrible. Tree-worship still survives to-day. Wood-cutters...those who take the life of trees... you see, a race of haunted men...'

He stopped abruptly, a singular catch in his voice. Bittacy felt something even before the sentences were over. His wife, he knew, felt it still more strongly. For it was in the middle of the heavy silence following upon these last remarks, that Mrs. Bittacy, rising with a violent abruptness from her chair, drew the attention of the others to something moving towards them across the lawn. It came silently. In outline it was large and curiously spread. It rose high, too, for the sky above the shrubberies, still pale gold from the sunset, was dimmed by its passage. She declared afterwards that it moved in 'looping circles', but what she perhaps meant to convey was 'spirals'.

She screamed faintly. 'It's come at last! And it's you that brought it!'

She turned excitedly, half afraid, half angry, to Sanderson. With a breathless sort of gasp she said it, politeness all forgotten. 'I knew it... if you went on. I knew it. Oh! Oh!' And she cried again, 'Your talking has brought it out!' The terror that shook her voice was rather dreadful.

But the confusion of her vehement words passed unnoticed in the first surprise they caused. For a moment nothing happened.

'What is it you think you see, my dear?' asked her husband, startled. Sanderson said nothing. All three leaned forward, the men still sitting, but Mrs. Bittacy had rushed hurriedly to the window, placing herself of a purpose, as it seemed, between her husband and the lawn. She pointed. Her little hand made a silhouette against the sky, the yellow shawl hanging from the arm like a cloud.

'Beyond the cedar—between it and the lilacs.' The voice had lost its shrillness; it was thin and hushed. 'There... now you see it going round upon itself again—going back, thank God! .... going back to the Forest.' It sank to a whisper, shaking. She repeated, with a great dropping sigh of relief—'Thank God! I thought ... at first... it was coming here ... to us!... David... to *you*!'

She stepped back from the window, her movements confused, feeling in the darkness for the support of a chair, and finding her husband's outstretched hand instead. 'Hold me, dear, hold me, please... tight. Do not let me go.' She was in what he called afterwards 'a regular state'. He drew her firmly down upon her chair again.

'Smoke, Sophie, my dear,' he said quickly, trying to make his voice calm and natural. 'I see it, yes. It's smoke blowing over from the gardener's cottage...'

'But, David,'—and there was new horror in her whisper now—'it made a noise. It makes it still. I hear it swishing.' Some such word she used—swishing, sishing, rushing, or something of the kind. 'David, I'm very frightened. It's something awful! That man has called it out...!'

'Hush, hush,' whispered her husband. He stroked her trembling hand beside him.

'It is in the wind,' said Sanderson, speaking for the first time, very quietly. The expression on his face was not visible in the gloom, but his voice was soft and unafraid. At the sound of it, Mrs. Bittacy started violently again. Bittacy drew his chair a little forward to obstruct her view of him. He felt bewildered himself, a little, hardly knowing quite what to say or do. It was all so very curious and sudden.

But Mrs. Bittacy was badly frightened. It seemed to her that what she saw came from the enveloping forest just beyond their little garden. It emerged in a sort of secret way, moving towards them as with a purpose, stealthily, difficultly. Then something stopped it. It could not advance beyond the cedar. The cedar—this impression remained with her afterwards too—prevented, kept it back. Like a rising sea the Forest had surged a moment in their direction through the covering darkness, and this visible movement was its first wave. Thus to her mind it seemed... like that mysterious turn of the tide that used to frighten and mystify her in childhood on the sands. The outward surge of some enormous Power was what she felt... something to which every instinct in her being rose in opposition because it threatened her and hers. In that moment she realised the Personality of the Forest... menacing.

In the stumbling movement that she made away from the window and towards the bell she barely caught the sentence Sanderson—or was it her husband?—murmured to himself: 'It came because we talked of it; our thinking made it aware of us and brought it out. But the cedar stops it. It cannot cross the lawn, you see...'

All three were standing now, and her husband's voice broke in with authority while his wife's fingers touched the bell.

'My dear, I should *not* say anything to Thompson.' The anxiety he felt was manifest in his voice, but his outward composure had returned. 'The gardener can go...'

Then Sanderson cut him short. 'Allow me,' he said quickly.

'I'll see if anything's wrong.' And before either of them could answer or object, he was gone, leaping out by the open window. They saw his figure vanish with a run across the lawn into the darkness.

A moment later the maid entered, in answer to the bell, and with her came the loud barking of the terrier from the hall.

'The lamps,' said her master shortly, and as she softly closed the door behind her, they heard the wind pass with a mournful sound of singing round the outer walls. A rustle of foliage from the distance passed within it.

'You see, the wind *is* rising. It *was* the wind!' He put a comforting arm about her, distressed to feel that she was trembling. But he knew that he was trembling too, though with a kind of odd elation rather than alarm. 'And it *was* smoke that you saw coming from Stride's cottage, or from the rubbish heaps he's been burning in the kitchen garden. The noise we heard was the branches rustling in the wind. Why should you be so nervous?'

A thin whispering voice answered him:

'I was afraid for *you*, dear. Something frightened me for *you*. That man makes me feel so uneasy and uncomfortable for his influence upon you. It's very foolish, I know. I think... I'm tired; I feel so overwrought and restless.' The words poured out in a hurried jumble and she kept turning to the window while she spoke.

'The strain of having a visitor,' he said soothingly, 'has taxed you. We're so unused to having people in the house. He goes to-morrow.' He warmed her cold hands between his own, stroking them tenderly. More, for the life of him, he could not say or do. The joy of a strange, internal excitement made his heart beat faster. He knew not what it was. He knew only, perhaps, whence it came.

She peered close into his face through the gloom, and said a curious thing. 'I thought, David, for a moment... you seemed... different. My nerves are all on edge to-night.' She made no further reference to her husband's visitor.

A sound of footsteps from the lawn warned of Sanderson's return, as he answered quickly in a lowered tone—'There's no need to be afraid on my account, dear girl. There's nothing wrong with me, I assure you; I never felt so well and happy in my life.'

Thompson came in with the lamps and brightness, and scarcely had she gone again when Sanderson in turn was seen climbing through the window.

'There's nothing,' he said lightly, as he closed it behind him. 'Somebody's been burning leaves, and the smoke is drifting a little through the trees. The wind,' he added, glancing at his host a moment significantly, but in so discreet a way that Mrs. Bittacy did not observe it, 'the wind, too, has begun to roar... in the Forest... further out.'

But Mrs. Bittacy noticed about him two things which increased her uneasiness. She noticed the shining of his eyes, because a similar light had suddenly come into her husband's; and she noticed, too, the apparent depth of meaning he put into those simple words that 'the wind had begun to roar in the Forest... further out.' Her mind retained the disagreeable impression that he meant more than he said. In his tone lay quite another implication. It was not actually 'wind' he spoke of, and it would not remain 'further out'... rather, it was coming in. Another impression she got too—still more unwelcome—was that her husband understood his hidden meaning.

## IV

'David, dear,' she observed gently as soon as they were alone upstairs, 'I have a horrible uneasy feeling about that man. I cannot get rid of it.' The tremor in her voice caught all his tenderness.

He turned to look at her. 'Of what kind, my dear? You're so imaginative sometimes, aren't you?'

'I think,' she hesitated, stammering a little, confused, still frightened, 'I mean—isn't he a hypnotist, or full of those theosofical ideas, or something of the sort? You know what I mean—'

He was too accustomed to her little confused alarms to explain them away seriously as a rule, or to correct her verbal inaccuracies, but to-night he felt she needed careful, tender treatment. He soothed her as best he could.

'But there's no harm in that, even if he is,' he answered quietly. 'Those are only new names for very old ideas, you know, dear.' There was no trace of impatience in his voice.

'That's what I mean,' she replied, the texts he dreaded rising in an unuttered crowd behind the words. 'He's one of those things that we are warned would come—one of the Latter-Day things.' For her mind still bristled with the bogeys of Antichrist and Prophecy, and she had only escaped the Number of the Beast, as it were, by the skin of her teeth. The Pope drew most of her fire usually, because she could understand him; the target was plain and she could shoot. But this tree-and-forest business was so vague and horrible. It terrified her. 'He makes me think,' she went on, 'of Principalities and Powers in high places, and of things that walk in darkness. I did *not* like the way he spoke of trees getting alive in the night, and all that; it made me think of wolves in sheep's clothing. And when I saw that awful thing in the sky above the lawn—'

But he interrupted her at once, for that was something he had decided it was best to leave unmentioned. Certainly it was better not discussed.

'He only meant, I think, Sophie,' he put in gravely, yet with a little smile, 'that trees may have a measure of conscious life—rather a nice idea on the whole, surely,—something like that bit we read in the *Times* the other night, you remember—and that a big forest may possess a sort of Collective Personality. Remember, he's an artist, and poetical.'

'It's dangerous,' she said emphatically. 'I feel it's playing with fire, unwise, unsafe—'

'Yet all to the glory of God,' he urged gently. 'We must not shut our ears and eyes to knowledge—of any kind, must we?'

'With you, David, the wish is always farther than the thought,' she rejoined. For, like the child who thought that 'suffered under Pontius Pilate' was 'suffered under a bunch of violets,' she heard her proverbs phonetically and reproduced them thus. She hoped to convey her warning in the quotation. 'And we must always try the spirits whether they be of God,' she added tentatively.

'Certainly, dear, we can always do that,' he assented, getting into bed.

But, after a little pause, during which she blew the light out, David Bittacy settling down to sleep with an excitement in his blood that was new and bewilderingly delightful, realised that perhaps he had not said quite enough to comfort her. She was lying awake by his side, still frightened. He put his head up in the darkness.

'Sophie,' he said softly, 'you must remember, too, that in any case between us and—and all that sort of thing—there is a great gulf fixed, a gulf that cannot be crossed—er—while we are still in the body.'

And hearing no reply, he satisfied himself that she was already asleep and happy. But Mrs. Bittacy was not asleep. She heard the sentence, only she said nothing because she felt her thought was better unexpressed. She was afraid to hear the words in the darkness. The Forest outside was listening and might hear them too—the Forest that was 'roaring further out'.

And the thought was this: That gulf, of course, existed, but Sanderson had somehow bridged it.

It was much later that night when she awoke out of troubled, uneasy dreams and heard a sound that twisted her very nerves with fear. It passed immediately with full waking, for, listen as she might, there was nothing audible but the inarticulate murmur of the night. It was in her dreams she heard it, and the dreams had vanished with it. But the sound was recognisable, for it was that rushing noise that had come across the lawn; only this time closer. Just above her face while she slept had passed this murmur as of rustling branches in the very room, a sound of foliage whispering. 'A going in the tops of the mulberry trees,' ran through her mind. She had dreamed that she lay beneath a spreading tree somewhere, a tree that whispered with ten thousand soft lips of green; and the dream continued for a moment even after waking.

She sat up in bed and stared about her. The window was open at the top; she saw the stars; the door, she remembered, was locked as usual; the room, of course, was empty. The deep hush of the summer night lay over all, broken only by another sound that now issued from the shadows close beside the bed, a human sound, yet unnatural, a sound that seized the fear with which she had waked and instantly increased it. And, although it was one she recognised as familiar, at first she could not name it. Some seconds certainly passed—and they were very long ones—before she understood that it was her husband talking in his sleep.

The direction of the voice confused and puzzled her, moreover, for it was not, as she first supposed, beside her. There was distance in it. The next minute, by the light of the sinking candle flame, she saw his white figure standing out in the middle of the room, half-way towards the window. The candle-light slowly grew. She saw him move then nearer to the window, with arms outstretched. His speech was low and mumbled, the words running together too much to be distinguishable.

And she shivered. To her, sleep-talking was uncanny to the point of horror; it was like the talking of the dead, mere parody of a living voice, unnatural.

'David!' she whispered, dreading the sound of her own voice, and half afraid to interrupt him and see his face. She could not bear the sight of the wide-opened eyes. 'David, you're walking in your sleep. Do—come back to bed, dear, *please*!'

Her whisper seemed so dreadfully loud in the still darkness. At the sound of her voice he paused, then turned slowly round to face her. His widely-opened eyes stared into her own without recognition; they looked through her into something beyond; it was as though he knew the direction of the sound, yet could not see her. They were shining, she noticed, as the eyes of Sanderson had shone several hours ago; and his face was flushed, distraught. Anxiety was written upon every feature. And, instantly, recognising that the fever was upon him, she forgot her terror temporarily in practical considerations. He came back to bed without waking. She closed his eyelids. Presently he composed himself quietly to sleep, or rather to deeper sleep. She contrived to make him swallow something from the tumbler beside the bed.

Then she rose very quietly to close the window, feeling the night air blow in too fresh and keen. She put the candle where it could not reach him. The sight of the big Baxter Bible beside it comforted her a little, but all through her underbeing ran the warnings of a curious alarm. And it was while in the act of fastening the catch with one hand and pulling the string of the blind with the other, that her husband sat up again in bed, and spoke in words this time that were distinctly audible. The eyes had opened wide again. He pointed. She stood stock still and listened, her shadow distorted on the blind. He did not come out towards her as at first she feared.

The whispering voice was very clear, horrible, too, beyond all she had ever known.

'They are roaring in the Forest further out... and I... must go and see.' He stared beyond her as he said it, to the woods. 'They are needing me. They sent for me...' Then his eyes wandering back again to things within the room, he lay down, his purpose suddenly changed. And that change was horrible as well, more horrible, perhaps, because of its revelation of another detailed world he moved in far away from her.

The singular phrase chilled her blood; for a moment she was utterly terrified. That tone of the somnambulist, differing so slightly yet so distressingly from normal, waking speech, seemed to her somehow wicked. Evil and danger lay waiting thick behind it. She leaned against the window-sill, shaking in every limb. She had an awful feeling for a moment that something was coming in to fetch him.

'Not yet, then,' she heard in a much lower voice from the bed, 'but later. It will be better so... I shall go later...'

The words expressed some fringe of these alarms that had haunted her so long, and that the arrival and presence of Sanderson seemed to have brought to the very edge of a climax she could not even dare to think about. They gave it form; they brought it closer; they sent her thoughts to her Deity in a wild, deep prayer for help and guidance. For here was a direct, unconscious betrayal of a world of inner purposes and claims her husband recognised while he kept them almost wholly to himself.

By the time she reached his side and knew the comfort of his touch, the eyes had closed again, this time of their own accord, and the head lay calmly back upon the pillows. She gently straightened the bed clothes. She watched him for some minutes, shading the candle carefully with one hand. There was a smile of strangest peace upon the face.

Then, blowing out the candle, she knelt down and prayed before getting back into bed. But no sleep came to her. She lay awake all night thinking, wondering, praying, until at length with the chorus of the birds and the glimmer of the dawn upon the green blind, she fell into a slumber of complete exhaustion.

But while she slept the wind continued roaring in the Forest further out. The sound came closer—sometimes very close indeed.

## V

With the departure of Sanderson the significance of the curious incidents waned, because the moods that had produced them passed away. Mrs. Bittacy soon afterwards came to regard them as some growth of disproportion that had been very largely, perhaps, in her own mind. It did not strike her that this change was sudden, for it came about quite naturally. For one thing her husband never spoke of the matter, and for another she remembered how many things in life that had seemed inexplicable and singular at the time turned out later to have been quite commonplace.

Most of it, certainly, she put down to the presence of the artist and to his wild, suggestive talk. With his welcome removal, the world turned ordinary again and safe. The fever, though it lasted as usual a short time only, had not allowed of her husband's getting up to say good-bye, and she had conveyed his regrets and adieux. In the morning Mr. Sanderson had seemed ordinary enough. In his town hat and gloves, as she saw him go, he seemed tame and unalarming.

'After all,' she thought as she watched the pony-cart bear him off, 'he's only an artist!' What she had thought he might be otherwise her slim imagination did not venture to disclose. Her change of feeling was wholesome and refreshing. She felt a little ashamed of her behaviour. She gave him a smile—genuine because the relief she felt was genuine—as he bent over her hand and kissed it, but she did not suggest a second visit, and her husband, she noted with satisfaction and relief, had said nothing either.

The little household fell again into the normal and sleepy routine to which it was accustomed. The name of Arthur Sanderson was rarely if ever mentioned. Nor, for her part, did she mention to her husband the incident of his walking in his sleep and the wild words he used. But to forget it was equally impossible. Thus it lay buried deep within her like a centre of some unknown disease of which it was a mysterious symptom, waiting to spread at the first favourable opportunity. She prayed against it every night and morning: prayed that she might forget it—that God would keep her husband safe from harm.

For in spite of much surface foolishness that many might have read as weakness, Mrs. Bittacy had balance, sanity, and a fine deep faith. She was greater than she knew. Her love for her husband and her God were somehow one, an achievement only possible to a single-hearted nobility of soul.

There followed a summer of great violence and beauty; o beauty, because the refreshing rains at night prolonged the glory of the spring and spread it all across July, keeping the foliage young and sweet; of violence, because the winds that tore about the south of England brushed the whole country into dancing movement. They swept the woods magnificently, and kept them roaring with a perpetual grand voice. Their deepest notes seemed never to leave the sky. They sang and shouted, and torn leaves raced and fluttered through the air long before their usually appointed time. Many a tree, after days of this roaring and dancing, fell exhausted to the ground. The cedar on the lawn gave up two limbs that fell upon successive days, at the same hour too—just before dusk. The wind often makes its most boisterous effort at that time, before it drops with the sun, and these two huge branches lay in dark ruin covering half the lawn. They spread across it and towards the house. They left an ugly gaping space upon the tree, so that the Lebanon looked unfinished, half destroyed, a monster shorn of its old-time comeliness and splendour. Far more of the Forest was now visible than before; it peered through the breach of the broken defences. They could see from the windows of the house now—especially from the drawing-room and bedroom windows--straight out into the glades and depths beyond.

Mrs. Bittacy's niece and nephew, who were staying on a visit at the time, enjoyed themselves immensely helping the gardeners carry off the fragments. It took two days to do this, for Mr. Bittacy insisted on the branches being moved entire. He would not allow them to be chopped; also, he would not consent to their use as firewood. Under his superintendence the unwieldy masses were dragged to the edge of the garden and arranged upon the frontier line between the Forest and the lawn. The children were delighted with the scheme. They entered into it with enthusiasm. At all costs this defence against the inroads of the Forest must be made secure. They caught their uncle's earnestness, felt even something of a hidden motive that he had, and the visit, usually rather dreaded, became the visit of their lives instead. It vas Aunt Sophia this time who seemed discouraging and dull.

'She's got so old and funny,' opined Stephen.

But Alice, who felt in the silent displeasure of her aunt some thing that half alarmed her, said:

'I think she's afraid of the woods. She never comes into them with us, you see.'

'All the more reason then for making this wall impreg—all fat and thick and solid,' he concluded, unable to manage the longer word. 'Then nothing—simply *nothing*—can get through. Can it, Uncle David?' And Mr. Bittacy, jacket discarded and working in his speckled waistcoat, went puffing to their aid, arranging the masive limb of the cedar like a hedge.

'Come on,' he said, 'whatever happens, you know, we must finish before it's dark. Already the wind is roaring in the Forest further out.' And Alice caught the phrase and instantly echoed it. 'Stevie,' she cried below her breath, 'look sharp, you lazy lump. Didn't you hear what Uncle David said? It'll come in and catch us before we've done!'

They worked like Trojans, and, sitting beneath the wistaria tree that climbed the southern wall of the cottage, Mrs. Bittacy with her knitting watched them, calling from time to time insignificant messages of counsel and advice. The messages passed, of course, unheeded. Mostly, indeed, they were unheard, for the workers were too absorbed. She warned her husband not to get too hot, Alice not to tear her dress, Stephen not to strain his back with pulling. Her mind hovered between the homoeopathic medicine-chest upstairs and her anxiety to see the business finished.

For this breaking up of the cedar had stirred again her slumbering alarms. It revived memories of the visit of Mr. Sanderson that had been sinking into oblivion; she recalled his queer and odious way of talking, and many things she hoped forgotten drew their heads up from that subconscious region to which all forgetting is impossible. They looked at her and nodded. They were full of life; they had no intention of being pushed aside and buried permanently. 'Now look!' they whispered, 'didn't we tell you so?' They had been merely waiting the right moment to assert their presence. And all her former vague distress crept over her. Anxiety, uneasiness returned. That dreadful sinking of the heart came too.

This incident of the cedar's breaking up was actually so unimportant, and yet her husband's attitude towards it made it so significant. There was nothing that he said in particular, or did, or left undone that frightened her, but his general air of earnestness seemed so unwarranted. She felt that he deemed the thing important. He was so exercised about it. This evidence of sudden concern and interest, buried all the summer from her sight and knowledge, she realised now had been buried purposely; he had kept it intentionally concealed. Deeply submerged in him there ran this tide of other thoughts, desires, hopes. What were they? Whither did they lead? The accident to the tree betrayed it most unpleasantly; and, doubtless, more than he was aware.

She watched his grave and serious face as he worked there with the children, and as she watched she felt afraid. It vexed her that the children worked so eagerly. They unconsciously supported him. The thing she feared she would not even name. But it was waiting.

Moreover, as far as her puzzled mind could deal with a dread so vague and incoherent, the collapse of the cedar somehow brought it nearer. The fact that, all so ill-explained and formless, the thing yet lay in her consciousness, out of reach but moving and alive, filled her with a kind of puzzled, dreadful wonder. Its presence was so very real, its power so gripping, its partial concealment so abominable. Then, out of the dim confusion, she grasped one thought and saw it stand quite clear before her eyes. She found difficulty in clothing it in words, but its meaning perhaps was this: That cedar stood in their life for something friendly; its downfall meant disaster; a sense of some protective influence about the cottage, and about her husband in particular, was thereby weakened.

'Why do you fear the big winds so?' he had asked her several days before, after a particularly boisterous day; and the answer she gave surprised her while she gave it. One of those heads poked up unconsciously, and let slip the truth:

'Because, David, I feel they—bring the Forest with them,' she faltered. 'They blow something from the trees—into the mind —into the house.'

He looked at her keenly for a moment.

'That must be why I love them then,' he answered. 'They blow the souls of the trees about the sky like clouds.'

The conversation dropped. She had never heard him talk in quite that way before.

And another time, when he had coaxed her to go with him down one of the nearer glades, she asked why he took the small hand-axe with him, and what he wanted it for.

'To cut the ivy that clings to the trunks and takes their life away,' he said.

'But can't the verdurers do that?' she asked. 'That's what they're paid for, isn't it?'

Whereupon he explained that ivy was a parasite the trees knew not how to fight alone, and that the verdurers were careless and did not do it thoroughly. They gave a chop here and there, leaving the tree to do the rest for itself if it could.

'Besides, I like to do it for them. I love to help them and protect,' he added, the foliage rustling all about his quiet words as they went.

And these stray remarks, as his attitude towards the broken cedar, betrayed this curious, subtle change that was going forward in his personality. Slowly and surely all the summer it had increased.

It was growing—the thought startled her horribly—just as a tree grows, the outer evidence from day to day so slight as to be unnoticeable, yet the rising tide so deep and irresistible. The alteration spread all through and over him, was in both mind and actions, sometimes almost in his face as well. Occasionally, thus, it stood up straight outside himself and frightened her.

His life was somehow becoming linked so intimately with trees, and with all that trees signified. His interests became more and more their interests, his activity combined with theirs, his thoughts and feelings theirs, his purpose, hope, desire, his fate——

His fate! The darkness of some vague, enormous terror dropped its shadow on her when she thought of it. Some instinct in her heart she dreaded infinitely more than death—for death meant sweet translation for his soul—came gradually to associate the thought of him with the thought of trees, in particular with these Forest trees. Sometimes, before she could face the thing, argue it away, or pray it into silence, she found the thought of him running swiftly through her mind like a thought of the Forest itself, the two most intimately linked and joined together, each a part and complement of the other, one being.

The idea was too dim for her to see it face to face. Its mere possibility dissolved the instant she focussed it to get the truth behind it. It was too utterly elusive, mad, protean. Under the attack of even a minute's concentration the very meaning of it vanished, melted away. The idea lay really behind any words that she could ever find, beyond the touch of definite thought. Her mind was unable to grapple with it. But, while it vanished the trail of its approach and disappearance flickered a moment before her shaking vision. The horror certainly remained.

Reduced to the simple human statement that her temperament sought instinctively it stood perhaps at this: her husband loved her, and he loved the trees as well; but the trees came first, claimed parts of him she did not know. *She* loved her God and him. *He* loved the trees and her.

Thus, in guise of some faint, distressing compromise, the matter shaped itself for her perplexed mind in the terms of conflict. A silent, hidden battle raged, but as yet raged far away. The breaking of the cedar was a visible outward fragment of a distant and mysterious encounter that was coming daily closer to them both. The wind, instead of roaring in the

Forest further out, now came nearer, booming in fitful gusts about its edge and frontiers.

Meanwhile the summer dimmed. The autumn winds went sighing through the woods; leaves turned to golden red, and the evenings were drawing in with cosy shadows before the first sign of anything seriously untoward made its appearance. It came then with a flat, decided kind of violence that indicated mature preparation beforehand. It was not impulsive nor ill-considered. In a fashion it seemed expected, and indeed inevitable. For within a fortnight of their annual change to the little village of Seillans above St. Raphael—a change so regular for the past ten years that it was not even discussed between them—David Bittacy abruptly refused to go.

Thompson had laid the tea-table, prepared the spirit lamp beneath the urn, pulled down the blinds in that swift and silent way she had, and left the room. The lamps were still unlit. The fire-light shone on the chintz armchairs, and Boxer lay asleep on the black horse-hair rug. Upon the walls the gilt picture frames gleamed faintly, the pictures themselves indistinguishable. Mrs. Bittacy had warmed the tea-pot and was in the act of pouring the water in to heat the cups when her husband, looking up from his chair across the hearth, made the abrupt announcement:

'My dear,' he said, as though following a train of thought of which she only heard this final phrase, 'it's really quite impossible for me to go.'

And so abrupt, inconsequent, it sounded that she at first misunderstood. She thought he meant go out into the garden or the woods. But her heart leaped all the same. The tone of his voice was ominous.

'Of course not,' she answered, 'it would be *most* unwise. Why should you——?' She referred to the mist that always spread on autumn nights upon the lawn; but before she finished the sentence she knew that *he* referred to something else. And her heart then gave its second horrible leap.

'David! You mean abroad?' she gasped.

'I mean abroad, dear, yes.'

It reminded her of the tone used when saying good-bye years ago before one of those jungle expeditions she dreaded. His voice then was so serious, so final. It was serious and final now. For several moments she could think of nothing to say. She busied herself with the tea-pot. She had filled one cup with hot water till it overflowed, and she emptied it slowly into the slop-basin, trying with all her might not to let him see the trembling of her hand. The firelight and the dimness of the room both helped her. But in any case he would hardly have noticed it. His thoughts were far away. ...

## VI

Mrs. Bittacy had never liked their present home. She preferred a flat, more open country that left approaches clear. She liked to see things coming. This cottage on the very edge of the old hunting grounds of William the Conqueror had never satisfied her ideal of a safe and pleasant place to settle down in. The sea-coast, with treeless downs behind and a clear horizon in front, as at Eastbourne, say, was her ideal of a proper home.

It was curious, this instinctive aversion she felt to being shut in—by trees especially; a kind of claustrophobia almost; probably due, as has been said, to the days in India when the trees took her husband off and surrounded him with dangers. In those weeks of solitude the feeling had matured. She had fought it in her fashion, but never conquered it. Apparently routed, it had a way of creeping back in other forms. In this particular case, yielding to his strong desire, she thought the battle won, but the terror of the trees came back before the first month had passed. They laughed in her face.

She never lost knowledge of the fact that the leagues of forest lay about their cottage like a mighty wall, a crowding, watching, listening presence that shut them in from freedom and escape. Far from morbid naturally, she did her best to deny the thought, and so simple and unartificial was her type of mind that for weeks together she would wholly lose it. Then, suddenly it would return upon her with a rush of bleak reality. It was not only in her mind; it existed apart from any mere mood; a separate fear that walked alone; it came and went, yet when it went—went only to watch her from another point of view. It was in abeyance—hidden round the corner.

The Forest never let her go completely. It was ever ready to encroach. All the branches, she sometimes fancied, stretched one way—towards their tiny cottage and garden, as though it sought to draw them in and merge them in itself. Its great deep-breathing soul resented the mockery, the insolence, the irritation of the prim garden at its very gates. It would absorb and smother them if it could. And every wind that blew its thundering message over the huge sounding-board of the million, shaking trees conveyed the purpose that it had. They had angered its great soul. At its heart was this deep, incessant roaring.

All this she never framed in words; the subtleties of language lay far beyond her reach. But instinctively she felt it; and more besides. It troubled her profoundly. Chiefly, moreover, for her husband. Merely for herself, the nightmare might have left her cold. It was David's peculiar interest in the trees that gave the special invitation.

Jealousy, then, in its most subtle aspect came to strengthen this aversion and dislike, for it came in a form that no reasonable wife could possibly object to. Her husband's passion, she reflected, was natural and inborn. It had decided his vocation, fed his ambition, nourished his dreams, desires, hopes. All his best years of active life had been spent in the care and guardianship of trees. He knew them, understood their secret life and nature, 'managed' them intuitively as other men 'managed' dogs and horses. He could not live for long away from them without a strange, acute nostalgia that stole his peace of mind and consequently his strength of body. A forest made him happy and at peace; it nursed and fed and soothed his deepest moods. Trees influenced the sources of his life, lowered or raised the very heart-beat in him. Cut off from them he languished as a lover of the sea can droop inland, or a mountaineer may pine in the flat monotony of the plains.

This she could understand, in a fashion at least, and make allowances for. She had yielded gently, even sweetly, to his choice of their English home; for in the little island there is nothing that suggests the woods of wilder countries so nearly as the New Forest. It has the genuine air and mystery, the depth and splendour, the loneliness, and here and there the strong, untamable quality of old-time forests as Bittacy of the Department knew them.

In a single detail only had he yielded to her wishes. He consented to a cottage on the edge, instead of in the heart of it. And for a dozen years now they had dwelt in peace and happiness at the lips of this great spreading thing that covered so many leagues with its tangle of swamps and moors and splendid ancient trees.

Only with the last two years or so—with his own increasing age, and physical decline perhaps—had come this marked growth of passionate interest in the welfare of the Forest. She had watched it grow, at first had laughed at it, then talked sympathetically so far as sincerity permitted, then had argued mildly, finally come to realise that its treatment lay altogether beyond her powers, and so had come to fear it with all her heart.

The six weeks they annually spent away from their English home, each regarded very differently of course. For her husband it meant a painful exile that did his health no good; he yearned for his trees—the sight and sound and smell of them; but for herself it meant release from a haunting dread—escape. To renounce those six weeks by the sea on the sunny, shining coast of France, was almost more than this little woman, even with her unselfishness, could face.

After the first shock of the announcement, she reflected as deeply as her nature permitted, prayed, wept in secret—and made up her mind. Duty, she felt clearly, pointed to renouncement.

The discipline would certainly be severe—she did not dream at the moment how severe!—but this fine, consistent little Christian saw it plain; she accepted it, too, without any sighing of the martyr, though the courage she showed was of the martyr order. Her husband should never know the cost. In all but this one passion his unselfishness was ever as great as her own. The love she had borne him all these years, like the love she bore her anthropomorphic deity, was deep and real. She loved to suffer for them both. Besides, the way her husband had put it to her was singular. It did not take the form of a mere selfish predilection. Something higher than two wills in conflict seeking compromise was in it from the beginning.

'I feel, Sophia, it would be really more than I could manage,' he said slowly, gazing into the fire over the tops of his stretched-out muddy boots. 'My duty and my happiness lie here with the Forest and with you. My life is deeply rooted in this place. Something I can't define connects my inner being with these trees, and separation would make me ill—might even kill me. My hold on life would weaken; here is my source of supply. I cannot explain it better than that.' He looked up steadily into her face across the table so that she saw the gravity of his expression and the shining of his steady eyes.

'David, you feel it as strongly as that!' she said, forgetting the tea things altogether.

'Yes,' he replied, 'I do. And it's not of the body only; I feel it in my soul.'

The reality of what he hinted at crept into that shadow-covered room like an actual Presence and stood beside them. It came not by the windows of the door, but it filled the entire space between the walls and ceiling. It took the heat from the fire before her face. She felt suddenly cold, confused a little, frightened. She almost felt the rush of foliage in the wind. It stood between them.

'There are things—some things,' she faltered, 'we are not intended to know, I think.' The words expressed her general attitude to life, not alone to this particular incident.

And after a pause of several minutes, disregarding the criticism as though he had not heard it—'I cannot explain it better than that, you see,' his grave voice answered. 'There *is* this deep, tremendous link,—some secret power they emanate that keeps me well and happy and—alive. If you cannot understand, I feel at least you may be able to—forgive.' His tone grew tender, gentle, soft. 'My selfishness, I know, must seem quite unforgivable. I cannot help it somehow; these trees, this ancient Forest, both seem knitted into all that makes me live, and if I go——'

There was a little sound of collapse in his voice. He stopped abruptly, and sank back in his chair. And, at that, a distinct lump came up into her throat which she had great difficulty in managing while she went over and put her arms about him.

'My dear,' she murmured, 'God will direct. We will accept His guidance. He has always shown the way before.'

'My selfishness afflicts me—' he began, but she would not let him finish.

'David, He will direct. Nothing shall harm you. You've never once been selfish, and I cannot bear to hear you say such things. The way will open that is best for you—for both of us.' She kissed him; she would not let him speak; her heart was in her throat, and she felt for him far more than for herself.

And then he had suggested that she should go alone perhaps for a shorter time, and stay in her brother's villa with the children, Alice and Stephen. It was always open to her as she well knew.

'You need the change,' he said, when the lamps had been lit and the servant had gone out again 'you need it as much as I dread it. I could manage somehow till you returned, and should feel happier that way if you went. I cannot leave this Forest that I love so well. I even feel, Sophie dear'—he sat up straight and faced her as he half whispered it—'that I can *never* leave it again. My life and happiness lie here together.'

And even while scorning the idea that she could leave him alone with the influence of the Forest all about him to have its unimpeded way, she felt the pangs of that subtle jealousy bite keen and close. He loved the Forest better than herself, for he placed it first. Behind the words, moreover, hid the unuttered thought that made her so uneasy. The terror Sanderson had brought revived and shook its wings before her very eyes. For the whole conversation, of which this was a fragment, conveyed the unutterable implication that while he could not spare the trees, they equally could not spare him. The vividness with which he managed to conceal and yet betray the fact brought a profound distress that crossed the border between presentiment and warning into positive alarm.

He clearly felt that the trees would miss him—the trees he tended, guarded, watched over, loved.

'David, I shall stay here with you. I think you need me, really,—don't you?' Eagerly, with a touch of heart-felt passion the words poured out.

'Now more than ever, dear. God bless you for your sweet unselfishness. And your sacrifice,' he added, 'is all the greater because you cannot understand the thing that makes it necessary for me to stay.'

'Perhaps in the spring instead——' she said, with a tremor in the voice.

'In the spring—perhaps,' he answered gently, almost beneath his breath. 'For they will not need me then. All the world can love them in the spring. It's in the winter that they're lonely and neglected. I wish to stay with them particularly then. I even feel I ought to—and I must.'

And in this way, without further speech, the decision was made. Mrs. Bittacy, at least asked no more questions. Yet she could not bring herself to show more sympathy than was necessary. She felt, for one thing, that if she did, it might lead him to speak freely, and to tell her things she could not possibly bear to know. And she dared not take the risk of that.

## VII

This was at the end of summer, but the autumn followed close. The conversation really marked the threshold between the two seasons, and marked at the same time the line between her husband's negative and aggressive state. She almost felt she had done wrong to yield, he grew so bold, concealment all discarded. He went, that is, quite openly to the woods, forgetting all his duties, all his former occupations. He even sought to coax her to go with him. The hidden thing blazed out without disguise. And, while she trembled at his energy, she admired the virile passion he displayed. Her jealousy had long ago retired before her fear, accepting the second place, one desire now was to protect. The wife turned wholly mother.

He said so little, but—he hated to come in. From morning to night he wandered in the Forest; often he went out after dinner; his mind was charged with trees—their foliage, growth, development; their wonder, beauty, strength; their loneliness in isolation, their power in a herded mass. He knew the effect of every wind upon them; the danger from the boisterous north, the glory from the west, the eastern dryness, and the soft, moist tenderness that a south wind left upon their thinning boughs. He spoke all day of their sensations; how they drank the fading sunshine, dreamed in the moonlight, thrilled to the kiss of stars. The dew could bring them half the passion of the night, but frost sent them plunging beneath the ground to dwell with hopes of a later coming softness in their roots. They nursed the life they carried—insects, larvae, chrysalis—and when the skies above them melted, he spoke of them standing 'motionless in an ecstasy of rain', or in the noon of sunshine 'self-poised upon their prodigy of shade'.

And once in the middle of the night she woke at the sound of his voice, and heard him—wide awake, not talking in his sleep—but talking towards the window where the shadow of the cedar fell at noon:

> O art thou sighing for Lebanon
> In the long breeze that streams to thy delicious East?
> Sighing for Lebanon,
> Dark cedar;

and, when, half charmed, half terrified, she turned and called to him by name, he merely said—

'My dear, I felt the loneliness—suddenly realised it—the alien desolation of that tree, set here upon our little lawn in England when all her Eastern brothers call to her in sleep.' And the answer seemed so queer, so 'un-evangelical', that she waited in silence till he slept again. The poetry passed her by. It seemed unnecessary and out of place. It made her ache with suspicion, fear, jealousy.

The fear, however, seemed somehow all lapped up and banished soon afterwards by her unwilling admiration of the rushing splendour of her husband's state. Her anxiety, at any rate, shifted from the religious to the medical. She thought he might be losing his steadiness of mind a little. How often in her prayers she offered thanks for the guidance that made her stay with him to help and watch is impossible to say. It certainly was twice a day.

She even went so far once, when Mr. Mortimer, the vicar, called, and brought with him a more or less distinguished doctor —as to tell the professional man privately some symptoms of her husband's queerness. And his answer that there was 'nothing he could prescribe for' added not a little to her sense of unholy bewilderment. No doubt Sir James had never been 'consulted' under such unorthodox conditions before. His sense of what was becoming naturally overrode his acquired instincts as a skilled instrument that might help the race.

'No fever, you think?' she asked insistently with hurry, determined to get something from him.

'Nothing that *I* can deal with, as I told you, Madam,' was the reply.

Evidently he did not care about being invited to examine patients in this surreptitious way before a tea-pot on the lawn, chance of a fee most problematical. He liked to see a tongue and feel a thumping pulse; to know the pedigree and bank account of his questioner as well. It was most unusual, in abominable taste besides. Of course it was. But the drowning woman seized the only straw she could.

For now the aggressive attitude of her husband overcame her

to the point where she found it difficult even to question him. Yet in the house he was so kind and gentle, doing all he could to make her sacrifice as easy as possible.

'David, you really *are* unwise to go out now. The night is damp and very chilly. The ground is soaked in dew. You'll catch your death of cold.'

His face lightened. 'Won't you come with me, dear,—just for once? I'm only going to the corner of the hollies to see the beech that stands so lonely by itself.'

She had been out with him in the short dark afternoon, and they had passed that evil group of hollies where the gipsies camped. Nothing else would grow there, but the hollies throve upon the stony soil.

'David, the beech is all right and safe.' She had learned his phraseology a little, made clever out of due season by her love. 'There's no wind to-night.'

'But it's rising,' he answered, 'rising in the east. I heard it in the bare and hungry larches. They need the sun and dew, and always cry out when wind's upon them from the east.'

She sent a short unspoken prayer most swiftly to her deity as she heard him say it. For every time now, when he spoke in this familiar, intimate way of the life of the trees, she felt a sheet of cold fasten tight against her very skin and flesh. She shivered. How *could* he possibly know such things?

Yet, in all else, and in the relations of his daily life, he was sane and reasonable, loving, kind and tender. It was only on the subject of the trees he seemed unhinged and queer. Most curiously it seemed that, since the collapse of the cedar they both loved, though in different fashion, his departure from the normal had increased. Why else did he watch them as a man might watch a sickly child? Why did he linger especially in the dusk to catch their 'mood of night' as he called it? Why think so carefully upon them when the frost was threatening of the wind appeared to rise?

As she put it so frequently now to herself—How could he possibly *know* such things?

He went. As she closed the front door after him she heard the distant roaring in the Forest. ...

And then it suddenly struck her: How could she know them too?

It dropped upon her like a blow that she felt at once all over, upon body, heart and mind. The discovery rushed out from its ambush to overwhelm. The truth of it, making all arguing futile, numbed her faculties. But though at first it deadened her, she soon revived, and her being rose into aggressive opposition. A wild yet calculated courage like that which animates the leaders of splendid forlorn hopes flamed in her little person—flamed grandly, and invincible. While knowing herself insignificant and weak, she knew at the same time that power at her back which moves the worlds. The faith that filled her was the weapon in her hands, and the right by which she claimed it; but the spirit of utter, selfless sacrifice that characterised her life was the means by which she mastered its immediate use. For a kind of white and faultless intuition guided her to the attack. Behind her stood her Bible and her God.

How so magnificent a divination came to her at all may well be a matter for astonishment, though some clue of explanation lies, perhaps, in the very simpleness of her nature. At any rate, she saw quite clearly certain things; saw them in moments only—after prayer, in the still silence of the night, or when left alone those long hours in the house with her knitting and her thoughts—and the guidance which then flashed into her remained, even after the manner of its coming was forgotten.

They came to her, these things she saw, formless, wordless; she could not put them into any kind of language; but by the very fact of being uncaught in sentence they retained their original clear vigour.

Hours of patient waiting brought the first, and the others followed easily afterwards, by degrees, on subsequent days, a little and a little. Her husband had been gone since early morning, and had taken his luncheon with him. She was sitting by the tea things, the cups and tea-pot warmed, the muffins in the fender keeping hot, all ready for his return, when she realised quite abruptly that this thing which took him off, which kept him out so many hours day after day, this that was against her own little will and instinct—was enormous as the sea. It was no mere prettiness of single Trees, but something massed and mountainous. About her rose the wall of its huge opposition to the sky, its scale gigantic, its power utterly prodigious. What she knew of it hitherto as green and delicate forms waving and rustling in the winds was but, as it were, the spray of foam that broke into sight upon the nearer edge of viewless depths far, far away. The trees, indeed, were sentinels set visibly about the limits of a camp that itself remained invisible. The awful hum and murmur of the main body in the distance passed into that still room about her with the firelight and hissing kettle. Out yonder—in the Forest further out—the thing that was ever roaring at the centre was dreadfully increasing.

The sense of definite battle, too—battle between herself and the Forest for his soul—came with it. Its presentment was as clear as though Thompson had come into the room and quietly told her that the cottage was surrounded. 'Please, ma'am, there are trees come up about the house,' she might have suddenly announced. And equally might have heard her own answer: 'It's all right, Thompson. The main body is still far away.'

Immediately upon its heels, then, came another truth, with a close reality that shocked her. She saw that jealousy was not confined to the human and animal world alone, but ran through all creation. The Vegetable Kingdom knew it too. So-called inanimate nature shared it with the rest. Trees felt it. This Forest just beyond the window—standing there in the silence of the autumn evening across the little lawn—this Forest understood it equally. The remorseless, branching power that sought to keep exclusively for itself the thing it loved and needed, spread like a running desire through all its million leaves and stems and roots. In humans, of course, it was consciously directed; in animals it acted with frank instinctiveness; but in trees this jealousy rose in some blind tide of impersonal and unconscious wrath that would sweep opposition from its path as the wind sweeps powdered snow from the surface of the ice. Their number was a host with endless reinforcements, and once it realised its passion was returned the power increased. Her husband loved the trees... They had become aware of it. ... They would take him from her in the end. ... For, equally, the trees loved him.

Then, while she heard his footsteps in the hall and the closing of the front door, she saw a third thing clearly;—realised the widening of the gap between herself and him. This other love had made it. All these weeks of the summer when she felt so close to him, now especially when she had made the biggest sacrifice of her life to stay by his side and help him, he had been slowly, surely—drawing away. The estrangement was here and now—a fact accomplished. It had been all this time maturing; there yawned this broad deep space between them. Across the empty distance she saw the change in merciless perspective. It revealed his face and figure, dearly-loved, once fondly worshipped, far on the other side in shadowy distance, small, the back turned from her, and moving while she watched—moving away from her.

They had their tea in silence then. She asked no questions, he volunteered no information of this day. The heart was big within her, the terrible loneliness of age spread through her like a rising icy mist. She watched him, filling all his wants. His hair was untidy and his boots were caked with blackish mud. He moved with a restless, swaying motion that somehow blanched her cheek and sent a miserable shivering down her back. It reminded her of trees. His eyes were very bright.

He brought in with him an odour of the earth and forest that seemed to choke her and make it difficult to breathe; and—what she noticed with a climax of almost uncontrollable alarm—upon his face beneath the lamplight shone traces of a mild, faint glory that made her think of moonlight falling upon a wood through speckled shadows. It was his new-found happiness that shone there, a happiness uncaused by her and in which she had no part.

In his coat was a spray of faded yellow beach leaves. 'I brought this from the Forest for you,' he said, with all the air that belonged to his little acts of devotion long ago. And she took the spray of leaves mechanically with a smile and a murmured 'thank you, dear,' as though he had unknowingly put into her hands the weapon for her own destruction and she had accepted it.

And when the tea was over and he left the room, he did not go to his study, or to change his clothes. She heard the front door softly shut behind him as he again went out towards the Forest.

A moment later she was in her room upstairs, kneeling beside the bed—the side he slept on—and praying wildly through a flood of tears that God would save and keep him to her. Wind brushed the window panes behind her while she knelt.

## VIII

One sunny November morning, when the strain had reached a pitch that made repression almost unmanageable, she came to an impulsive decision, and obeyed it. Her husband had again gone out with luncheon for the day. She took adventure in her hands and followed him. The power of clear-seeing was strong upon her, forcing her up to some unnatural level of understanding. To stay indoors and wait inactive for his return seemed suddenly impossible. She meant to know what he knew, feel what he felt, put herself in his place. She would dare the fascination of the Forest—share it with him. It was greatly daring; but it would give her greater understanding how to help and save him and therefore greater Power. She went upstairs a moment first to pray.

In a thick, warm skirt, and wearing heavy boots—those walking boots she used with him upon the mountains about Seillans—she left the cottage by the back way and turned towards the

Forest. She could not actually follow him, for he had started off an hour before and she knew not exactly his direction. What was so urgent in her was the wish to be with him in the woods, to walk beneath the leafless branches just as he did: to be there when he was there, even though not together. For it had come to her that she might thus share with him for once this horrible mighty life and breathing of the trees he loved. In winter, he had said, they needed him particularly; and winter now was coming. Her love *must* bring her something of what he felt himself—the huge attraction, the suction and the pull of all the trees. Thus, in some vicarious fashion, she might share, though unknown to himself, this very thing that was taking him away from her. She might thus even lessen its attack upon himself.

The impulse came to her clairvoyantly, and she obeyed without a sign of hesitation. Deeper comprehension would come to her of the whole awful puzzle. And come it did, yet not in the way she imagined and expected.

The air was very still, the sky a cold pale blue, but cloudless. The entire Forest stood silent, at attention. It knew perfectly well that she had come. It knew the moment when she entered; watched and followed her; and behind her something dropped without a sound and shut her in. Her feet upon the glades of mossy grass fell silently, as the oaks and beeches shifted past in rows and took up their positions at her back. It was not pleasant, this way they grew so dense behind her the instant she had passed. She realised that they gathered in an ever-growing army, massed, herded, trooped, between her and the cottage, shutting off escape. They let her pass so easily, but to get out again she would know them differently—thick, crowded, branches all drawn and hostile. Already their increasing numbers bewildered her. In front, they looked so sparse and scattered, with open spaces where the sunshine fell; but when she turned it seemed they stood so close together, a serried army, darkening the sunlight. They blocked the day, collected all the shadows, stood with their leafless and forbidding rampart like the night. They swallowed down into themselves the very glade by which she came. For when she glanced behind her—rarely—the way she had come was shadowy and lost.

Yet the morning sparkled overhead, and a glance of excitement ran quivering through the entire day. It was what she always knew as 'children's weather', so clear and harmless, without a sign of danger, nothing ominous to threaten or alarm. Steadfast in her purpose, looking back as little as she dared, Sophia Bittacy marched slowly and deliberately into the heart of the silent woods, deeper, ever deeper. ...

And then, abruptly, in an open space where the sunshine fell unhindered, she stopped. It was one of the breathing-places of the forest. Dead, withered bracken lay in patches of unsightly grey. There were bits of heather too. All round the trees stood looking on—oak, beech, holly, ash, pine, larch, with here and there small groups of juniper. On the lips of this breathing-space of the woods she stopped to rest, disobeying her instinct for the first time. For the other instinct in her was to go on. She did not really want to rest.

This was the little act that brought it to her—the wireless message from a vast Emitter.

'I've been stopped,' she thought to herself with a horrid qualm.

She looked about her in this quiet, ancient place. Nothing stirred. There was no life nor sign of life; no birds sang; no rabbits scuttled off at her approach. The stillness was bewildering, and gravity hung down upon it like a heavy curtain. It hushed the heart in her. Could this be part of what her husband felt—this sense of thick entanglement with stems, boughs, roots, and foliage?

'This has always been as it is now,' she thought, yet not knowing why she thought it. 'Ever since the Forest grew it has been still and secret here. It has never changed.' The curtain of silence drew closer while she said it, thickening round her. 'For a thousand years—I'm here with a thousand years. And behind this place stand all the forests of the world!'

So foreign to her temperament were such thoughts, and so

alien to all she had been taught to look for in Nature, that she strove against them. She made an effort to oppose. But they clung and haunted just the same; they refused to be dispersed. The curtain hung dense and heavy as though its texture thickened. The air with difficulty came through.

And then she thought that curtain stirred. There was movement somewhere. That obscure dim thing which ever broods behind the visible appearance of trees came nearer to her. She caught her breath and stared about her, listening intently. The trees, perhaps because she saw them more in detail now, it seemed to her had changed. A vague, faint alteration spread over them, at first so slight she scarcely would admit it, then growing steadily, though still obscurely, outwards. 'They tremble and are changed,' flashed through her mind the horrid line that Sanderson had quoted. Yet the change was graceful for all the uncouthness attendant upon the size of so vast a movement. They had turned in her direction. That was it. *They saw her*.

In this way the change expressed itself in her groping, terrified thought. Till now it had been otherwise: she had looked at them from her own point of view; now they looked at her from theirs. They stared her in the face and eyes; they stared at her all over. In some unkind, resentful, hostile way, they watched her. Hitherto in life she had watched them variously, in superficial ways, reading into them what her own mind suggested. Now they read into her the things they actually *were,* and not merely another's interpretation of them.

They seemed in their motionless silence there instinct with life, a life, moreover, that breathed about her a species of terrible soft enchantment that bewitched. It branched all through her, climbing to the brain. The Forest held her with its huge and giant fascination. In this secluded breathing-spot that the centuries had left untouched, she had stepped close against the hidden pulse of the whole collective mass of them. They were aware of her and had turned to gaze with their myriad, vast sight upon the intruder. They shouted at her in the silence. For she wanted to look back at them, but it was like staring at a crowd, and her glance merely shifted from one tree to another, hurriedly, finding in none the one she sought. They saw her so easily, each and all. The rows that stood behind her also stared. But she could not return the gaze. Her husband, she realised, could. And their steady stare shocked her as though in some sense she knew that she was naked. They saw so much of her: she saw of them—so little.

Her efforts to return their gaze were pitiful. The constant shifting increased her bewilderment. Conscious of this awful and enormous sight all over her, she let her eyes first rest upon the ground; and then she closed them altogether. She kept the lids as tight together as ever they would go.

But the sight of the trees came even into that inner darkness behind the fastened lids, for there was no escaping it. Outside, in the light, she still knew that the leaves of the hollies glittered smoothly, that the dead foliage of the oaks hung crisp in the air above her, that the needles of the little junipers were pointing all one way. The spread perception of the Forest was focussed on herself, and no mere shutting of the eyes could hide its scattered yet concentrated stare—the all-inclusive vision of great woods.

There was no wind, yet here and there a single leaf hanging by its dried-up stalk shook all alone with great rapidity—rattling. It was the sentry drawing attention to her presence. And then, again, as once long weeks before, she felt their Being as a tide about her. The tide had turned. That memory of her childhood sands came back, when the nurse said, 'The tide has turned now; we must go in,' and she saw the mass of piled-up waters, green and heaped to the horizon, and realised that it was slowly coming in. The gigantic mass of it, too vast for hurry, loaded with massive purpose, she used to feel, was moving towards herself. The fluid body of the sea was creeping along beneath the sky to the very spot upon the yellow sands where she stood and played. The sight and thought of it had always overwhelmed her with a sense of awe—as though her puny self were the object of the whole sea's advance. 'The tide has turned; we had better now go in.'

This was happening now about her—the same thing was happening in the woods—slow, sure, and steady, and its motion as little discernible as the sea's. The tide had turned. The small human presence that had ventured among its green and mountainous depths, moreover, was its objective.

That all was clear within her while she sat and waited with tight-shut lids. But the next moment she opened her eyes with a sudden realisation of something more. The presence that it sought was after all not hers. It was the presence of some one other than herself. And then she understood. Her eyes had opened with a click, it seemed; but the sound, in reality, was outside herself. Across the clearing where her sunshine lay so calm and still, she saw the figure of her husband moving among the trees—a man, like a tree, walking.

With hands behind his back, and head uplifted, he moved quite slowly, as though absorbed in his own thoughts. Hardly fifty paces separated them, but he had no inkling of her presence there so near. With mind intent and senses all turned inwards, he marched past her like a figure in a dream, and like a figure in a dream she saw him go. Love, yearning, pity rose in a storm within her, but as in nightmare she found no words or movement possible. She sat and watched him go—go from her—go into the deeper reaches of the green enveloping woods. Desire to save, to bid him stop and turn, ran in a passion through her being, but there was nothing she could do. She saw him go away from her, go of his own accord and willingly beyond her; she saw the branches drop about his steps and hide him. His figure faded out among the speckled shade and sunlight. The trees covered him. The tide just took him, all unresisting and content to go. Upon the bosom of the green soft sea he floated away beyond her reach of vision. Her eyes could follow him no longer. He was gone.

And then for the first time she realised, even at that distance, that the look upon his face was one of peace and happiness—

rapt, and caught away in joy, a look of youth. That expression now he never showed to her. But she *had* known it. Years ago, in the early days of their married life, she had seen it on his face. Now it no longer obeyed the summons of her presence and her love. The woods alone could call it forth; it answered to the trees; the Forest had taken every part of him—from her —his very heart and soul. ...

Her sight that had plunged inwards to the fields of faded memory now came back to outer things again. She looked about her, and her love, returning empty-handed and unsatisfied, left her open to the invading of the bleakest terror she had ever known. That such things could be real and happen found her utterly helpless. Terror invaded the quietest corners of her heart, that had never yet known quailing. She could not—for moments at any rate—reach either her Bible or her God. Desolate in an empty world of fear she sat with eyes too dry and hot for tears, yet with a coldness as of ice upon her very flesh. She stared, unseeing, about her. That horror which stalks in the stillness of the noonday, when the glare of an artificial sunshine lights up the motionless trees, moved all about her. In front and behind she was aware of it. Beyond this stealthy silence, just within the edge of it, the things of another world were passing. But she could not know them. Her husband knew them, knew their beauty and their awe, yes, but for her they were out of reach. She might not share with him the very least of them. It seemed that behind and through the glare of this wintry noonday in the heart of the woods there brooded another universe of life and passion, for her all unexpressed. The silence veiled it, the stillness hid it; but he moved with it all and understood. His love interpreted it.

She rose to her feet, tottered feebly, and collapsed again upon the moss. Yet for herself she felt no terror; no little personal fear could touch her whose anguish and deep longing streamed all out to him whom she bravely loved. In this time of utter self-forgetfulness, when she realised that the battle was hopeless, thinking she had lost even her God, she found Him again quite close beside her like a little Presence in this terrible heart of the hostile Forest. But at first she did not recognise that He was there; she did not know Him in that strangely unacceptable guise. For He stood so very close, so very intimate, so very sweet and comforting, and yet so hard to understand—as Resignation.

Once more she struggled to her feet, and this time turned successfully and slowly made her way along the mossy glade by which she came. And at first she marvelled, though only for a moment, at the ease with which she found the path. For a moment only, because almost at once she saw the truth. The trees were glad that she should go. They helped her on her way. The Forest did not want her.

The tide was coming in, indeed, yet not for her.

And so, in another of those flashes of clear vision that of late had lifted life above the normal level, she saw and understood the whole terrible thing complete.

Till now, though unexpressed in thought or language, her fear had been that the woods her husband loved would somehow take him from her—to merge his life in theirs—even to kill him in some mysterious way. This time she saw her deep mistake, and so seeing, let in upon herself the fuller agony of horror. For their jealousy was not the petty jealousy of animals or humans. They wanted him because they loved him, but they did not want him dead. Full charged with his splendid life and enthusiasm they wanted him. They wanted him—alive.

It was she who stood in their way, and it was she whom they intended to remove.

This was what brought the sense of abject helplessness. She stood upon the sands against an entire ocean slowly rolling in against her. For, as all the forces of a human being combine unconsciously to eject a grain of sand that has crept beneath the skin to cause discomfort, so the entire mass of what Sanderson had called the Collective Consciousness of the Forest strove to eject this human atom that stood across the path of its desire.

Loving her husband, she had crept beneath its skin. It was her they would eject and take away; it was her they would destroy, not him. Him, whom they loved and needed, they would keep alive. They meant to take him living.

She reached the house in safety, though she never remembered how she found her way. It was made all simple for her. The branches almost urged her out.

But behind her, as she left the shadowed precincts, she felt as though some towering Angel of the Woods let fall across the threshold the flaming sword of a countless multitude of leaves that formed behind her a barrier, green, shimmering, and impassable. Into the Forest she never walked again.

. . . .

And she went about her daily duties with a calm and quietness that was a perpetual astonishment even to herself, for it hardly seemed of this world at all. She talked to her husband when he came in for tea—after dark. Resignation brings a curious large courage—when there is nothing more to lose. The soul takes risks, and dares. Is it a curious short-cut sometimes to the heights?

'David, I went into the Forest, too, this morning; soon after you I went. I saw you there.'

'Wasn't it wonderful?' he answered simply, inclining his head a little. There was no surprise or annoyance in his look; a mild and gentle *ennui* rather. He asked no real question. She thought of some garden tree the wind attacks too suddenly, bending it over when it does not want to bend—the mild unwillingness with which it yields. She often saw him this way now, in the terms of trees.

'It was very wonderful indeed, dear, yes,' she replied low, her voice not faltering though indistinct. 'But for me it was too—too strange and big.'

The passion of tears lay just below the quiet voice all unbetrayed. Somehow she kept them back.

There was a pause, and then he added:

'I find it more and more so every day.' His voice passed through the lamp-lit room like a murmur of the wind in branches. The look of youth and happiness she had caught upon his face out there had wholly gone, and an expression of weariness was in its place, as of a man distressed vaguely at finding himself in uncongenial surroundings where he is slightly ill at ease. It was the house he hated—coming back to rooms and walls and furniture. The ceilings and closed windows confined him. Yet, in it, no suggestion that he found *her* irksome. Her presence seemed of no account at all; indeed, he hardly noticed her. For whole long periods he lost her, did not know that she was there. He had no need of her. He lived alone. Each lived alone.

The outward signs by which she recognised that the awful battle was against her and the terms of surrender accepted were pathetic. She put the medicine-chest away upon the shelf; she gave the orders for his pocket-luncheon before he asked; she went to bed alone and early, leaving the front door unlocked, with milk and bread and butter in the hall beside the lamp—all concessions that she felt impelled to make. For more and more, unless the weather was too violent, he went out after dinner even, staying for hours in the woods. But she never slept until she heard the front door close below, and knew soon afterwards his careful step come creeping up the stairs and into the room so softly. Until she heard his regular deep breathing close beside her, she lay awake. All strength or desire to resist had gone for good. The thing against her was too huge and powerful. Capitulation was complete, a fact accomplished. She dated it from the day she followed him to the Forest.

Moreover, the time for evacuation—her own evacuation—seemed approaching. It came stealthily ever nearer, surely and slowly as the rising tide she used to dread. At the high-water mark she stood waiting calmly—waiting to be swept away. Across the lawn all those terrible days of early winter the encircling Forest watched it come, guiding its silent swell and currents towards her feet. Only she never once gave up her Bible or her praying. This complete resignation, moreover, had somehow brought to her a strange great understanding, and if she could not share her husband's horrible abandonment to powers outside himself, she could, and did, in some half-groping way grasp at shadowy meanings that might make such abandonment—possible, yes, but more than merely possible—in some extraordinary sense not evil.

Hitherto she had divided the beyond-world into two sharp halves—spirits good or spirits evil. But thoughts came to her now, on soft and very tentative feet, like the footsteps of the gods which are on wool, that besides these definite clases, there might be other Powers as well, belonging definitely to neither one nor the other. Her thought stopped dead at that. But the big idea found lodgment in her little mind, and, owing to the largeness of her heart, remained there unejected. It even brought a certain solace with it.

The failure—or unwillingness, as she preferred to state it—of her God to interfere and help, that also she came in a measure to understand. For here, she found it more and more possible to imagine, was perhaps no positive evil at work, but only something that usually stands away from humankind, something alien and not commonly recognised. There *was* a gulf fixed between the two, and Mr. Sanderson *had* bridged it, by his talk, his explanations, his attitude of mind. Through these her husband had found the way into it. His temperament and natural passion for the woods had prepared the soul in him, and the moment he saw the way to go he took it—the line of least resistance. Life was, of course, open to all, and her husband had the right to choose it where he would. He had chosen it—away from her, away from other men, but not necessarily away from God. This was an enormous concession that she skirted, never really faced; it was too revolutionary to face. But its possibility peeped into her bewildered mind. It might delay his progress, or it might advance it. Who could know? And why should God, who ordered all things with such magnificent detail, from the pathway of a sun to the falling of a sparrow, object to his free choice, or interfere to hinder him and stop?

She came to realise resignation, that is, in another aspect. It gave her comfort, if not peace. She fought against all belittling of her God. It was, perhaps, enough that He—knew.

'You are not alone, dear, in the trees out there?' she ventured one night, as he crept on tiptoe into the room not far from midnight. 'God is with you?'

'Magnificently,' was the immediate answer, given with enthusiasm, 'for He is everywhere. And I only wish that you——'

But she stuffed the clothes against her ears. That invitation on his lips was more than she could bear to hear. It seemed like asking her to hurry to her own execution. She buried her face among the sheets and blankets, shaking all over like a leaf.

## IX

And so the thought that she was the one to go remained and grew. It was, perhaps, the first sign of that weakening of the mind which indicated the singular manner of her going. For it was her mental opposition, the trees felt, that stood in their way. Once that was overcome, obliterated, her physical presence did not matter. She would be harmless.

Having accepted defeat, because she had come to feel that his obsession was not actually evil, she accepted at the same time the conditions of an atrocious loneliness. She stood now from her husband farther than from the moon. They had no visitors. Callers were few and far between, and less encouraged than before. The empty dark of winter was before them. Among the neighbours was none in whom, without disloyalty to her husband, she could confide. Mr. Mortimer, had he been single, might have helped her in this desert of solitude that preyed upon her mind, but his wife was there the obstacle; for Mrs. Mortimer wore sandals, believed that nuts were the complete food of man, and indulged in other idiosyncrasies that classed her inevitably among the 'latter signs' which Mrs. Bittacy had been taught to dread as dangerous. She stood most desolately alone.

Solitude, therefore, in which the mind unhindered feeds upon its own delusions, was the assignable cause of her gradual mental disruption and collapse.

With the definite arrival of the colder weather her husband gave up his rambles after dark; evenings were spent together over the fire; he read *The Times*; they even talked about their postponed visit abroad in the coming spring. No restlessness was on him at the change; he seemed content and easy in his mind; spoke little of the trees and woods; enjoyed far better health than if there had been change of scene, and to herself was tender, kind, solicitous over trifles, as in the distant days of their first honeymoon.

But this deep calm could not deceive her; it meant, she fully understood, that he felt sure of himself, sure of her, and sure of the trees as well. It all lay buried in the depths of him, too secure and deep, too intimately established in his central being to permit of those surface fluctuations which betray disharmony within. His life was hid with trees. Even the fever, so dreaded in the damp of winter, left him free. She now knew why. The fever was due to their efforts to obtain him, his efforts to respond and go—physical results of a fierce unrest he had never understood till Sanderson came with his wicked explanations. Now it was otherwise. The bridge was made. And—he had gone.

And she, brave, loyal, and consistent soul, found herself utterly alone, even trying to make his passage easy. It seemed that she stood at the bottom of some huge ravine that opened in her mind, the walls whereof instead of rock were trees that reached enormous to the sky, engulfing her. God alone knew that she was there. He watched, permitted, even perhaps approved. At any rate—He knew.

During those quiet evenings in the house, moreover, while they sat over the fire listening to the roaming winds about the house her husband knew continual access to the world his alien love had furnished for him. Never for a single instant was he cut off from it. She gazed at the newspaper spread before his face and knees, saw the smoke of his cheroot curl up above the edge, noticed the little hole in his evening socks, and listened to the paragraphs he read aloud as of old. But this was all a veil he spread about himself of purpose. Behind it—he escaped. It was the conjurer's trick to divert the sight to unimportant details while the essential thing went forward unobserved. He managed wonderfully; she loved him for the pains he took to spare her distress; but all the while she knew that the body lolling in that armchair before her eyes contained the merest fragment of his actual self. It was little better than a corpse. It was an empty shell. The essential soul of him was out yonder with the Forest—farther out near that ever-roaring heart of it.

And, with the dark, the Forest came up boldly and pressed against the very walls and windows, peering in upon them, joining hands above the slates and chimneys. The winds were always walking on the lawn and gravel paths; steps came and went and came again; some one seemed always talking in the woods, some one was in the building too. She passed them on the stairs, or running soft and muffled, very large and gentle, down the passages and landings after dusk, as though loose fragments of the Day had broken off and stayed there caught among the shadows, trying to get out. They blundered silently all about the house. They waited till she passed, then made a run for it. And her husband always knew. She saw him more than once deliberately avoid them because—*she* was there. More than once, too, she saw him stand and listen when he thought she was not near, then heard herself the long bounding stride of their approach across the silent garden. Already *he* had heard them in the windy distance of the night, far, far away. They sped, she well knew, along that glade of mossy turf by which she last came out; it cushioned their tread exactly as it had cushioned her own.

It seemed to her the trees were always in the house with him, and in their very bedroom. He welcomed them, unaware that she also knew, and trembled.

One night in their bedroom it caught her unawares. She

woke out of deep sleep and it came upon her before she could gather her forces for control.

The day had been wildly boisterous, but now the wind had dropped; only its rags went fluttering through the night. The rays of the full moon fell in a shower between the branches. Overhead still raced the scud and wrack, shaped like hurrying monsters; but below the earth was quiet. Still and dripping stood the hosts of trees. Their trunks gleamed wet and sparkling where the moon caught them. There was a strong smell of mould and fallen leaves. The air was sharp—heavy with odour.

And she knew all this the instant that she woke; for it seemed to her that she had been elsewhere—following her husband—as though she had been *out*! There was no dream at all, merely this definite, haunting certainty. It dived away, lost, buried in the night. She sat upright in bed. She had come back.

The room shone pale in the moonlight reflected through the windows, for the blinds were up, and she saw her husband's form beside her, motionless in deep sleep. But what caught her unawares was the horrid thing that by this fact of sudden, unexpected waking she had surprised these other things in the room, beside the very bed, gathered close about him while he slept. It was their dreadful boldness—herself of no account as it were—that terrified her into screaming before she could collect her powers to prevent. She screamed before she realised what she did — a long, high shriek of terror that filled the room, yet made so little actual sound. For wet and shimmering presences stood grouped all round that bed. She saw their outline underneath the ceiling, the green, spread bulk of them, their vague extension over walls and furniture. They shifted to and fro, massed yet translucent, mild yet thick, moving and turning within themselves to a hushed noise of multitudinous soft rustling. In their sound was something very sweet and winning that fell into her with a spell of horrible enchantment. They were so mild, each one alone, yet so terrific in their combination. Cold seized her. The sheets against her body turned to ice.

She screamed a second time, though the sound hardly issued from her throat. The spell sank deeper, reaching to the heart; for it softened all the currents of her blood and took life from her in a stream—towards themselves. Resistance in that moment seemed impossible.

Her husband then stirred in his sleep, and woke. And, instantly, the forms drew up, erect, and gathered themselves in some amazing way together. They lessened in extent—then scattered through the air like an effect of light when shadows seek to smother it. It was tremendous, yet most exquisite. A sheet of pale-green shadow that yet had form and substance filled the room. There was a rush of silent movement, as the Presences drew past her through the air,—and then were gone.

But, clearest of all, she saw the manner of their going; for she recognised in their tumult of escape by the window open at the top, the same wide 'looping circles'—spirals it seemed—that she had seen upon the lawn those weeks ago when Sanderson had talked. The room once more was empty.

In the collapse that followed, she heard her husband's voice, as though coming from some great distance. Her own replies she heard as well. Both were so strange and unlike their normal speech, the very words unnatural:

'What is it, dear? Why do you wake me *now*?' And his voice whispered it with a sighing sound, like wind in pine boughs.

'A moment since something went past me through the air of the room. Back to the night outside it went.' Her voice, too, held the same note as of wind entangled among too many leaves.

'My dear, it *was* the wind.'

'But it called, David. It was calling *you*—by name!'

'The stir of the branches, dear, was what you heard. Now, sleep again, I beg you, sleep.'

'It had a crowd of eyes all through and over it—before and behind——' Her voice grew louder. But his own in reply sank lower, far away, and oddly hushed.

'The moonlight, dear, upon the sea of twigs and boughs in the rain, was what you saw.'

'But it frightened me. I've lost my God—and you—I'm cold as death!'

'My dear, it is the cold of the early morning hours. The whole world sleeps. Now sleep again yourself.'

He whispered close to her ear. She felt his hand stroking her. His voice was soft and very soothing. But only a part of him was there; only a part of him was speaking; it was a half-emptied body that lay beside her and uttered these strange sentences, even forcing her own singular choice of words. The horrible, dim enchantment of the trees was close about them in the room—gnarled, ancient, lonely trees of winter, whispering round the human life they loved.

'And let me sleep again,' she heard him murmur as he settled down among the clothes, 'sleep back into that deep, delicious peace from which you called me. ...'

His dreamy, happy tone, and that look of youth and joy she discerned upon his features even in the filtered moonlight, touched her again as with the spell of those shining, mild green presences. It sank down into her. She felt sleep grope for her. On the threshold of slumber one of those strange vagrant voices that loss of consciousness lets loose cried faintly in her heart—

'There is joy in the Forest over one sinner that——'

Then sleep took her before she had time to realise even that she was vilely parodying one of her most precious texts, and that the irreverence was ghastly. ...

And though she quickly slept again, her sleep was not as usual, dreamless. It was not woods and trees she dreamed of, but a small and curious dream that kept coming again and again upon her: that she stood upon a wee, bare rock in the sea, and that the tide was rising. The water first came to her feet, then to her knees, then to her waist. Each time the dream returned, the tide seemed higher. Once it rose to her neck, once even to her mouth, covering her lips for a moment so that she could not breathe. She did not wake between the dreams; a period of drab and dreamless slumber intervened. But, finally, the water rose above her eyes and face, completely covering her head.

And then came explanation—the sort of explanation dreams bring. She understood. For, beneath the water, she had seen the world of seaweed rising from the bottom of the sea like a forest of dense green—long, sinuous stems, immense thick branches, millions of feelers spreading through the darkened watery depths the power of their ocean foliage. The Vegetable Kingdom was even in the sea. It was everywhere. Earth, air, and water helped it, way of escape there was none.

And even underneath the sea she heard that terrible sound of roaring—was it surf or wind or voices?—further out, yet coming steadily towards her.

And so, in the loneliness of that drab English winter, the mind of Mrs. Bittacy, preying upon itself, and fed by constant dread, went lost in disproportion. Dreariness filled the weeks with dismal, sunless skies and a clinging moisture that knew no wholesome tonic of keen frosts. Alone with her thoughts, both her husband and her God withdrawn into distance, she counted the days to Spring. She groped her way, stumbling down the long dark tunnel. Through the arch at the far end lay a brilliant picture of the violet sea sparkling on the coast of France. There lay safety and escape for both of them, could she but hold on. Behind her the trees blocked up the other entrance. She never once looked back.

She drooped. Vitality passed from her, drawn out and away as by some steady suction. Immense and incessant was this sensation of her powers draining off. The taps were all turned on. Her personality, as it were, streamed steadily away, coaxed outwards by this Power that never wearied and seemed inexhaustible. It won her as the full moon wins the tide. She waned; she faded; she obeyed.

At first she watched the process, and recognised exactly what was going on. Her physical life, and that balance of the mind which depends on physical well-being, were being slowly undermined. She saw that clearly. Only the soul, dwelling like a star apart from these and independent of them, lay safe somewhere—with her distant God. That she knew—tranquilly. The spiritual love that linked her to her husband was safe from all attack. Later, in His good time, they would merge together again because of it. But, meanwhile, all of her that had kinship with the earth was slowly going. This separation was being remorselessly accomplished. Every part of her the trees could touch was being steadily drained from her. She was being—removed.

After a time, however, even this power of realisation went, so that she no longer 'watched the process' or knew exactly what was going on. The one satisfaction she had known—the feeling that it was sweet to suffer for his sake—went with it. She stood utterly alone with this terror of the trees... mid the ruins of her broken and disordered mind.

She slept badly; woke in the morning with hot and tired eyes; her head ached dully; she grew confused in thought and lost the clues of daily life in the most feeble fashion. At the same time she lost sight, too, of that brilliant picture at the exit of the tunnel; it faded away into a tiny semicircle of pale light, the violet sea and the sunshine the merest point of white, remote as a star and equally inaccessible. She knew now that she could never reach it. And through the darkness that stretched behind, the power of the trees came close and caught her, twining about her feet and arms, climbing to her very lips. She woke at night, finding it difficult to breathe. There seemed wet leaves pressed against her mouth, and soft green tendrils clinging to her neck. Her feet were heavy, half rooted, as it were, in deep, thick earth. Huge creepers stretched along the whole of that black tunnel, feeling about her person for points where they might fasten well, as ivy or the giant parasites of the Vegetable Kingdom settle down on the trees themselves to sap their life and kill them.

Slowly and surely the morbid growth possessed her life and held her. She feared those very winds that ran about the wintry forest. They were in league with it. They helped it everywhere.

'Why don't you sleep, dear?' It was her husband now who played the role of nurse, tending her little wants with an honest care that at least aped the services of love. He was so utterly unconscious of the raging battle he had caused. 'What is it that keeps you so wide awake and restless?'

'The winds,' she whispered in the dark. For hours she had lain watching the tossing of the trees through the blindless windows. 'They go walking and talking everywhere to-night, keeping me awake. And all the time they call so loudly to you.'

And this strange whispered answer appalled her for a moment until the meaning of it faded and left her in a dark confusion of the mind that was now becoming almost permanent.

'The trees excite them in the night. The winds are the great swift carriers. Go with them, dear—and not against. You'll find sleep that way if you do.'

'The storm is rising,' she began, hardly knowing what she said.

'All the more then—go with them. Don't resist. They'll take you to the trees, that's all.'

Resist! The word touched on the button of some text that once had helped her.

'Resist the devil and he will flee from you,' she heard her whispered answer, and the same second had buried her face beneath the clothes in a flood of hysterical weeping.

But her husband did not seem disturbed. Perhaps he did not hear it, for the wind ran just then against the windows with a booming shout, and the roaring of the Forest further out came behind the blow, surging into the room. Perhaps, too, he was already asleep again. She slowly regained a sort of dull composure. Her face emerged from the tangle of sheets and blankets. With a growing terror over her—she listened. The storm was rising. It came with a sudden and impetuous rush that made all further sleep for her impossible.

Alone in a shaking world, it seemed, she lay and listened. That storm interpreted for her mind the climax. The Forest bellowed out its victory to the winds; the winds in turn proclaimed it to the Night. The whole world knew of her complete defeat, her loss, her little human pain. This was the roar and shout of victory that she listened to.

For, unmistakably, the trees were shouting in the dark. There were sounds, too, like the flapping of great sails, a thousand at a time, and sometimes reports that resembled more than anything else the distant booming of enormous drums. The trees stood up—the whole beleaguering host of them stood up—and with the uproar of their million branches drummed the thundering message out across the night. It seemed as if they all had broken loose. Their roots swept trailing over field and hedge and roof. They tossed their bushy heads beneath the clouds with a wild, delighted shuffling of great boughs. With trunks upright they raced leaping through the sky. There was upheaval and adventure in the awful sound they made, and their cry was like the cry of a sea that has broken through its gates and poured loose upon the world. ...

Through it all her husband slept peacefully as though he heard it not. It was, as she well knew, the sleep of the semi-dead. For he was out with all that clamouring turmoil. The part of him hat she had lost was there. The form that slept so calmly at her side was but the shell, half emptied. ...

And when the winter's morning stole upon the scene at length, with a pale, washed sunshine that followed the departing tempest, the first thing she saw, as she crept to the window and looked out, was the ruined cedar lying on the lawn. Only the gaunt and crippled trunk of it remained. The single giant bough that had been left to it lay dark upon the grass, sucked endways towards the Forest by a great wind eddy. It lay there like a mass of driftwood from a wreck, left by the ebbing of a high spring-tide upon the sands—remnant of some friendly, splendid vessel that once had sheltered men.

And in the distance she heard the roaring of the Forest further out. Her husband's voice was in it.

# THE VALLEY OF THE BEASTS

## I

As they emerged suddenly from the dense forest the Indian halted, and Grimwood, his employer, stood beside him, gazing into the beautiful wooded valley that lay spread below them in the blaze of a golden sunset. Both men leaned upon their rifles, caught by the enchantment of the unexpected scene.

'We camp here,' said Tooshalli abruptly, after a careful survey. 'To-morrow we make a plan.'

He spoke excellent English. The note of decision, almost of authority, in his voice was noticeable, but Grimwood set it down to the natural excitement of the moment. Every track they had followed during the last two days, but one track in particular as well, had headed straight for this remote and hidden valley, and the sport promised to be unusual.

'That's so,' he replied, in the tone of one giving an order. 'You can make camp ready at once.' And he sat down on a fallen hemlock to take off his moccasin boots and grease his feet that ached from the arduous day now drawing to a close. Though under ordinary circumstances he would have pushed on for another hour or two he was not averse to a night here, for exhaustion had come upon him during the last bit of rough going, his eye and muscles were no longer steady, and it was doubtful if he could have shot straight enough to kill. He did not mean to miss a second time.

With his Canadian friend, Iredale, the latter's half-breed, and his own Indian, Tooshalli, the party had set out three weeks ago to find the 'wonderful big moose' the Indians reported were travelling in the Snow River country. They soon found that the tale was true; tracks were abundant; they saw fine animals nearly every day, but though carrying good heads, the hunters expected better still and left them alone. Pushing up the river to a chain of small lakes near its source, they then separated into two parties, each with its nine-foot bark canoe, and packed in for three days after the yet bigger animals the Indians agreed would be found in the deeper woods beyond. Excitement was keen, expectation keener still. The day before they separated, Iredale shot the biggest moose of his life, and its head, bigger even than the grand Alaskan heads, hangs in his house to-day. Grimwood's hunting blood was fairly up. His blood was of the fiery, not to say ferocious, quality. It almost seemed he liked killing for its own sake.

Four days after the party broke into two he came upon a gigantic track, whose measurements and length of stride keyed every nerve he possessed to its highest tension.

Tooshalli examined the tracks for some minutes with care. 'It is the biggest moose in the world,' he said at length, a new expression on his inscrutable red visage.

Following it all that day, they yet got no sight of the big fellow that seemed to be frequenting a little marshy dip of country, too small to be called valley, where willow and undergrowth abounded. He had not yet scented his pursuers. They were after him again at dawn. Towards the evening of the second day Grimwood caught a sudden glimpse of the monster among a thick clump of willows, and the sight of the magnificent head that easily beat all records set his heart beating like a hammer with excitement. He aimed and fired. But the moose, instead of crashing, went thundering away through the farther scrub and disappeared, the sound of his plunging canter presently dying away. Grimwood had missed, even if he had wounded.

They camped, and all next day, leaving the canoe behind, they followed the huge track, but though finding signs of blood, these were not plentiful, and the shot had evidently only grazed the animal. The travelling was of the hardest. Towards evening, utterly exhausted, the spoor led them to the ridge they now stood upon, gazing down into the enchanting valley that opened at their feet. The giant moose had gone down into this valley. He would consider himself safe there. Grimwood agreed with the Indian's judgment. They would camp for the night and continue at dawn the wild hunt after 'the biggest moose in the world'.

Supper was over, the small fire used for cooking dying down, when Grimwood became first aware that the Indian was not behaving quite as usual. What particular detail drew his attention is hard to say. He was a slow-witted, heavy man, full-blooded, unobservant; a fact had to hurt him through his comfort, through his pleasure, before he noticed it. Yet anyone else must have observed the changed mood of the Redskin long ago. Tooshalli had made the fire, fried the bacon, served the tea, and was arranging the blankets, his own and his employer's, before the latter remarked upon his—silence. Tooshalli had not uttered a word for over an hour and a half, since he had first set eyes upon the new valley, to be exact. And his employer now noticed the unaccustomed silence, because after food he liked to listen to wood talk and hunting lore.

'Tired out, aren't you?' said big Grimwood, looking into the dark face across the firelight. He resented the absence of conversation, now that he noticed it. He was over-weary himself, he felt more irritable than usual, though his temper was always vile.

'Lost your tongue, eh?' he went on with a growl, as the Indian returned his stare with solemn, expressionless face. That dark inscrutable look got on his nerves a bit. 'Speak up, man!' he exclaimed sharply. 'What's it all about?'

The Englishman had at last realised that there was something to 'speak up' about. The discovery, in his present state, annoyed him further. Tooshalli stared gravely, but made no reply. The silence was prolonged almost into minutes. Presently the head turned sideways, as though the man listened. The other watched him very closely, anger growing in him.

But it was the way the Redskin turned his head, keeping his body rigid, that gave the jerk to Grimwood's nerves, providing him with a sensation he had never known in his life before—it gave him what is generally called 'the goose-flesh'. It seemed to jangle his entire system, yet at the same time made him cautious. He did not like it, this combination of emotions puzzled him.

'Say something, I tell you,' he repeated in a harsher tone, raising his voice. He sat up, drawing his great body closer to the fire. 'Say something, damn it!'

His voice fell dead against the surrounding trees, making the silence of the forest unpleasantly noticeable. Very still the great woods stood about them: there was no wind, no stir of branches; only the crackle of a snapping twig was audible from time to time, as the night-life moved unwarily sometimes, watching the humans round their little fire. The October air had a frosty touch that nipped.

The Redskin did not answer. No muscle of his neck nor of his stiffened body moved. He seemed all ears.

'Well?' repeated the Englishman, lowering his voice this time instinctively. 'What d'you hear, God damn it?' The touch of odd nervousness that made his anger grow betrayed itself in his language.

Tooshalli slowly turned his head back again to its normal position, the body rigid as before.

'I hear nothing, Mr. Grimwood,' he said, gazing with quiet dignity into his employer's eyes.

This was too much for the other, a man of savage temper at the best of times. He was the type of Englishman who held strong views as to the right way of treating 'inferior' races.

'That's a lie, Tooshalli, and I won't have you lie to me. Now what was it? Tell me at once!'

'I hear nothing,' repeated the other. 'I only think.'

'And what is it you're pleased to think?' Impatience made a nasty expression round the mouth.

'I go not,' was the abrupt reply, unalterable decision in the voice.

The man's rejoinder was so unexpected that Grimwood found

nothing to say at first. For a moment he did not take its meaning; his mind, always slow, was confused by impatience, also by what he considered the foolishness of the little scene. Then in a flash he understood; but he also understood the immovable obstinacy of the race he had to deal with. Tooshalli was informing him that he refused to go into the valley where the big moose had vanished. And his astonishment was so great at first that he merely sat and stared. No words came to him.

'It is——' said the Indian, but used a native term.

'What's that mean?' Grimwood found his tongue, but his quiet tone was ominous.

'Mr. Grimwood, it mean the "Valley of the Beasts",' was the reply in a tone quieter still.

The Englishman made a great, a genuine effort at self-control. He was dealing, he forced himself to remember, with a superstitious Redskin. He knew the stubbornness of the type. If the man left him his sport was irretrievably spoilt, for he could not hunt in this wilderness alone, and even if he got the coveted head, he could never, never get it out alone. His native selfishness seconded his effort. Persuasion, if only he could keep back his rising anger, was his role to play.

'The Valley of the Beasts,' he said, a smile on his lips rather than in his darkening eyes; 'but that's just what we want. It's beasts we're after, isn't it?' His voice had a false cheery ring that could not have deceived a child. 'But what d'you mean, anyhow—the Valley of the Beasts?' He asked it with a dull attempt at sympathy.

'It belong to Ishtot, Mr. Grimwood.' The man looked him full in the face, no flinching in the eyes.

'My—our—big moose is there,' said the other, who recognised the name of the Indian Hunting God, and understanding better, felt confident he would soon persuade his man. Tooshalli, he remembered, too, was nominally a Christian. 'We'll follow him at dawn and get the biggest head the world has ever seen. You will be famous,' he added, his temper better in hand again. 'Your tribe will honour you. And the white hunters will pay you much money.'

'He go there to save himself. I go not.'

The other's anger revived with a leap at this stupid obstinacy. But, in spite of it, he noticed the old choice of words. He began to realise that nothing now would move the man. At the same time he also realised that violence on his part must prove worse than useless. Yet violence was natural to his 'dominant' type.

'That brute Grimwood' was the way most men spoke of him.

'Back at the settlement you're a Christian, remember,' he tried, in his clumsy way, another line. 'And disobedience means hell-fire. You know that!'

'I a Christian—at the post,' was the reply, 'but out here the Red God rule. Ishtot keep that valley for himself. No Indian hunt there.' It was as though a granite boulder spoke.

The savage temper of the Englishman, enforced by the long difficult suppression, rose wickedly into sudden flame. He stood up, kicking his blankets aside. He strode across the dying fire to the Indian's side. Tooshalli also rose. They faced each other, two humans alone in the wilderness, watched by countless invisible forest eyes.

Tooshalli stood motionless, yet as though he expected violence from the foolish, ignorant white-face. 'You go alone, Mr. Grimwood.' There was no fear in him.

Grimwood choked with rage. His words came forth with difficulty, though he roared them into the silence of the forest:

'I pay you, don't I? You'll do what *I* say, not what *you* say!' His voice woke the echoes.

The Indian, arms hanging by his side, gave the old reply.

'I go not,' he repeated firmly.

It stung the other into uncontrollable fury.

The beast then came uppermost; it came out. 'You've said that once too often, Tooshalli!' and he struck him brutally in the face. The Indian fell, rose to his knees again, collapsed sideways beside the fire, then struggled back into a sitting position. He never once took his eyes from the white man's face.

Beside himself with anger, Grimwood stood over him. 'Is that enough? Will you obey me now?' he shouted.

'I go not,' came the thick reply, blood streaming from his mouth. The eyes had no flinching in them. 'That valley Ishtot keep. Ishtot see us now. *He see you.*' The last words he uttered with strange, almost uncanny emphasis.

Grimwood, arm raised, fist clenched, about to repeat his terrible assault, paused suddenly. His arm sank to his side. What exactly stopped him he could never say. For one thing he feared his own anger, feared that if he let himself go he would not stop till he had killed—committed murder. He knew his own fearful temper and stood afraid of it. Yet it was not only that. The calm firmness of the Redskin, his courage under pain, and something in the fixed and burning eyes arrested him. Was it also something in the words he had used—'Ishtot see *you*'—that stung him into a queer caution midway in his violence?

He could not say. He only knew that a momentary sense of awe came over him. He became unpleasantly aware of the enveloping forest, so still, listening in a kind of impenetrable, remorseless silence. This lonely wilderness, looking silently upon what might easily prove murder, laid a faint, inexplicable chill upon his raging blood. The hand dropped slowly to his side again, the fist unclenched itself, his breath came more evenly.

'Look you here,' he said, adopting without knowing it the local way of speech. 'I ain't a bad man, though your going-on do make a man damned tired. I'll give you another chance.' His voice was sullen, but a new note in it surprised even himself. 'I'll do that. You can have the night to think it over, Tooshalli—see? Talk it over with your——'

He did not finish the sentence. Somehow the name of the Redskin God refused to pass his lips. He turned away, flung himself into his blankets, and in less than ten minutes, exhausted as much by his anger as by the day's hard going, he was sound asleep.

The Indian, crouching beside the dying fire, had said nothing.

Night held the woods, the sky was thick with stars, the life of the forest went about its business quietly, with that wondrous skill which millions of years have perfected. The Redskin, so close to this skill that he instinctively used and borrowed from it, was silent, alert and wise, his outline as inconspicuous as though he merged, like his four-footed teachers, into the mass of the surrounding bush.

He moved perhaps, yet nothing knew he moved. His wisdom, derived from that eternal, ancient mother who from infinite experience makes no mistakes, did not fail him. His soft tread made no sound; his breathing, as his weight, was calculated. The stars observed him, but they did not tell; the light air knew his whereabouts, yet without betrayal. ...

The chill dawn gleamed at length between the trees, lighting the pale ashes of an extinguished fire, also of a bulky, obvious form beneath a blanket. The form moved clumsily. The cold was penetrating.

And that bulky form moved because a dream had come to trouble it. A dark figure stole across its confused field of vision. The form started, but it did not wake. The figure spoke: 'Take this,' it whispered, handing a little stick, curiously carved. 'It is the totem of great Ishtot. In the valley all memory of the White Gods will leave you. Call upon Ishtot. ... Call on Him if you dare' and the dark figure glided away out of the dream and out of all remembrance. ...

## II

The first thing Grimwood noticed when he woke was that Tooshalli was not there. No fire burned, no tea was ready. He felt exceedingly annoyed. He glared about him, then got up with a curse to make the fire. His mind seemed confused and troubled. At first he only realised one thing clearly—his guide had left him in the night.

It was very cold. He lit the wood with difficulty and made his tea, and the actual world came gradually back to him. The Red

Indian had gone; perhaps the blow, perhaps the superstitious terror, perhaps both, had driven him away. He was alone, that was the outstanding fact. For anything beyond outstanding facts, Grimwood felt little interest. Imaginative speculation was beyond his compass. Close to the brute creation, it seemed, his nature lay.

It was while packing his blankets—he did it automatically, a dull, vicious resentment in him—that his fingers struck a bit of wood that he was about to throw away when its unusual shape caught his attention suddenly. His odd dream came back then. But was it a dream? The bit of wood was undoubtedly a totem stick. He examined it. He paid it more attention than he meant to, wished to. Yes, it was unquestionably a totem stick. The dream, then, was not a dream. Tooshalli had quit, but, following with Redskin faithfulness some code of his own, had left him the means of safety. He chuckled sourly, but thrust the stick inside his belt. 'One never knows,' he mumbled to himself.

He faced the situation squarely. He was alone in the wilderness. His capable, experienced woodsman had deserted him. The situation was serious. What should he do? A weakling would certainly retrace his steps, following the track they had made, afraid to be left alone in this vast hinterland of pathless forest. But Grimwood was of another build. Alarmed he might be, but he would not give in. He had the defects of his own qualities. The brutality of his nature argued force. He was determined and a sportsman. He would go on. And ten minutes after breakfast, having first made a *cache* of what provisions were left over, he was on his way—down across the ridge and into the mysterious valley, the Valley of the Beasts.

It looked, in the morning sunlight, entrancing. The trees closed in behind him, but he did not notice. It led him on. ...

He followed the track of the gigantic moose he meant to kill, and the sweet, delicious sunshine helped him. The air was like wine, the seductive spoor of the great beast, with here and there a faint splash of blood on leaves or ground, lay for ever just before his eyes. He found the valley, though the actual word did not occur to him, enticing; more and more he noticed the beauty, the desolate grandeur of the mighty spruce and hemlock, the splendour of the granite bluffs which in places rose above the forest and caught the sun.... The valley was deeper, vaster than he had imagined. He felt safe, at home in it, though, again, these actual terms did not occur to him. ... Here he could hide for ever and find peace. ... He became aware of a new quality in the deep loneliness. The scenery for the first time in his life appealed to him, and the form of the appeal was curious—he felt the comfort of it.

For a man of his habit, this was odd, yet the new sensations stole over him so gently, their approach so gradual, that they were first recognised by his consciousness indirectly. They had already established themselves in him before he noticed them; and the indirectness took this form—that the passion of the chase gave place to an interest in the valley itself. The lust of the hunt, the fierce desire to find and kill, the keen wish, in a word, to see his quarry within range, to aim, to fire, to witness the natural consummation of the long expedition—these had all become measurably less, while the effect of the valley upon him had increased in strength. There was a welcome about it that he did not understand.

The change was singular, yet, oddly enough, it did not occur to him as singular; it was unnatural, yet it did not strike him so. To a dull mind of his unobservant, unanalytical type, a change had to be marked and dramatic before he noticed it; something in the nature of a shock must accompany it for him to recognise it had happened. And there had been no shock. The spoor of the great moose was much clearer, now that he caught up with the animal that made it; the blood more frequent; he had noticed the spot where it had rested, its huge body leaving a marked imprint on the soft ground; where it had reached up to eat the leaves of saplings here and there was also visible; he had come undoubtedly very near to it, and any minute now might see its great bulk within range of an easy shot. Yet his ardour had somehow lessened.

He first realised this change in himself when it suddenly occurred to him that the animal itself had grown less cautious. It must scent him easily now, since a moose, its sight being indifferent, depends chiefly for its safety upon its unusually keen sense of smell, and the wind came from behind him. This now struck him as decidedly uncommon: the moose itself was obviously careless of his close approach. It felt no fear.

It was this inexplicable alteration in the animal's behaviour that made him recognise, at last, the alteration in his own. He had followed it now for a couple of hours and had descended some eight hundred to a thousand feet; the trees were thinner and more sparsely placed; there were open park-like places where silver birch, sumach and maple splashed their blazing colours; and a crystal stream, broken by many waterfalls, foamed past towards the bed of the great valley, yet another thousand feet below. By a quiet pool against some over-arching rocks, the moose had evidently paused to drink, paused at its leisure, moreover. Grimwood, rising from a close examination of the direction the creature had taken after drinking—the hoofmarks were fresh and very distinct in the marshy ground about the pool—looked suddenly straight into the great creature's eyes. It was not twenty yards from where he stood, yet he had been standing on that spot for at least ten minutes, caught by the wonder and loneliness of the scene. The moose, therefore, had been close beside him all this time. It had been calmly drinking, undisturbed by his presence, unafraid.

The shock came now, the shock that woke his heavy nature into realisation. For some seconds, probably for minutes, he stood rooted to the ground, motionlesss, hardly breathing. He stared as though he saw a vision. The animal's head was lowered, but turned obliquely somewhat, so that the eyes, placed sideways in its great head, could see him properly; its immense proboscis hung as though stuffed upon an English wall; he saw the fore-feet planted wide apart, the slope of the enormous shoulders dropping back towards the fine hind-quarters and lean flanks. It was a magnificent bull. The horns and head justified his wildest expectations, they were superb, a record specimen, and a phrase—where had he heard it?—ran vaguely, as from far distance, through his mind: 'the biggest moose in the world'.

There was the extraordinary fact, however, that he did not shoot; nor feel the wish to shoot. The familiar instinct, so strongly hitherto in his blood, made no sign; the desire to kill apparently had left him. To raise his rifle, aim and fire had become suddenly an absolute impossibility.

He did not move. The animal and the human stared into each other's eyes for a length of time whose interval he could not measure. Then came a soft noise close beside him: the rifle had slipped from his grasp and fallen with a thud into the mossy earth at his feet. And the moose, for the first time now, was moving. With slow, easy stride, its great weight causing a squelching sound as the feet drew out of the moist ground, it came towards him, the bulk of the shoulders giving it an appearance of swaying like a ship at sea. It reached his side, it almost touched him, the magnificent head bent low, the spread of the gigantic horns lay beneath his very eyes. He could have patted, stroked it. He saw, with a touch of pity, that blood trickled from a sore in its left shoulder, matting the thick hair. It sniffed the fallen rifle.

Then, lifting its head and shoulders again, it sniffed the air, this time with an audible sound that shook from Grimwood's mind the last possibility that he witnessed a vision or dreamed a dream. One moment it gazed into his face, its big brown eyes shining and unafraid, then turned abruptly, and swung away at a speed ever rapidly increasing across the park-like spaces till it was lost finally in the dark tangle of undergrowth beyond. And the Englishman's muscles turned to paper, his paralysis passed, his legs refused to support his weight, and he sank heavily to the ground.

## III

It seems he slept, slept long and heavily; he sat up, stretched himself, yawned and rubbed his eyes. The sun had moved across the sky, for the shadows, he saw, now ran from west to east, and they were long shadows. He had slept evidently for hours, and evening was drawing in. He was aware that he felt hungry. In his pouch-like pockets he had dried meat, sugar, matches, tea, and the little billy that never left him. He would make a fire, boil some tea and eat.

But he took no steps to carry out his purpose, he felt disinclined to move, he sat thinking, thinking ... What was he thinking about? He did not know, he could not say exactly; it was more like fugitive pictures that passed across his mind. Who, and where, was he? This was the Valley of the Beasts, that he knew; he felt sure of nothing else. How long had he been here, and where had he come from, and why? The questions did not linger for their answers, almost as though his interest in them was merely automatic. He felt happy, peaceful, unafraid.

He looked about him, and the spell of this virgin forest came upon him like a charm; only the sound of falling water, the murmur of wind sighing among innumerable branches, broke the enveloping silence. Overhead, beyond the crests of the towering trees, a cloudless evening sky was paling into transparent orange, opal, mother of pearl. He saw buzzards soaring lazily. A scarlet tanager flashed by. Soon would the owls begin to call and the darkness fall like a sweet black veil and hide all detail, while the stars sparkled in their countless thousands ...

A glint of something that shone upon the ground caught his eye—a smooth, polished strip of rounded metal: his rifle. And he started to his feet impulsively, yet not knowing exactly what he meant to do. At the sight of the weapon, something had leaped to life in him, then faded out, died down, and was gone again.

'I'm—I'm——' he began muttering to himself, but could not finish what he was about to say. His name had disappeared completely. 'I'm in the Valley of the Beasts,' he repeated in place of what he sought but could not find.

This fact, that he was in the Valley of the Beasts, seemed the only positive item of knowledge that he had. About the name something known and familiar clung, though the sequence that led up to it he could not trace. Presently, nevertheless, he rose to his feet, advanced a few steps, stooped and picked up the shining metal thing, his rifle. He examined it a moment, a feeling of dread and loathing rising in him, a sensation of almost horror that made him tremble, then, with a convulsive movement that betrayed an intense reaction of some sort he could not comprehend, he flung the thing far from him into the foaming torrent. He saw the splash it made, he also saw that same instant a large grizzly bear swing heavily along the bank not a dozen yards from where he stood. It, too, heard the splash, for it started, turned, paused a second, then changed its direction and came towards him. It came up close. Its fur brushed his body. It examined him leisurely, as the moose had done, sniffed, half rose upon its terrible hind legs, opened its mouth so that red tongue and gleaming teeth were plainly visible, then flopped back upon all fours again with a deep growl that yet had no anger in it, and swung off at a quick trot back to the bank of the torrent. He had felt its hot breath upon his face, but he had felt no fear. The monster was puzzled but not hostile. It disappeared.

'They know not——' he sought for the word 'man', but could not find it. 'They have never been hunted.'

The words ran through his mind, if perhaps he was not entirely certain of their meaning; they rose, as it were, automatically; a familiar sound lay in them somewhere. At the same time there rose feelings in him that were equally, though in another way, familiar and quite natural, feelings he had once known intimately but long since laid aside.

What were they? What was their origin? They seemed distant as the stars, yet were actually in his body, in his blood and nerves, part and parcel of his flesh. Long, long ago ... Oh, how long, how long?

Thinking was difficult; feeling was what he most easily and naturally managed. He could not think for long; feeling rose up and drowned the effort quickly.

That huge and awful bear—not a nerve, not a muscle quivered in him as its acrid smell rose to his nostrils, its fur brushed down his legs. Yet he was aware that somewhere there was danger, though not here. Somewhere there was attack, hostility, wicked and calculated plans against him—as against that splendid, roaming animal that had sniffed, examined, then gone its own way, satisfied. Yes, active attack, hostility and careful, cruel plans against his safety, but—not here. Here he was safe, secure, at peace; here he was happy; here he could roam at will, no eye cast sideways into forest depths, no ear pricked high to catch sounds not explained, no nostrils quivering to scent alarm. He felt this, but he did not think it. He felt hungry, thirsty too.

Something prompted him now at last to act. His billy lay at his feet, and he picked it up; the matches—he carried them in a metal case whose screw top kept out all moisture—were in his hand. Gathering a few dry twigs, he stooped to light them, then suddenly drew back with the first touch of fear he had yet known.

Fire! What *was* fire? The idea was repugnant to him, it was impossible, he was afraid of fire. He flung the metal case after the rifle and saw it gleam in the last rays of sunset, then sink with a little splash beneath the water. Glancing down at his billy, he realised next that he could not make use of it either, nor of the dark dry dusty stuff he had meant to boil in water. He felt no repugnance, certainly no fear, in connection with these things, only he could not handle them, he did not need them, he had forgotten, yes, 'forgotten', what they meant exactly. This strange forgetfulness was increasing in him rapidly, becoming more and more complete with every minute. Yet his thirst must be quenched.

The next moment he found himself at the water's edge; he stooped to fill his billy; paused, hesitated, examined the rushing water, then abruptly moved a few feet higher up the stream, leaving the metal can behind him. His handling of it had been oddly clumsy, his gestures awkward, even unnatural. He now flung himself down with an easy, simple motion of his entire body, lowered his face to a quiet pool he had found, and drank his fill of the cool, refreshing liquid. But, though unaware of the fact, he did not drink. He lapped.

Then, crouching where he was, he ate the meat and sugar from his pockets, lapped more water, moved back a short distance again into the dry ground beneath the trees, but moved this time without rising to his feet, curled his body into a comfortable position and closed his eyes again to sleep ... No single question now raised its head in him. He felt contentment, satisfaction only...

He stirred, shook himself, opened half an eye and saw, as he had felt already in slumber, that he was not alone. In the park-like spaces in front of him, as in the shadowed fringe of the trees at his back, there was sound and movement, the sound of stealthy feet, the movement of innumerable dark bodies. There was the pad and tread of animals, the stir of backs, of smooth and shaggy beasts, in countless numbers. Upon this host fell the light of a half moon sailing high in a cloudless sky; the gleam of stars, sparkling in the clear night air like diamonds, shone reflected in hundreds of ever-shifting eyes, most of them but a few feet above the ground. The whole valley was alive.

He sat upon his haunches, staring, staring, but staring in wonder, not in fear, though the foremost of the great host were so near that he could have stretched an arm and touched them. It was an ever-moving, ever-shifting throng he gazed at, spell-bound, in the pale light of moon and stars, now fading slowly towards the approaching dawn. And the smell of the forest itself was not sweeter to him in that moment than the mingled perfume, raw, pungent, acrid, of this furry host of beautiful wild animals that moved like a sea, with a strange murmuring, too, like sea, as the myriad feet and bodies passed to and fro together. Nor was the gleam of the starry, phosphorescent eyes less pleasantly friendly than those happy lamps that light home-lost wanderers to cosy rooms and safety. Through the wild army, in a word, poured to him the deep comfort of the entire valley, a comfort which held both the sweetness of invitation and the welcome of some magical home-coming.

No thoughts came to him, but feeling rose in a tide of wonder and acceptance. He was in his rightful place. His nature had come home. There was this dim, vague consciousness in him that after long, futile straying in another place where uncongenial conditions had forced him to be unnatural and therefore terrible, he had returned at last where he belonged. Here, in the Valley of the Beasts, he had found peace, security and happiness. He would be—he was at last—himself.

It was a marvellous, even a magical, scene he watched, his nerves at highest tension yet quite steady, his senses exquisitely alert, yet no uneasiness in the full accurate reports they furnished. Strong as some deep flood-tide, yet dim, as with untold time and distance, rose over him the spell of long-forgotten memory of a state where he was content and happy, where he was *natural.* The outlines, as it were, of mighty, primitive pictures, flashed before him, yet were gone again before the detail was filled in.

He watched the great army of the animals, they were all about him now; he crouched upon his haunches in the centre of an ever-moving circle of wild forest life. Great timber wolves he saw pass to and fro, loping past him with long stride and graceful swing; their red tongues lolling out; they swarmed in hundreds. Behind, yet mingling freely with them, rolled the huge grizzlies, not clumsy as their uncouth bodies promised, but swiftly, lightly, easily, their half tumbling gait masking agility and speed. They gambolled, sometimes they rose and stood half upright, they were comely in their mass and power, they rolled past him so close that he could touch them. And the black bear and the brown went with them, bears beyond counting, monsters and little ones, a splendid multitude. Beyond them, yet only a little farther back, where the park-like spaces made free movement easier, rose a sea of horns and antlers like a miniature forest in the silvery moonlight.

The immense tribe of deer gathered in vast throngs beneath

the starlit sky. Moose and caribou, he saw, the mighty wapiti, and the smaller deer in their crowding thousands. He heard the sound of meeting horns, the tread of innumerable hoofs, the occasional pawing of the ground as the bigger creatures manoeuvred for more space about them. A wolf, he saw, was licking gently at the shoulder of a great bull-moose that had been injured. And the tide receded, advanced again, once more receded, rising and falling like a living sea whose waves were animal shapes, the inhabitants of the Valley of the Beasts.

Beneath the quiet moonlight they swayed to and fro before him. They watched him, knew him, recognised him. They made him welcome.

He was aware, moreover, of a world of smaller life that formed an under-sea, as it were, numerous under-currents rather, running in and out between the great upright legs of the larger creatures. These, though he could not see them clearly, covered the earth, he was aware, in enormous numbers, darting hither and thither, now hiding, now reappearing, too intent upon their busy purposes to pay him attention like their huger comrades, yet ever and anon tumbling against his back, cannoning from his sides, scampering across his legs even, then gone again with a scuttering sound of rapid little feet, and rushing back in to the general host beyond. And with this smaller world also he felt at home.

How long he sat gazing, happy in himself, secure, satisfied, contented, natural, he could not say, but it was long enough for the desire to mingle with what he saw, to know closer contact, to become one with them all—long enough for this deep blind desire to assert itself, so that at length he began to move from his mossy seat towards them, to move, moreover, as they moved, and not upright on two feet.

The moon was lower now, just sinking behind a towering cedar whose ragged crest broke its light into silvery spray. The stars were a little paler too. A line of faint red was visible beyond the heights at the valley's eastern end.

He paused and looked about him, as he advanced slowly,

aware that the host already made an opening in their ranks and that the bear even nosed the earth in front, as though to show the way that was easiest to follow. Then, suddenly, a lynx leaped past him into the low branches of a hemlock, and he lifted his head to admire its perfect poise. He saw in the same instant the arrival of the birds, the army of the eagles, hawks and buzzards, birds of prey—the awakening flight that just precedes the dawn. He saw the flock and streaming lines, hiding the whitening stars a moment as they passed with a prodigious whirr of wings. There came the hooting of an owl from the tree immediately overhead where the lynx now crouched, but not maliciously, along its branch.

He started. He half rose to an upright position. He knew not why he did so, knew not exactly why he started. But in the attempt to find his new, and, as it now seemed, his unaccustomed balance, one hand fell against his side and came in contact with a hard straight thing that projected awkwardly from his clothing. He pulled it out, feeling it all over with his fingers. It was a little stick. He raised it nearer to his eyes, examined it in the light of dawn now growing swiftly, remembered, or half remembered what it was—and stood stock still.

'The totem stick,' he mumbled to himself, yet audibly, finding his speech, and finding another thing—a glint of peering memory—for the first time since entering the valley.

A shock of fire ran through his body; he straightened himself, aware that a moment before he had been crawling upon his hands and knees; it seemed that something broke in his brain, lifting a veil, flinging a shutter free. And Memory peered dreadfully through the widening gap.

'I'm—I'm Grimwood,' his voice uttered, though below his breath. 'Tooshalli's left me. I'm alone... !'

He was aware of a sudden change in the animals surrounding him. A big, grey wolf sat three feet away, glaring into his face; at its side an enormous grizzly swayed itself from one foot to the other; behind it, as if looking over its shoulder, loomed a gigantic wapiti, its horns merged in the shadows of the drooping cedar boughs. But the northern dawn was nearer, the sun already close to the horizon. He saw details with sharp distinctness now- The great bear rose, balancing a moment on its massive hind-quarters, then took a step towards him, its front paws spread like arms. Its wicked head lolled horribly, as a huge bull-moose, lowering its horns as if about to charge, came up with a couple of long strides and joined it. A sudden excitement ran quivering over the entire host; the distant ranks moved in a new, unpleasant way; a thousand heads were lifted, ears were pricked, a forest of ugly muzzles pointed up to the wind. And the Englishman, beside himself suddenly with a sense of ultimate terror that saw no possible escape, stiffened and stood rigid. The horror of his position petrified him. Motionless and silent he faced the awful army of his enemies, while the white light of breaking day added fresh ghastliness to the scene which was the setting for his cruel death in the Valley of the Beasts.

Above him crouched the hideous lynx, ready to spring the instant he sought safety in the tree; above it again, he was aware of a thousand talons of steel, fierce hooked beaks of iron, and the angry beating of prodigious wings.

He reeled, for the grizzly touched his body with its outstretched paw; the wolf crouched just before its deadly spring; in another second, he would have been torn to pieces, crushed, devoured, when terror, operating naturally as ever, released the muscles of his throat and tongue. He shouted with what he believed was his last breath on earth. He called aloud in his frenzy. It was a prayer to whatever gods there be, it was an anguished cry for help to heaven.

'Ishtot! Great Ishtot, help me!' his voice rang out, while his hand still clutched the forgotten totem stick.

And the Red Heaven heard him.

Grimwood that same instant was aware of a presence that, but for his terror of the beasts, must have frightened him into sheer unconsciousness. A gigantic Red Indian stood before him. Yet, while the figure rose close in front of him, causing the birds to settle and the wild animals to crouch quietly where they stood, it rose also from a great distance, for it seemed to fill the entire valley with its influence, its power, its amazing majesty. In some way, moreover, that he could not understand, its vast appearance included the actual valley itself with all its trees, its running streams, its open spaces and its rocky bluffs. These marked its outline, as it were, the outline of a superhuman shape. There was a mighty bow, there was a quiver of enormous arrows, there was this Redskin figure to whom they belonged.

Yet the appearance, the outline, the face and figure too—these *were* the valley; and when the voice became audible, it was the valley itself that uttered the appalling words. It was the voice of trees and wind, and of running, falling water that woke the echoes in the Valley of the Beasts, as, in that same moment, the sun topped the ridge and filled the scene, the outline of the majestic figure too, with a flood of dazzling light:

'You have shed blood in this my valley... *I will not save*...!'

The figure melted away in to the sunlit forest, merging with the new-born day. But Grimwood saw close against his face the shining teeth, hot fetid breath passed over his cheeks, a power enveloped his whole body as though a mountain crushed him. He closed his eyes. He fell. A sharp, crackling sound passed through his brain, but already unconscious, he did not hear it.

* * *

His eyes opened again, and the first thing they took in was fire. He shrank back instinctively.

'It's all right, old man. We'll bring you round. Nothing to be frightened about.' He saw the face of Iredale looking down into his own. Behind Iredale stood Tooshalli. His face was swollen. Grimwood remembered the blow. The big man began to cry.

'Painful still, is it?' Iredale said sympathetically. 'Here, swallow a little more of this. It'll set you right in no time.'

Grimwood gulped down the spirit. He made a violent effort to control himself, but was unable to keep the tears back. He felt no pain. It was his heart that ached, though why or wherefore, he had no idea.

'I'm all to pieces,' he mumbled, ashamed yet somehow not ashamed. 'My nerves are rotten. What's happened?' There was as yet no memory in him.

'You've been hugged by a bear, old man. But no bones broken. Tooshalli saved you. He fired in the nick of time—a brave shot, for he might easily have hit you instead of the brute.'

'The other brute,' whispered Grimwood, as the whisky worked in him and memory came slowly back.

'Where are we?' he asked presently, looking about him.

He saw a lake, canoes drawn up on the shore, two tents, and figures moving. Iredale explained matters briefly, then left him to sleep a bit. Tooshalli, it appeared, travelling without rest, had reached Iredale's camping ground twenty-four hours after leaving his employer. He found it deserted, Iredale and his Indian being on the hunt. When they returned at nightfall, he had explained his presence in his brief native fashion: 'He struck me and I quit. He hunt now alone in Ishtot's Valley of the Beasts. He is dead, I think. I come to tell you.'

Iredale and his guide, with Tooshalli as leader, started off then and there, but Grimwood had covered a considerable distance, though leaving an easy track to follow. It was the moose tracks and the blood that chiefly guided them. They came up with him suddenly enough—in the grip of an enormous bear.

It was Tooshalli that fired.

* * *

The Indian lives now in easy circumstances, all his needs cared for, while Grimwood, his benefactor but no longer his employer, had given up hunting. He is a quiet, easy-tempered, almost gentle sort of fellow, and people wonder rather why he hasn't married. 'Just the fellow to make a good father,' is what they say; 'so kind, good-natured and affectionate.' Among his pipes, in a glass case over the mantelpiece, hangs a totem stick. He declares it saved his soul, but what he means by the expression he has never quite explained.

## THE SOUTH WIND

It is impossible to say through which sense, or combination of senses, I knew that Someone was approaching—was already near; but most probably it was the deep underlying 'mother-sense' including them all that conveyed the delicate warning. At any rate, the scene-shifters of my moods knew it too, for very swiftly they prepared the stage; then, ever soft-footed and invisible, stood aside to wait.

As I went down the village street on my way to bed after midnight, the high Alpine valley lay silent in its frozen stillness. For days it had now lain thus, even the mouths of its cataracts stopped with ice; and for days, too, the dry, tight cold had drawn up the nerves of the humans in it to a sharp, thin pitch of exhilaration that at last began to call for the gentler comfort of relaxation. The key had been a little too high, the inner tautness too prolonged. The tension of that implacable north-east wind, the *bise noire,* had drawn its twisted wires too long through our very entrails. We all sighed for some loosening of the bands—the comforting touch of something damp, soft, less penetratingly acute.

And now, as I turned, midway in the little journey from the inn to my room above La Poste, this sudden warning that Someone was approaching repeated its silent wireless message, and I paused to listen and to watch.

Yet at first I searched in vain. The village street lay empty—a white ribbon between the black walls of the big-roofed chalets; there were no lights in any of the houses; the hotels stood gaunt and ugly with their myriad shuttered windows; and the church, topped by the Crown of Savoy in stone, was so engulfed by the shadows of the mountains that it seemed almost a part of them.

Beyond, reared the immense buttresses of the Dent du Midi, terrible and stalwart against the sky, their feet resting among the crowding pines, their streaked precipices tilting up at violent angles towards the stars. The bands of snow, belting their enormous flanks, stretched for miles, faintly gleaming, like Saturn's rings. To the right I could just make out the pinnacles of the Dents Blanches, cruelly pointed; and, still farther, the Dent de Bonnaveau, as of iron and crystal, running up its gaunt and dreadful pyramid into relentless depths of night. Everywhere in the hard, black sparkling air was the rigid spell of winter. It seemed as if this valley could never melt again, never know currents of warm wind, never taste the sun, nor yield its million flowers.

And now, dipping down behind me out of the reaches of the darkness, the New Comer moved close, heralded by this subtle yet compelling admonition that had arrested me in my very tracks. For, just as I turned in at the door, kicking the crunched snow from my boots against the granite step, I *knew* that, from the heart of all this tightly frozen winter's night, the 'Someone' whose message had travelled so delicately in advance was now, quite suddenly, at my very heels. And while my eyes lifted to sift their way between the darkness and the snow I became aware that It was already coming down the village street. It ran on feathered feet, pressing close against the enclosing walls, yet at the same time spreading from side to side, brushing the window-panes, rustling against the doors, and even including the shingled roofs in its enveloping advent. It came, too—*against the wind*...

It flew up close and passed me, very faintly singing, running down between the chalets and the church, very swift, very soft, neither man nor animal, neither woman, girl, nor child, turning the corner of the snowy road beyond the *Curé's* house with a rushing cantering motion, that made me think of a Body of water —something of fluid and generous shape, too mighty to be confined in common forms. And, as it passed, it touched me— touched me through all skin and flesh upon the naked nerves, loosening, relieving, setting free the congealed sources of life which the *bise* so long had mercilessly bound, so that magic currents, flowing and released, washed down all the secret byways of the spirit and flooded again with full tide into a thousand dried-up cisterns of the heart.

The thrill I experienced is quite incommunicable in words. I ran upstairs and opened all my windows wide, knowing that soon the Messenger would return with a million others—only to find that already it had been there before me. Its taste was in the air, fragrant and alive; in my very mouth—and all the currents of the inner life ran sweet again, and full. Nothing in the whole village was quite the same as it had been before. The deeply slumbering peasants, even behind their shuttered windows and barred doors; the *Curé*, the servants at the inn, the consumptive man opposite, the children in the house behind the church, the horde of tourists in the caravanserai—all knew—more or less, according to the delicacy of their receiving apparatus—that Something charged with fresh and living force had swept on viewless feet down the village street, passed noiselessly between the cracks of doors and windows, touched nerves and eyelids, and—set them free. In response to the great Order of Release that the messenger had left everywhere behind her, even the dreams of the sleepers had shifted into softer and more flowing keys...

And the Valley—the Valley also knew! For, as I watched from my window, something loosened about the trees and stones and boulders; about the massed snows on the great slopes; about the roots of the hanging icicles that fringed and sheeted the dark cliffs; and down in the deepest beds of the killed and silent streams. Far overhead, across those desolate bleak shoulders of the mountains, ran some sudden softness like the rush of awakening life... and was gone. A touch, lithe yet dewy, as of silk and water mixed, dropped softly over all... and, silently, without resistance, the *bise noire,* utterly routed, went back to the icy caverns of the north and east, where it sleeps, hated of men, and dreams its keen black dreams of death and desolation...

... And some five hours later, when I woke and looked

towards the sunrise, I saw those strips of pearly grey, just tinged with red, the Messenger had been to summon... charged with the warm moisture that brings relief. On the wings of a rising South Wind they came down hurriedly to cap the mountains and to unbind the captive forces of life; then moved with flying streamers up our own valley, sponging from the thirsty woods their richest perfume...

And farther down, in soft, wet fields, stood the leafless poplars, with little pools of water gemming the grass between and pouring their musical overflow through runnels of dark and sodden leaves to join the rapidly increasing torrents descending from the mountains. For across the entire valley ran magically that sweet and welcome message of relief which Job knew when he put the whole delicious tenderness and passion of it into less than a dozen words: '*He comforteth the earth with the south wind.*'

# THE MAN WHO WAS MILLIGAN

Milligan looked round the dingy rooms with an appraising air, while he landlady stood behind him, wondering whether he would decide to take them. She stood with her arms crossed; her eye was observant. She, in her turn, was appraising Milligan, of course. He was a clerk in a tourist agency, and in his spare time he wrote stories for the cinema. What attracted him just now in the very ordinary lodgings was the big folding-doors. All he really needed was a bed-sitting-room, with breakfast, but he suddenly saw himself sitting in that front room writing his scenarios—successfully at last. It was rather tempting. He would be a literary man—with a study! 'Your price seems a trifle high, Mrs.—er—?' he opened the bargain.

'Bostock, sir, Mrs. Bostock,' she informed him, then recited her tale of woe about the high cost of living. It was an unnecessary recitation, for Milligan was not listening, having already decided in his mind to take the rooms.

While Mrs. Bostock droned monotonously on, his eye fell casually upon a picture that hung above the plush mantelpiece—a Chinese scene showing a man in a boat upon a little lake. He glanced at it, no more than that. It was better than glancing at Mrs. Bostock. The landlady, however, instantly caught that glance and noticed its direction.

'Me 'usband'—she switched off her main theme—'brought it 'ome from China. From Hong-Kong, I *should* say.' And the way she aspirated the 'H' in Hong made Milligan smile. He perceived that she was proud of the picture evidently.

'It's wonderful,' he said. 'Probably it's worth something, too. These Chinese drawings—some of 'em—are very rare, I believe.'

The little picture was worth perhaps two shillings, and he knew it; but he had found his way to Mrs. Bostock's heart, and, incidentally, had persuaded her to take a shilling off the rent.

The picture, he felt sure, had been stolen by her late husband, a sea captain. To her it was a kind of nest-egg. If she ever found herself in difficulties, it would fetch money. Milligan, by chance, had stumbled upon what he called a 'good line'.

Being an honest creature, he had no wish to use his knowledge, but every week thereafter, almost every day, indeed, some remark concerning the Chinese drawing passed between them; with the natural result that, while it bored him a good deal, he cultivated the theme, and in so doing gazed much and often at the Chinaman. That Celestial, sitting in the boat with his back to the room, rowing, rowing eternally across the placid lake without advancing, he came to know in every detail.

Every time Mrs. Bostock chatted with him, his eye wandered from her grimy visage to the drawing. He used it to end the chat with.

'I like your picture so much,' he observed. 'It's nice to live with.' He put it straight, he flicked dust from the frame with his handkerchief. 'It's so much better than these modern things. It's worth a bit—I dare say——'

It chanced, at the time, that Lafcadio Hearn, the writer about Japan, was in his mind. He had once arranged a successful trip to Japan for a client of his firm, and the client had made him a present of one of Hearn's strange and wonderful books. It was hardly in the line of Milligan's reading, for it had no 'film value', and he had sold the book—a collection of Chinese stories—to a secondhand bookseller for a shilling. But he had glanced at it first, and a story in it had remained sharply in his mind: a story about a picture of a man in a boat. An observer, watching the picture, had seen the man move. The man actually began to row. Finally, the man rowed right out of the picture and into the place—a temple—where the observer stood.

Milligan thought it foolish, yet his memory retained the details vividly. They stuck in his head. The graphic description was realistic. Milligan caught himself thinking of it every time he met a Chinaman in the street, every time he sold a ticket to China or Japan. It rose, it flitted by, it vanished. The memory persisted. And the moment his eye first saw Mrs. Bostock's treasure over the plush mantelpiece, this vivid memory of Hearn's story had again risen, flitted by, and vanished. It betrayed its vitality, at any rate. Wonderful chap, that Hearn, thought Milligan.

All this was natural enough, without mystery, without a hint of anything queer or out of the ordinary. What was a little queer—it struck Milligan so, at any rate—was an idea that began to grow in him from the very first week of his tenancy.

'That *might* be the very drawing the fellow wrote about,' occurred to him one night as he laboured at a lurid scenario which was to make his fortune. 'Not impossible at all. It's an old picture probably. Exactly what Hearn described, too. I wonder! Why not?'

Why not, indeed? A fellow—especially a literary fellow—should use his imagination. Milligan used his. Sometimes he used it in prolonged labour till the early hours. The gas-light flickered across his pages, across that lake in China, across the boat, across the back and arms and pigtail of that diminutive Chink who rowed eternally over a placid Chinese lake without advancing an inch. The scenario of the moment brought in China, aptly enough. A glance at the picture, he found, was not unhelpful in the way of stimulating a flagging imagination.

Milligan glanced often. The gas-light was always flickering. Shadows were for ever shifting to and fro across Mrs. Bostock's worthless nest-egg. It was easy to imagine that the boat, the water, even the figure moved. Those dancing shadows! How they played about the arms, the back, the outline of the boat, the oars!

And when it was two in the morning, and the London streets lay hushed, and a great stillness blanketed the whole city, Milligan felt even a little thrilled. It was, he thought, 'imaginative', to catch these slight, elusive movements in the drawing. He imagined the fellow rowing about, changing his position, landing. It helped his own mood, his incidents, his atmosphere. He had read Thomas Burke, of course. His scenarios always referred to Chinamen as 'Chinks'.

'That Chink's alive!' he whispered to himself. 'By Jove! He moves in the picture. His place changes. It's an inspiration. I must use it somehow——!' And imagination, eerily stimulated in the deep silence of the sleeping city, was at work again.

This was the beginning of the strange adventure which befell the literary Milligan, whose imagination worked in the stillness of the small hours, but whose scenarios were never used.

'For why write scenarios,' he said to me, 'when you can *live* them?'

In Peking, ten or twelve years later, he said this to me, and I am probably the only person to whom this scenario he 'lived' was ever confided.

In Peking his name was not Milligan at all. He was not working in a tourist agency. He was a rich man, aged thirty-eight, a 'figure' in the English community there, a man of influence and position. But all that does not matter. What matters is the story of how he came to be in China at all—and this he does not know. He does not know how he came to be in China at all. There is no recollection of the journey even. Nor can he state precisely how he began the speculations and enterprises that made him prosperous, beyond that he suddenly found himself concerned in big, fortunate undertakings in the Chinese city.

There is this deep gap in the years.

'Loss of memory, I suppose they call it,' he mentioned, after our chance acquaintanceship had grown into a friendship that gave me his confidence. What he *could* tell he told me frankly and without reserve, glad to talk of it, I think, to someone who did not mock, and making no condition of secrecy, moreover.

There was some link, apparently, between myself and the man who had been Milligan. Chance, that some call destiny, revealed it. And, as I listened to his amazing tale, I swore that on my return to London I would visit Mrs. Bostock and buy the picture. I wanted that Chinese drawing badly. I wanted to examine it myself. Her nest-egg at last should be worth something, as Milligan, ten years before, had told her.

What happened was, apparently, as follows: Milligan, first of all, discovered in himself, somewhat suddenly it seemed, a new interest in China and things Chinese. If the birth of this interest was abrupt, its growth was extremely rapid. China fairly leapt at him. He read books, talked with travellers, studied the map, the history, the civilisation of China. The psychology of the Celestial race absorbed him. The subject obsessed him. He longed to go to China. It became a yearning that left him no peace day or night. In practical terms of time, money and opportunity, the journey was, of course, impossible. He lived on in London, but actually he lived already in China, for where a man's thought is there shall his consciousness be also.

All this I could readily understand, for others, similarly, have felt the call and spell of countries like Egypt, Africa, the desert. There was nothing incomprehensible nor peculiar in the fascination China exercised upon the imaginative Milligan. It was his business, moreover, to sell exciting tickets to travellers, and China happened to have fired his particular temperament. Natural enough!

Natural enough, too, that, through this, the picture in his lodgings should have acquired more meaning for him, and that he should have studied it more closely and more frequently. It was the only Chinese object he had within constant reach, and he told me at wearisome length how he knew every tiniest detail of the drawing, and how it became for him a kind of symbol, almost a kind of sacred symbol, upon which he focussed his intense desires—frustrated desires. Wearisome, yes, until he reached a point in his story that suddenly galvanised my interest, so that I began to listen with uncommon, if a rather creepy, curiosity.

The picture, he informed me, altered. There was movement among its details that he already knew by heart.

'*Movement!*' he half-whispered to me, his eyes shining, a faint shudder running through his big body.

The sincerity of deep conviction with which he described what happened left a lasting impression on my mind. His words, his manner, conveyed the truth of a genuine experience. Hitherto only the back of the Chink's head had been visible. Then, one night, Milligan saw his profile. The face was turned. It now looked a little over the shoulder, and towards the room.

From this moment, though he never detected actual movement when it occurred, the alteration in the drawing was marked and rapid. The face retained its new position; the angle of the profile did not widen, but the position of oars and boat, the attitude of arms and back, their size as well, these now changed from day to day.

There was a dreadful rapidity about these changes. The figure of the Chink grew bigger; the boat grew bigger too. They were coming nearer. 'I had the awful conviction,' whispered the man who had been Milligan, 'that they were coming—to fetch me. I used to get all of a sweat each time I saw the size and nearness grow. It was appalling, but also it was delightful somehow——'

I permitted myself a question: 'Did your landlady notice it too?' I enquired, concealing my scepticism.

'Mrs. Bostock was ill in bed the whole time. She never came into the room once.'

'The servant?' I persisted. 'Or any of your friends?'

He hesitated. 'The girl who did the room,' he said honestly, 'observed nothing. She gave notice suddenly without a reason. So did the next girl. I never asked them anything. As for my friends'—he smiled faintly—'I was too scared—to bring them in.'

'You were afraid they might *not* see what you saw?'

He shrugged his shoulders. 'It scared me,' he repeated, looking past me towards the shuttered windows of his study where we sat.

The account he gave of it all made my flesh creep even in that bright Peking sunshine. He certainly described what he saw, or believed he saw, as, day after day, night after night, that Chink rowed his boat slowly, slowly, surely, surely, very gradually, but with remorseless purpose, nearer, nearer—and nearer. The lodger watched. He also waited.

'The man,' he whispered, 'was rowing into the room. It was his purpose to row into the room. He was *coming to fetch me*.' And he mopped his forehead at the thought of what had happened ten years ago.

Suddenly he leant forward.

'In the end,' his thin voice rattled almost against my face, 'he —did fetch me. I'm in that picture with him now. I'm not in China, as *you* think I am. This'—he tapped his chest, the chest of a successful business man—'is not me. I'm not Milligan. Milligan is in that picture with the Chink. He's in that boat. Sitting beside that Chink. Motionless. Being stared at by a succession of lodgers. Sitting in that stiff little boat. Very tiny. Not dead, but captive. Sitting without breath. Without feeling. Painted, yet alive. Caught on the surface of that placid Chinese lake until time or death dissolve the drawing——'

I thought he was going to faint, but, oddly enough, I did *not* think him merely mad. His mood, his crawling horror, his intense sincerity took me bodily into his own deep nightmare. He recovered quickly. He was a man who had himself always well in hand. He told me the end at once.

He had been to a dance and he came home tired, sober, having well enjoyed himself, it seems, about four in the morning. The time was early spring, and dawn was just giving faint signs of breaking, but the hall and passage of the house were still dark.

He entered his room and lit the gas, going at once to the mirror to have a look at himself. This was the first thing he did, he assured me, and in the mirror he saw, behind himself, the boat and the Chinaman, both of them—gigantic.

Gigantic was the word he used, though he used it, of course, relatively. The Chinaman was standing in the room. He was in the lake in front of the plush mantelpiece. The wall was gone—there was a sort of hazy space. Close at the Chinaman's heels lay the boat, both oars resting sideways on the water, their heads still in the rowlocks. Water was up to his feet, to Milligan's feet, for he not only felt his shoes soaked through, but he also heard the lapping sound of diminutive wavelets on the 'shore'.

He gave a great sigh. No cry, either of terror or surprise, he said, escaped him. His only sound was this great sigh—of acceptance, of resignation, of a mind benumbed and yet secretly delighted. The big Chink beckoned, smiled, nodded his yellow face, retreating very slowly as he did so. And Milligan obeyed. He followed. He stepped into the boat. The Chink took up the oars, and rowed him slowly, very slowly, across the placid lake, into the picture and out of his familiar, known surroundings, rowed him slowly, very slowly, into the land of his heart's deep desire.

* * *

All the way home to England in the steamer this strangest of strange narratives haunted me. I still saw the man who was Milligan sitting in the study of his big, expensive house as he told it to me. His shrewd business brain had built that house; the fortune he had made provided the good lunch and cigars we had enjoyed together. From the moment of entering the boat his memory had remained a blank. Continuity of personality though still, it seemed to me, rather uncertain somewhere, had revived only when he was already a rich man who had spent years in China. This big gap in the years remains.

In my mind lay every detail of the story; in my pocket-book lay the address of Mrs. Bostock's rooms. I prayed heaven she might still be living, even if aged and crumpled by ten more English winters.

I had arranged to cable 'Milligan' at once; we had selected the very words I was to use: 'Two figures in boat,' or 'One figure in boat.' He asked for the message in these words. Fortune favoured me; I found the rooms; Mrs. Bostock was alive; the rooms were unoccupied; I looked over them; I saw—the picture.

Before visiting Mrs. Bostock's however, I had visited the newspaper files in the British Museum, and the 'Disappearance of James Milligan' was there for all to read. Millions had evidently read it. It had been *the* news of the day. Columns of space were devoted to it; dozens of false clues were started; crime was suggested, of course. His disappearance was complete. Milligan was a case of 'sunk without trace', with a vengeance.

It was in the dingy front room that I experienced what was perhaps the most vivid thrill of wonder life has ever given me. I stood, appraising the room as a would-be lodger. Behind me, her arms crossed, appraising me in turn just as she had appraised her former lodger of ten years ago, stood Mrs. Bostock. Probably I looked more prosperous than he had looked; her attitude, at any rate, was attentive to a fault. Why I should have trembled a little is hard to say, but self-control was certainly not as full as it might have been, for my voice shook a trifle as, at length, I drew her attention with calculated purpose to the picture above the plush mantelpiece. I praised it.

'Me 'usband brought it back from Hong-Kong,' I heard her say.

My breath caught a little, so that there was a slight pause before I said the next thing. My voice went slightly husky.

'I have a collection of Chinese drawings,' I mentioned. 'If you cared to sell, perhaps——'

'Oh, many 'as wanted to buy it,' she lied easily, hoping to increase its value.

I mentioned five pounds. I mentioned another figure too—the figure in the boat.

'That single figure,' I explained in as calm a tone as I could muster, 'is so good, you see. The Chinese artists never overcrowded their paintings. Now, if—instead of that single figure—there were two'—I moved closer to the picture, hoping she would follow—'the value,' I went on, 'would, of course, be less.'

Mrs. Bostock had followed me. I had tempted her greed; I had tested her truth as well. We stood side by side immediately beneath the drawing. We examined it together.

At the mention of five pounds the woman had given a little gasp, jerking her body at the same time. Now, at such close quarters with the thing she hoped to sell me, her voice was dumb at first. At first. For a moment later a strange sound escaped her lips, a sound that was meant to be a cry, but only succeeded in being a wheezy struggle to get her breath. Her mouth opened wide, her eyes popped almost from her face. She staggered, recovered her balance by putting a hand on my arm for support, she stepped still nearer to the mantelpiece and thrust her head and shoulders close against the drawing. Her blind eyes peered. Her skin was already white.

'Two of 'em!' she exclaimed in a terrified whisper. 'Two of 'em, so 'elp me, Gawd! And the other's *him*!'

I was ready to support. I had expected her to collapse perhaps. I felt rather like collapsing myself. She swayed, turning her horror-stricken countenance to mine.

'Mr. Milligan!' she screamed aloud, then, her voice returning in full volume: 'It's Mr. Milligan. All this time that's where 'e's been. And I never noticed it till now!'

She swooned away.

The second figure faced the room, for the boat was in the position of being pushed by the oars, not rowed. The features were unmistakable. ... Half an hour later I sent a cable to Peking: '*Two figures in boat.*'

The real climax, I think, came three days later, when, with the picture safely in my rooms, I had arranged for 'specialists' to call and examine it. A chemist, an experienced dealer, and a sort of expert psychic investigator were already upstairs when I reached my flat.

The picture was in my bedroom. I had examined it myself—examined Milligan's face and figure—hour after hour, my flesh crawling, my hair almost rising, as I did so. My guests were in the sitting-room, the servant informed me, handing me a telegram as I hurried up in the lift. My three friends were already known to each other, and, after apologising for the delay, I brought in the drawing and laid it before them on the small table. I intended to tell them the story after their examination; the psychic investigator I meant to keep when the other two had left. Setting the drawing in front of them, I looked over their shoulders at it.

There was only one figure—the Chink. He sat alone in the little boat. He was rowing, not pushing; his back was to the room.

The dealer said the drawing was worth a shilling; the chemist said nothing; I, too, said nothing; but the psychic investigator turned sharply and complained that I was hurting him. My hand, it seems, had clutched the shoulder nearest to me, and it happened to be his. I allowed him to leave when the other two left. ...

I was alone. I remembered the telegram. More to steady my mind than for any interest I felt in it, my fingers tore it open. It was a cablegram from—Peking, signed by a friend of Milligan and myself:

'Milligan died heart failure yesterday.'

# THE TROD

Young Norman was being whirled in one of the newest stream-lined expresses towards the north. He leaned back in his first-class Smoker and lit a cigarette. On the rack in front of him was his gun-case with the pair of guns he never willingly allowed out of his sight, his magazine with over a thousand cartridges beside it, and the rest of his luggage, he knew, was safely in the van. He was looking forward to a really good week's shooting at Greystones, one of the best moors in England.

He realised that he was uncommonly lucky to have been invited at alll. Yet a question mark lay in him. Why precisely, he wondered, had he been asked? For one thing, he knew his host, Sir Hiram Digby, very slightly. He had met him once or twice at various shoots in Norfolk, and while he had acquitted himself well when standing near him, he could not honestly think this was the reason for the invitation. There had been too many good shots present, and far better shots, for him to have been specially picked out. There was another reason, he was certain. His thoughts, as he puffed his cigarette reflectively, turned easily enough in another direction—towards Diana Travers, Sir Hiram Digby's niece.

The wish, he remembered, is often father to the thought, yet he clung to it obstinately, and with lingering enjoyment. It was Diana Travers who had suggested his name; it well might be, it probably was, and the more he thought it over, the more positive he felt. It explained the invitation, at any rate.

A curious thrill of excitement and delight ran through him as memory went backwards and played about her. A curious being, he saw her, quite unlike the usual run of girls, but curious, in the way that he himself perhaps was curious, for he was just old enough to have discovered that he was curious, standing apart somehow from the young men of his age and station.

Well born, rich, sporting and all the rest, he yet did not quite belong to his time in certain ways. He could drink, revel, go wild, enjoy himself with his companions, but up to a point only —when he withdrew unsatisfied. There were 'other things' that claimed him with some terrible inner power; and the two could not mix. These other things he could not quite explain even to himself, but to his boon companions—never. Were they things of the spirit? He could not say. Wild, pagan things belonging to an older day. He knew not. They were of unspeakable loveliness and power, drawing him away from ordinary modern life—*that* he knew. He could not define them to himself, much less speak of them to others.

And then he met Diana Travers and knew, though he did not dare put his discovery into actual words, that she felt something similar.

He came across her first at a dance in town, he remembered, remembering also how bored he had been until the casual introduction, and after it, how happy, enchanted, satisfied. It was assuredly not that he had fallen suddenly in love, nor that she was wildly beautiful—a tall, fair girl with a radiant, yet not lovely face, soft voice, graceful movements—for there were thousands, Norman knew, who excelled her in all these qualities. No, it was not the usual love attack, the mating fever, the herd-instinct that she might be *his* girl, but the old conviction, rather, that there lay concealed in her the same nameless, mysterious longings that lay also in himself—the terrible and lovely power that drew him from his human kind towards unknown 'other things'.

As they stood together on the balcony, where they had escaped from the heat and clamour of the ball-room, he acknowledged to himself, yet without utterance, this overpowering, strange conviction that their fates were in some way linked together. He could not explain it at the time, he could not explain it now—while he thought it over in the railway carriage, and his conscious mind rejected it as imagination. Yet it remained. Their talk, indeed, had been ordinary enough, nor was he conscious of the slightest desire to flirt or make love; it was just that, as the saying is, they 'clicked' and that each felt delightfully easy in the other's company, happy and at home. It was almost, he reflected, as though they shared some rather wonderful deep secret that had no need of words, a secret that lay, indeed, beyond the reach of words altogether.

They had met several times since, and on each occasion he had been aware of the same feeling; and once when he ran across her by chance in the park they walked together for over an hour and she had talked more freely. Talked suddenly about herself, moreover, openly and naturally, as though she knew he would understand. In the open air, it struck him, she was more spontaneous than in the artificial surroundings of walls and furniture. It was not so much that she said anything significant, but rather the voice and manner and gestures that she used.

She had been admitting how she disliked London and all its works, loathing especially the Season with its glittering routine of so-called gaiety, adding that she always longed to get back to Marston, Sir Hiram's place in Essex. 'There are the marshes,' she said, with quiet enthusiasm, 'and the sea, and I go with my uncle duck-flighting in the twilight, or in the dawn when the sun comes up like a red ball out of the sea, and the mists over the marshes drift away ... and things, you know, may happen...'

He had been watching her movements with admiration as she spoke, thinking the name of huntress was well chosen, and now there was a note of strange passion in her voice that he heard for the first time. Her whole being, moreover, conveyed the sense that he would understand some emotional yearning in her that her actual words omitted.

He stopped and stared at her.

'That's to be alive,' she added with a laugh that made her eyes shine. 'The wind and the rain blowing in your face and the ducks streaming by. You feel yourself part of nature. Gates open, as it were. It was how we were meant to live, I'm sure.'

Such phrases from any other girl must have made him feel shy and embarrassed, from her they were merely natural and true. He had not taken her up, however, beyond confessing that he agreed with her, and the conversation had passed on to other things. Yet the reason he had not become enthusiastic or taken up the little clue she offered, was because his inmost heart knew what she meant.

Her confession, not striking in itself, concealed, while it revealed, a whole region of significant, mysterious 'other things' best left alone in words. 'You and I think alike,' was what she had really said. 'You and I share this strange, unearthly longing, only for God's sake, don't let us talk about it... !'

'A queer girl, anyhow,' he now smiled to himself, as the train rushed northwards, and then asked himself what exactly he knew about her? Very little, practically nothing, beyond that, both parents being dead, she lived with her elderly bachelor uncle and was doing the London Season. 'A thoroughbred anyhow,' he told himself, 'lovely as a nymph into the bargain...' and his thoughts went dreaming rather foolishly. Then suddenly, as he lit another cigarette, a much more definite thought emerged. It gave him something of a start, for it sprang up abruptly out of his mood of reverie in the way that a true judgment sometimes leaps to recognition in the state between sleeping and waking.

'She *knows*. Knows about these other lovely and mysterious things that have always haunted me. She has—yes, experienced them. She can explain them to me. She wants to share them with me. ...'

Norman sat up with a jerk, as though something had scared him. He had been dreaming, these ideas were the phantasmagoria of a dream. Yet his heart, he noticed, was beating rather rapidly, as though a deep inner excitement had touched him in his condition of half-dream.

He looked up at his gun-cases and cartridges in the rack, then shaded his eyes and gazed out of the window. The train was doing at least sixty. The character of the country it rushed through was changing. The hedges of the midlands had gone, and stone walls were beginning to take their place. The country was getting wilder, lonelier, less inhabited. He drew unconsciously a deep breath of satisfaction. He must actually have slept for a considerable time, he realised, for his watch told him that in a few minutes he would reach the junction where he had to change. Bracendale, the local station for Greystones, he remembered, was on a little branch line that wandered away among the hills. And some fifteen minutes later he found himself, luggage and all, in the creaky, grunting train that would land him at Bracendale towards five o'clock. The dusk had fallen when, with great effort apparently, the struggling engine deposited him with his precious guns and cartridges on the deserted platform amid swirling mists a damp wind prepared for his reception. To his considerable relief a car was there to carry him the remaining ten miles to the Lodge, and he was soon comfortably installed among its luxurious rugs for the drive across the hills.

He settled back comfortably to enjoy the keen mountain air.

After leaving the station, the car followed a road up a narrow valley for a time; a small beck fell tumbling from the hills on the left, where occasionally dark plantations of fir trooped down to the side of the road; but what struck him chiefly was the air of desolation and loneliness that hung over all the countryside. The landscape seemed to him wilder and less inhabited even than the Scottish Highlands. Not a house, not a croft, was to be seen. A sense of desertion, due partly to the dusk no doubt, hung brooding over everything, as though human influence was not welcomed here, perhaps not possible. Bleak and inhospitable it looked certainly, though for himself this loneliness held a thrill of wild beauty that appealed to him.

A few black-faced sheep strung occasionally across the road, and once they passed a bearded shepherd hurrying downhill with his dog. They vanished into the mist like wraiths. It seemed impossible to Norman that the country could be so desolate and uninhabited when he knew that only a few score miles away lay the large manufacturing towns of Lancashire. The car, meanwhile, was steadily climbing up the valley and presently they came to more open country and passed a few scattered farmhouses with an occasional field of oats beside them.

Norman asked the chauffeur if many people lived hereabouts, and the man was clearly delighted to be spoken to.

'No, sir,' he said, 'it's a right desolate spot at the best of times, and I'm glad enough,' he added, 'when it's time for us to go back south again.' It had been a wonderful season for the grouse, and there was every promise of a record year.

Norman noticed an odd thing about the farmhouses they passed, for many of them, if not all, had a large cross carved over the lintel of the doors, and even some of the gates leading from the road into the fields had a smaller cross cut into the top bar. The car's flash-light picked them out. It reminded him of the shrines and crosses scattered over the countryside in Catholic countries abroad, but seemed a little incongruous in England. He asked the chauffeur if most of the people hereabout were Catholics, and the man's answer, given with emphasis, touched his curiosity.

'Oh, no, I don't think so,' was the reply. 'In fact, sir, if you ask me, the people round here are about as heathen as you could find in any Christian country.'

Norman drew his attention to the crosses everywhere, asking him how he accounted for them if the inhabitants were heathen, and the man hesitated a moment before replying, as though, glad to talk otherwise, the subject was not wholly to his liking.

'Well, sir,' he said at length, watching the road carefully in front of him, 'they don't tell *me* much about what they think, counting me for a foreigner like, as I come from the south. But they're a rum lot to my way of thinking. What I'm told,' he added after a further pause, 'is that they carve these crosses to protect themselves.'

'Protect themselves!' exclaimed Norman a little startled. 'Protect themselves from—what?'

'Ah, there, sir,' said the man after hesitating again, 'that's more than I can say. I've heard of a haunted house before now, but never a haunted countryside. Yet that's what they believe, I take it. It's all haunted, sir—everywhere. It's the devil of a job to get any of them to turn out after dark, as I know well, and even in the daytime they won't stir far without a crucifix hung round their neck. Even the men won't.'

The car had put on speed while he spoke and Norman had to ask him to ease up a bit; the man, he felt sure, was prey to a touch of superstitious fear as they raced along the darkening road, yet glad enough to talk, provided he was not laughed at. After his last burst of speech he had drawn a deep breath, as though glad to have got it off his chest.

'What you tell me is most interesting,' Norman commented invitingly. 'I've come across that sort of thing abroad, but never yet in England. There's something in it, you know,' he added persuasively, 'if we only knew what. I wish I knew the reason, for I'm sure it's a mistake just to laugh it all away.' He lit a cigarette, handing one also to his companion, and making him slow down while they lighted them. 'You're an observant fellow, I see,' he went on, 'and I'll be bound you've come across some queer things. I wish I had your opportunity. It interests me very much.'

'You're right, sir,' the chauffeur agreed, as they drove on again, 'and it can't be laughed away, not *all* of it. There's something about the whole place 'ere that ain't right, as you might say. It "got" me a bit when I first came 'ere some years ago, but now I'm kind of used to it.'

'I don't think I should ever get *quite* used to it,' said Norman, 'till I'd got to the bottom of it. Do tell me anything you've noticed. I'd like to know—and I'll keep it to myself.'

Feeling sure the man had interesting things to tell and having now won his confidence, he begged him to drive more slowly; he was afraid they would reach the house before there had been time to tell more, possibly even some personal experiences.

'There's a funny sort of road, or track rather, you may be

seeing out shooting,' the chauffeur went on eagerly enough, yet half nervously. 'It leads across the moor, and no man or woman will set foot on it to save their lives, not even in the daytime, let alone at night.'

Norman said eagerly that he would like to see it, asking its whereabouts, but of course the directions only puzzled him.

'You'll be seeing it, sir, one of these days out shooting and if you watch the natives, you'll find I'm telling you right.'

'What's wrong with it?' Norman asked. 'Haunted—eh?'

'That's it, sir,' the man admitted, after a longish pause. 'But a queer kind of 'aunting. They do say it's just too lovely to look at—and keep your senses.'

It was the other's turn to hesitate, for something in him trembled.

Now, young Norman was aware of two things very clearly: first, that it wasn't quite the thing to pump his host's employee in this way; second, that what the man told him held an extraordinary, almost alarming interest for him. All folk-lore interested him intensely, legends and local superstitions included. Was this, perhaps a 'fairy-ridden' stretch of country, he asked himself? Yet he was not in Ireland, where it would have been natural, but in stolid, matter-of-fact England. The chauffeur was obviously an observant, commonplace southerner, and yet he had become impressed, even a little scared, by what he had noticed. That lay beyond question: the man was relieved to talk to someone who would not laugh at him, while at the same time he was obviously a bit frightened.

A third question rose in his mind as well: this talk of haunted country, of bogies, fairies and the rest, fantastic though it was, perhaps, stirred a queer, yet delicious feeling in him—in his heart, doubtless—that his host's niece, Diana, had a link with it somewhere. The origin of a deep intuition is hardly discoverable. He made no attempt to probe it. This was Diana's country, she must know all the chauffeur hinted, and more besides. There must be something in the atmosphere that attracted her. She had been instrumental in making her uncle invite him. She wanted him to come, she wanted him to taste and share things, 'other things', that to her were vital.

These thoughts flashed across him with an elaboration of detail impossible to describe. That the wish was, again, father to the thoughts, doubtless operated, yet the conviction persistently remained and the intuitive flash provided, apparently, inspiration, so that he plied the chauffeur with further questions that produced valuable results. He referred even to the Little People, the Fairies, without exciting contempt or laughter—with the result that the man gave him finally a somewhat dangerous confidence. Solemnly warning his passenger that 'Sir Hiram mustn't hear of it' or he'd lose his job, the man described a remarkable incident that had happened, so to speak, under his own eyes. Sir Hiram's sister was lost on the moors some years ago and was never found...and the local talk and belief had it that she had been 'carried off'. Yet not carried off against her will: she had wanted to go.

'Would that be Mrs. Travers?' Norman asked.

'That's who it was, sir, exactly, seeing as 'ow you know the family. And it was the strangest disappearance that ever came *my* way.' He gave a slight shudder and, if not quite to his listener's surprise, suddenly crossed himself.

Diana's mother!

A pause followed the extraordinary story, and then, for once, Norman used words first spoken (to Horatio) to a man who had never heard them before and received them with appropriate satisfaction.

'Yes, sir.' he went on, 'and now he's got her up here for the first time since it happened years ago—in the very country where her mother was taken—and I'm told his idea is that he 'opes it will put her right—'

'Put her right?'

'I should say—cure her, sir. She's supposed to have the same—the same—' he fumbled for a word—'unbalance as wot her mother had.' A strange rush of hope and terror swept across Norman's heart and mind, but he made a great effort and denied them both, so that his companion little guessed this raging storm. Changing the subject as best he could, controlling his voice with difficulty so as to make it sound normal, he asked casually:

'Do other people—I mean, *have* other people disappeared here?'

'They do say so, sir,' was the reply. 'I've heard many a tale, though I couldn't say as I proved anything. Natives, according to the talk, 'ave disappeared, nor no trace of them ever found. Children mostly. But the people round here won't speak of it and it's difficult to find out, as they never go to the Police and keep it dark among themselves—'

'Couldn't they have fallen into potholes, or something like that?' Norman interrupted, to which the man replied that there was only one pothole in the whole district and the danger spot most carefully fenced round. 'It's the place itself, sir,' he added finally with conviction, as though he could tell of a first-hand personal experience if he dared, 'it's the whole country that's so strange.'

Norman risked the direct question.

'And what you've seen yourself, with your own eyes,' he asked, 'did it—sort of frighten you? I mean, you observe so carefully that anything you reported would be valuable.'

'Well, sir,' came the reply after a little hesitation, 'I can't say 'frightened' exactly, though—if you ask me—I didn't like it. It made me feel queer all over, and I ain't a religious man—'

'Do tell me,' Norman pressed, feeling the house was now not far away and time was short. 'I shall keep it to myself—and I shall believe you. I've had odd experiences myself.'

The man needed no urging, however: he seemed glad to tell his tale.

'It's not really very much,' he said lowering his voice. 'It was like this, you see, sir. The garage and my rooms lie down at an old farmhouse about a quarter-mile from the Lodge, and from my bedroom window I can see across the moor quite a way. It takes in that trail I was speaking of before, and along that track exactly I sometimes saw lights moving in a sort of wavering line. A bit faint, they were, and sort of dancing about and going out and coming on again, and at first I took them for marsh lights—I've seen marsh lights down at our marshes at home—marsh gas we call it. That's what I thought at first, but I know better now.'

'You never went out to examine them closer?'

'No, sir, I did *not*,' came the emphatic reply.

'Or asked any of the natives what they thought?'

The chauffeur gave a curious little laugh; it was a half shy, half embarrassed laugh. Yes, he had once got a native who was willing to say something, but it was only with difficulty that Norman persuaded him to repeat it.

'Well, sir, what he told me'—again that embarrassed little laugh—'the words *he* used were "It was the Gay People changing their hunting grounds." That's what *he* said and crossed himself as he said it. They always changed their grounds at what he called the Equinox.'

'The Gay People... the Equinox. ...'

The odd phrases were not new to Norman, but he heard them now as though for the first time, they had meaning. The equinox, the solstice, he knew naturally what the words meant, but the 'Gay People' belonged to some inner phantasmagoria of his own he had hitherto thought of only imaginatively. It pertained, that is, to some private 'imaginative creed' he believed in when he had been reading Yeats, James Stephens, A.E., or when he was trying to write poetry of his own.

Now, side by side with this burly chauffeur from the sceptical South, he came up against it—bang. And he admitted frankly to himself, it gave him a half-incredible thrill of wonder, delight and passion.

'The Gay People,' he repeated, half to himself, half to the driver. 'The fellow called them *that*?'

'That's wot he called them,' repeated the matter-of-fact chauffeur. 'And they were passing,' he added, almost defiantly, as though he expected to be called a liar and deserved it, 'passing in a stream of dancing lights along the Trod.'

'The Trod,' murmured Norman under his breath.

'The Trod,' repeated the man in a whisper, 'that track I spoke of—' and the car swerved, as though the touch on the wheel was unsteady for a second, though it instantly recovered itself as they swung into the drive.

The Lodge flew past, carrying a cross, Norman noticed, like all the other buildings; and a few minutes later the grey stone shooting-box, small and unpretentious, came in sight. Diana herself was on the step to welcome him, to his great delight.

'What a picture,' he thought, as he saw her in her tweeds, her retriever beside her, the hall lamp blazing on her golden hair, one hand shading her eyes. Radiant, intoxicating, delicious, unearthly—he could not find the words—and he knew in that sudden instant that he loved her far beyond all that language could express. The dark background of the grey stone building, with the dim, mysterious moors behind, was exactly right. She stood there, framed in the wonder of two worlds—his girl!

Yet her reception chilled him to the bone. Excited, bubbling over as he was, his words of pleasure ready to tumble about each other, his heart primed with fairy tales and wonder, she had nothing to say except that tea was waiting, and that she hoped he had had a good journey. Response to his own inner convulsions there was none: she was polite, genial, cordial even, but beyond that—nothing. They exchanged commonplaces and she mentioned that the grouse were plentiful, that her uncle had got some of the best 'guns' in England—which pleased his vanity for a moment—and that she hoped he would enjoy himself.

Her leaden reaction left him speechless. He felt convicted of boyish, idiotic fantasy.

'I asked particularly for you to come,' she admitted frankly, as they crossed the hall. 'I had an idea somehow you'd like to be here.'

He thanked her, but betrayed nothing of his first delight, now chilled and rendered voiceless.

'It's your sort of country,' she added, turning towards him with a swish of her skirts. 'At least, I think it is.'

'If *you* like it,' he returned quietly, 'I certainly shall like it too.'

She stopped a moment and looked hard at him. 'But of course I like it,' she said with conviction. 'And it's much lovelier than those Essex marshes.'

Remembering her first description of those Essex marshes, he thought of a hundred answers, but before the right one came to him he found himself in the drawing-room chatting to his hostess, Lady Digby. The rest of the house-party were still out on the moor.

'Diana will show you the garden before the darkness comes,' Lady Digby suggested presently. 'It's quite a pretty view.'

The 'pretty view' thrilled Norman with its wild beauty, for the moor beyond stretched right down to the sea at Saltbeck, and in the other direction the hills ran away, fold upon fold, into a dim blue distance. The Lodge and its garden seemed an oasis in a wilderness of primeval loveliness, unkempt and wild as when God first made it. He was aware of its intense, seductive loveliness that appealed to all the strange, unearthly side of him, but at the same time he felt the powerful, enticing human seductiveness of the girl who was showing him round. And the two conflicted violently in his soul. The conflict left him puzzled, distraught, stupid, since first one, then the other, took the upper hand. What saved him from a sudden tumultuous confession of his imagined passion, probably, was the girl's calm, almost cold, indifference. Obviously without response she felt nothing of the tumult that possessed him.

Exchanging commonplaces, they admired the 'pretty view' together, then turned back in due course to the house. 'I catch their voices,' remarked Diana. 'Let's go in and hear all about it and how many birds they got.' And it was on the door of the french window that she suddenly amazed—and, truth to tell—almost frightened him.

'Dick,' she said, using his first name, to his utter bewilderment and delight, and grasping his hand tightly in both of her own, 'I may need your help.' She spoke with a fiery intensity. Her eyes went blazing suddenly. 'It was here, you know, that mother—went. And I think—I'm certain of it—they're *after me, too.* And I don't know which is right—to go or to stay. All this'—she swept her arm to include the house, the chattering room, the garden—'is such rubbish—cheap, nasty, worthless. The other is so satisfying—its eternal loveliness, and yet—' her voice dropped to a whisper—'*soulless*, without hope or future. You may help me.' Her eyes turned upon him with a sudden amazing fire. 'That's why I asked you here.'

She kissed him on the eyes—an impersonal, passionless kiss, and the next minute they were in the room, crowded, with the 'guns' from a large shooting brake which had just arrived.

How Norman staggered in among the noisy throng and played his part as a fellow guest, he never understood. He managed it somehow, while in his heart sang the wild music of the Irish Fairy's enticing whisper: 'I kiss you and the world begins to fade,' A queer feeling came to him that he was going lost to life as he knew it, that Diana with her sweet passionless kiss had sealed his fate, that the known world must fade and die because she knew the way to another, lovelier region where nothing could ever pass or die because it was literally everlasting—the state of evolution belonging to fairy-land, the land of the deathless Gay People. ...

Sir Hiram welcomed him cordially, then introduced him to the others, upon which followed the usual description by the guns of the day's sport. They drank their whiskies and sodas, in due course they went up to dress for dinner, but after dinner there was no carousing, for their host bundled them all off to an early bed. The next day they were going to shoot the best beat on the moor and clear eyes and steady hands were important. The two drives for which Greystones was celebrated were to be taken—Telegraph Hill and Silvermine—both well known wherever shooting men congregated so that anticipation and exitement were understandable. An early bed was a small price to pay and Norman, keen and eager as any of them, was glad enough to get to his room when the others trooped upstairs. To be included as a crack shot among all these famous guns was, naturally, a great event to him. He longed to justify himself.

Yet his heart was heavy and dissatisfied, a strange uneasiness gnawed at him despite all his efforts to think only of the morrow's thrill. For Diana had not come down to dinner, nor had he set eyes on her the whole evening. His polite enquiry about her was met by his host's cheery laugh: 'Oh, she's all right, Norman, thank ee; she keeps to herself a bit when a shoot's on. Shooting, you see, ain't her line exactly, but she may come out with us to-morrow.' He brushed her tastes aside. 'Try and persuade her, if you can. The air'll do her good.'

Once in his room, his thoughts and emotions tried in vain to sort themselves out satisfactorily: there was a strange confusion in his mind, an uneasy sense of excitement that was half delight, half fearful anticipation, yet anticipation of he knew not exactly what. That sudden use of his familiar first name, the extraordinary kiss, establishing an unprepared intimacy, deep if passionless, had left him the entire evening in a state of hungry expectancy with nerves on edge. If only she had made an appearance at dinner, if only he could have had a further word with her! He wondered how he would ever get to sleep with this inner turmoil in his brain, and if he slept badly he would shoot badly.

It was this reflection about shooting badly that convinced him abruptly that his sudden 'love' was not of the ordinary accepted kind; had he been humanly 'in love', no consideration of that sort could have entered his head for a moment. His queer uneasiness, half mixed with delight as it was, increased. The tie was surely of another sort.

Turning out the electric light, he looked from his window across the moor, wondering if he might see the strange lights the chauffeur had told him about. He saw only the dim carpet of the rolling moorland fading into darkness where a moon hid behind fleecy, drifting clouds. A soft, sweet, fragrant air went past him; there was a murmur of falling water. It was intoxicating; he drew in a deep delicious breath. For a second he imagined a golden-haired Diana, with flying hair and flaming eyes, pursuing her lost mother midway between the silvery clouds and shadowy moor... then turned back into his room and flooded it with light... in which instant he saw something concrete lying on his pillow—a scrap of paper—no, an envelope. He tore it open.

'Always wear this when you go out. I wear one too. They cannot come up with you unless you wish, if you wear it. Mother...'

The word 'mother', full of imaginative suggestion, was crossed out; the signature was 'Diana'. With a faint musical tinkle, a little silver crucifix slipped from the pencilled note and fell to the floor.

As Norman stood beside the bed with the note in his hand, and before he stooped to recover the crucifix, there fell upon him with an amazing certainty the eerie conviction that all this had happened before. As a rule this odd sensation is too fleeting to be retained for analysis; yet he held it now for several seconds without effort. Startled, he saw quite clearly that it was not passing in ordinary time, but somewhere outside ordinary time as he knew it. It had happened 'before' because it was happening 'always'. He had caught it in the act.

For a flashing instant he understood; the crucifix symbolised security among known conditions, and if he held to it he would be protected, mentally and spiritually, against a terrific draw into unknown conditions. It meant no more than that—a support to the mind.

That antagonistic 'draw' of terrific power, involved the nameless, secret yearnings of his fundamental nature. Diana, aware of this inner conflict, shared the terror and the joy. Her mother, whence she derived the opportunity, had yielded—and had disappeared from life as humans know it. Diana herself was now tempted and afraid. She asked his help. Both he and she together, in some condition outside ordinary time, had met this conflict many times already. He had experienced all this before—the incident of the crucifix, its appeal for help, the delight, the joy, the fear involved. And even as he realised all this, the strange, eerie sensation vanished and was gone, as though it never had been. It became unseizable, lost beyond recapture. It left him with a sensation of loss, of cold, of isolation, a realisaiton of homelessness, yet of intense attraction towards a world unrealised.

He stooped, picked up the small silver crucifix, re-read the pencilled note letter by letter, kissed the paper that her hand had touched, then sat down on the bed and smiled with a sudden gush of human relief and happiness. The eerie sensation had gone its way beyond recovery. That Diana had thought about him was all that mattered. This little superstition about wearing the crucifix was sweet and touching, and of course he would wear the thing against his heart. And see that she came out tomorrow with him too! His relief was sincere. Now he could sleep. And tomorrow he might not shoot too badly. But before he climbed into bed, he looked in his diary to find out when the equinox was due, and found to his astonishment that it was on the 23rd of September, and that tonight was the 21st! The discovery gave him something of a turn, but he soon fell asleep with the letter against his cheek and the little silver crucifix hung round his neck.

He woke next morning when he was called to find the sun streaming into his room, promising perfect shooting weather. In broad daylight the normal reactions followed as they usually do; the incidents of the day before now seemed slightly ridiculous—his talk with Diana, the crucifix, the chauffeur's fairy-tales above all. He had stumbled upon a nest of hysterical delusions, born of a mysterious disappearance many years ago. It was natural he thought, as he shaved himself, that his host disliked all reference to the subject and its aftermath. For all that, as he went down to breakfast, he felt secretly comforted that he had hung the little silver crucifix round his neck. No one, at any rate, he reflected, could see it.

He had done full justice to the well stocked sideboard and was just finishing his coffee when Diana came into the empty room, and his mind, now charged with the prosaic prospects of the coming shoot, acknowledged a shock. Fact and imagination clashed. The girl was white and drawn. Before he could rise to greet her, she came straight across to the chair beside him.

'Dick,' she began at once, 'have you got it on?'

He produced the crucifix after a moment's fumbling.

'Of course I have,' he said. 'You asked me to wear it.' Remembering the hesitation in his bedroom, he felt rather foolish. He felt foolish anyhow, wearing a superstitious crucifix on a day's shooting.

Her next words dispelled the feeling of incongruity.

'I was out early,' she said in a tense, low voice, 'and I heard mother's voice calling me on the moor. It was unmistakable. Close in my ear, then far away. I was with the dog and the dog heard it too and ran for shelter. His hair was up.'

'What did you hear?' Norman asked gently, taking her hand.

'My pet name—"Dis",' she told him, 'the name only mother used.'

'What words did you hear?' he asked, trembling in spite of himself.

'Quite distinctly—in that distant muffled voice—I heard her call: "Come to me, Dis, oh, come to me quickly!" '

For a moment Norman made no answer. He felt her hand trembling in his. Then he turned and looked straight into her eyes.

'Did you *want* to go?' he asked.

There was a pause before she replied. 'Dick,' she said, 'when I heard that voice, *nothing else in the world seemed to matter*—!' at which moment her uncle's figure, bursting in through the door, shouted that the cars were ready and waiting, and the conversation came to an abrupt end.

This abrupt interruption at the moment of deepest interest left

Norman, as may be imagined, excusably and dreadfully disturbed. A word from his host on this particular shooting party was of course, a command. He dared not keep these great 'guns' waiting. Diana, too, shot out as though a bullet had hit her. But her last words went on ringing in his ears, in his heart as well: 'Nothing else in the world seemed to matter.' He understood in his deepest being what she meant. There was a 'call' away from human things, a call into some unimaginable state of bliss no words described, and she had heard it, heard it in her *mother's* voice—the strongest tie humanity knows. Her mother, having left the world, sent back a message.

Norman, trembling unaccountably, hurried to fetch his gun and join the car, and Diana, obeying the orders of her uncle, was shoved into the Ford with her retriever. She had just time to whisper to him 'Keep off the Trod—don't put a foot on it,' and the two cars whisked off and separated them.

The 'shoot' took place, nevertheless, ordinarily, so far as Norman was concerned, for the hunter's passion was too strong in him to be smothered. If his mind was mystical, his body was primitive. He was by nature a hunter before the Lord. The imaginative, mystical view of life, as with peasants and woodsmen, lay deep below, The first birds put an end to all reflection. He was soon too busy to bother about anything else but firing as fast as he could and changing his guns swiftly and smoothly. Breaking through this practical excitement, none the less, flashed swift, haunting thoughts and fancies—Diana's face and voice and eyes, her mother's supernatural call, his own secret yearnings, and, above all, her warning about the Trod. Both sides of his mixed nature operated furiously. Apparently, he shot well, but how he managed it, heaven only knew.

The drive in due course was over and the pick-up completed. Sir Hiram came over and asked if he would mind taking the outside butt at the next drive.

'You see,' he explained courteously, 'I always ask the youngest of the party to take the outside, as it's a devil of a walk for the old 'uns. Probably,' he added, 'you'll get more shooting than anyone, as the birds slip away over yonder butt down a little gully. So you'll find it worth the extra swot!'

Norman and his loader set off on their long tramp, while the rest of the guns made their way down to the road where the cars would carry them as far as the track allowed. After nearly a mile's detour Norman was puzzled by his loader striking across the heather instead of following the obvious path. He himself, naturally, kept to the smooth track. He had not gone ten yards along the track before the loader's startled voice shouted at him:

'For the love of God, sir, come off! You're walking on the Trod!'

'It's a good path,' cried Norman. 'What's wrong with it?'

The man eyed him a moment. 'It's the Trod, sir,' he said gravely, as though that were enough. 'We don't walk on it—not at this time o' year especially.' He crossed himself. 'Come off it, sir, into the heather.'

The two men stood facing one another for a minute.

'If you don't believe me, sir, just watch them sheep,' said the man in a voice full of excitement and emotion. 'You'll see they won't put foot on it. Nor any other animal either.'

Norman watched a band of black-faced sheep move hesitatingly down the moorland slope. He was impatient to get on, half angry. For the moment he had forgotten all about Diana's warning. Fuming and annoyed, he watched. To his amazement, the little band of black-faced sheep, on reaching the obvious path, jumped clear over it. They jumped the Trod. Not one of them would touch it. It was an astonishing sight. Each animal leapt across, as though the Trod might burn or injure them. They went their way across the rough heather and disappeared from sight.

Norman, remembering the warning uncomfortably, paused and lit a cigarette.

'That's odd,' he said. 'It's the easiest way.'

'Maybe,' replied the loader. 'But the easiest way may not be the best—or safest.'

'The safest?'

'I've got children of me own,' said the loader.

It was a significant statement. It made Norman reflect a moment.

'Safest,' he repeated, remembering all he had heard, yet longing eagerly to hear more. 'You mean, children especially are in danger? Young folks—eh?—is that it?' A moment later, he added, 'I can quite believe it, you know, it's a queer bit of country—to my way of thinking.'

The understanding sympathy won the man's confidence, as it was meant to do.

'And it's equinox time, isn't it?' Norman ventured further.

The man responded quickly enough, finding a 'gun' who wouldn't laugh at him. As with the chauffeur, he was evidently relieved to give some kind of utterance to fears and superstitions he was at heart ashamed of and yet believed in.

'I don't mind for myself, sir,' he broke out, obviously glad to talk, 'for I'm leaving these parts as soon as the grouse shooting's over, but I've two little 'uns up here just now, and I want to keep 'em. Too many young 'uns get lost on the moor for my liking. I'm sending 'em tomorrow down to my aunt at Crossways—'

'Good for you,' put in Norman. 'It's the equinox just now, isn't it? And that's the dangerous time, they say.'

The loader eyed him cautiously a moment, weighing perhaps his value as a recipient of private fears, beliefs, fancies and the rest, yet deciding finally that Norman was worthy of his confidences.

'That's what my father always said,' he agreed.

'Your father? It's always wise to listen to what a father tells,' the other suggested. 'No doubt he'd seen something—worth seeing.'

A silence fell between them. Norman felt he had been, perhaps, too eager to draw the man out; yet the loader was reflecting merely. There was something he yearned to tell.

'Worth seeing,' the man repeated, 'well—that's as may be. But not of this world, and wonderful, it certainly was. It put ice into his bones, that's all I can swear to. And he wasn't the sort to be fooled easy, let me tell you. It was on his dying bed he told me—and a man doesn't lie with death in his eyes.'

That Norman was standing idly on this important shoot was sufficient proof of his tremendous interest, and the man beyond question was aware of it.

'In daylight,' Norman asked quietly, assuming the truth of what he hoped to hear.

'It was just at nightfall,' the other said, 'and he was coming from a sick friend at a farm beyond the Garage. The doctor had frightened him, I take it, so it was a bit late when he started for home across the moor and, without realising that it was equinox time, he found himself on the Trod before he knew it. And, to his terror, the whole place was lit up, and he saw a column of figures moving down it towards him. They was all bright and lovely, he described 'em, gay and terrible, laughing and singing and crying, and jewels shining in their hair, and—worst of all—he swears he saw young children who had gone lost on the moor years before, and a girl he had loved these twenty years back, no older than when he saw her last, and as gay and happy and laughing as though the passing years was nothing—'

'They called to him?' asked Norman, strangely moved. 'They asked him to join them?'

'The girl did,' replied the man. 'The girl, he said, with no years to her back, drew him something terrible. "Come with us," he swears she sang to him, "come with us and be happy and young forever," and, if my father hadn't clutched hold of his crucifix in time—my God—he would have gone—'

The loader stopped, embarrassed lest he had told too much.

'If he'd gone, he'd have lost his soul,' put in Norman, guided by a horrible intuition of his own.

'That's what they say, sir,' agreed the man, obviously relieved.

Simultaneously, they hurried on, Sir Hiram's practical world breaking in upon this strange interlude. A big shoot was in progress. They must not be late at their appointed place.

'And where does the Trod start?' Norman asked presently, and the man described the little cave of the Black Waters whence the beck, dark with the peat, ran thence towards the sea across the bleak moors. The scenery provided an admirable setting for the 'fairy-tale' he had just listened to; yet his thoughts, as they ploughed forward through the heather, went back to the lovely, fascinating tale, to the superstitious dream of the 'Gay People' changing their hunting grounds along that unholy Trod when the equinox flamed with unearthly blazing, when the human young, unsatisfied with earthly pleasures, might be invited to join another ageless evolution that, if it knew no hope, shared at least an unstained, eternal, happy present. Diana's temptation, her mother's incredible disappearance, his own heart-searing yearnings in the balance to boot, took strange shape as practical possibilities.

The cumulative effect of all he had heard, from chauffeur, loader, and from the girl herself, began, it may be, to operate, since the human mind, especially the imaginative human mind, is ever open to attack along the line of least resistance.

He stumbled on, holding his gun firmly, as though a modern weapon of destruction helped to steady his feet, to say nothing of his mind, now full of seething dreams. They reached the appointed butt. And hardly had they settled themselves in it than the first birds began to come, and all conversation was impossible. This was the celebrated 'Silvermine Drive', and Norman had never in his life seen so many grouse as he now saw. His guns got too hot to hold, yet still the grouse poured over. ...

The Drive finished in due course, and after a hurried lunch came the equally famous Telegraph Hill Drive, where there were even more birds than before, and when this came to an end Norman found that his shoulder was sore from the recoil and that he had developed a slight gun-headache, so that he was glad enough to climb into the car that took him back to the Lodge and tea. The excitement, naturally, had been great, the nervous hope that he had shot well enough to justify his inclusion in the great shoot had also played upon his vitality. He found himself exhausted, and after tea he was relieved to slip up to his bedroom for a quiet hour or two.

Lying comfortably on his sofa with a cigarette, thinking over the fire and fury of the recent hours, his thoughts turned gradually aside to other things. The hunter, it seemed, withdrew; the dreamer, never wholly submerged, re-appeared. His mind reviewed the tales he had heard from the chauffeur and the loader, while the story of Diana's mother, the strange words of the girl herself, took possession of his thoughts. Too weary to be critical, he remembered them. His own natural leaning enforced their possible truth, while fatigue made analysis too difficult to bother about, so that imagination cast its spell of glamour undefied.... He burned to know the truth. In the end he made up his mind to creep out the following night and watch the Trod. It would be the night of the equinox. That ought to settle things one way or the other—proof or disproof. Only he must examine it in the daylight first.

It was disturbing at dinner to find that the girl was absent, had in fact, according to Sir Hiram, gone away for a day or so to see an old school-friend in a neighbouring town. She would be back, however, for the final shoot, he added, an explanation which Norman interpreted to mean that her uncle had deliberately sent her out of danger. He felt positive he was right. Sir Hiram might scorn such 'rubbishy tales', but he was taking no chances. It was at the equinox that his sister had mysteriously disappeared. The girl was best elsewhere. Nor could all the pleasant compliments about Norman's good shooting on the two Drives conceal his host's genuine uneasiness. Diana was 'best elsewhere'.

Norman fell asleep with the firm determination that he must explore the Trod next day in good light, making sure of his landmarks and then creep out at night when the household was quiet, and see what happened.

There was no shooting next day. His task was easy. Keepers and dogs went out to pick up any birds that had been left from the previous day. After breakfast he slipped off across the waste of heather and soon found it—a deep smooth groove running through occasional hollows where no water lay, nor any faintest track of man or beast upon its soft, black peaty surface. Obviously, it was a track through the deep heather no one—neither man nor animal—used. He again noted the landmarks carefully, and felt sure he could find it again in the darkness... and, in due course, the day passed along its normal course, the 'guns' after dinner discussed the next day's beat, and all turned in early in pleasurable anticipation of the shoot to come.

Norman went up to bed with a beating heart, for his plan to slip out of the sleeping house later and explore the moorland with its 'haunted Trod', was not exactly what a host expected of a guest. The absence of Diana, moreover, deliberately planned, added to his deep uneasiness. Her sudden disappearance to visit 'an old school friend' was not convincing. Nor had she even left a line of explanation. It came to him that others besides the chauffeur and the loader took these fantastic fairy-tales seriously. His thoughts flew buzzing like bees outside a bee-hive...

From his window he looked out upon the night. The moon, in her second quarter, shone brightly at moments, then became hidden behind fleecy clouds. Higher up, evidently, a raging wind was driving, but below over the moorland a deathly stillness reigned. This stillness touched his nerves, and the dogs, howling in their kennels, added to a sense of superstitious uneasiness in his blood. The deep stillness seemed to hide a busy activity behind the silence. Something was stirring in the night, something out on the moor.

He turned back from the window and saw the lighted room, its cosy comfort, its well-lit luxury, its delicious bed waiting for weary limbs. He hesitated. The two sides of his nature clashed ... but in the end the strange absence of Diana, her words, her abrupt sensational kiss, her odd silence... the quixotic feeling that he *might* help—these finally decided him.

Changing quickly into his shooting clothes, and making sure that the lights in all the bedroom windows he could see were out, he crept down in stockinged feet to the front door, carrying a pair of tennis shoes in his hand. The front door was unlocked, opening without noise, so that he slipped quietly across the gravel drive on to the grass, and thence, having now put on his shoes, on to the moor beyond.

The house faded behind him, patches of silvery moonlight shone through thin racing clouds, the taste of the night air was intoxicating. How could he ever have hesitated? The wonder and mystery of the wild country-side, haunted or otherwise, caught him by the throat. As he climbed the railings leading from the cultivated garden to the moor, there came a faint odd whispering sound behind him, so that he paused and listened for a moment. Was it wind or footsteps? It was neither—merely the flap of his open coat trailing across the fence. Bah! his nerves were jumpy. He laughed—almost laughed aloud, such was the exhilaration in him—and moved on quickly through the weird half lights. And for some reason his spirits rose, his blood went racing: here was an adventure the other side of his nature delighted in, yet his 'other side' now took ominously the upper hand.

How primitive, after all, these 'shooting parties' were! For men of brains and character, the best that England could produce, to spend all this time and money, hunting as the cave-men hunted! The fox, the deer, the bird—earlier men needed these for food, yet thousands of years later the finest males of the twentieth century—sportsmen all—spent millions on superior weapons, which gave the hunted animal no chance, to bring them down. Not to be a 'sportsman' was to be an inferior Englishman...! The 'sportsman' was the flower of the race. It struck him, not for the first time, as a grim, a cheap, ideal. Was there no other climax of chivalric achievement more desirable?

This flashed across his mind as a hundred times before, while yet he himself, admittedly, was a 'sportsman' born. Against it, at the same time, rose some strange glamour of eternal, deathless things that took no account of killing, things that caught his soul away in ecstasy. Fairy tales, of course, were fairy tales, yet they enshrined the undying truths of life and human nature within their golden 'nonsense', catching at the skirts of radiant wonder, whispering ageless secrets of the soul, giving hints of ineffable glories that lay outside the normal scales of space and time as accepted by the reasoning mind. And this attitude now rose upon him like a wild ungovernable wind of spring, fragrant, delicious, intoxicating. Fairies, the Little People, the 'Gay People', happy dwellers in some non-human state...

Diana's mother had disappeared, yearning with secret, surreptitious calls for her daughter to come and join her. The girl herself acknowledged the call and was afraid, while yet her practical, hard-boiled uncle took particular trouble to keep her out of the way. Even for him, typical 'sportsman', the time of the equinox was dangerous. These reflections, tumbling about his mind and heart, flooded Norman's being, while his yearning and desire for the girl came over him like a flame.

The moor, meanwhile, easy enough to walk on in the daytime, seemed unexpectedly difficult at night, the heather longer, the ground very uneven. He was always putting his legs into little hollows that he could not see, and he was relieved when at last he could make out the loom of the garage which was one of his landmarks. He knew that he had not much further to go before he reached the Trod.

The turmoil in his mind had been such that he had paid little attention to the occasional slight sounds he heard as though somebody were at his heels, but now, on reaching the Trod, he became uneasily convinced that someone was not far behind him. So certain, indeed, was he of someone else that he let himself down silently into the deep heather and waited.

He listened intently, breathing very softly. The same instant he knew that he was right. Those sounds were not imagination. Footsteps were at his heels. The swish through the heather of a moving body was unmistakable. He caught distinct footsteps then. The footsteps came to a pause quite near to where he crouched. At which moment exactly, the clouds raced past the moon, letting down a clear space of silvery light, so that he saw the 'follower' brilliantly defined.

It was Diana.

'I knew it,' he said half aloud, 'I was sure of it long ago,' while his heart, faced with a yearning hope and fear, both half fulfilled, yet gave no leap of relief or pleasure. A shiver ran up and down his spine. Crouching there deep among the heather on the edge of the Trod, he knew more of terror than of happiness. It was all too clear for misunderstanding. She had been drawn irresistibly on the night of the equinox to the danger zone where her mother had so mysteriously 'disappeared'.

'I'm here,' he added with a great effort in the same low whisper. 'You asked my help. I'm here to meet you... dear...'

The words, even if he actually uttered them, died on his lips. The girl, he saw, stood still a moment, gazing in a dazed way, as though puzzled by something that obstructed her passage. Like a sleep walker, she stared about her, beautiful as a dream, yet only half conscious of her surrounding. Her eyes shone in the moonlight, her hands were half outstretched, yet not towards himself.

'Diana,' he heard himself crying, 'can you see me? Do you see who I am? Don't you recognise me? I've come to help—to save—you!'

It was plain she neither heard nor saw him standing there in front of her. She was aware of an obstructing presence, no more than that. Her glazed, shining eyes looked far beyond him—along the Trod. And a terror clutched him that, unless he quickly did the right thing, she would be lost to him for ever.

He sprang to his feet and went towards her, but with the extraordinary sensation that he at once came up against some intervening wall of resistance that made normal movement difficult. It was almost like forcing his way through moving water or a drift of wind, and it was with an effort that he reached her side and stood now close against her.

'Diana!' he cried, 'Dis—Dis,' using the name her mother used. 'Can't you see who I am? Don't you know me? I've come to save you—' and he stretched his hands towards her.

There was no response; she made no sign.

'I've come to lead you back—to lead you home—for God's sake, answer me, look into my eyes!'

She turned her head in his direction, as though to look into his face, but her eyes went past him towards the moonlit moor beyond. He noticed only, while she stared with those unseeing eyes, that her left hand fumbled weakly at a tiny crucifix that hung on a thin silver chain about her neck. He put out his hand and seized her by the arm, but the instant he touched her he found himself suddenly powerless to move. There came this strange arrest. And at the same instant, the whole Trod became startlingly lit up with a kind of unearthly radiance, and a strange greenish light shone upon the track right across the moor beyond where they stood. A deep terror for himself as well as for her rose over him simultaneously. It came to him, with a shock of ice, that his own soul as well as hers, lay in sudden danger.

His eyes turned irresistibly towards the Trod, so strangely shining in the night. Though his hand still touched the girl, his mind was caught away in phantasmal possibilities. For two passions seized and fought within him: the fierce desire to possess her in the world of men and women, or to go with her headlong, recklessly, and share some ineffable ecstasy of happiness beyond the familiar world where ordinary time and space held sway. Her own nature already held the key and knew the danger. ... His whole being rocked.

The two incompatible passions gored the very heart in him. In a flash he realised his alternative—the dreary desolation of human progress with its grinding future, the joy and glory of a soulless happiness that reason denied and yet the heart welcomed as an ultimate truth. These two!

Yet of what value and meaning could she ever be to him as wife and mother if she were now drawn away—away to where her mother now eternally passed her golden, time-less life? How could he face this daily exile of her soul, this hourly isolation, this rape of her normal being his earthly nature held so dear and precious? While—should he save her, keeping her safe against the *human* hearth—how should he hold her to him, he himself tainted with the golden poison...?

Norman saw both sides with remorseless clarity in that swift instant while the Trod took on its shining radiance. His reasoning mind, he knew, had sunk away; his heart, wildly beating, was uppermost. With a supreme effort he kept his touch upon Diana's arm. His fingers clutched at the rough tweed of her sleeve. His entire being seemed rapt in some incredible ecstasy. He stood, he stared, he wondered, lost in an ineffable dream of beauty. One link only with the normal he held to like a vice—his touch upon her rough tweed sleeve, and, in his fading memory, the picture of a crucifix her weakening fingers weakly fumbled.

Figures were now moving fast and furious along the Trod; he could see them approaching from the distance. It was an inspiring, an intoxicating vision, and yet quite credible, with no foolish phantasmagoria of any childish sort. He saw everything as plainly as though he watched a parade in Whitehall, or a procession at some southern Battle of Flowers. Yet lovely, happy, radiant—and irresistibly enticing. As the figures came nearer, the light increased, so that it was obvious *they* emanated light of their own against the dark moorland. Nor were the individual figures particularly striking, least of all sensational. They seemed 'natural', yet natural only because they were true and justified.

In the lead, as they drew nearer, Norman saw a tall dark man riding a white horse, close behind him a fair shining woman in a green dress, her long, golden hair falling to her waist. On her head he saw a circlet of gold in which was set a red stone that shone and glowed like burning flame. Beside her was another woman, dark and beautiful, with white stones sparkling in her hair as diamonds or crystals sparkle. It was a gorgeous and a radiant sight. Their faces shone with the ecstasy of youth. In some indescribable way they all spread happiness and joy about them, their eyes blazing with a peace and beneficence he had never seen in any human eyes.

These passed, and more and more poured by, some riding, some walking, young and old and children, men with hunting spears and unstrung bows, then youthful figures with harps and lyres, and one and all making friendly gestures of invitation to come and join them, as they flowed past silently. Silently, yes, silently, without a sound of footsteps or of rustling heather, silently along the illuminated Trod, and yet, silent though their passing was, there came to him an impression of singing, laughter, even an air of dancing. Such figures, he realised, could not move without rhythm, rhythm of sound and gesture, for it was as essential to them as breathing. Happy, radiant, gay they were for ever from the grinding effort and struggle of the world's strenuous evolutionary battles—free, if soulless. The 'Gay People' as the natives called them. And the sight wrenched at the deepest roots of his own mixed being. To go with them and share their soulless bliss forever... or to stay and face the grim battle of Humanity's terrific—noble, yes—but almost hopeless, evolution?

That he was torn in two seemed an understatement. The pain seared and burned him in his very vitals. Diana, the girl, drew him as with some power of the stars themselves, and his hand still felt the tweed of her cloth beneath his fingers. His mind and heart, his nerves, his straining muscles, seemed fused in a fury of contradictions and acceptances. The glorious procession flowed streaming by, as though the stars had touched the common moorland earth, dripping their lavish gold in quiet glory—when suddenly Diana wrenched herself away and ran headlong towards them.

A golden-haired woman, he saw, had stepped out of the actual Trod, and had come to a halt directly in front of where he stood. Radiant and wonderful, she stood for a moment poised.

'Dis... Dis...' he heard in tones like music. 'Come... come to me. Come and join us! The way is always open. There are no regrets... !'

The girl was half way to her mother before he could break the awful spell that held him motionless. But the rough cloth of her sleeve held clutched between his fingers, and with it the broken chain that caught her little crucifix. The silver cross swung and dangled a moment, then dropped among the heather.

It was as he stooped frantically to recover it that Fate played that strange, unusual card she keeps in reserve for moments when the world seems lost; for, as he fell, his own chain and crucifix, to which he had not once given a thought, flicked up and caught him on the lip. Thinking it was a broken edge of torn heather that stung him into pain, he dashed it aside—only to find it was the foolish metal symbol Diana had made him promise to wear, in his own safety. It was the sharp stab of pain, not the superstitious mental reaction, that roused immediate action in him.

In a second he was on his feet again, and a second later he had overtaken the striding girl and had both arms possessingly round her figure. An instant afterwards his lips were on her own, her head and shoulders torn backwards against his breast.

'Dis!' he cried wildly, 'we must stay here together! You belong to me. I hold you tight—forever... here!'

What else he cried he hardly knows. He felt her weight sink back into his arms. It seems he carried her. He felt her convulsive weeping sobs against his heart. Her arms clung tightly round him.

In the distance he saw the line of moving figures die fading off into the enveloping moorland, dipping down into the curving dimness. Clouds raced back across the moon. There was no sound, the wind lay still, no tumbling beck was audible, the peewits slept.

Putting his own coat about her, he carried her home... and in due course he married her; he married Diana, he married Dis as well, a queer, lovely girl, but a girl without a soul, almost without a mind—a girl as commonplace as the radiant nonentity pictured with shining teeth on the cover of a popular magazine —a standardised creature whose essence had 'gone elsewhere'.

# THE TERROR OF THE TWINS

That the man's hopes had built upon a son to inherit his name and estates—a single son, that is—was to be expected; but no one could have foreseen the depth and bitterness of his disappointment, the cold, implacable fury, when there arrived instead—twins. For, though the elder legally must inherit, that other ran him so deadly close. A daughter would have been a more reasonable defeat. But twins——! To miss his dream by so feeble a device——!

The complete frustration of a hope deeply cherished for years may easily result in strange fevers of the soul, but the violence of the father's hatred, existing as it did side by side with a love he could not deny, was something to set psychologists thinking. More than unnatural, it was positively uncanny. Being a man of rigid self-control, however, it operated inwardly, and doubtless along some morbid line of weakness little suspected even by those nearest to him, preying upon his thought to such dreadful extent that finally the mind gave way. The suppressed rage and bitterness deprived him, so the family decided, of his reason, and he spent the last years of his life under restraint. He was possessed naturally of immense forces—of will, feeling, desire; his dynamic value truly tremendous, driving through life like a great engine; and the intensity of this concentrated and buried hatred was guessed by few. The twins themselves, however, knew it. They divined it, at least, for it operated ceaselessly against them side by side with the genuine soft love that occasionally sweetened it, to their great perplexity. They spoke of it only to each other, though.

'At twenty-one,' Edward, the elder, would remark sometimes, unhappily, 'we shall know more.' 'Too much,' Ernest would reply, with a rush of unreasoning terror the thought never failed to evoke—*in him*. 'Things father said always happened—in life.' And they paled perceptibly. For the hatred, thus compressed into a veritable bomb of psychic energy, had found at the last a singular expression in the cry of the father's distraught mind. On the occasion of their final visit to the asylum, preceding his death by a few hours only, very calmly, but with an intensity that drove the words into their hearts like points of burning metal, he had spoken. In the presence of the attendant, at the door of the dreadful padded cell, he said it: 'You are not two, but *one*. I still regard you as one. And at the coming of age, by h——, you shall find it out!'

The lads perhaps had never fully divined that icy hatred which lay so well concealed against them, but that this final sentence was a curse, backed by all the man's terrific force, they quite well realised; and accordingly, almost unknown to each other, they had come to dread the day inexpressibly. On the morning of that twenty-first birthday—their father gone these five years into the Unknown, yet still sometimes so strangely close to them—they shared the same biting, inner terror, just as they shared all other emotions of their life—intimately, without speech. During the daytime they managed to keep it at a distance, but when the dusk fell about the old house they knew the stealthy approach of a kind of panic sense. Their self-respect weakened swiftly... and they persuaded their old friend, and once tutor, the vicar, to sit up with them till midnight. ... He had humoured them to that extent, willing to forgo his sleep, and at the same time more than a little interested in their singular belief—that before the day was out, before midnight struck, that is, the curse of that terrible man would somehow come into operation against them.

Festivities over and the guests departed, they sat up in the library, the room usually occupied by their father, and little used since. Mr. Curtice, a robust man of fifty-five, and a firm believer in spiritual principalities and powers, dark as well as good, affected (for their own good) to regard the youths' obsession with a kindly cynicism. 'I do not think it likely for one moment,' he said gravely, 'that such a thing would be permitted. All spirits are in the hands of God, and the violent ones more especially.' To which Edward made the extraordinary reply: 'Even if father does not come himself he will—*send*!' And Ernest agreed: 'All this time he's been making preparations for this very day. We've both known it for a long time—by odd things that have happened, by our dreams, by nasty little dark hints of various kinds, and by these persistent attacks of terror that come from nowhere, especially of late. Haven't we, Edward?' Edward assenting with a shudder. 'Father has been *at us* of late with renewed violence. To-night it will be a regular assault upon our lives, or minds, or souls!'

'Strong personalities *may* possibly leave behind them forces that continue to act,' observed Mr. Curtice with caution, while the brothers replied almost in the same breath: 'That's exactly what we feel so curiously. Though—nothing has actually happened yet, you know, and it's a good many years now since——'

This was the way the twins spoke of it all. And it was their profound conviction that had touched their old friend's sense of duty. The experiment should justify itself—and cure them. Meanwhile none of the family knew. Everything was planned secretly.

The library was the quietest room in the house. It had shuttered bow-windows, thick carpets, heavy doors. Books lined the walls, and there was a capacious open fireplace of brick in which the woodlogs blazed and roared, for the autumn night was chilly. Round this the three of them were grouped, the clergyman reading aloud from the Book of Job in low tones; Edward and Ernest, in dinner-jackets, occupying deep leather arm-chairs, listening. They looked exactly what they were—Cambridge 'undergrads', their faces pale against their dark hair, and alike as two peas. A shaded lamp behind the clergyman threw the rest of the room into shadow. The reading voice was steady, even monotonous, but something in it betrayed an underlying anxiety, and although the eyes rarely left the printed page, they took in every movement of the young men opposite, and noted every change upon their faces. It was his aim to produce an unexciting atmosphere, yet to miss nothing; if anything did occur to see it from the very beginning. Not to be taken by surprise was his main idea. ... And thus, upon this falsely peaceful scene, the minutes passed the hour of eleven and slipped rapidly along towards midnight.

The novel element in his account of this distressing and dreadful occurrence seems to be that what happened—happened without the slightest warning or preparation. There was no gradual presentiment of any horror; no strange blast of cold air; no dwindling of heat or light; no shaking of windows or mysterious tapping upon furniture. Without preliminaries it fell with its black trappings of terror upon the scene.

The clergyman had been reading aloud for some considerable time, one or other of the twins—Ernest usually—making occasional remarks, which proved that his sense of dread was disappearing. As the time grew short and nothing happened they grew more at their ease. Edward, indeed, actually nodded, dozed, and finally fell asleep. It was a few minutes before midnight. Ernest, slightly yawning, was stretching himself in the big chair. 'Nothing's going to happen,' he said aloud, in a pause. 'Your good influence has prevented it.' He even laughed now. 'What superstitious asses we've been, sir; haven't we——?'

Curtice, then, dropping his Bible, looked hard at him under the lamp. For in that second, even while the words sounded, there had come about a most abrupt and dreadful change; and so swiftly that the clergyman, in spite of himself, was taken utterly by surprise and had no time to think. There had swooped down upon the quiet library—so he puts it—an immense hushing silence, so profound that the peace already reigning there seemed clamour by comparison; and out of this enveloping stillness there rose through the space about them a living and abominable Invasion—soft, motionless, terrific. It was as though vast engines, working at full speed and pressure, yet too swift and delicate to be appreciable to any definite sense, had suddenly dropped down upon them—from nowhere. 'It made me think,' the vicar used to say afterwards, 'of the *Mauretania* machinery compressed into a nutshell, yet losing none of its awful power.'

'... haven't we?' repeated Ernest, still laughing. And Curtice, making no audible reply, heard the true answer in his heart: 'Because everything has *already happened*—even as you feared.'

Yet, to the vicar's supreme astonishment, Ernest still noticed —nothing!

'Look,' the boy added, 'Eddy's sound asleep—sleeping like a pig. Doesn't say much for your reading, you know, sir!' And he laughed again—lightly, even foolishly. But that laughter jarred, for the clergyman understood now that the sleep of the elder twin was either feigned—or *unnatural*.

And while the easy words fell so lightly from his lips, the monstrous engines worked and pulsed against him and against his sleeping brother, all their huge energy concentrated down into points fine as Suggestion, delicate as Thought. The Invasion affected everything. The very objects in the room altered incredibly, revealing suddenly behind their normal exteriors horrid little hearts of darkness. It was truly amazing, this vile metamorphosis. Books, chairs, pictures, all yielded up their pleasant aspect, and betrayed, as with silent mocking laughter, their inner soul of blackness—their *decay*. This is how Curtice tries to body forth in words what he actually witnessed. ... And Ernest, yawning, talking lightly, half foolishly —still noticed nothing!

For all this, as described, came about in something like ten seconds; and with it swept into the clergyman's mind, like a blow, the memory of that sinister phrase used more than once by Edward: 'If father doesn't come, he will certainly—*send*.' And Curtice understood that he had done both—both sent and come himself. ... That violent mind, released from its spell of madness in the body, yet still retaining the old implacable hatred, was now directing the terrible, unseen assault. This silent room, so hushed and still, was charged to the brim. The horror of it, as he said later, 'seemed to peel the very skin from my back.' ... And, while Ernest noticed nothing, Edward slept!... The soul of the clergyman, strong with the desire to help or save, yet realising that he was alone against a Legion, poured out in wordless prayer to his Deity. The clock just then, whirring before it struck, made itself audible.

'By Jove! It's all right, you see!' exclaimed Ernest, his voice oddly fainter and lower than before. 'There's midnight —and nothing's happened. Bally nonsense, all of it!' His voice had dwindled curiously in volume. 'I'll get the whisky and soda from the hall.' His relief was great and his manner showed it. But in him somewhere was a singular change. His voice, manner, gestures, his very tread as he moved over the thick carpet toward the door, all showed it. He seemed less *real,* less alive, reduced somehow to littleness, the voice without timbre or quality, the appearance of him diminished in some fashion quite ghastly. His presence, if not actually shrivelled, was at least impaired. Ernest had suffered a singular and horrible *decrease*. ...

The clock was still whirring before the strike. One heard the chain running up softly. Then the hammer fell upon the first stroke of midnight.

'I'm off,' he laughed faintly from the door; 'it's all been pure funk—on my part, at least...!' He passed out of sight into the hall. *The Power that throbbed so mightily about the room followed him out.* Almost at the same moment Edward woke up. But he woke with a tearing and indescribable cry of pain and anguish on his lips: 'Oh, oh, oh! But it hurts! It hurts! I can't hold you; leave me. It's breaking me asunder——'

The clergyman had sprung to his feet, but in the same instant everything had become normal once more—the room as it was before, the horror gone. There was nothing he could do or say, for there was no longer anything to put right, to defend, or to attack. Edward was speaking; his voice, deep and full as it never had been before: 'By Jove, how that sleep has refreshed me! I feel twice the chap I was before—twice the chap. I feel quite splendid. Your voice, sir, must have hypnotised me to sleep. ...' He crossed the room with great vigour. 'Where's—er—where's—Ernie, by the bye?' he asked casually, hesitating—almost searching—for the name. And a shadow as of a vanished memory crossed his face and was gone. The tone conveyed the most complete indifference where once the least word or movement of his twin had wakened solicitude, love. 'Gone away, I suppose—gone to bed, I mean, of course.'

Curtice has never been able to describe the dreadful conviction that overwhelmed him as he stood there staring, his heart in his mouth—the conviction, the positive certainty, that Edward had changed interiorly, had suffered an incredible accession to his existing personality. But he *knew* it as he watched. His mind, spirit, soul had most wonderfully increased. Something that hitherto the lad had known from the outside only, or by the magic of loving sympathy, had now passed, to be incorporated with his own being. And, being himself, it required no expression. Yet this visible increase was somehow terrible. Curtice shrank back from him. The instinct—he has never grasped the profound psychology of *that*, nor why it turned his soul dizzy with a kind of nausea—the instinct to strike him where he stood, passed, and a plaintive sound from the hall, stealing softly into the room between them, sent all that was left to him of self-possession onto his feet. He turned and ran. Edward followed him—very leisurely.

They found Ernest, or what had been Ernest, crouching behind the table in the hall, weeping foolishly to himself. On his face lay blackness. The mouth was open, the jaw dropped; he dribbled hopelessly; and from the face had passed all signs of intelligence—of spirit.

For a few weeks he lingered on, regaining no sign of spiritual or mental life before the poor body, hopelessly disorganised, released what was left of him, from pure inertia—from complete and utter loss of vitality.

And the horrible thing—so the distressed family thought, at least—was that all those weeks Edward showed an indifference that was singularly brutal and complete. He rarely even went to visit him. I believe, too, it is true that he only once spoke of him by name; and that was when he said—

'Ernie? Oh, but Ernie is much better and happier where he is——!'

## THE DEFERRED APPOINTMENT

The little 'Photographic Studio' in the side-street beyond Shepherd's Bush had done no business all day, for the light had been uninviting to even the vainest sitter, and the murky sky that foreboded snow had hung over London without a break since dawn. Pedestrians went hurrying and shivering along the pavements disappearing into the gloom of countless ugly little houses the moment they passed beyond the glare of the big electric standards that lit the thundering motor-buses in the main street. The first flakes of snow, indeed, were already falling slowly, as though they shrank from settling in the grime. The wind moaned and sang dismally, catching the ears and lifting the shabby coat-tails of Mr. Mortimer Jenkyn, 'Photographic Artist', as he stood outside and put the shutters up with his own cold hands in despair of further trade. It was five minutes to six.

With a lingering glance at the enlarged portrait of a fat man in masonic regalia who was the pride and glory of his window-front, he fixed the last hook of the shutter, and turned to go indoors. There was developing and framing to be done upstairs, not very remunerative work, but better, at any rate, than waiting in an empty studio for customers who did not come—wasting the heat of two oil-stoves into the bargain. And it was then, in the act of closing the street-door behind him, that he saw a man standing in the shadows of the narrow passage, staring fixedly into his face.

Mr. Jenkyn admits that he jumped. The man was so very close, yet he had not seen him come in; and in the eyes was such a curiously sad and appealing expression. He had already sent his assistant home, and there was no other occupant of the little two-storey house. The man must have slipped past him from the dark street while his back was turned. Who in the world could he be, and what could he want? Was he beggar, customer, or rogue?

'Good evening,' Mr. Jenkyn said, washing his hands, but using only half the oily politeness of tone with which he favoured sitters. He was just going to add 'sir', feeling it wiser to be on the safe side, when the stranger shifted his position so that the light fell directly upon his face, and Mr. Jenkyn was aware that he—recognised him. Unless he was greatly mistaken, it was the second-hand bookseller in the main street.

'Ah, it's you, Mr. Wilson!' he stammered, making half a question of it, as though not quite convinced. 'Pardon me; I did not quite catch your face—er—I was just shutting up.' The other bowed his head in reply. 'Won't you come in? Do, please.'

Mr. Jenkyn led the way. He wondered what was the matter. The visitor was not among his customers; indeed, he could hardly claim to know him, having only seen him occasionally when calling at the shop for slight purchases of paper and what not. The man, he now realised, looked fearfully ill and wasted, his face pale and haggard. It upset him rather, this sudden, abrupt call. He felt sorry, pained. He felt uneasy.

Into the studio they passed, the visitor going first as though he knew the way, Mr. Jenkyn noticing through his flurry that he was in his 'Sunday best'. Evidently he had come with a definite purpose. It was odd. Still without speaking, he moved straight across the room and posed himself in front of the dingy back-ground of painted trees, facing the camera. The studio was brightly lit. He seated himself in the faded armchair, crossed his legs, drew up the little round table with the artificial roses upon it in a tall, thin vase, and struck an attitude. He meant to be photographed. His eyes, staring straight into the lens, draped as it was with the black velvet curtain, seemed, however, to take no account of the Photographic Artist. But Mr. Jenkyn, standing still beside the door, felt a cold air playing over his face that was not merely the winter cold from the street. He felt his hair rise. A slight shiver ran down his back. In that pale, drawn face, and in those staring eyes across the room that gazed so fixedly into the draped camera, he read the signature of illness that no longer knows hope. It was Death that he saw.

In a flash the impression came and went—less than a second. The whole business, indeed, had not occupied two minutes. Mr. Jenkyn pulled himself together with a strong effort, dismissed his foolish obsession, and came sharply to practical considerations. 'Forgive me,' he said, a trifle thickly, confusedly, 'but I—er—did not quite realise. You desire to sit for your portrait, of course. I've had such a busy day, and—'ardly looked for a customer so late.' The clock, as he spoke, struck six. But he did not notice the sound. Through his mind ran another reflection: 'A man shouldn't 'ave his picture taken when he's ill and next door to dying. Lord! He'll want a lot of touching-up and finishin', too!'

He began discussing the size, price, and length—the usual rigmarole of his 'profession', and the other, sitting there, still vouchsafed no comment or reply. He simply made the impression of a man in a great hurry, who wished to finish a disagreeable business without unnecessary talk. Many men, reflected the photographer, were the same; being photographed was worse to them than going to the dentist. Mr. Jenkyn filled the pauses with his professional running talk and patter, while the sitter, fixed and motionless, kept his first position and stared at the camera. The photographer rather prided himself upon his ability to make sitters look bright and pleasant; but this man was hopeless. It was only afterwards Mr. Jenkyn recalled the singular fact that he never once touched him—that, in fact, something connected possibly with his frail appearance of deadly illness had prevented his going close to arrange the details of the hastily assumed pose.

'It must be a flashlight, of course, Mr. Wilson,' he said, fidgeting at length with the camera-stand, shifting it slightly nearer; while the other moved his head gently yet impatiently in agreement. Mr. Jenkyn longed to suggest his coming another time when he looked better, to speak with sympathy of his illness; to say something, in fact, that might establish a personal relation. But his tongue in this respect seemed utterly tied. It was just this personal relation which seemed impossible to approach—absolutely and peremptorily impossible. There seemed a barrier between the two. He could only chatter the usual professional commonplaces. To tell the truth, Mr. Jenkyn thinks he felt a little dazed the whole time—not quite his usual self. And, meanwhile, his uneasiness oddly increased. He hurried. He too, wanted the matter done with and his visitor gone.

At length everything was ready, only the flashlight waiting to be turned on, when stooping, he covered his head with the velvet cloth and peered through the lens—at no one! When he says 'at no one', however, he qualifies it thus: 'There was a quick flash of brilliant white light and a face in the middle of it —my gracious Heaven! But such a face—*'im*, yet not *'im*—like a sudden rushing glory of a face! It shot off like lightning out of the camera's field of vision. It left me blinded, I assure you, 'alf blinded, and that's a fac'. It was sheer dazzling!'

It seems Mr. Jenkyn remained entangled a moment in the cloth, eyes closed, breath coming in gasps, for when he got clear and straightened up again, staring once more at his customer over the top of the camera, he stared for the second time at—no one. And the cap that he held in his left hand he clapped feverishly over the uncovered lens. Mr. Jenkyn staggered... looked hurriedly round the empty studio, then ran, knocking a chair over as he went, into the passage. The hall was deserted, the front door closed. His visitor had disappeared 'almost as though he hadn't never been there at all'—thus he described it to himself in a terrified whisper. And again he felt the hair rise on his scalp; his skin crawled a little, and something put back the ice against his spine.

After a moment he returned to the studio and somewhat feverishly examined it. There stood the chair against the dingy background of trees; and there, close beside it, was the round table with the flower vase. Less than a minute ago Mr. Thomas Wilson, looking like death, had been sitting in that very chair.

'It wasn't *all* a sort of dreamin', then,' ran through his disordered and frightened mind. 'I did see something...!' He remembered vaguely stories he had read in the newspapers, stories of queer warnings that saved people from disasters, apparitions, faces seen in dream, and so forth. 'Maybe,' he thought with confusion, 'something's going to 'appen to *me*!' Further than that he could not get for some little time, as he stood there staring about him, almost expecting that Mr. Wilson might reappear as strangely as he had disappeared. He went over the whole scene again and again, reconstructing it in minutest detail. And only then for the first time, did he plainly realise two things which somehow or other he had not thought strange before, but now thought very strange. For his visitor, he remembered, had not uttered a single word, nor had he, Mr. Jenkyn, once touched his person... And, thereupon, without more ado, he put on his hat and coat and went round to the little shop in the main street to buy some ink and stationery, which he did not in the least require.

The shop seemed all as usual, though Mr. Wilson himself was not visible behind the littered desk. A tall gentleman was talking in low tones to the partner. Mr. Jenkyn bowed as he went in, then stood examining a case of cheap stylographic pens, waiting for the others to finish. It was impossible to avoid overhearing. Besides, the little shop had distinguished customers sometimes, he had heard, and this evidently was one of them. He only understood part of the conversation, but he remembers all of it. 'Singular, yes, these last words of dying men,' the tall man was saying, 'very singular. You remember Newman's: "More light", wasn't it?' The bookseller nodded. 'Fine,' he said, 'fine, that!' There was a pause. Mr. Jenkyn stooped lower over the pens. 'This, too, was fine in its way,' the gentleman added, straightening up to go; 'the old promise, you see, unfulfilled but not forgotten. Cropped up suddenly out of the delirium. Curious, very curious! A good, conscientious man to the last. In all the twenty years I've known him he never broke his word...'

A motor-bus drowned a sentence, and then was heard in the

bookseller's voice, as he moved towards the door: '... You see, he was half-way down the stairs before they found him, always repeating the same thing, "I promised the wife, I promised the wife." And it was a job, I'm told, getting him back again... he struggled so. That's what finished him so quick, I suppose. Fifteen minutes later he was gone, and his last words were always the same, "I promised the wife"...'

The tall man was gone, and Mr. Jenkyn forgot about his purchases. 'When did it 'appen?' he heard himself asking in a voice he hardly recognised as his own. And the reply roared and thundered in his ears as he went down the street a minute later to his house: 'Close on six o'clock—a few minutes before the hour. Been ill for weeks, yes. Caught him out of bed with high fever on his way to your place, Mr. Jenkyn, calling at the top of his voice that he'd forgotten to see you about his picture being taken. Yes, very sad, very sad indeed.'

But Mr. Jenkyn did not return to his studio. He left the light burning there all night. He went to the little room where he slept out, and next day gave the plate to be developed by his assistant. 'Defective plate, sir,' was the report in due course; 'shows nothing but a flash of light—uncommonly brilliant.'

'Make a print of it all the same,' was the reply. Six months later, when he examined the plate and print, Mr. Jenkyn found that the singular streaks of light had disappeared from both. The uncommon brilliance had faded out completely as though it had never been there.

## ACCESSORY BEFORE THE FACT

At the moorland cross-roads Martin stood examining the sign-post for several minutes in some bewilderment. The names on the four arms were not what he expected, distances were not given, and his map, he concluded with impatience, must be hopelessly out of date. Spreading it against the post, he stooped to study it more closely. The wind blew the corners flapping against his face. The small print was almost indecipherable in the fading light. It appeared, however—as well as he could make out—that two miles back he must have taken the wrong turning.

He remembered that turning. The path had looked inviting; he had hesitated a moment, then followed it, caught by the usual lure of walkers that it 'might prove a short cut'. The short-cut snare is old as human nature. For some minutes he studied the sign-post and the map alternately. Dusk was falling, and his knapsack had grown heavy. He could not make the two guides tally, however, and a feeling of uncertainty crept over his mind. He felt oddly baffled, frustrated. His thought grew thick. Decision was most difficult. 'I'm muddled,' he thought; 'I must be tired,' as at length he chose the most likely arm. 'Sooner or later it will bring me to an inn, though not the one I intended.' He accepted his walker's luck, and started briskly. The arm read, 'Over Litacy Hill' in small, fine letters that danced and shifted every time he looked at them; but the name was not discoverable on the map. It was, however, inviting like the short-cut. A similar impulse again directed his choice. Only this time it seemed more insistent, almost urgent.

And he became aware, then, of the exceeding loneliness of the country about him. The road for a hundred yards went straight, then curved like a white river running into space; the deep blue-green of heather lined the banks, spreading upwards through the twilight; and occasional small pines stood solitary here and there, all unexplained. The curious adjective, having made its appearance, haunted him. So many things that afternoon were similarly—unexplained: the short cut, the darkened map, the names on the sign-post, his own erratic impulses, and the growing strange confusion that crept upon his spirit. The entire country-side needed explanation, though perhaps 'interpretation' was the truer word. Those little lonely trees had made him see it. Why had he lost his way so easily? Why did he suffer vague impressions to influence his direction? Why was he here—exactly *here*? And why did he go now 'over Litacy Hill'?

Then, by a green field that shone like a thought of day-light amid the darkness of the moor, he saw a figure lying in the grass. It was a blot upon the landscape, a mere huddled patch of dirty rags, yet with a certain horrid picturesqueness too; and his mind—though his German was of the schoolroom order—at once picked out the German equivalents as against the English. *Lump* and *Lumpen* flashed across his brain most oddly. They seemed in that moment right, and so expressive, almost like onomatopoeic words, if that were possible of sight. Neither 'rags' nor 'rascal' would have fitted what he saw. The adequate description was in German.

Here was a clue tossed up by the part of him that did not reason. But it seems he missed it. And the next minute the tramp rose to a sitting posture and asked the time of evening. In German he asked it. And Martin, answering without a second's hesitation, gave it, also in German, '*halb sieben*'—half-past six. The instinctive guess was accurate. A glance at his watch when he looked a moment later proved it. He heard the man say, with the covert insolence of tramps, 'T'ank you; much opliged.' For Martin had not shown his watch—another intuition subconsciously obeyed.

He quickened his pace along that lonely road, a curious jumble of thoughts and feelings surging through him. He had somehow known the question would come, and come in German. Yet it flustered and dismayed him. Another thing had also flustered and dismayed him. He had expected it in the same queer fashion:

it was right. For when the ragged brown thing rose to ask the question, a part of it remained lying on the grass—another brown, dirty thing. There were two tramps. And he saw both faces clearly. Behind the untidy beards, and below the slouch hats, he caught the look of unpleasant, clever faces that watched him closely while he passed. The eyes followed him. For a second he looked straight into those eyes, so that he could not fail to know them. And he understood, quite horridly, that both faces were too sleek, refined, and cunning for those of ordinary tramps. The men were not really tramps at all. They were disguised.

'How covertly they watched me!' was his thought, as he hurried along the darkening road, in dead earnestness now aware of the loneliness and desolation of the moorland all about him.

Uneasy and distressed, he increased his pace. Midway in thinking what an unnecessarily clanking noise his nailed boots made upon the hard white road, there came upon him with a rush together the company of these things that haunted him as 'unexplained'. They brought a single definite message: That all this business was not really meant for him at all, and hence his confusion and bewilderment; that he had intruded into someone else's scenery, and was trespassing upon another's map of life. By some wrong *inner* turning he had interpolated his person into a group of foreign forces which operated in the little world of someone else. Unwittingly, somewhere, he had crossed the threshold, and now was fairly in—a trespasser, an eavesdropper, a Peeping Tom. He was listening, peeping; overhearing things he had no right to know, because they were intended for another. Like a ship at sea he was intercepting wireless messages he could not properly interpret, because his Receiver was not accurately tuned to their reception. And more—these messages were warnings!

Then fear dropped upon him like the night. He was caught in a net of delicate, deep forces he could not manage, knowing neither their origin nor purpose. He had walked into some huge psychic trap elaborately planned and baited, yet calculated for another than himself. Something had lured him in, something in the landscape, the time of day, his mood. Owing to some undiscovered weakness in himself he had been easily caught. His fear slipped easily into terror.

What happened next happened with such speed and concentration that it all seemed crammed into a moment. At once and in a heap it happened. It was quite inevitable. Down the white road to meet him a man came swaying from side to side in drunkenness quite obviously feigned—a tramp; and while Martin made room for him to pass, the lurch changed in a second to attack, and the fellow was upon him. The blow was sudden and terrific, yet even while it fell Martin was aware that behind him rushed a second man, who caught his legs from under him and bore him with a thud and crash to the ground. Blows rained then; he saw a gleam of something shining; a sudden deadly nausea plunged him into utter weakness where resistance was impossible. Something of fire entered his throat, and from his mouth poured a thick sweet thing that choked him. The world sank far away into darkness... Yet through all the horror and confusion ran the trail of two clear thoughts: he realised that the first tramp had sneaked at a fast double through the heather and so come to meet him; and that something heavy was torn from fastenings that clipped it tight and close beneath his clothes against his body...

Abruptly then the darkness lifted, passed utterly away. He found himself peering into the map against the sign-post. The wind was flapping the corners against his cheek, and he was poring over names that now he saw quite clear. Upon the arms of the sign-post above were those he had expected to find, and the map recorded them quite faithfully. All was accurate again and as it should be. He read the name of the village he had meant to make—it was plainly visible in the dusk, two miles the distance given. Bewildered, shaken, unable to think of anything, he stuffed the map into his pocket unfolded, and hurried forward like a man who has just wakened from an awful dream that had compressed into a single second all the detailed misery of some prolonged, oppressive nightmare.

He broke into a steady trot that soon became a run; the perspiration poured from him; his legs felt weak, and his breath was difficult to manage. He was only conscious of the overpowering desire to get away as fast as possible from the sign-post at the cross-roads where the dreadful vision had flashed upon him. For Martin, accountant on a holiday, had never dreamed of any world of psychic possibilities. The entire thing was torture. It was worse than a 'cooked' balance of the books that some conspiracy of clerks and directors proved at his innocent door. He raced as though the country-side ran crying at his heels. And always still ran with him the incredible conviction that none of this was really meant for himself at all. He had overheard the secrets of another. He had taken the warning for another into himself, and so altered its direction. He had thereby prevented its right delivery. It all shocked him beyond words. It dislocated the machinery of his just and accurate soul. The warning was intended for another, who could not—would not—now receive it.

The physical exertion, however, brought at length a more comfortable reaction and some measure of composure. With the lights in sight, he slowed down and entered the village at a reasonable pace. The inn was reached, a bedroom inspected and engaged, and supper ordered with the solid comfort of a large Bass to satisfy an unholy thirst and complete the restoration of balance. The unusual sensations largely passed away, and the odd feeling that anything in his simple, wholesome world required explanation was no longer present. Still with a vague uneasiness about him, though actual fear quite gone, he went into the bar to smoke an after-supper pipe and chat with the natives, as his pleasure was upon a holiday, and so saw two men leaning upon the counter at the far end with their backs towards him. He saw their faces instantly in the glass, and the pipe nearly slipped from between his teeth. Clean-shaven, sleek clever faces—and he caught a word or two as they talked over their drinks—German words. Well dressed they were, both men, with nothing about them calling for particular attention; they might have been two tourists holiday-making like himself in tweeds and walking-boots. And they presently paid for their drinks and went out. He never saw them face to face at all; but the sweat broke out afresh all over him, a feverish rush of heat and ice together ran about his body; beyond question he recognised the two tramps, this time not disguised—*not yet* disguised.

He remained in his corner without moving, puffing violently at an extinguished pipe, gripped helplessly by the return of that first vile terror. It came again to him with an absolute clarity of certainty that it was not with himself they had to do, these men, and, further, that he had no right in the world to interfere. He had no *locus standi* at all; it would be immoral... even if the opportunity came. And the opportunity, he felt, would come. He had been an eavesdropper, and had come upon private information of a secret kind that he had no right to make use of, even that good might come—even to save life. He sat on in his corner, terrified and silent, waiting for the thing that should happen next.

But night came without explanation. Nothing happened. He slept soundly. There was no other guest at the inn but an elderly man, apparently a tourist like himself. He wore gold-rimmed glasses, and in the morning Martin overheard him asking the landlord what direction he should take for Litacy Hill. His teeth began then to chatter and a weakness came into his knees. 'You turn to the left at the cross-roads,' Martin broke in before the landlord could reply; 'you'll see the sign-post about two miles from here, and after that it's a matter of four miles more.' How in the world did he know, flashed horribly through him. 'I'm going that way myself,' he was saying next; 'I'll go with you for a bit—if you don't mind!' The words came out impulsively and ill-considered; of their own accord they came. For his own direction was exactly opposite. *He did not want the man to go alone.* The stranger, however, easily evaded his offer of companionship.

He thanked him with the remark that he was starting later in the day... They were standing, all three, beside the horse-trough in front of the inn, when at that very moment a tramp, slouching along the road, looked up and asked the time of day. And it was the man with the gold-rimmed glasses who told him.

'T'ank you; much opliged,' the tramp replied, passing on with his slow, slouching gait, while the landlord, a talkative fellow, proceeded to remark upon the number of Germans that lived in England and were ready to swell the Teutonic invasion which *he*, for his part, deemed imminent.

But Martin heard it not. Before he had gone a mile upon his way he went into the woods to fight his conscience all alone. His feebleness, his cowardice were surely criminal. Real anguish tortured him. A dozen times he decided to go back upon his steps, and a dozen times the singular authority that whispered he had no right to interfere prevented him. How could he act upon knowledge gained by eavesdropping? How interfere in the private business of another's hidden life merely because he had overheard, as at the telephone, its secret dangers? Some inner confusion prevented straight thinking altogether. The stranger would merely think him mad. He had no 'fact' to go upon... He smothered a hundred impulses... and finally went on his way with a shaking, troubled heart.

The last two days of his holiday were ruined by doubts and questions and alarms—all justified later when he read of the murder of a tourist upon Litacy Hill. The man wore gold-rimmed glasses, and carried in a belt about his person a large sum of money. His throat was cut. And the police were hard upon the trail of a mysterious pair of tramps, said to be—Germans.

# THE GLAMOUR OF THE SNOW

## I

Hibbert, always conscious of two worlds, was in this mountain village conscious of three. It lay on the slopes of the Valais Alps, and he had taken a room in the little post office, where he could be at peace to write his book, yet at the same time enjoy the winter sports and find companionship in the hotels when he wanted it.

The three worlds that met and mingled here seemed to his imaginative temperament very obvious, though it is doubtful if another mind less intuitively equipped would have seen them so well-defined. There was the world of tourist English, civilised, quasi-educated, to which he belonged by birth, at any rate; there was the world of peasants to which he felt himself drawn by sympathy—for he loved and admired their toiling, simple life; and there was this other—which he could only call the world of Nature. To this last, however, in virtue of a vehement poetic imagination, and a tumultuous pagan instinct fed by his very blood, he felt that most of him belonged. The others borrowed from it, as it were, for visits. Here, with the soul of Nature, hid his central life.

Between all three was conflict—potential conflict. On the skating-rink each Sunday the tourists regarded the natives as intruders; in the church the peasants plainly questioned: 'Why do you come? We are here to worship; you to stare and whisper!' For neither of these two worlds accepted the other. And neither did Nature accept the tourists, for it took advantage of their least mistakes, and indeed, even of the peasant-world 'accepted' only those who were strong and bold enough to invade her savage domain with sufficient skill to protect themselves from several forms of—death.

Now Hibbert was keenly aware of this potential conflict and

want of harmony; he felt outside, yet caught by it—torn in the three directions because he was partly of each world, but wholly in only one. There grew in him a constant, subtle effort—or, at least, desire—to unify them and decide positively to which he should belong and live in. The attempt, of course, was largely subconscious. It was the natural instinct of a richly imaginative nature seeking the point of equilibrium, so that the mind could feel at peace and his brain be free to do good work.

Among the guests no one especially claimed his interest. The men were nice but undistinguished—athletic schoolmasters, doctors snatching a holiday, good fellows all; the women, equally various—the clever, the would-be-fast, the dare-to-be-dull, the women 'who understood', and the usual pack of jolly dancing girls and 'flappers'. And Hibbert, with his forty odd years of thick experience behind him, got on well with the lot; he understood them all; they belonged to definite, predigested types that are the same the world over, and that he had met the world over long ago.

But to none of them did he belong. His nature was too 'multiple' to subscribe to the set of shibboleths of any one class. And, since all liked him, and felt that somehow he seemed outside of them—spectator, looker-on—all sought to claim him.

In a sense, therefore, the three worlds fought for him: natives, tourists, Nature...

It was thus began the singular conflict for the soul of Hibbert. *In* his own soul, however, it took place. Neither the peasants nor the tourists were conscious that they fought for anything. And Nature, they say, is merely blind and automatic.

The assault upon him of the peasants may be left out of account, for it is obvious that they stood no chance of success. The tourist world, however, made a gallant effort to subdue him to themselves. But the evenings in the hotel, when dancing was not in order, were—English. The provincial imagination was set upon a throne and worshipped heavily through incense of the stupidest conventions possible. Hibbert used to go back early to his room in the post office to work.

'It is a mistake on my part to have *realised* that there is any conflict at all,' he thought, as he crunched home over the snow at midnight after one of the dances. 'It would have been better to have kept outside it all and done my work. Better,' he added, looking back down the silent village street to the church tower, 'and—safer.'

The adjective slipped from his mind before he was aware of it. He turned with an involuntary start and looked about him. He knew perfectly well what it meant—this thought that had thrust its head up from the instinctive region. He understood, without being able to express it fully, the meaning that betrayed itself in the choice of the adjective. For if he had ignored the existence of this conflict he would at the same time have remained outside the arena. Whereas now he had entered the lists. Now this battle for his soul must have issue. And he knew that the spell of Nature was greater for him than all other spells in the world combined—greater than love, revelry, pleasure, greater even than study. He had always been afraid to let himself go. His pagan soul dreaded her terrific powers of witchery even while he worshipped.

The little village already slept. The world lay smothered in snow. The chalet roofs shone white beneath the moon, and pitch-black shadows gathered against the walls of the church. His eye rested a moment on the square stone tower with its frosted cross that pointed to the sky: then travelled with a leap of many thousand feet to the enormous mountains that brushed the brilliant stars. Like a forest rose the huge peaks above the slumbering village, measuring the night and heavens. They beckoned him. And something born of the snowy desolation, born of the midnight and the silent grandeur, born of the great listening hollows of the night, something that lay 'twixt terror and wonder, dropped from the vast wintry spaces down into his heart—and called him. Very softly, unrecorded in any word or thought his brain could compass, it laid its spell upon him. Fingers of snow brushed the surface of his heart. The power and quiet majesty of the winter's night appalled him...

Fumbling a moment with the big unwieldy key, he let himself in and went upstairs to bed. Two thoughts went with him—apparently quite ordinary and sensible ones:

'What fools these peasants are to sleep through such a night!' And the other:

'Those dances tire me. I'll never go again. My work only suffers in the morning.' The claims of peasants and tourists upon him seemed thus in a single instant weakened.

The clash of battle troubled half his dreams. Nature had sent her Beauty of the Night and won the first assault. The others, routed and dismayed, fled far away.

## II

'Don't go back to your dreary old post office. We're going to have supper in my room—something hot. Come and join us. Hurry up!'

There had been an ice carnival, and the last party, trailing up the snow-slope to the hotel, called him. The Chinese lanterns smoked and sputtered on the wires; the band had long since gone. The cold was bitter and the moon came only momentarily between high, driving clouds. From the shed where the people changed from skates to snow-boots he shouted something to the effect that he was 'following'; but no answer came; the moving shadows of those who had called were already merged high up against the village darkness. The voice died away. Doors slammed. Hibbert found himself alone on the deserted rink.

And it was then, quite suddenly, the impulse came to—stay and skate alone. The thought of the stuffy hotel room, and of those noisy people with their obvious jokes and laughter, oppressed him. He felt a longing to be alone with the night, to taste her wonder all by himself there beneath the stars, gliding over the ice. It was not yet midnight, and he could skate for half an hour. That supper party, if they noticed his absence at all, would merely think he had changed his mind and gone to bed.

It was an impulse, yes, and not an unnatural one; yet even at the time it struck him that something more than impulse lay concealed behind it. More than invitation, yet certainly less than command, there was a vague queer feeling that he stayed because he had to, almost as though there was something he had forgotten, overlooked, left undone. Imaginative temperaments are often thus; and impulse is ever weakness. For with such ill-considered opening of the doors to hasty action may come an invasion of other forces at the same time—forces merely waiting their opportunity perhaps!

He caught the fugitive warning even while he dismissed it as absurd, and the next minute he was whirling over the smooth ice in delightful curves and loops beneath the moon. There was no fear of collision. He could take his own speed and space as he willed. The shadows of the towering mountains fell across the rink, and a wind of ice came from the forests, where the snow lay ten feet deep. The hotel lights winked and went out. The village slept. The high wire netting could not keep out the wonder of the winter night that grew about him like a presence. He skated on and on, keen exhilarating pleasure in his tingling blood, and weariness all forgotten.

And then, midway in the delight of rushing movement, he saw a figure gliding behind the wire netting, watching him. With a start that almost made him lose his balance—for the abruptness of the new arrival was so unlooked for—he paused and stared. Although the light was dim he made out that it was the figure of a woman and that she was feeling her way along the netting, trying to get in. Against the white background of the snow-field he watched her rather stealthy efforts as she passed with a silent step over the banked-up snow. She was tall and slim and graceful; he could see that even in the dark. And then, of course, he understood. It was another adventurous skater like himself, stolen down unawares from hotel or chalet, and searching for the opening. At once, making a sign and pointing with one hand, he turned swiftly and skated over to the little entrance on the other side.

But, even before he got there, there was a sound on the ice behind him, and with an exclamation of amazement he could not suppress, he turned to see her swerving up to his side across the width of the rink. She had somehow found another way in.

Hibbert, as a rule, was punctilious, and in these free-and-easy places, perhaps, especially so. If only for his own protection he did not seek to make advances unless some kind of introduction paved the way. But for these two to skate together in the semi-darkness without speech, often of necessity brushing shoulders almost, was too absurd to think of. Accordingly he raised his cap and spoke. His actual words he seems unable to recall, nor what the girl said in reply, except that she answered him in accented English with some common place about doing figures at midnight on an empty rink. Quite natural it was, and right. She wore grey clothes of some kind, though not the customary long gloves or sweater, for indeed her hands were bare, and presently when he skated with her, he wondered with something like astonishment at their dry and icy coldness.

And she was delicious to skate with—supple, sure, and light, fast as a man yet with the freedom of a child, sinuous and steady at the same time. Her flexibility made him wonder, and when he asked where she had learned she murmured—he caught the breath against his ear and recalled later that it was singularly cold—that she could hardly tell, for she had been accustomed to the ice ever since she could remember.

But her face he never properly saw. A muffler of white fur buried her neck to the ears, and her cap came over the eyes. He only saw that she was young. Nor could he gather her hotel or chalet, for she pointed vaguely, when he asked her, up the slopes. 'Just over there——' she said, quickly taking his hand again. He did not press her; no doubt she wished to hide her escapade. And the touch of her hand thrilled him more than anything he could remember; even through his thick glove he felt the softness of that cold and delicate softness.

The clouds thickened over the mountains. It grew darker.

They talked very little, and did not always skate together. Often they separated, curving about in corners by themselves, but always coming together again in the centre of the rink; and when she left him thus Hibbert was conscious of—yes, of missing her. He found a peculiar satisfaction, almost a fascination, in skating by her side. It was quite an adventure—these two strangers with the ice and snow and night!

Midnight had long since sounded from the old church tower before they parted. She gave the sign, and he skated quickly to the shed, meaning to find a seat and help her take her skates off. Yet when he turned—she had already gone. He saw her slim figure gliding away across the snow... and hurrying for the last time round the rink alone he searched in vain for the opening she had twice used in this curious way.

'How very queer!' he thought, referring to the wire netting. 'She must have lifted it and wriggled under... !'

Wondering how in the world she managed it, what in the world had possessed him to be so free with her, and who in the world she was, he went up the steep slope to the post office and so to bed, her promise to come again another night still ringing delightfully in his ears. And curious were the thoughts and sensations that accompanied him. Most of all, perhaps, was the half suggestion of some dim memory that he had known this girl before, had met her somewhere, more—that she knew him. For in her voice—a low, soft, windy little voice it was, tender and soothing for all its quiet coldness—there lay some faint reminder of two others he had known, both long since gone; the voice of the woman he had loved, and—the voice of his mother.

But this time through his dreams there ran no clash of battle. He was conscious, rather, of something cold and clinging that made him think of sifting snowflakes climbing slowly with entangling touch and thickness round his feet. The snow, coming without noise, each flake so light and tiny none can mark the spot whereon it settles, yet the mass of it able to smother whole villages, wove through the very texture of his mind—cold, bewildering, deadening effort with its clinging network of the million feathery touches.

## III

In the morning Hibbert realised he had done, perhaps, a foolish thing. The brilliant sunshine that drenched the valley made him see this, and the sight of his work-table with its type-writer, books, papers, and the rest, brought additional conviction. To have skated with a girl alone at midnight, no matter how innocently the thing had come about, was unwise—unfair, especially to her. Gossip in these little winter resorts was worse than in a provincial town. He hoped no one had seen them. Luckily the night had been dark. Most likely none had heard the ring of skates.

Deciding that in future he would be more careful, he plunged into work and sought to dismiss the matter from his mind.

But in his times of leisure the memory returned persistently to haunt him. When he 'ski-d', 'luged', or danced in the evenings, and especially when he skated on the little rink, he was aware that the eyes of his mind forever sought this strange companion of the night. A hundred times he fancied that he saw her, but always sight deceived him. Her face he might not know, but he could hardly fail to recognise her figure. Yet nowhere among the others did he catch a glimpse of that slim young creature he had skated with alone beneath the clouded stars. He searched in vain. Even his inquiries as to the occupants of the private chalets brought no results. He had lost her. But the queer thing was that he felt as though she were somewhere close; he *knew* she had not really gone. While people came and left with every day, it never once occurred to him that she had left. On the contrary, he felt assured that they would meet again.

This thought he never quite acknowledged. Perhaps it was the wish that fathered it only. And, even when he did meet her, it was a question how he would speak and claim acquaintance, or whether *she* would recognise himself. It might be awkward. He almost came to dread a meeting, though 'dread', of course, was far too strong a word to describe an emotion that was half delight, half wondering anticipation.

Meanwhile the season was in full swing. Hibbert felt in perfect health, worked hard, ski-d, skated, luged, and at night danced fairly often—in spite of his decision. This dancing was, however, an act of subconscious surrender; it really meant he hoped to find her among the whirling couples. He was searching for her without quite acknowledging it to himself; and the hotel-world, meanwhile, thinking it had won him over, teased and chaffed him. He made excuses in a similar vein; but all the time he watched and searched and—waited.

For several days the sky held clear and bright and frosty, bitterly cold, everything crisp and sparkling in the sun; but there was no sign of fresh snow, and the skiers began to grumble. On the mountains was an icy crust that made 'running' dangerous; they wanted the frozen, dry, and powdery snow that makes for speed, renders steering easier and falling less severe. But the keen east wind showed no signs of changing for a whole ten days. Then, suddenly, there came a touch of softer air and the weather-wise began to prophesy.

Hibbert, who was delicately sensitive to the least change in earth or sky, was perhaps the first to feel it. Only he did not prophesy. He knew through every nerve in his body that moisture had crept into the air, was accumulating, and that presently a fall would come. For he responded to the moods of Nature like a fine barometer.

And the knowledge, this time, brought into his heart a strange little wayward motion that was hard to account for—a feeling of unexplained uneasiness and disquieting joy. For behind it, woven through it rather, ran a faint exhilaration that connected remotely somewhere with that touch of delicious alarm, that tiny anticipating 'dread', that so puzzled him when he thought of his next meeting with his skating companion of the night. It lay beyond all words, all telling, this queer relationship between the two; but somehow the girl and snow ran in a pair across his mind.

Perhaps for imaginative writing-men, more than for other workers, the smallest change of mood betrays itself at once. His work at any rate revealed this slight shifting of emotional values in his soul. Not that his writing suffered, but that it altered, subtly as those changes of sky or sea or landscape that come with the passing of afternoon into evening—imperceptibly. A subconscious excitement sought to push outwards and express itself... and, knowing the uneven effect such moods produced in his work, he laid his pen aside and took instead to reading what he had to do.

Meanwhile the brilliance passed form the sunshine, the sky grew slowly overcast; by dusk the mountain tops came singularly close and sharp; the distant valley rose into absurdly near perspective. The moisture increased, rapidly approaching saturation point, when it must fall in snow. Hibbert watched and waited.

And in the morning the world lay smothered beneath its fresh white carpet. It snowed heavily till noon, thickly, incessantly, chokingly, a foot or more; then the sky cleared, the sun came out in splendour, the wind shifted back to the east, and frost came down upon the mountains with its keenest and most biting tooth. The drop in the temperature was tremendous, but the skiers were jubilant. Next day the 'running' would be fast and perfect. Already the mass was settling, and the surface freezing into those moss-like, powdery crystals that make the skis run almost of their own accord with the faint 'sishing' as of a bird's wings through the air.

## IV

That night there was excitement in the little hotel-world, first because there was a *bal costumé*, but chiefly because the new snow had come. And Hibbert went—felt drawn to go; he did not go in costume, but he wanted to talk about the slopes and skiing with the other men, and at the same time...

Ah, there was the truth, the deeper necessity that called. For the singular connection between the stranger and the snow again betrayed itself, utterly beyond explanation as before, but vital and insistent. Some hidden instinct in his pagan soul—heaven knows how he phrased it even to himself, if he phrased it at all—whispered that with the snow the girl would be somewhere about, would emerge from her hiding place, would even look for him.

Absolutely unwarranted it was. He laughed while he stood before the little glass and trimmed his moustache, tried to make his black tie sit straight, and shook down his dinner jacket so that it should lie upon the shoulders without a crease. His brown eyes were very bright. 'I look younger than I usually do,' he thought. It was unusual, even significant, in a man who had no vanity about his appearance and certainly never questioned his age or tried to look younger than he was. Affairs of the heart, with one tumultuous exception, that left no fuel for lesser subsequent fires, had never troubled him. The forces of his soul and mind not called upon for 'work' and obvious duties, all went to Nature. The desolate, wild places of the earth were what he loved; night, and the beauty of the stars and snow. And this evening he felt their claims upon him mightily stirring. A rising wildness caught his blood, quickened his pulse, woke longing and passion too. But chiefly snow. The snow whirred softly through his thoughts like white, seductive dreams... For the snow had come; and She, it seemed, had somehow come with it—into his mind.

And yet he stood before that twisted mirror and pulled his tie and coat askew a dozen times, as though it mattered. 'What in the world is up with me?' he thought. Then, laughing a little, he turned before leaving the room to put his private papers in order. The green morocco desk that held them he took down from the shelf and laid upon the table. Tied to the lid was the visiting card with his brother's London address 'in case of accident'. On the way down to the hotel he wondered why he had done this, for though imaginative, he was not the kind of man who dealt in presentiments. Moods with him were strong, but ever held in leash.

'It's almost like a warning,' he thought, smiling. He drew his thick coat tightly round the throat as the freezing air bit at him. 'These warnings one reads of in stories sometimes...!'

A delicious happiness was in his blood. Over the edge of the hills across the valley rose the moon. He saw her silver sheet the world of snow. Snow covered all. It smothered sound and distance. It smothered houses, streets, and human beings. It smothered—life.

## V

In the hall there was light and bustle; people were already arriving from the other hotels and chalets, their costumes hidden beneath many wraps. Groups of men in evening dress stood about smoking, talking 'snow' and 'skiing'. The band was tuning up. The claims of the hotel-world clashed about him faintly as of old. At the big glass windows of the verandah, peasants stopped a moment on their way home from the *café* to peer. Hibbert thought laughingly of that conflict he used to imagine. He laughed bacause it suddenly seemed so unreal. He belonged so utterly to Nature and the mountains, and especially to those desolate slopes where now the snow lay thick and fresh and sweet, that there was no question of a conflict at all. The power of the newly fallen snow had caught him, proving it without effort. Out there, upon those lonely reaches of the moonlit ridges, the snow lay ready—masses and masses of it—cool, soft, inviting. He longed for it. It awaited him. He thought of the intoxicating delight of skiing in the moonlight. ...

Thus, somehow, in vivid flashing vision, he thought of it while he stood there smoking with the other men and talking all the 'shop' of skiing.

And, ever mysteriously blended with this power of the snow, poured also through his inner being the power of the girl. He could not disabuse his mind of the insinuating presence of the two together. He remembered that queer skating-impulse of ten days ago, the impulse that had let her in. That any mind, even an imaginative one, could pass beneath the sway of such a fancy was strange enough; and Hibbert, while fully aware of the disorder, yet found curious joy in yielding to it. This insubordinate centre that drew him towards old pagan beliefs had assumed command. With a kind of sensuous pleasure he let himself be conquered.

And snow that night seemed in everybody's thoughts. The dancing couples talked of it; the hotel proprietors congratulated one another; it meant good sport and satisfied their guests; every one was planning trips and expeditions, talking of slopes and telemarks, of flying speed and distance, of drifts and crust and frost. Vitality and enthusiasm pulsed in the very air; all were alert and active, positive, radiating currents of creative life even into the stuffy atmosphere of that crowded ball-room. And the snow had caused it, the snow had brought it; all this discharge of eager sparkling energy was due primarily to the—Snow.

But in the mind of Hibbert, by some swift alchemy of his pagan yearnings, this energy became transmuted. It rarefied itself, gleaming in white and crystal currents of passionate anticipation which he transferred, as by a species of electrical imagination into the personality of the girl—the Girl of the Snow. She somewhere was waiting for him, expecting him, calling to him softly from those leagues of moonlit mountain. He remembered the touch of that cool, dry hand; the soft and icy breath against his cheek; the hush and softness of her presence in the way she came and the way she had gone again—like a flurry of snow the wind sent gliding up the slopes. She, like himself, belonged out there. He fancied that he heard her little windy voice come sifting to him through the snowy branches of the trees, calling his name... that haunting little voice that dived straight to the centre of his life as once, long years ago, two other voices used to do. ...

But nowhere among the costumed dancers did he see her slender figure. He danced with one and all, distrait and absent, a stupid partner as each girl discovered, his eyes ever turning towards the door and windows, hoping to catch the luring face, the vision that did not come... and at length, hoping even against hope. For the ball-room thinned; groups left one by one, going home to their hotels and chalets; the band tired obviously; people sat drinking lemon-squashes at the little tables, the men mopping their foreheads, everybody ready for bed.

It was close on midnight. As Hibbert passed through the hall to get his overcoat and snow-boots, he saw men in the passage by the 'sport-room', greasing their skis against an early start. Knapsack luncheons were being ordered by the kitchen swing doors. He sighed. Lighting a cigarette a friend offered him, he returned a confused reply to some question as to whether he could join their party in the morning. It seemed he did not hear it properly. He passed through the outer vestibule between the double glass doors, and went into the night.

The man who asked the question watched him go, an expression of anxiety momentarily in his eyes.

'Don't think he heard you,' said another, laughing. 'You've got to shout to Hibbert, his mind's so full of his work.'

'He works too hard,' suggested the first, 'full of queer ideas and dreams.'

But Hibbert's silence was not rudeness. He had not caught the invitation, that was all. The call of the hotel world had faded. He no longer heard it. Another wilder call was sounding in his ears.

For up the street he had seen a little figure moving. Close against the shadows of the baker's shop it glided—white, slim, enticing.

## VI

And at once into his mind passed the hush and softness of the snow—yet with it a searching, crying wildness for the heights. He knew by some incalculable, swift instinct she would not meet him in the village street. It was not there, amid crowding houses, she would speak to him. Indeed, already she had disappeared, melted from view up the white vista of the moonlit road. Yonder, he divined, she waited where the highway narrowed abruptly into the mountain path beyond the chalets.

It did not even occur to him to hesitate; mad though it seemed, and was—this sudden craving for the heights with her, at least for open spaces where the snow lay thick and fresh—it was too imperious to be denied. He does not remember going up to his room putting the sweater over his evening clothes, and getting into the fur gauntlet gloves and the helmet cap of wool. Most certainly he has no recollection of fastening on his skis; he must have done it automatically. Some faculty of normal observation was in abeyance, as it were. His mind was out beyond the village—out with the snowy mountains and the moon.

Henri Défago, putting up the shutters over his *café* windows, saw him pass, and wondered mildly: 'Un monsieur qui fait du ski à cette heure! Il est Anglais, donc...!' He shrugged his shoulders, as though a man had the right to choose his own way of death. And Marthe Perotti, the hunchback wife of the shoemaker, looking by chance from her window, caught his figure moving swiftly up the road. She had other thoughts, for she knew and believed the old traditions of the witches and snow-beings that steal the souls of men. She had even heard, 'twas said, the dreaded 'synagogue' pass roaring down the street at night and now, as then, she hid her eyes. 'They've called to him... and he must go,' she murmured, making the sign of the cross.

But no one sought to stop him. Hibbert recalls only a single incident until he found himself beyond the houses, searching for her along the fringe of forest where the moonlight met the snow in a bewildering frieze of fantastic shadows. And the incident was simply this—that he remembered passing the church. Catching the outline of this tower against the stars, he was aware of a faint sense of hesitation. A vague uneasiness came and went—jarred unpleasantly across the flow of his excited feelings, chilling exhilaration. He caught the instant's discord, dismissed it, and—passed on. The seduction of the snow smothered the mind before he realised that it had brushed the skirts of warning.

And then he saw her. She stood there waiting in a little clear space of shining snow, dressed all in white, part of the moonlight and the glistening background, her slender figure just discernible.

'I waited, for I knew you would come,' the silvery little voice of windy beauty floated down to him. 'You *had* to come.'

'I'm ready,' he answered, 'I knew it too.'

The world of Nature caught him to its heart in those few words—the wonder and the glory of the night and snow. Life leaped within him. The passion of his pagan soul exulted, rose in joy, flowed out to her. He neither reflected nor considered, but let himself go like the veriest schoolboy in the wildness of first love.

'Give me your hand,' he cried, 'I'm coming... !'

'A little farther on, a little higher,' came her delicious answer. 'Here it is too near the village—and the church.'

And the words seemed wholly right and natural; he did not dream of questioning them; he understood that, with this little touch of civilisation in sight, the familiarity he suggested was impossible. Once out upon the open mountains, 'mid the freedom of huge slopes and towering peaks, the stars and moon to witness and the wilderness of snow to watch, they could taste an innocence of happy intercourse free from the dead conventions that imprison liberal minds.

He urged his pace, yet did not quite overtake her. The girl kept always just a little bit ahead of his best efforts.... And soon they left the trees behind and passed on to the enormous slopes of the sea of snow that rolled in mountainous terror and beauty to the stars. The wonder of the white world caught him away. Under the steady moonlight it was more than haunting. It was a living, white, bewildering power that deliciously confused the senses and laid a spell of wild perplexity upon the heart. It was a personality that cloaked, and yet revealed, itself through all this sheeted whiteness of snow. It rose, went with him, fled before, and followed after. Slowly it dropped lithe, gleaming arms about his neck, gathering him in. ...

Certainly some soft persuasion coaxed his very soul, urging him ever forwards, upwards, on towards the higher icy slopes. Judgment and reason left their throne, it seemed, completely, as in the madness of intoxication. The girl, slim and seductive, kept always just ahead, so that he never quite came up with her. He saw the white enchantment of her face and figure, something that streamed about her neck flying like a wreath of snow in the wind, and heard the alluring accents of her whispering voice that called from time to time: 'A little farther on, a little higher. ... Then we'll run home together!'

Sometimes he saw her hand stretched out to find his own, but each time, just as he came up with her, he saw her still in front, the hand and arm withdrawn. They took a gentle angle of ascent. The toil seemed nothing. In this crystal, wine-like air fatigue vanished. The sishing of the skis through the powdery surface of the snow was the only sound that broke the stillness; this, with his breathing and the rustle of her skirts, was all he heard. Cold moonshine, snow, and silence held the world. The sky was black and the peaks beyond cut into it like frosted wedges of iron and steel. Far below the valley slept the village long since hidden out of sight. He felt that he could never tire. ... The sound of the church clock rose from time to time faintly through the air—more and more distant.

'Give me your hand. It's time now to turn back.'

'Just one more slope,' she laughed. 'That ridge above us. Then we'll make for home.' And her low voice mingled pleasantly with the purring of their skis. His own seemed harsh and ugly by comparison.

'But I have never come so high before. It's glorious! This world of silent snow and moonlight—and *you*. You're a child of the snow, I swear. Let me come up—closer—to see your face—and touch your little hand.'

Her laughter answered him.

'Come on! A little higher. Here we're quite alone together.'

'It's magnificent,' he cried. 'But why did you hide away so long? I've looked and searched for you in vain ever since we skated——' he was going to say 'ten days ago', but the accurate memory of time had gone from him; he was not sure whether it was days or years or minutes. His thoughts of earth were scattered and confused.

'You looked for me in the wrong places,' he heard her murmur just above him. 'You looked in places where I never go. Hotels and houses kill me. I avoid them.' She laughed—a fine, shrill, windy little laugh.

'I loathe them too——'

He stopped. The girl had suddenly come quite close. A breath of ice passed through his very soul. She had touched him.

'But this awful cold!' he cried out sharply, 'this freezing cold that takes me. The wind is rising; it's a wind of ice. Come, let us turn...!'

But when he plunged forward to hold her, or at least to look, the girl was gone again. And something in the way she stood there a few feet beyond, and stared down into his eyes so steadfastly in silence, made him shiver. The moonlight was behind her, but in some odd way he could not focus sight upon her face, although so close. The gleam of eyes he caught, but all the rest seemed white and snowy as though he looked beyond her—out into space...

The sound of the church bell came up faintly from the valley far below, and he counted the strokes—five. A sudden, curious weakness seized him as he listened. Deep within it was, deadly yet somehow sweet, and hard to resist. He felt like sinking down upon the snow and lying there. ... They had been climbing for five hours. ... It was, of course, the warning of complete exhaustion.

With a great effort he fought and overcame it. It passed away as suddenly as it came.

'We'll turn,' he said with a decision he hardly felt. 'It will be dawn before we reach the village again. Come at once. It's time for home.'

The sense of exhilaration had utterly left him. An emotion that was akin to fear swept coldly through him. But her whispering answer turned it instantly to terror—a terror that gripped him horribly and turned him weak and unresisting.

'Our home is—*here*!' A burst of wild, high laughter, loud and shrill, accompanied the words. It was like a whistling wind.

The wind *had* risen, and clouds obscured the moon. 'A little higher—where we cannot hear the wicked bells,' she cried, and for the first time seized him deliberately by the hand. She moved, was suddenly close against his face. Again she touched him.

And Hibbert tried to turn away in escape, and so trying, found for the first time that the power of the snow—that other power which does not exhilarate but deadens effort—was upon him. The suffocating weakness that it brings to exhausted men, luring them to the sleep of death in her clinging soft embrace, lulling the will and conquering all desire for life—this was awfully upon him. His feet were heavy and entangled. He could not turn or move.

The girl stood in front of him, very near; he felt her chilly breath upon his cheeks; her hair passed blindingly across his eyes; and that icy wind came with her. He saw her whiteness close; again, it seemed, his sight passed through her into space as though she had no face. Her arms were round his neck. She drew him softly downwards to his knees. He sank; he yielded utterly; he obeyed. Her weight was upon him, smothering, delicious. The snow was to his waist. ... She kissed him softly on the lips, the eyes, all over his face. And then she spoke his name in that voice of love and wonder, the voice that held the accent of two others—both taken over long ago by Death—the voice of his mother, and of the woman he had loved.

He made one more feeble effort to resist. Then, realising even while he struggled that this soft weight about his heart was sweeter than anything life could ever bring, he let his muscles relax, and sank back into the soft oblivion of the covering snow. Her wintry kisses bore him into sleep.

## VII

They say that men who know the sleep of exhaustion in the snow find no awakening on the hither side of death. ... The hours passed and the moon sank down below the white world's rim. Then, suddenly, there came a little crash upon his breast and neck, and Hibbert—woke.

He slowly turned bewildered, heavy eyes upon the desolate mountains, stared dizzily about him, tried to rise. At first his muscles would not act; a numbing, aching pain possessed him. He uttered a long, thin cry for help, and heard its faintness swallowed by the wind. And then he understood vaguely why he was only warm—not dead. For this very wind that took his cry had built up a sheltering mound of driven snow against his body while he slept. Like a curving wave it ran beside him. It was the breaking of its over-toppling edge that caused the crash, and the coldness of the mass against his neck that woke him.

Dawn kissed the eastern sky; pale gleams of gold shot every peak with splendour; but ice was in the air, and the dry and frozen snow blew like powder from the surface of the slopes. He saw the points of his skis projecting just below him. Then he—remembered. It seems he had just strength enough to realise that, could he but rise and stand, he might fly with terrific impetus towards the woods and village far beneath. The skis would carry him. But if he failed and fell... !

How he contrived it Hibbert never knew; this fear of death somehow called out his whole available reserve force. He rose slowly, balanced a moment, then, taking the angle of an immense zigzag, started down the awful slopes like an arrow from a bow. And automatically the splendid muscles of the practised skier and athlete saved and guided him, for he was hardly conscious of controlling either speed or direction. The snow stung face and eyes like fine steel shot; ridge after ridge flew past; the summits raced across the sky; the valley leaped up with bounds to meet him. He scarcely felt the ground beneath his feet as the huge slopes and distance melted before the lightning speed of that descent from death to life.

He took it in four mile-long zigzags, and it was the turning at each corner that nearly finished him, for then the strain of balancing taxed to the verge of collapse the remnants of his strength.

Slopes that have taken hours to climb can be descended in a

short half-hour on skis, but Hibbert had lost all count of time. Quite other thoughts and feelings mastered him in that wild, swift dropping through the air that was like the flight of a bird. For ever close upon his heels came following forms and voices with the whirling snow-dust. He heard that little silvery voice of death and laughter at his back. Shrill and wild, with the whistling of the wind past his ears, he caught its pursuing tones; but in anger now, no longer soft and coaxing. And it was accompanied; she did not follow alone. It seemed a host of these flying figures of the snow chased madly just behind him. He felt them furiously smite his neck and cheeks, snatch at his hands and try to entangle his feet and skis in drifts. His eyes they blinded, and they caught his breath away.

The terror of the heights and snow and winter desolation urged him forward in the maddest race with death a human being ever knew; and so terrific was the speed that before the gold and crimson had left the summits to touch the ice-lips of the lower glaciers, he saw the friendly forest far beneath swing up and welcome him.

And it was then, moving slowly along the edge of the woods, he saw a light. A man was carrying it. A procession of human figures was passing in a dark line laboriously through the snow. And—he heard the sound of chanting.

Instinctively, without a second's hesitation, he changed his course. No longer flying at an angle as before, he pointed his skis straight down the mountain-side. The dreadful steepness did not frighten him. He knew full well it meant a crashing tumble at the bottom, but he also knew it meant a doubling of his speed—with safety at the end. For, though no definite thought passed through his mind, he understood that it was the village *curé* who carried that little gleaming lantern in the dawn, and that he was taking the Host to a chalet on the lower slopes—to some peasant *in extremis.* He remembered her terror of the church and bells. She feared the holy symbols.

There was one last wild cry in his ears as he started, a shriek of the wind before his face, and a rush of stinging snow against closed eyelids—and then he dropped through empty space. Speed took sight from him. It seemed he flew off the surface of the world.

* * *

Indistinctly he recalls the murmur of men's voices, the touch of strong arms that lifted him, and the shooting pains as the skis were unfastened from the twisted ankle... for when he opened his eyes again to normal life he found himself lying in his bed at the post office with the doctor at his side. But for years to come the story of 'mad Hibbert's' skiing at night is recounted in that mountain village. He went, it seems, up slopes, and to a height that no man in his senses ever tried before. The tourists were agog about it for the rest of the season, and the very same day two of the bolder men went over the actual ground and photographed the slopes. Later Hibbert saw these photographs. He noticed one curious thing about them—though he did not mention it to any one:

There was only a single track.

# THE HOUSE OF THE PAST

One night a Dream came to me and brought with her an old and rusty key. She led me across fields and sweet smelling lanes, where the hedges were already whispering to one another in the dark of the spring, till we came to a huge, gaunt house with staring windows and lofty roof half hidden in the shadows of very early morning. I noticed that the blinds were of heavy black, and that the house seemed wrapped in absolute stillness.

'This,' she whispered in my ear, 'is the House of the Past. Come with me and we will go through some of its rooms and passages; but quickly, for I have not the key for long, and the night is very nearly over. Yet, perchance, you shall remember!'

The key made a dreadful noise as she turned it in the lock, and when the great door swung open into an empty hall and we went in, I heard sounds of whispering and weeping, and the rustling of clothes, as of people moving in their sleep and about to wake. Then, instantly, a spirit of intense sadness came over me, drenching me to the soul; my eyes began to burn and smart, and in my heart I became aware of a strange sensation as of the uncoiling of something that had been asleep for ages. My whole being, unable to resist, at once surrendered itself to the spirit of deepest melancholy, and the pain of my heart, as the Things moved and woke, became in a moment of time too strong for words...

As we advanced, the faint voices and sobbings fled away before us into the interior of the House, and I became conscious that the air was full of hands held aloft, of swaying garments, of drooping tresses, and of eyes so sad and wistful that the tears, which were already brimming in my own, held back for wonder at the sight of such intolerable yearning.

'Do not allow all this sadness to overwhelm you,' whispered the Dream at my side. 'It is not often They wake. They sleep for years and years and years. The chambers are all full, and unless visitors such as we come to disturb them, they will never wake of their own accord. But, when one stirs, the sleep of the others is troubled, and they too awake, till the motion is communicated from one room to another and thus finally throughout the whole House... Then, sometimes, the sadness is too great to be borne, and the mind weakens. For this reason Memory gives to them the sweetest and deepest sleep she has, and she keeps this old key rusty from little use. But, listen now,' she added, holding up her hand: 'do you not hear all through the House that trembling of the air like the distant murmur of falling water? And do you not now... perhaps... *remember*?'

Even before she spoke, I had already caught faintly the beginning of a new sound; and, now, deep in the cellars beneath our feet, and from the upper regions of the great House as well, I heard the whispering, and the rustling and the inward stirring of the sleeping Shadows. It rose like a chord swept softly from huge unseen strings stretched somewhere among the foundations of the House, and its tremblings ran gently through its walls and ceilings. And I knew that I heard the slow awakening of the Ghosts of the Past.

Ah, me, with what terrible inrushing of sadness I stood with brimming eyes and listened to the faint dead voices of the long ago... For, indeed, the whole House was awakening; and there presently rose to my nostrils the subtle, penetrating perfume of age: of letters, long preserved, with ink faded and ribbons pale; of scented tresses, golden and brown, laid away, ah, how tenderly! among pressed flowers that still held the inmost delicacy of their forgotten fragrance; the scented presence of lost memories—the intoxicating incense of the past. My eyes o'erflowed, my heart tightened and expanded, as I yielded myself up without reserve to these old, old influences of sound and smell. These Ghosts of the Past—forgotten in the tumult of more recent memories—thronged round me, took my hands in theirs, and, ever whispering of what I had so long forgot, ever sighing, shaking from their hair and garments the ineffable odours of the dead ages, led me through the vast House, from room to room, from floor to floor.

And the Ghosts—were not all equally clear to me. Some had indeed but the faintest life, and stirred me so little that they left only an indistinct, blurred impression in the air; while others gazed half reproachfully at me out of faded, colourless eyes, as if longing to recall themselves to my recollection; and then, seeing they were not recognised, floated back gently into the shadows of their room, to sleep again undisturbed till the Final Day, when I should not fail to know them.

'Many of them have slept so long,' said the Dream beside me, 'that they wake only with the greatest difficulty. Once awake, however, they know and remember *you* even though you fail to remember them. For it is the rule in this House of the Past that, unless you recall them distinctly, remembering precisely when you knew them and with what particular causes in your past evolution they were associated, they cannot stay awake. Unless you remember them when your eyes meet, unless their look of recognition is returned by you, they are obliged to go back to their sleep, silent and sorrowful, their hands unpressed, their voices unheard, to sleep and dream, deathless and patient, till...'

At this moment, her words died away suddenly into the distance, and I became conscious of an overpowering sensation of delight and happiness. Something had touched me on the lips, and a strong, sweet fire flashed down into my heart and sent blood rushing tumultuously through my veins. My pulses beat wildly, my skin glowed, my eyes grew tender, and the terrible sadness of the place was instantly dispelled as if by magic. Turning with a cry of joy, that was at once swallowed up in the chorus of weeping and sighing round me, I looked... and instinctively stretched forth my arms in a rapture of happiness towards... towards a vision of a Face... hair, lips, eyes; a cloth of gold lay about the fair neck, and the old, old perfume of the East—ye stars, how long ago—was in her breath. Her lips were again on mine; her hair over my eyes; her arms about my neck, and the love of her ancient soul pouring into mine out of eyes still starry and undimmed. Oh, the fierce tumult, the untold wonder, if I could only remember!... That subtle, mist-dispelling odour of many ages ago, once so familiar... before the Hills of Atlantis were above the blue sea, or the sands had begun to form the bed of the Sphinx. Yet wait; it comes back; I begin to remember. Curtain upon curtain rises in my soul, and I can almost see beyond. But that hideous stretch of the years, awful and sinister, thousands upon thousands... My heart shakes, and I am afraid. Another curtain rises and a new vista, farther than the others, comes into view, interminable, running to a point among thick mists. Lo, they too are moving, rising, lightening. At last, I shall see... already I begin to recall... the dusky skin... the Eastern grace, the wondrous eyes that held the knowledge of Buddha and the wisdom of Christ before these had even dreamed of attainment. As a dream within a dream, it steals over me again, taking compelling possession of my whole being... the slender form... the stars in that magical Eastern sky... the whispering winds among the palm trees... the murmur of the river's waves and the music of the reeds where they bend and sigh in the shallows on the golden sand. Thousands of years ago in some aeonian distance. It fades a little and begins to pass; then seems again to rise. Ah me, that smile of the shining teeth... those lace-veined lids. Oh, who will help me to recall, for it is too far away, too dim, and I cannot wholly remember; though my lips are still tingling, and my arms still outstretched, it again begins to fade. Already there is a look of sadness too deep for words, as she realises that she is unrecognised... she, whose mere presence could once extinguish for me the entire universe... and she goes back slowly, mournfully, silently to her dim, tremendous sleep, to dream and dream of the day when I *must* remember her and she *must* come where she belongs...

She peers at me from the end of the room where the Shadows already cover her and win her back with outstretched arms to her age-long sleep in the House of the Past.

Trembling all over, with the strange odour still in my nostrils and the fire in my heart, I turned away and followed my Dream up a broad staircase into another part of the House.

As we entered the upper corridors I heard the wind pass singing over the roof. Its music took possession of me until I felt as though my whole body were a single heart, aching, straining, throbbing as if it would break; and all because I heard the wind singing round this House of the Past.

'But, remember,' whispered the Dream, answering my unspoken wonder, 'that you are listening to the song it has sung for untold ages into untold myriad ears. It carries back so appallingly far; and in that simple dirge, profound in its terrible monotony, are the associations and recollections, of the joys, griefs, and struggles of all your previous existence. The wind, like the sea, speaks to the inmost memory,' she added, 'and that is why its voice is one of such deep spiritual sadness. It is the song of things for ever incomplete, unfinished, unsatisfying.'

As we passed through the vaulted rooms, I noticed that no one stirred. There was no actual sound, only a general impression of deep, collective breathing, like the heave of a muffled ocean. But the rooms, I knew at once, were full to the walls, crowded, rows upon rows... And, from the floors below, rose ever the murmur of the weeping Shadows as they returned to their sleep, and settled down again in the silence, the darkness, and the dust. The dust... Ah, the dust that floated in this House of the Past, so thick, so penetrating; so fine, it filled the throat and eyes without pain; so fragrant, it soothed the senses and stilled the aching of the heart; so soft, it parched the tongue, without offence; yet so silently falling, gathering, settling over everything, that the air held it like a fine mist and the sleeping Shadows wore it for their shrouds.

'And these are the oldest,' said my Dream, 'the longest asleep,' pointing to the crowded rows of silent sleepers. 'None here have wakened for ages too many to count; and even if they woke, you would not know them. They are, like the others, all your own, but they are the memories of your earliest stages along the great Path of Evolution. Some day, though, they will awake, and you must know them, and answer their questions, for they cannot die till they have exhausted themselves again through you who gave them birth.'

'Ah me,' I thought, only half listening to or understanding these last words, 'what mothers, fathers, brothers may then be asleep in this room; what faithful lovers, what true friends, what ancient enemies! And to think that some day they will step forth and confront me, and I shall meet their eyes again, claim them, know them, forgive, and be forgiven... the memories of all my Past...'

I turned to speak to the Dream at my side, but she was already fading into dimness, and, as I looked again, the whole House melted away into the flush of the eastern sky, and I heard the birds singing and saw the clouds overhead veiling the stars in the light of coming day.

# THE DECOY

It belonged to the category of unlovely houses about which an ugly superstition clings, one reason being, perhaps, its inability to inspire interest in itself without assistance. It seemed too ordinary to possess individuality, much less to exert an influence. Solid and ungainly, its huge bulk dwarfing the park timber, its best claim to notice was a negative one—it was unpretentious.

From the little hill its expressionless windows stared across the Kentish Weald, indifferent to weather, dreary in winter, bleak in spring, unblessed in summer. Some colossal hand had tossed it down, then let it starve to death, a country mansion that might well strain the adjectives of advertisers and find inheritors with difficulty. Its soul had fled, said some; it had committed suicide, thought others; and it was an inheritor, before he killed himself in the library, who thought this latter, yielding, apparently, to an hereditary taint in the family. For two other inheritors followed suit, with an interval of twenty years between them, and there was no clear reason to explain the three disasters. Only the first owner, indeed, lived permanently in the house, the others using it in the summer months and then deserting it with relief. Hence, when John Burley, present inheritor, assumed possession, he entered a house about which clung an ugly superstition, based, nevertheless, upon a series of undeniably ugly facts.

This century deals harshly with superstitious folk, deeming them fools or charlatans; but John Burley, robust, contemptuous of half lights, did not deal harshly with them, because he did not deal with them at all. He was hardly aware of their existence. He ignored them as he ignored, say, the Esquimaux, poets, and other human aspects that did not touch his scheme of life. A successful business man, he concentrated on what was real; he dealt with business people. His philanthropy, on a big scale, was also real; yet, though he would have denied it vehemently, he had his superstition as well. No man exists without some taint of superstition in his blood; the racial heritage is too rich to be escaped entirely. Burley's took this form—that unless he gave his tithe to the poor he would not prosper. This ugly mansion, he decided, would make an ideal Convalescent Home.

'Only cowards or lunatics kill themselves,' he declared flatly, when his use of the house was criticised. 'I'm neither one nor t'other.' He let out his gusty, boisterous laugh. In his invigorating atmosphere such weakness seemed contemptible, just as superstition in his presence seemed feeblest ignorance. Even its picturesqueness faded. 'I can't conceive,' he boomed, 'can't even imagine to myself,' he added emphatically, 'the state of mind in which a man can *think* of suicide, much less do it.' He threw his chest out with a challenging air. 'I tell you, Nancy, it's either cowardice or mania. And I've no use for either.'

Yet he was easy-going and good-humoured in his denunciation. He admitted his limitations with a hearty laugh his wife called noisy. Thus he made allowances for the fairy fears of sailorfolk, and had even been known to mention haunted ships his Companies owned. But he did so in the terms of tonnage and £ s. d. His scope was big; details were made for clerks.

His consent to pass a night in the mansion was the consent of a practical business man and philanthropist who dealt condescendingly with foolish human nature. It was based on the common-sense of tonnage and £ s. d. The local newspapers had revived the silly story of the suicides, calling attention to the effect of the superstition upon the fortunes of the house, and so, possibly, upon the fortunes of its present owner. But the mansion, otherwise a white elephant, was precisely ideal for his purpose, and so trivial a matter as spending a night in it should not stand in the way. 'We must take people as we find them, Nancy.'

His young wife had her motive, of course, in making the proposal, and, if she was amused by what she called 'spook-hunting', he saw no reason to refuse her the indulgence. He loved her, and took her as he found her—late in life. To allay the superstitions of prospective staff and patients and supporters, all, in fact, whose goodwill was necessary to success, he faced this boredom of a night in the building before its opening was announced. 'You see, John, if you, the owner, do this, it will nip damaging talk in the bud. If anything went wrong later it would only be put down to this suicide idea, this haunting influence. The Home will have a bad name from the start. There'll be endless trouble. It will be a failure.'

'You think my spending a night there will stop the nonsense?' he enquired.

'According to the old legend it breaks the spell,' she replied. 'That's the condition, anyhow.'

'But somebody's sure to die there sooner or later,' he objected. 'We can't prevent that.'

'We can prevent people whispering that they died unnaturally.' She explained the working of the public mind.

'I see,' he replied, his lip curling, yet quick to gauge the truth of what she told him about collective instinct.

'Unless *you* take poison in the hall,' she added laughingly, 'or elect to hang yourself with your braces from the hat peg.'

'I'll do it,' he agreed, after a moment's thought. 'I'll sit up with you. It will be like a honeymoon over again, you and I on the spree—eh?' He was even interested now; the boyish side of him was touched perhaps; but his enthusiasm was less when she explained that three was a better number than two on such an expedition.

'I've often done it before, John. We were always three.'

'Who?' he asked bluntly. He looked wonderingly at her, but she answered that if anything went wrong a party of three provided a better margin for help. It was sufficiently obvious. He listened and agreed. 'I'll get young Mortimer,' he suggested. 'Will he do?'

She hesitated. 'Well—he's cheery; he'll be interested, too. Yes, he's as good as another.' She seemed indifferent.

'And he'll make the time pass with his stories,' added her husband.

So Captain Mortimer, late officer on a T.B.D., a 'cheery lad', afraid of nothing, cousin of Mrs. Burley, and now filling a good post in the company's London offices, was engaged as third hand in the expedition. But Captain Mortimer was young and ardent, and Mrs. Burley was young and pretty and ill-mated, and John Burley was a neglectful and self-satisfied husband.

Fate laid the trap with cunning, and John Burley, blind-eyed, careless of detail, floundered into it. He also floundered out again, though in a fashion none could have expected of him.

The night agreed upon eventually was as near to the shortest in the year as John Burley could contrive—June 18th—when the sun set at 8.18 and rose about a quarter to four. There would be barely three hours of true darkness. 'You're the expert,' he admitted, as she explained that sitting through the actual darkness only was required, not necessarily from sunset to sunrise. 'We'll do the thing properly. Mortimer's not very keen, he had a dance or something,' he added, noticing the look of annoyance that flashed swiftly in her eyes; 'but he got out of it. He's coming.' The pouting expression of the spoilt woman amused him. 'Oh, no, he didn't need much persuading really,' he assured her. 'Some girl or other, of course. He's young, remember.' To which no comment was forthcoming, though the implied comparison made her flush.

They motored from South Audley Street after an early tea, in due course passing Sevenoaks and entering the Kentish Weald; and, in order that the necessary advertisement should be given, the chauffeur, warned strictly to keep their purpose quiet, was to put up at the country inn and fetch them an hour after sunrise; they would breakfast in London. 'He'll tell everybody,' said his practical and cynical master; 'the local newspaper will have it all next day. A few hours' discomfort is worth while if it ends the nonsense. We'll read and smoke, and Mortimer shall tell us yarns about the sea.' He went with the driver into the house to superintend the arrangement of the room, the lights, the hampers of food, and so forth, leaving the pair upon the lawn.

'Four hours isn't much, but it's something,' whispered Mortimer, alone with her for the first time since they started. 'It's simply ripping of you to have got me in. You look divine to-night. You're the most wonderful woman in the world.' His blue eyes shone with the hungry desire he mistook for love. He looked as if he had blown in from the sea, for his skin was tanned and his light hair bleached a little by the sun. He took her hand, drawing her out of the slanting sunlight towards the rhododendrons.

'I didn't, you silly boy. It was John suggested your coming.' She released her hand with an affected effort. 'Besides, you overdid it—pretending you had a dance.'

'You could have objected,' he said eagerly, 'and didn't. Oh, you're too lovely, you're delicious!' He kissed her suddenly with passion. There was a tiny struggle, in which she yielded too easily, he thought.

'Harry, you're an idiot!' she cried breathlessly, when he let her go. 'I really don't know how you dare! And John's your friend. Besides, you know'—she glanced round quickly— 'it isn't safe her.' Here eyes shone happily, her cheeks were flaming. She looked what she was, a pretty, young, lustful animal, false to ideals, true to selfish passion only. 'Luckily,' she added, 'he trusts me too fully to think anything.'

The young man, worship in his eyes, laughed gaily. 'There's no harm in a kiss,' he said. 'You're a child to him, he never thinks of you as a woman. Anyhow, his head's full of ships and kings and sealing-wax,' he comforted her, while respecting her sudden instinct which warned him not to touch her again, 'and he never sees anything. Why, even at ten yards——'

From twenty yards away a big voice interrupted him, as John Burley came round a corner of the house and across the lawn towards them. The chauffeur, he announced, had left the hampers in the room on the first floor and gone back to the inn. 'Let's take a walk round,' he added, joining them, 'and see the garden. Five minutes before sunset we'll go in and feed.' He laughed. 'We must do the thing faithfully, you know, mustn't we, Nancy? Dark to dark, remember. Come on, Mortimer'—he took the young man's arm—'a last look round before we go in and hang ourselves from adjoining hooks in the matron's room!' He reached out his free hand towards his wife.

'Oh, hush, John!' she said quickly. 'I don't like—especially now the dusk is coming.' She shivered, as though it were a genuine little shiver, pursing her lips deliciously as she did so; whereupon he drew her forcibly to him, saying he was sorry, and kissed her exactly where she had been kissed two minutes before, while young Mortimer looked on. 'We'll take care of you between us,' he said. Behind a broad back the pair exchanged a swift but meaning glance, for there was that in his tone which enjoined wariness, and perhaps after all he was not so blind as he appeared. They had their code, these two. 'All's well,' was signalled; 'but another time be more careful!'

There still remained some minutes' sunlight before the huge red ball of fire would sink behind the wooded hills, and the trio, talking idly, a flutter of excitement in two hearts certainly, walked among the roses. It was a perfect evening, windless, perfumed, warm. Headless shadows preceded them gigantically across the lawn as they moved, and one side of the great building lay already dark; bats were flitting, moths darted to and fro above the azalea and rhododendron clumps. The talk turned chiefly on the uses of the mansion as a Convalescent Home, its probable running cost, suitable staff, and so forth.

'Come along,' John Burley said presently, breaking off and turning abruptly, 'we must be inside, actually inside, before the sun's gone. We must fulfil the conditions faithfully,' he repeated as though fond of the phrase. He was in earnest over everything in life, big or little, once he set his hand to it.

They entered, this incongruous trio of ghost-hunters, no one of them really intent upon the business in hand, and went slowly upstairs to the great room where the hampers lay. Already in the hall it was dark enough for three electric torches to flash usefully and help their steps as they moved with caution, lighting one corner after another. The air inside was chill and damp. 'Like an unused museum,' said Mortimer. 'I can smell the specimens.' They looked about them, sniffing. 'That's humanity,' declared his host, employer, friend, 'with cement and whitewash to flavour it'; and all three laughed as Mrs. Burley said she wished they had picked some roses and brought them in. Her husband was again in front on the broad staircase. Mortimer just behind him, when she called out. 'I don't like being last,' she exclaimed. 'It's so black behind me in the hall. I'll come between you two,' and the sailor took her outstretched hand, squeezing it, as he passed her up. 'There's a figure, remember,' she said hurriedly turning to gain her husband's attention, as when she touched wood at home. 'A figure is seen; that's part of the story. The figure of a man.' She gave a tiny shiver of pleasure, half-imagined alarm as she took his arm.

'I hope we shall see it,' he mentioned prosaically.

'I hope we shan't,' she replied with emphasis. 'It's only seen before—something happens.' Her husband said nothing, while Mortimer remarked facetiously that it would be a pity if they had their trouble for nothing. 'Something can hardly happen to all three of us,' he said lightly, as they entered a large room where the paper-hangers had conveniently left a rough table of bare planks. Mrs. Burley, busy with her own thoughts, began to unpack the sandwiches and wine. Her husband strolled over to the window. He seemed restless.

'So this'—his deep voice startled her—'is where one of us'—he looked round him—'is to——'

'John!' She stopped him sharply, with impatience. 'Several times already I've begged you.' Her voice rang rather shrill and querulous in the empty room, a new note in it. She was beginning to feel the atmosphere of the place, perhaps. On the sunny lawn it had not touched her, but now, with the fall of night, she was aware of it, as shadow called to shadow and the kingdom of darkness gathered power. Like a great whispering gallery, the whole house listened.

'Upon my word, Nancy,' he said with contrition, as he came and sat down beside her, 'I quite forgot again. Only I cannot take it seriously. It's utterly unthinkable to me that a man——'

'But why evoke the idea at all?' she insisted in a lowered voice, that snapped despite its faintness. 'Men, after all, don't do such things for nothing.'

'We don't know everything in the universe, do we?' Mortimer put in, trying clumsily to support her. 'All I know just now is that I'm famished and this veal and ham pie is delicious.' He was very busy with his knife and fork. His foot rested lightly on her own beneath the table; he could not keep his eyes off her face; he was continually passing new edibles to her.

'No,' agreed John Burley, 'not everything. You're right there.'

She kicked the younger man gently, flashing a warning with her eyes as well, while her husband, emptying his glass, his head thrown back, looked straight at them over the rim, apparently seeing nothing. They smoked their cigarettes round the table, Burley lighting a big cigar. 'Tell us about the figure, Nancy?' he inquired. 'At least there's no harm in that. It's new to me. I hadn't heard about a figure.' And she did so willingly, turning her chair sideways from the dangerous, reckless feet. Mortimer could now no longer touch her. 'I know very little,' she confessed; 'only what the paper said. It's a man... And he changes.'

'How changes?' asked her husband. 'Clothes, you mean, or what?'

Mrs. Burley laughed, as though she was glad to laugh. Then she answered: 'According to the story he shows himself each time to the man——'

'The man who——?'

'Yes, yes, of course. He appears to the man who dies—as himself.'

'H'm,' grunted her husband, naturally puzzled. He stared at her.

'Each time the chap saw his own double — Mortimer came this time usefully to the rescue—'before he did it.'

Considerable explanation followed, involving much psychic

jargon from Mrs. Burley, which fascinated and impressed the sailor, who thought her as wonderful as she was lovely, showing it in his eyes for all to see. John Burley's attention wandered. He moved over to the window, leaving them to finish the discussion between them; he took no part in it, made no comment even, merely listening idly and watching them with an air of absent-mindedness through the cloud of cigar smoke round his head. He moved from window to window, ensconcing himself in turn in each deep embrasure, examining the fastenings, measuring the thickness of the stonework with his handkerchief. He seemed restless, bored, obviously out of place in this ridiculous expedition. On his big massive face lay a quiet, resigned expression his wife had never seen before. She noticed it now as, the discussion ended, the pair tidied away the *débris* of dinner, lit the spirit lamp for coffee and laid out a supper which would be very welcome with the dawn. A draught passed through the room, making the papers flutter on the table. Mortimer turned down the smoking lamps with care.

'Wind's getting up a bit—from the south,' observed Burley from his niche, closing one-half of the casement window as he said it. To do this, he turned his back a moment, fumbling for several seconds with the latch, while Mortimer, noting it, seized his sudden opportunity with the foolish abandon of his age and temperament. Neither he nor his victim perceived that, against the outside darkness, the interior of the room was plainly reflected in the window-pane. One reckless, the other terrified, they snatched the fearful joy, which might, after all, have been lengthened by another full half-minute, for the head they feared, followed by the shoulders, pushed through the side of the casement still open, and remained outside, taking in the night.

'A grand air,' said his deep voice, as the head drew in again. 'I'd like to be at sea a night like this.' He left the casement open and came across the room towards them. 'Now,' he said cheerfully, arranging a seat for himself, 'let's get comfortable for the night. Mortimer, we expect stories from you without ceasing, until dawn or the ghost arrives. Horrible stories of chains and headless men, remember. Make it a night we shan't forget in a hurry.' He produced his gust of laughter.

They arranged their chairs, with other chairs to put their feet on, and Mortimer contrived a footstool by means of a hamper for the smallest feet; the air grew thick with tobacco smoke; eyes flashed and answered, watched perhaps as well; ears listened and perhaps grew wise; occasionally, as a window shook, they started and looked round; there were sounds about the house from time to time, when the entering wind, using broken or open windows, set loose objects rattling.

But Mrs. Burley vetoed horrible stories with decision. A big, empty mansion, lonely in the country, and even with the comfort of John Burley and a lover in it, has its atmosphere. Furnished rooms are far less ghostly. This atmosphere now came creeping everywhere, through spacious halls and sighing corridors, silent, invisible, but all-pervading, John Burley alone impervious to it, unaware of its soft attack upon the nerves. It entered possibly with the summer night wind, but possibly it was always there... And Mrs. Burley looked often at her husband, sitting near her at an angle; the light fell on his fine strong face; she felt that, though apparently so calm and quiet, he was really very restless; something about him was a little different; she could not define it; his mouth seemed set as with an effort; he looked, she thought curiously to herself, patient and very dignified; he was rather a dear after all. Why did she think the face inscrutable? Her thoughts wandered vaguely, unease, discomfort among them somewhere, while the heated blood—she had taken her share of wine—seethed in her.

Burley turned to the sailor for more stories. 'Sea and wind in them,' he asked. 'No horrors, remember!' And Mortimer told a tale about the shortage of rooms at a Welsh seaside place where spare rooms fetched fabulous prices, and one man alone refused to let—a retired captain of South Seas trader, very poor, a bit crazy apparently. He had two furnished rooms in his house worth twenty guineas a week. The rooms faced south; he kept them full of flowers; but he would not let. An explanation of his unworldily obstinacy was not forthcoming until Mortimer—they fished together—gained his confidence. 'The South Wind lives in them,' the old fellow told him. 'I keep them free for her.'

'For *her*?'

'It was on the South Wind my love came to me,' said the other softly; 'and it was on the South Wind that she left——'

It was an odd tale to tell in such company, but he told it well.

'Beautiful,' thought Mrs. Burley. Aloud she said a quiet, 'Thank you. By "left" I suppose he meant she died or ran away?'

John Burley looked up with a certain surprise. 'We ask for a story,' he said, 'and you give us a poem.' He laughed. 'You're in love, Mortimer,' he informed him, 'and with my wife, probably.'

'Of course I am, sir,' replied the young man gallantly. 'A sailor's heart, you know,' while the face of the woman turned pink, then white. She knew her husband more intimately than Mortimer did, and there was something in his tone, his eyes, his words, she did not like. Harry was an idiot to choose such a tale. An irritated annoyance stirred in her, close upon dislike. 'Anyhow, it's better than horrors,' she said hurriedly.

'Well,' put in her husband, letting forth a minor gust of laughter, 'it's possible, at any rate. Though one's as crazy as the other.' His meaning was not wholly clear. 'If a man really loved,' he added in his blunt fashion, 'and was tricked by her, I could almost conceive his——'

'Oh, don't preach, John, for Heaven's sake. You're so dull in the pulpit.' But the interruption only served to emphasise the sentence which, otherwise, might have been passed over.

'Could conceive his finding life so worthless,' persisted the other, 'that——' He hesitated. 'But there, now, I promised I wouldn't,' he went on, laughing good-humouredly. Then, suddenly, as though in spite of himself, driven it seemed: 'Still, under such conditions, he might show his contempt for human nature and for life by——'

It was a tiny stifled scream that stopped him this time.

'John, I hate, I loathe you, when you talk like that. And you've broken your word again.' She was more than petulant; a nervous anger sounded in her voice. It was the way he had said it, looking from them towards the window, that made her quiver. She felt him suddenly as a man; she felt afraid of him.

Her husband made no reply; he rose and looked at his watch, leaning sideways towards the lamp, so that the expression of his face was shaded. 'Two o'clock,' he remarked. 'I think I'll take a turn through the house. I may find a workman asleep or something. Anyhow, the light will soon come now.' He laughed; the expression of his face, his tone of voice, relieved her momentarily. He went out. They heard his heavy tread echoing down the carpetless long corridor.

Mortimer began at once. 'Did he mean anything?' he asked breathlessly. 'He doesn't love you the least little bit, anyhow. He never did. I do. You're wasted on him. You belong to me.' The words poured out. He covered her face with kisses. 'Oh. I didn't mean *that*,' he caught between the kisses.

The sailor released her, staring. 'What then?' he whispered. 'Do you think he saw us on the lawn?' He paused a moment, as she made no reply. The steps were audible in the distance still. 'I know!' he exclaimed suddenly. 'It's the blessed house he feels. That's what it is. He doesn't like it.'

A wind sighed through the room, making the papers flutter; something rattled; and Mrs. Burley started. A loose end of rope swinging from the paperhanger's ladder caught her eye. She shivered slightly.

'He's different,' she replied in a low voice, nestling very close again, 'and so restless. Didn't you notice what he said just now—that under certain conditions he could understand a man'—she hesitated—'doing it,' she concluded, a sudden drop in her voice. 'Harry,' she looked full into his eyes, 'that's not like him. He didn't say that for nothing.'

'Nonsense! He's bored to tears, that's all. And the house is getting on your nerves, too.' He kissed her tenderly. Then, as she responded, he drew her nearer still and held her passionately, mumbling incoherent words, among which 'nothing to be afraid of' was distinguishable. Meanwhile, the steps were coming nearer. She pushed him away. 'You must behave yourself. I insist. You shall, Harry.' Then buried herself in his arms, her face hidden against his neck—only to disentagle herself the next instant and stand clear of him. 'I hate you, Harry,' she exclaimed sharply, a look of angry annoyance flashing across her face. 'And I *hate* myself. Why do you treat me——?' She broke off as the steps came closer, patted her hair straight, and stalked over to the open window.

'I believe after all you're only playing with me,' he said viciously. He stared in surprised disappointment, watching her. 'It's him you really love,' he added jealously. He looked and spoke like a petulant spoilt boy.

She did not turn her head. 'He's always been fair to me, kind and generous. He never blames me for anything. Give me a cigarette, and don't play the stage hero. My nerves are on edge, to tell you the truth.' Her voice jarred harshly, and as he lit her cigarette he noticed that her lips were trembling; his own hand trembled too. He was still holding the match, standing beside her at the window-sill, when the steps crossed the threshold and John Burley came into the room. He went straight up to the table and turned the lamp down. 'It was smoking,' he remarked. 'Didn't you see?'

'I'm sorry, sir.' And Mortimer sprang forward too late to help him. 'It was the draught as you pushed the door open.' The big man said, 'Ah!' and drew a chair over, facing them. 'It's just *the* very house,' he told them. 'I've been through every room on this floor. It will make a splendid Home, with very little alteration, too.' He turned round in his creaking wicker chair and looked up at his wife, who sat swinging her legs and smoking in the window embrasure. 'Lives will be saved inside these old walls. It's a good investment,' he went on, talking rather to himself it seemed. 'People will die here, too——'

'Hark!' Mrs. Burley interrupted him. 'That noise—what is it?' A faint thudding sound in the corridor or in the adjoining room was audible, making all three look round quickly, listening for a repetition, which did not come. The papers fluttered on the table, the lamps smoked an instant.

'Wind,' observed Burley calmly, 'our little friend, the South Wind. Something blown over again, that's all.' But, curiously, the three of them stood up. 'I'll go and see,' he continued. 'Doors and windows are all open to let the paint dry.' Yet he did not move; he stood there watching a white moth that dashed round and round the lamp, flopping heavily now and again upon the bare deal table.

'Let me go, sir,' put in Mortimer eagerly. He was glad of the chance; for the first time he, too, felt uncomfortable. But there was another, who, apparently, suffered a discomfort greater than his own and was accordingly even more glad to get away. 'I'll go,' Mrs. Burley announced, with decision. 'I'd like to. I haven't been out of this room since we came. I'm not an atom afraid.'

It was strange that for a moment she did not make a move either; it seemed as if she waited for something. For perhaps fifteen seconds no one stirred or spoke. She knew by the look in her lover's eyes that he had now become aware of the slight, indefinite change in her husband's manner, and was alarmed by it. The fear in him woke her contempt; she suddenly despised the youth, and was conscious of a new, strange yearning towards her husband; against her worked nameless pressure, troubling her being. There was an alteration in the room, she thought; something had come in. The trio stood listening to the gentle wind outside, waiting for the sound to be repeated; two careless, passionate young lovers and a man stood waiting, listening, watching in that room; yet it seemed there were five persons altogether and not three, for two guilty consciences stood apart and separate from their owners. John Burley broke the silence.

'Yes, you go, Nancy. Nothing to be afraid of—there. It's only wind.' He spoke as though he meant it.

Mortimer bit his lips. 'I'll come with you,' he said instantly. He was confused. 'Let's all three go. I don't think we ought to be separated.' But Mrs. Burley was already at the door. 'I insist,' she said, with a forced laugh. 'I'll call if I'm frightened,' while her husband, saying nothing, watched her from the table.

'Take this,' said the sailor, flashing his electric torch as he went over to her. 'Two are better than one.' He saw her figure exquisitely silhouetted against the black corridor beyond; it was clear she wanted to go; any nervousness in her was mastered by a stronger emotion still; she was glad to be out of their presence for a bit. He had hoped to snatch a word of explanation in the corridor, but her manner stopped him. Something else stopped him, too.

'First door on the left,' he called out, his voice echoing down the empty length. 'That's the room where the noise came from. Shout if you want us.'

He watched her moving away, the light held steadily in front of her, but she made no answer, and he turned back to see John Burley lighting his cigar at the lamp chimney, his face thrust forward as he did so. He stood a second, watching him, as the lips sucked hard at the cigar to make it draw; the strength of the features was emphasised to sternness. He had meant to stand by the door and listen for the least sound from the adjoining room, but now found his whole attention focussed on the face above the lamp. In that minute he realised that Burley had wished—had meant—his wife to go. In that minute also he forgot his love, his shameless, selfish little mistress, his worthless, caddish little self. For John Burley looked up. He straightened slowly, puffing hard and quickly to make sure his cigar was lit, and faced him. Mortimer moved forward into the room, self-conscious, embarrassed, cold.

'Of course it was only wind,' he said lightly, his one desire being to fill the interval while they were alone with commonplaces. He did not wish the other to speak. 'Dawn wind, probably.' He glanced at his wrist-watch. 'It's half-past two already and the sun gets up at a quarter to four. It's light by now, I expect. The shortest night is never quite dark.' He rambled on confusedly, for the other's steady, silent stare embarrassed him.

A faint sound of Mrs. Burley moving in the next room made him stop a moment. He turned instinctively to the door, eager for an excuse to go.

'That's nothing,' said Burley, speaking at last and in a firm quiet voice. 'Only my wife, glad to be alone—my young and pretty wife. She's all right. I know her better than you do. Come in and shut the door.'

Mortimer obeyed. He closed the door and came close to the table, facing the other, who at once continued.

'If I thought,' he said, in that quiet deep voice, 'that you two were serious'—he uttered his words very slowly, with emphasis, with intense severity—'do you know what I should do? I will tell you, Mortimer. I should like one of us two—you or myself—to remain in this house, dead.'

His teeth gripped his cigar tightly; his hands were clenched; he went on through a half-closed mouth. His eyes blazed steadily.

'I trust her so absolutely—understand me?—that my belief in women, in human beings, would go. And with it the desire to live. Understand me?'

Each word to the young careless fool was a blow in the face, yet it was the softest blow, the flash of a big deep heart, that hurt the most. A dozen answers—denial, explanation, confession, taking all guilt upon himself—crowded his mind, only to be dismissed. He stood motionless and silent, staring hard into the other's eyes. No word passed his lips; there was no time in any case. It was in this position that Mrs. Burley, entering at that moment, found them. She saw her husband's face; the other man stood with his back to her. She came in with a little nervous laugh. 'A bell-rope swinging in the wind and hitting a sheet of metal before the fireplace,' she informed them. And all three laughed together then, though each laugh had a different sound. 'But I hate this house,' she added. 'I wish we had never come.'

'The moment there's light in the sky,' remarked her husband quietly, 'we can leave. That's the contract; let's see it through. Another half-hour will do it. Sit down, Nancy, and have a bit of something.' He got up and placed a chair for her. 'I think I'll take another look round.' He moved slowly to the door. 'I may go out on to the lawn a bit, and see what the sky is doing.'

It did not take half a minute to say the words, yet to Mortimer it seemed as though the voice would never end. His mind was confused and troubled. He loathed himself, he loathed the woman through whom he had got into this awkward mess.

The situation had suddenly become extremely painful; he had never imagined such a thing; the man he had thought blind had after all seen everything—known it all along, watched them, waited. And the woman, he was now certain, loved her husband; she had fooled him, Mortimer, all along, amusing herself.

'I'll come with you, sir. Do let me,' he said suddenly. Mrs. Burley stood pale and uncertain between them. She looked scared. What has happened, she was clearly wondering.

'No, no, Harry'—he called him 'Harry' for the first time—'I'll be back in five minutes at most. My wife mustn't be alone either.' And he went out.

The young man waited till the footsteps sounded some distance down the corridor, then turned, but he did not move forward; for the first time he let pass unused what he called 'an opportunity'. His passion had left him; his love, as he once thought it, was gone. He looked at the pretty woman near him, wondering blankly what he had ever seen there to attract him so wildly. He wished to Heaven he was out of it all. He wished he were dead. John Burley's words suddenly appalled him.

One thing he saw plainly—she was frightened. This opened his lips.

'What's the matter?' he asked, and his hushed voice shirked the familiar Christian name. 'Did you see anything?' He nodded his head in the direction of the adjoining room. It was the sound of his own voice addressing her coldly that made him abruptly see himself as he really was, but it was her reply, honestly given, in a faint even voice, that told him she saw her own self too with similar clarity. God, he thought, how revealing a tone, a single word can be!

'I saw—nothing. Only I feel uneasy—dear.' That 'dear' was a call for help.

'Look here,' he cried, so loud that she held up a warning finger, 'I'm—I've been a damned fool, a cad! I'm most frightfully ashamed. I'll do anything—*anything* to get it right.' He felt cold, naked, his worthlessness laid bare; she felt, he knew, the same. Each revolted suddenly from the other. Yet he knew not quite how or wherefore this great change had thus abruptly come about, especially on her side. He felt that a bigger, deeper emotion than he could understand was working on them, making mere physical relationships seem empty, trivial, cheap and vulgar. His cold increased in face of this utter ignorance.

'Uneasy?' he repeated, perhaps hardly knowing exactly why he said it. 'Good Lord, but he can take care of himself——'

'Oh, *he* is a man,' she interrupted; 'yes.'

Steps were heard, firm, heavy steps, coming back along the corridor. It seemed to Mortimer that he had listened to this sound of steps all night, and would listen to them till he died. He crossed to the lamp and lit a cigarette, carefully this time, turning the wick down afterwards. Mrs. Burley also rose, moving over towards the door, away from him. They listened a moment to these firm and heavy steps, the tread of a man, John Burley. A man... and a philanderer, flashed across Mortimer's brain like fire, contrasting the two with fierce contempt for himself. The tread became less audible. There was distance in it. It had turned in somewhere.

'There!' she exclaimed in a hushed tone. 'He's gone in.'

'Nonsense! It passed us. He's going out on to the lawn.'

The pair listened breathlessly for a moment, when the sound of steps came distinctly from the adjoining room, walking across the boards, apparently towards the window.

'There!' she repeated. 'He did go in.'

Silence of perhaps a minute followed, in which they heard each other's breathing. 'I don't like being alone—in there,' Mrs. Burley said in a thin faltering voice, and moved as though to go out. Her hand was already on the knob of the door, when Mortimer stopped her with a violent gesture.

'Don't! For God's sake, don't!' he cried, before she could turn it. He darted forward. As he laid a hand upon her arm a thud was audible through the wall. It was a heavy sound, and this time there was no wind to cause it.

It's only that loose swinging thing,' he whispered thickly, a dreadful confusion blotting out clear thought and speech.

'There was no loose swaying thing at all,' she said in a failing voice, then reeled and swayed against him. 'I invented that. There was nothing.' As he caught her, staring helplessly, it seemed to him that a face with lifted lids rushed up at him. He saw two terrified eyes in a patch of ghastly white. Her whisper followed, as she sank into his arms. 'It's John, he's——'

At which instant, with terror at its climax, the sound of steps suddenly became audible once more—the firm and heavy tread of John Burley coming out again into the corridor. Such was their amazement and relief that they neither moved nor spoke. The steps drew nearer. The pair seemed petrified; Mortimer did not remove his arms, nor did Mrs. Burley attempt to release herself. They stared at the door and waited. It was pushed wider the next second, and John Burley stood beside them. He was so close he almost touched them—there in each other's arms.

'Jack, dear!' cried his wife, with a searching tenderness that made her voice seem strange.

He gazed a second at each in turn. 'I'm going out on to the lawn for a moment,' he said quietly. There was no expression on his face; he did not smile, he did not frown; he showed no feeling, no emotion—just looked into their eyes, and then withdrew round the edge of the door before either could utter a word in answer. The door swung to behind him. He was gone.

'He's going to the lawn. He said so.' It was Mortimer speaking, but his voice shook and stammered. Mrs. Burley had released herself. She stood now by the table, silent, gazing with fixed eyes at nothing, her lips parted, her expression vacant. Again she was aware of an alteration in the room: something had gone out. ... He watched her a second, uncertain what to say or do. It was the face of a drowned person, occurred to him. Something intangible, yet almost visible stood between them in that narrow space. Something had ended, there before his eyes, definitely ended. The barrier between them rose higher, denser. Through this barrier her words came to him with an odd whispering remoteness.

'Harry. ... You saw? You noticed?'

'What d'you mean?' he said gruffly. He tried to feel angry, contemptuous, but his breath caught absurdly.

'Harry—he was different. The eyes, the hair, the'—her face grew like death—'the twist in his face——'

'What on earth are you saying? Pull yourself together.' He saw that she was trembling down the whole length of her body, as she leaned against the table for support. His own legs shook. He stared hard at her.

'Altered, Harry ... altered.' Her horrified whisper came at him like a knife. For it was true. He, too, had noticed something about the husband's appearance that was not quite normal. Yet, even while they talked, they heard him going down the carpetless stairs; the sounds ceased as he crossed the hall; then came the noise of the front door banging, the reverberation even shaking the room a little where they stood.

Mortimer went over to her side. He walked unevenly.

'My dear! For God's sake—this is sheer nonsense. Don't let yourself go like this. I'll put it straight with him—it's all my fault.' He saw by her face that she did not understand his words; he was saying the wrong thing altogether; her mind was utterly elsewhere. 'He's all right,' he went on hurriedly. 'He's not on the lawn now——'

He broke off at sight of her. The horror that fastened on her brain plastered her face with deathly whiteness.

'That was not John at all,' she cried, a wail of misery and terror in her voice. She rushed to the window and he followed. To his immense relief a figure moving below was plainly visible. It was John Burley. They saw him in the faint grey of the dawn, as he crossed the lawn, going away from the house. He disappeared.

'There you are! See?' whispered Mortimer reassuringly. 'He'll be back in——' when a sound in the adjoining room, heavier, louder than before, cut appallingly across his words, and Mrs. Burley, with that wailing scream, fell back into his arms. He caught her only just in time, for he stiffened into ice, daft with the uncomprehended terror of it all, and helpless as a child.

'Darling, my darling—oh, God!' He bent, kissing her face wildly. He was utterly distraught.

'Harry! Jack—oh, oh!' she wailed in her anguish. 'It took on his likeness. It deceived us... to give him time. He's done it.'

She sat up suddenly. 'Go,' she said, pointing to the room beyond, then sank fainting, a dead weight in his arms.

He carried her unconscious body to a chair, then entering the adjoining room he flashed his torch upon the body of her husband hanging from a bracket in the wall. He cut it down five minutes too late.

## THE TRADITION

The noises outside the little flat at first were very disconcerting after living in the country. They made sleep difficult. At the cottage in Sussex where the family had lived, night brought deep, comfortable silence, unless the wind was high, when the pine trees round the duck-pond made a sound like surf, or, if the gale was from the south-west, the orchard roared a bit unpleasantly.

But in London it was very different; sleep was easier in the daytime than at night. For, after nightfall, the rumble of the traffic became spasmodic instead of continuous; the motor-horns startled like warnings of alarm; after comparative silence the furious rushing of a taxicab touched the nerves. From dinner till eleven o'clock the streets subsided gradually; then came the army from theatres, parties, and late dinners, hurrying home to bed. The motor-horns during this hour were lively and incessant, like bugles of a regiment moving into battle. The parents rarely retired until this attack was over. If quick about it, sleep was possible then before the flying of the night-birds—an uncertain squadron—screamed half the street awake again. But, these finally disposed of, a delightful hush settled down upon the neighbourhood, profounder far than any peace of the countryside. The deep rumble of the produce wagons, coming in to the big London markets from the farms—generally about three a.m.—held no disturbing quality.

But sometimes in the stillness of very early morning, when streets were empty and pavements all deserted, there was a sound of another kind that was startling and unwelcome. For it was ominous. It came with a clattering violence that made nerves quiver and forced the heart to pause and listen. A strange resonance was in it, a volume of sound, moreover, that was hardly justified by its cause. For it was hoofs. A horse swept hurrying up the deserted street, and was close upon the building in a moment. It was audible suddenly, no gradual approach from a distance, but as though it turned a corner from soft ground that muffled the hoofs, on to the echoing, hard paving that emphasised the dreadful clatter. Nor did it die away again when once the house was reached. It ceased as abruptly as it came. The hoofs did not go away.

It was the mother who heard them first, and drew her husband's attention to their disagreeable quality.

'It is the mail-vans, dear,' he answered. 'They go at four a.m. to catch the early trains into the country.'

She looked up sharply, as though something in his tone surprised her.

'But there's no sound of wheels,' she said. And then, as he did not reply, she added gravely, 'You have heard it too, John. I can tell.'

'I have,' he said. 'I have heard it—twice.'

And they looked at one another searchingly, each trying to read the other's mind. She did not question him; he did not propose writing to complain in a newspaper; both understood something that neither of them quite believed.

'I heard it first,' she then said softly, 'the night before Jack got the fever. And, as I listened, I heard him crying. But when I went in to see he was asleep. The noise stopped just outside the building.' There was a shadow in her eyes as she said this, and a hush crept in between her words. 'I did not hear it *go*.' She said this almost beneath her breath.

He looked a moment at the ground; then, coming towards her, he took her in his arms and kissed her. And she clung very tightly to him.

'Sometimes,' he said in a quiet voice, 'a mounted policeman passes down the street, I think.'

'It is a horse,' she answered. But whether it was a question or mere corroboration he did not ask, for at that moment the doctor arrived, and the question of little Jack's health became the paramount matter of immediate interest. The great man's verdict was uncommonly disquieting.

All that night they sat up in the sick room. It was strangely still, as though by one accord the traffic avoided the house where a little boy hung between life and death. The motor-horns even had a muffled sound, and heavy drays and wagons used the side streets; there were fewer taxicabs about, or else they flew by noiselessly. Yet no straw was down, the expense prohibited that. And towards morning, very early, the mother decided to watch alone. She had been a trained nurse before her marriage, accustomed when she was younger to long vigils. 'You go down, dear, and get a little sleep,' she urged in a whisper. 'He's quiet now. At five o'clock I'll come for you to take my place.'

'You'll fetch me at once,' he whispered, 'if—' then hesitated—as though breath failed him. A moment he stood there staring from her face to the bed. 'If you hear anything,' he finished. She nodded, and he went downstairs to his study, not to his bedroom. He left the door ajar. He sat in darkness, listening. Mother, he knew, was listening, too, beside the bed. His heart was very full, for he did not believe the boy could live till morning. The picture of the room was all the time before his eyes—the shaded lamp, the table with the medicines, the little wasted figure beneath the blankets, and mother close beside it, listening. He sat alert, ready to fly upstairs at the smallest cry.

But no sound broke the stillness; the entire neighbourhood was silent; all London slept. He heard the clock strike three in the dining-room at the end of the corridor. It was still enough for that. There was not even the heavy rumble of a single produce wagon, though usually they passed about this time on their way to Smithfield and Covent Garden markets. He waited, far too anxious to close his eyes. ... At four o'clock he would go up and relieve her vigil. Four, he knew, was the time when life sinks to its lowest ebb. ... Then, in the middle of his reflections, thought stopped dead, and it seemed his heart stopped too.

Far away, but coming nearer with extraordinary rapidity, a

sharp, clear sound broke out of the surrounding stillness—a horse's hoofs. At first it was so distant that it might have been almost on the high roads of the country, but the amazing speed with which it came closer, and the sudden increase of the beating sound was such, that by the time he turned his head it seemed to have entered the street outside. It was within a hundred yards of the building. The next second it was before the very door. And something in him blenched. He knew a moment's complete paralysis. The abrupt cessation of the heavy clatter was strangest of all. It came like lightning, it struck, it paused. It did not go away again. Yet the sound of it was still beating in his ears as he dashed upstairs three steps at a time. It seemed in the house as well, on the stairs behind him, in the little passage-way, *inside the very bedroom*. It was an appalling sound. Yet he entered a room that was quiet, orderly, and calm. It was silent. Beside the bed his wife sat, holding Jack's hand, stroking it. She was soothing him; her face was very peaceful. No sound but her gentle whisper was audible.

He controlled himself by a tremendous effort, but his face betrayed his consternation and distress. 'Hush,' she said beneath her breath, 'he's sleeping much more calmly now. The crisis, bless God, is over, I do believe. I dared not leave him.'

He saw in a moment that she was right, and an untellable relief passed over him. He sat down beside her, very cold, yet perspiring with heat.

'You heard——?' he asked after a pause.

'Nothing,' she replied quickly, 'except his pitiful, wild words when the delirium was on him. It's passed. It lasted but a moment, or I'd have called you.'

He stared closely into her tired eyes. 'And his words?' he asked in a whisper. Whereupon she told him quietly that the little chap had sat up with wide-opened eyes and talked excitedly about a 'great, great horse' he heard, but that was not 'coming for him'. He laughed and said he would not go with it because he 'was not ready yet'. 'Some scrap of talk he had overheard from us,' she added, 'when we discussed the traffic once. ...'

'But *you* heard nothing?' he repeated almost impatiently.

No, she had heard nothing. After all, then, he *had* dozed a moment in his chair. ...

Four weeks later Jack, entirely convalescent, was playing a restricted game of hide-and-seek with his sister in the flat. It was really a forbidden joy, owing to noise and risk of breakages, but he had unusual privileges after his grave illness. It was dusk. The lamps in the street were being lit. 'Quietly, remember; your mother's resting in her room,' were the father's orders. She had just returned from a week by the sea, recuperating from the strain of nursing for so many nights. The traffic rolled and boomed along the streets below.

'Jack! Do come on and hide. It's your turn. I hid last.'

But the boy was standing spellbound by the window, staring hard at something on the pavement. Sybil called and tugged in vain. Tears threatened. Jack would not budge. He declared he saw something.

'Oh, you're always seeing something. I wish you'd go and hide. It's only because you can't think of a good place, really.'

'Look!' he cried in a voice of wonder. And as he said it his father rose quickly from his chair before the fire.

'Look,' the child repeated with delight and excitement. 'It's a great, great horse. And it's perfectly white all over.' His sister joined him at the window. 'Where? Where? I can't see it. Oh, *do* show me!'

Their father was standing close behind them now. 'I heard it,' he was whispering, but so low the children did not notice him. His face was very pale.

'Straight in front of our door, stupid! Can't you see it? Oh, I do wish it had come for me. It's *such* a beauty!' And he clapped his hands with pleasure and excitement. 'Quick, quick! I can hear it. It's going away again!'

But, while the children stood half squabbling by the window their father leaned over a sofa in the adjoining room above a figure whose heart in sleep had quietly stopped its beating. The great, great horse had come. But this time he had not only heard its wonderful arrival. He had also heard it go. It seemed he heard the awful hoofs beat down the sky, far far away, and very swiftly, dying into silence, finally up among the stars.

## THE TOUCH OF PAN

### I

An idiot, Heber understood, was a person in whom intelligence had been arrested—instinct acted, but not reason. A lunatic, on the other hand, was someone whose reason had gone awry—the mechanism of the brain was injured. The lunatic was out of relation with his environment; the idiot had merely been delayed *en route*.

Be that as it might, he knew at any rate that a lunatic was not to be listened to, whereas an idiot—well, the one he fell in love with, certainly had the secret of some instinctual knowledge that was not only joy, but a kind of sheer natural joy. Probably it was that sheer natural joy of living that reason argues to be untaught, degraded. In any case—at thirty—he married her instead of the daughter of a duchess he was engaged to. They lead to-day that happy, natural, vagabond life called idiotic, unmindful of that world the majority of reasonable people live only to remember.

Though born into an artificial social clique that made it difficult, Heber had always loved the simple things. Nature, especially, meant much to him. He would rather see a woodland misty with bluebells than all the châteaux on the Loire; the thought of a mountain valley in the dawn made his feet lonely in the grandest houses. Yet in these very houses was his home established. Not that he under-estimated worldly things—their value was too obvious—but that it was another thing he wanted. Only he did not know precisely *what* he wanted until this particular idiot made it plain.

Her case was a mild one, possibly; the title bestowed by implication rather than by specific mention. Her family did not say that she was imbecile or half-witted, but that she was 'not all there' they probably did say. Perhaps she saw men as trees walking, perhaps she saw through a glass darkly. ... Heber, who had met her once or twice, though never yet to speak to, did not analyse her degree of sight, for in him, personally, she woke a secret joy and wonder that almost involved a touch of awe. The part of her that was 'not all there' dwelt in an 'elsewhere' that he longed to know about. He wanted to share it with her. She seemed aware of certain happy and desirable things that reason and too much thinking hid.

He just felt this instinctively without analysis. The values they set upon the prizes of life were similar. Money to her was just stamped metal, fame a loud noise of sorts, position nothing. Of people she was aware as a dog or bird might be aware—they were kind or unkind. Her parents, having collected much metal and achieved position, proceeded to make a loud noise of sorts with some success; and since she did not contribute, either by her appearance or her tastes, to their ambitions, they neglected her and made excuses. They were ashamed of her existence. Her father in particular justified Nietzsche's shrewd remark that no one with a loud voice can listen to subtle thoughts.

She was, perhaps, sixteen; for, though she did not look it, eighteen or nineteen was probably more in accord with her birth certificate. Her mother was content, however, that she should dress the lesser age, preferring to tell strangers that she was childish, rather than admit that she was backward.

'You'll never marry at all, child, much less marry as you might,' she said, 'if you go about with that rabbit expression on your face. That's not the way to catch a nice young man of the sort we get down to stay with us now. Many a chorus-girl with less than you've got has caught them easily enough. Your sister's done well. Why not do the same? There's nothing to be shy or frightened about.'

'But I'm not shy or frightened, mother. I'm bored. I mean *they* bore me.'

It made no difference to the girl; she was herself. The bored expression in the eyes—the rabbit, not-all-there expression—gave place sometimes to another look. Yet not often, nor with anybody. It was this other look that stirred the strange joy in the man who fell in love with her. It is not to be easily described. It was very wonderful. Whether sixteen or nineteen, she then looked—a thousand.

* * *

The house-party was of that up-to-date kind prevalent in Heber's world. Husbands and wives were not asked together. There was a cynical disregard of the decent (not the stupid) conventions that savoured of abandon, perhaps of decadence. He only went himself in the hope of seeing the backward daughter once again. Her millionaire parents afflicted him, the smart folk tired him. Their peculiar affection of a special language, their strange belief that they were of importance, their treatment of the servants, their calculated self-indulgence, all jarred upon him more than usual. At bottom he heartily despised the whole vapid set. He felt uncomfortable and out of place. Though not a prig, he abhorred the way these folk believed themselves the climax of fine living. Their open immorality disgusted him, their indiscriminate love-making was merely rather nasty; he watched the very girl he was at last to settle down with behaving as the tone of the clique expected over her final fling—and bored by the strain of so much 'modernity', he tried to get away. Tea was long over, the sunset interval invited, he felt hungry for trees and fields that were not self-conscious—and he escaped. The flaming June day was turning chill. Dusk hovered over the ancient house, veiling the pretentious new wing that had been added. And he came across the idiot girl at the bend of the drive, where the birch trees shivered in the evening wind. His heart gave a sudden leap.

She was leaning against one of the dreadful statues—it was a satyr—that sprinkled the lawn. Her back was to him; she gazed at a group of broken pine trees in the park beyond. He paused an instant, then went on quickly, while his mind scurried, to recall her name. They were within easy speaking range.

'Miss Elizabeth!' he cried, yet not too loudly, lest she might vanish as suddenly as she had appeared. She turned at once.

Her eyes and lips were smiling welcome at him without pretence. She showed no surprise.

'You're the first one of the lot who's said it properly,' she exclaimed, as he came up. 'Everybody calls me Elizabeth instead of Elspeth. It's idiotic. They don't even take the trouble to get a name right.'

'It is,' he agreed, 'quite idiotic.' He did not correct her. Possibly he had said Elspeth after all—the names were similar. Her perfectly natural voice was grateful to his ear, and soothing. He looked at her all over with an open admiration that she noticed and, without concealment, liked. She was very untidy, the grey stockings on her slim, vigorous legs were torn, her short skirt was spattered with mud. Her nut-brown hair, glossy and plentiful, flew loose about neck and shoulders. In place of the usual belt she had tied a coloured handkerchief round her waist. She wore no hat. What she had been doing to get in such a state, while her parents entertained a 'distinguished' party, he did not know, but it was not difficult to guess. Climbing trees or riding bareback and astride was probably the truth. Yet her dishevelled state became her well, and the welcome in her face delighted him. She remembered him, she was glad. He, too, was glad, and a sense both happy and reckless stirred in his heart. 'Like a wild animal,' he said, 'you come out in the dusk——'

'To play with my kind,' she answered in a flash, throwing him a glance of invitation that made his blood go dancing.

He leaned against the statue a moment, asking himself why this young Cinderella of a parvenu family delighted him when all the London beauties left him cold. There was a lift through his whole being as he watched her, slim and supple, grace shining through the untidy modern garb—almost as though she wore no clothes. He thought of a panther standing upright. Her poise was so alert—one arm upon the marble ledge, one leg bent across the other, the hip-line showing like a bird's curved wing. Wild animal or bird flashed across his mind; something untamed and natural. Another second and she might leap away—or spring into his arms.

It was a deep, delicious sensation in him that produced the mental picture. 'Pure and natural,' a voice whispered with it in his heart, 'as surely as *they* are just the other thing!' And the thrill struck with unerring aim at the very root of that unrest he had always known in the state of life to which he was called. She made the natural clean and pure. This girl and himself were somehow kin. The primitive thing broke loose in him.

In two seconds, while he stood with her beside the vulgar statue, these thoughts passed through his mind. But he did not at first, give utterance to any of them. He spoke more formally, although laughter, due to his happiness, lay close behind.

'They haven't asked you to the party, then? Or you don't care about it? Which is it?'

'Both,' she said, looking fearlessly into his face. 'But I've been waiting here ten minutes already. Why were you so long?'

This outspoken honesty was hardly what he expected, yet in another sense he was not surprised. Her eyes were very penetrating, very innocent, very frank. He felt her as clean and sweet as some young fawn that asks plainly to be stroked and fondled. He told the truth: 'I couldn't get away before. I had to play about and——' when she interrupted with impatience:

'*They* don't want you,' she exclaimed scornfully. 'I do.'

And, before he could choose one out of the several answers that rushed into his mind, she nudged him with her foot, holding it out a little so that he saw the shoelace was unfastened. She nodded her head towards it, and pulled her skirt up half an inch as he at once stooped down.

'And, anyhow,' she went on as he fumbled with the lace, touching her ankle with his hand, 'you're going to marry one of them. I read it in the paper. You'll be miserable. It's idiotic.'

The blood rushed to his head, but whether owing to his stooping or to something else, he could not say.

'I only came—I only accepted,' he said quickly, 'because I wanted to see you again.'

'Of course. I made mother ask you.'

He did an impulsive thing. Kneeling as he was, he bent his

head a little lower and suddenly kissed the soft grey stocking—then stood up and looked her in the face. She was laughing happily, no sign of embarrassment in her anywhere, no trace of outraged modesty. She only looked very pleased.

'I've tied a knot that won't come undone in a hurry——' he began, then stopped dead. For as he said it, gazing into her smiling face, another expression looked forth at him from the two big eyes of hazel. Something rushed from his heart to meet it. It may have been that playful kiss, it may have been the way she took it; but, at any rate, there was a strength in the new emotion that made him unsure of who he was and of whom he looked at. He forgot the place, the time, his own identity and hers. ... The lawn swept from beneath his feet, the English sunset with it. He forgot his host and hostess, his fellow guests, even his father's name and his own into the bargain. He was carried away upon a great tide, the girl always beside him. He left the shore-line in the distance, already half forgotten, the shore-line of his education, learning, manners, social point of view—everything to which his father had most carefully brought him up as the scion of an old established English family. This girl had torn up the anchor. Only the anchor had previously been loosened a little, perhaps, by his own unconscious and restless efforts. ...

Where was she taking him to? Upon what island would they land...?

'I'm younger than you—a good deal,' she broke in upon his rushing mood. 'But that doesn't matter a bit, does it? We're about the same age really.'

With the happy sound of her voice the extraordinary sensation passed—or, rather, it became normal. But that it lasted an appreciable time was proved by the fact that they had left the statue on the lawn, the house was no longer visible behind them, and they were now walking side by side between the massive rhododendron clumps. They brought up against a five-barred gate into the park. They leaned upon the topmost bar, and he felt her shoulder touching his—edging into it—as they looked across to the grove of pines.

'I feel absurdly young,' he said without a sign of affectation, 'and yet I've been looking for you a thousand years and more.'

The afterglow lit up her face; it fell on her loose hair and tumbled blouse, turning them amber red. She looked not only soft and comely, but extraordinarily beautiful. The strange expression haunted the deep eyes again, the lips were a little parted, the young breast heaving slightly, joy and excitement in her whole presentment. And as he watched her he knew that all he had just felt was due to her close presence, her atmosphere, her perfume, her physical warmth and vigour. It had emanated directly from her being.

'Of course,' she said, and laughed so that he felt her breath upon his face. He bent lower to bring his own on a level, gazing straight into her eyes that were still fixed upon the field beyond. They were clear and luminous as pools of water, and in their centre, sharp as a photograph, he saw the reflection of the pine grove, perhaps a hundred yards away. With detailed accuracy he saw it, empty and motionless in the glimmering June dusk.

Then something caught his eye. He examined the picture more closely. He drew slightly nearer. He almost touched her face with his own, forgetting for a moment whose were the eyes that served him for a mirror. For, looking intently thus, it seemed to him that there was movement, a passing to and fro, a stirring as of figures among the trees... Then suddenly the entire picture was obliterated. She had dropped her lids. He heard her speaking—the warm breath was again upon his face:

'*In the heart of that wood dwell I*'.

His heart gave another leap—more violent than the first—for the sentence caught him like a spell. There was a lilt and rhythm in the words, a wonder and a beauty, that made it poetry. She laid emphasis upon the pronoun and the nouns. It seemed the last line of some delicious runic verse:

'In the *heart* of that *wood*—dwell *I*...'

And it flashed across him: that living, moving, inhabited pine wood was her thought. It was thus she thought it, saw it. Her nature flung back to a life she understood, a life that needed claimed her. The ostentatious and artificial values that surrounded her she denied, even as the distinguished house-party of her ambitious, masquerading family neglected her. Of course she was unnoticed by them—just as a swallow or a wild-rose were unnoticed.

He knew her secret then, for she had told it to him. It was his own secret too. They were akin, as the birds and animals were akin. They belonged together in some free and open life, natural, wild, untamed. That unhampered life was flowing about them now, rising, beating with delicious tumult in her veins and his, yet innocent as the sunlight and the wind—because it was as freely recognised.

'Elspeth!' he cried, 'come, take me with you! We'll go at once. Come—hurry—before we forget to be happy, or remember to be wise again——!'

His words stopped half-way towards completion, for a perfume floated past him, born of the summer dusk, perhaps, yet sweet with a penetrating magic that made his senses reel with some remembered joy. No flower, no scented garden-bush delivered it. It was the perfume of young, spendthrift life, sweet with the purity that season had not yet stained. The girl moved closer. Gathering her loose hair between her fingers, she brushed his cheeks and eyes with it, her slim, warm body pressing against him as she leaned over laughingly.

'*In the darkness,*' she whispered in his ear; '*when the moon puts the house upon the statue!*'

And he understood. Her world lay behind the vulgar, staring day. He turned. He heard the flutter of skirts—just caught the grey stockings, swift and light, and they flew behind the rhododendron masses. And she was gone.

He stood a long time, leaning upon that five-barred gate... It was the dressing-gong that recalled him at length to what seemed the present. By the conservatory door, as he went slowly in, he met his distinguished cousin—who was helping the girl he himself was to marry to enjoy her 'final fling'. He looked at his cousin. He realised suddenly that he was merely vicious. There was no sun and wind, no flowers—there was depravity only, lust instead of laughter, excitement in place of happiness. It was calculated, not spontaneous. His mind was in it. Without joy it was. He was not natural.

'Not a girl in the whole lot fit to look at,' his cousin exclaimed with peevish boredom, excusing himself stupidly for his illicit conduct. 'I'm off in the morning.' He shrugged his blue-blooded shoulders. 'These millionaires! Their shooting's all right, but their mixum-gatherum week-ends—bah!' His gesture completed all he had to say about this one in particular. He glanced sharply, nastily, at his companion. '*You* look as if you'd found something!' he added, with a suggestive grin. 'Or have you seen the ghost that was paid for with the house?' And he guffawed and let his eye-glass drop. 'Lady Hermione will be asking for an explanation—eh?'

'Idiot!' replied Heber, and ran upstairs to dress for dinner.

But the word was wrong, he remembered, as he closed his door. It was lunatic he had meant to say, yet something more as well. He saw the smart, modern philanderer somehow as a beast.

## II

It was nearly midnight when he went up to bed, after an evening of intolerable amusement. The abandoned moral attitude, the common rudeness, the contempt of all others but themselves, the ugly jests, the horseplay of tasteless minds that passed for gaiety, above all the shamelessness of the women that behind the cover of fine breeding aped emancipation, afflicted him to a boredom that touched desperation.

He understood now with a clarity unknown before. As with his cousin, so with these. They took life, he saw, with a brazen effrontery they thought was freedom, while yet it was life that they denied. He felt vampired and degraded; spontaneity went out of him. The fact that the geography of bedrooms was studied openly seemed an affirmation of vice that sickened him. Their ways were nauseous merely. He escaped—unnoticed.

He locked his door, went to the open window, and looked out into the night—then started. For silver dressed the lawn and park, the shadow of the building lay dark across the elaborate garden, and the moon, he noticed, was just high enough to put the house upon the statue. The chimney-stacks edged the pedestal precisely.

'Odd!' he exclaimed. 'Odd that I should come at the very moment——!' then smiled as he realised how his proposed adventure would be misinterpreted, its natural innocence and spirit ruined—if he were seen. 'And someone would be sure to see me on a night like this. There are couples still hanging about in the garden.' And he glanced at the shrubberies and secret paths that seemed to float upon the warm June air like islands.

He stood for a moment framed in the glare of the electric light, then turned back into the room; and at that instant a low sound like a bird-call rose from the lawn below. It was soft and flutey, as though someone played two notes upon a reed, a piping sound. He had been seen, and she was waiting for him. Before he knew it, he had made an answering call, of oddly similar kind, then switched the light out.

Three minutes later, dressed in simpler clothes, with a cap pulled over his eyes, he reached the back lawn by means of the conservatory and billiard-room. He paused a moment to look about him. There was no one, although the lights were still ablaze. 'I am an idiot,' he chuckled to himself. 'I'm acting on instinct!' He ran.

The sweet night air bathed him from head to foot; there was strength and cleansing in it. The lawn shone wet with dew. He could almost smell the perfume of the stars. The fumes of wine, cigars and artificial scent were left behind, the atmosphere exhaled by civilisation, by heavy thoughts, by bodies overdressed unwisely stimulated—all, all forgotten. He passed into a world of magical enchantment. The hush of the open sky came down. In black and white the garden lay, brimmed full with beauty, shot by the ancient silver of the moon, spangled with the stars' old-gold. And the night wind rustled in the rhododendron masses as he flew between them.

In a moment he was beside the statue, engulfed now by the shadow of the building, and the girl detached herself silently from the blur of darkness. Two arms were flung about his neck, a shower of soft hair fell on his cheek with a heady scent of earth and leaves and grass, and the same instant they were away together at full speed—towards the pine wood. Their feet were soundless on the soaking grass. They went so swiftly that they made a whir of following wind that blew her hair across his eyes.

And the sudden contrast caused a shock that put a blank, perhaps, upon his mind, so that he lost the standard of remembered things. For it was no longer merely a particular adventure; it seemed a habit and a natural joy resumed.

It was not new. He realised the momentum of an accustomed happiness, mislaid, it may be, but certainly familiar. They sped across the gravel paths that intersected the well-groomed lawn, they leaped the flower-beds, so laboriously shaped in mockery, they clambered over the ornamental iron railings, scorning the easier five-barred gate into the park. The longer grass then shook the dew in soaking showers against his knees. He stooped, as though in some foolish effort to turn up some thing, then realised that his legs, of course, were bare. *Her* garment was already high and free, for she, too, was barelegged like himself. He saw her little ankles, wet and shining in the moonlight, and flinging himself down, he kissed them happily, plunging his face into the dripping, perfumed grass. Her ringing laughter mingled with his own, as she stooped beside him the same instant; her hair hung in a silver cloud; her eyes gleamed through its curtain into his; then, suddenly, she soaked her hands in the heavy dew and passed them over his face with a softness that was like the touch of some scented southern wind.

'Now you are anointed with the Night,' she cried. 'No one will know you. You are forgotten of the world. Kiss me!'

'We'll play for ever and ever,' he cried, 'the eternal game that was old when still the world was young,' and lifting her in his arms he kissed her eyes and lips. There was some natural bliss of song and dance laughter in his heart, an elemental bliss that caught them together as wind and sunlight catch the branches of a tree. She leaped from the ground to meet his swinging arms, and in an instant was upon his shoulders. He ran with her, then tossed her off and caught her neatly as she fell. Evading a second capture, she danced ahead, holding out one shining arm that he might follow. Hand in hand they raced on together through the clean summer moonlight. Yet there remained a smooth softness as of fur against his neck and shoulders, and he saw then that she wore skins of tawny colour that clung to her body closely, that he wore them too, and that her skin, like his own, was of a sweet dusky brown.

Then, pulling her towards him, he stared into her face. She suffered the close gaze a second, but no longer, for with a burst of sparkling laughter again she leaped into his arms, and before he shook her free she had pulled and tweaked the two small horns that hid in the thick curly hair behind, and just above, the ears.

And that wilful tweaking turned him wild and reckless. That touch ran down him deep into the mothering earth. He leaped and ran and sang with a great laughing sound. The wine of eternal youth flushed all his veins with joy, and the old, old world was young again with every impulse of natural happiness intensified with the Earth's own foaming tide of life.

From head to foot he tingled with the delight of Spring, prodigal with creative power. Of course he could fly the bushes and fling wild across the open! Of course the wind and moonlight fitted close and soft about him like a skin! Of course he had youth and beauty for playmates, with dancing, laughter, singing, and a thousand kisses! For he and she were natural once again. They were free together of those long-forgotten days when 'Pan leaped through the roses in the month of June...!'

With the girl swaying this way and that upon his shoulders, tweaking his horns with mischief and desire, hanging her flying hair before his eyes, then bending swiftly over again to lift it, he danced to join the rest of their companions in the little moonlit grove of pines beyond...

## III

They rose somewhat pointed, perhaps, against the moonlight, those English pines—more with the shape of cypresses, some might have thought. A stream gushed down between their roots, there were mossy ferns, and rough grey boulders with lichen on them. But there was no dimness, for the silver of the moon sprinkled freely through the branches like the faint sunlight that it really was, and the air ran out to meet them with a heady fragrance that was wiser far than wine.

The girl, in an instant, was whirled from her perch on his shoulders and caught by a dozen arms that bore her into the heart of the merry, careless throng. Whisht! Whew! Whir! She was gone, but another, fairer still, was in her place, with skins as soft and knees that clung as tightly. Her eyes were liquid amber, grapes hung between her little breasts, her arms entwined about him, smoother than marble, and as cool. She had a crystal laugh.

But he flung her off, so that she fell plump among a group of bigger figures lolling against a twisted root and roaring with a jollity that boomed like wind through the chorus of a song. They seized her, kissed her, then sent her flying. They were happier, after all, with their glad singing. They held stone goblets, red and foaming in their broad-palmed hands.

'The mountains lie behind us!' cried someone dancing past. 'We are come at last into our valley of delight. Grapes, breasts, and rich red lips! Ho! Ho! It is time to press them that the juice of life may run!' The figure waved a cluster of ferns across the air and vanished amid a cloud of song and laughter.

'It is ours. Use it!' answered a deep, ringing voice. 'The valleys are our own. No climbing now!' And a wind of echoing cries gave answer from all sides. 'Life! Life! Life! Abundant, flowing over—use it, use it!'

A troop of nymphs rushed forth, escaped from clustering arms and lips they yet openly desired. He chased them in and out among the waving branches, while she who had brought him ever followed, and sped past him and away again. He caught three gleaming soft brown bodies, then fell beneath them, smothered, bubbling with joyous laughter—next freed himself and, while they sought to drag him captive again, escaped and raced with a leap upon a slimmer, sweeter outline that swung up—only just in time upon a lower bough, whence she leaned down above him with hanging net of hair and merry eyes. A few feet beyond his reach, she laughed and teased him—the one who had brought him in, the one he ever sought, and who for ever sought him too...

It became a riotous glory of wild children who romped and played with an impassioned glee beneath the moon. For the world was young and they, her happy offspring, glowed with the life she poured so freely into them. All intermingled, the laughing voices rose into a foam of song that broke against the stars. The difficult mountains had been climbed and were forgotten. Good! Then, enjoy the luxuriant, fruitful valley and be glad! And glad they were, brimful with spontaneous energy, natural as birds and animals that obeyed the big, deep rhythm of a simpler age—natural as wind and innocent as sunshine.

Yet, for all the untamed riot, there was a lift of beauty pulsing underneath. Even when the wildest abandon approached the heat of orgy, when the recklessness appeared excess—there hid that marvellous touch of loveliness which makes the natural sacred. There was coherence, purpose, the fulfilling of an exquisite law: and—there was worship. The form it took, haply, was strange as well as riotous, yet in its strangeness dreamed innocence and purity, and in its very riot flamed that spirit which is divine.

For he found himself at length beside her once again; breathless and panting, her sweet brown limbs aglow from the excitement of escape denied; eyes shining like a blaze of stars, and pulses beating with tumultuous life—helpless and yielding against the strength that pinned her down between the roots.

His eyes put mastery on her own. She looked up into his face, obedient, happy, soft with love, surrendering with the same delicious abandon that had swept her for a moment into other arms. 'You caught me in the end,' she sighed. 'I only played awhile.'

'I hold you for ever,' he replied, half wondering at the rough power in his voice.

It was here the hush of worship stole upon her little face, into her obedient eyes, about her parted lips. She ceased her wilful struggling.

'Listen!' she whispered. 'I hear a step upon the glades beyond. The iris and the lily open; the earth is ready, waiting; we must be ready too! *He* is coming!'

He released her and sprang up; the entire company rose too. All stood, all bowed the head. There was an instant's subtle panic, but it was the panic of reverent awe that preludes a descent of deity. For a wind passed through the branches with a sound that is the oldest in the world and so the youngest. Above it there rose the shrill, faint piping of a little reed...

Only the first, true sounds were audible—wind and water: the tinkling of the dewdrops as they fell, the murmur of the trees against the air. This was the piping that they heard. And in the hush the stars bent down to hear, the riot paused, the orgy passed and died. The figures waited, kneeling then with one accord. They listened with—the Earth.

'He comes... He comes...' the valley breathed about them.

A footfall from far away came treading across a world unruined and unstained. It fell with the wind and water, sweetening the valley into life as it approached. Across the rivers and forests it came gently, tenderly, but swiftly and with a power that knew majesty.

'He comes... He comes...!' rose with the murmur of the wind and water from the host of lowered heads.

The footfall came nearer, treading a world grown soft with worship. It reached the grove. It entered. There was a sense of intolerable loveliness, of brimming life, of rapture. The thousand faces lifted like a cloud. They heard the piping close... And so He came.

But He came with blessing. With the stupendous Presence there was joy, the joy of abundant, natural life, pure as the sunlight and the wind. He passed among them. There was great movement—as of a forest shaking, as of deep water falling, as of a cornfield swaying to the wind, gentle as of harebell shedding its burden of dew that it has held too long because of love. He passed among them, touching every head. The great hand swept with tenderness each face, lingered a moment on each beating heart. There was sweetness, peace, and loveliness; but above all, there was—life. He sanctioned every natural joy in them and blessed each passion with his power of creation... Yet each one saw him differently: some as a wife or maiden desired with fire, some as a youth or stalwart husband, others as a figure veiled with stars or cloaked in luminous mist, hardly attainable; others, again—the fewest these, not more than two or three—as that mysterious wonder which tempts the heart away from known familiar sweetness into a wilderness of undecipherable magic without flesh and blood.

To two, in particular, He came so near that they could feel his breath of hills and fields upon their eyes. He touched them with both mighty hands. He stroked the marble breasts, He felt the little hidden horns... and, as they bent lower so that their lips met together for an instant, He took her arms and twined them about the curved, brown neck that she might hold him closer still...

Again a footfall sounded far away upon an unruined world... and He was gone—back into the wind and water whence He came. The thousand faces lifted; all stood up; the hush of worship still among them. There was a quiet as of the dawn. The piping floated over woods and fields, fading into silence. All looked at one another... And then once more the laughter and the play broke loose.

## IV

'We'll go,' she cried, 'and peep upon that other world where life hangs like a prison on their eyes!'

And, in a moment, they were across the soaking grass, the lawn and flower-beds, and close to the walls of the heavy mansion. He peered in through a window, lifting her up to peer in with him. He recognised the world to which he outwardly belonged; he understood; a little gasp escaped him; and a slight shiver ran down the girl's body into his own. She turned her eyes away. 'See,' she murmured in his ear, 'it's ugly, it's not natural. They feel guilty and ashamed. There is no innocence!' She saw the men; it was the women that he saw chiefly.

Lolling ungracefully, with a kind of boldness that asserted independence, the women smoked their cigarettes with an air of invitation they sought to conceal and yet plainly showed. He saw his familiar world in nakedness. Their backs were bare, for all the elaborate clothes they wore; they hung their breasts uncleanly; in their eyes shone light that had never known the open sun. Hoping they were alluring and desirable, they feigned a guilty ignorance of that hope. They all pretended. Instead of wind and dew upon their hair, he saw flowers grown artificially to ape wild beauty, tresses without lustre borrowed from the slums of city factories. He watched them manoeuvring with the men; heard dark sentences; caught gestures half delivered whose meaning should just convey that glimpse of guilt they deemed to increase pleasure. The women were calculating, but nowhere glad; the men experienced, but nowhere joyous. Pretended innocence lay cloaked with a veil of something that whispered secretly, clandestine, ashamed, yet with a brazen air that laid mockery instead of sunshine in their smiles. Vice masqueraded in the ugly shape of pleasure; beauty was degraded into calculated tricks. They were not natural. They knew not joy.

'The forward ones, the civilised!' she laughed in his ear, tweaking his horns with energy. '*We* are the backward!'

'Unclean,' he muttered, recalling a catchword of the world he gazed upon.

They were the civilised! They were refined and educated—advanced. Generations of careful breeding, mate cautiously selecting mate, laid the polish of caste upon their hands and faces where gleamed ridiculous, untaught jewels—rings, bracelets, necklaces hanging absurdly from every possible angle.

'But—they are dressed up—for fun,' he exclaimed, more to himself than to the girl in skins who clung to his shoulder with her naked arms.

'Undressed!' she answered, putting her brown hand in play across his eyes. 'Only they have forgotten even that!' And another shiver passed through her into him. He turned and hid his face against the soft skins that touched his cheek. He kissed her body. Seizing his horns, she pressed him to her, laughing happily.

'Look!' she whispered, raising her head again; 'they're coming out.' And he saw that two of them, a man and a girl, with an interchange of secret glances, had stolen from the room and were already by the door of the conservatory that led into the garden. It was his wife to be—and his distinguished cousin.

'Oh, Pan!' she cried in mischief. The girl sprang from his arms and pointed. 'We will follow them. We will put natural life into their little veins!'

'Or panic terror,' he answered, catching the yellow panther skin and following her swiftly round the building. He kept in the shadow, though she ran full into the blaze of moonlight. 'But they can't see us,' she called, looking over her shoulder a moment. 'They can only feel our presence, perhaps.' And, as she danced across the lawn, it seemed a moonbeam slipped from a sapling birch tree that the wind curved earthwards, then tossed back against the sky.

Keeping just ahead, they led the pair, by methods known instinctively to elemental blood yet not translatable—led them towards the little grove of waiting pines. The night wind murmured in the branches; a bird woke into a sudden burst of song.

These sounds were plainly audible. But four little pointed ears caught other, wilder, notes behind the wind and music of the bird—the cries and ringing laughter, the leaping footsteps and the happy singing of their merry kin within the wood.

And the throng paused then amid the revels to watch the 'civilised' draw near. They presently reached the trees, halted, looked about them, hesitated a moment—then, with a hurried movement as of shame and fear lest they be caught, entered the zone of shadow.

'Let's go in here,' said the man, without music in his voice. 'It's dry on the pine needles, and we can't be seen.' He led the way; she picked up her skirts and followed over the strip of long wet grass. 'Here's a log all ready for us,' he added, sat down, and drew her into his arms with a sigh of satisfaction. 'Sit on my knee; it's warmer for your pretty figure.' He chuckled; evidently they were on familiar terms, for though she hesitated there was no real resistance in her, and she allowed the ungraceful roughness. 'But are we *quite* safe? Are you sure?' she asked between his kisses.

'What does it matter, even if we're not? he replied, establishing her more securely on his knees. 'But, as a matter of fact, we're safer here than in my own house.' He kissed her hungrily. 'By Jove, Hermione, but you're divine,' he cried passionately, 'divinely beautiful, I love you with every atom of my being—with my very soul.

'Yes, dear, I know—I mean, I know you do, but——'

'But what?' he asked impatiently.

'Those horrid detectives——'

He laughed. Yet it seemed to annoy him. 'My wife *is* a beast, isn't she?—to have me watched like that,' he said quickly.

'They're everywhere,' she replied, a sudden hush in her tone. She looked at the encircling trees a moment, then added bitterly: 'I hate her, simply *hate* her for it.'

'I love you,' he cried, crushing her to him, 'that's all that matters now. Don't let's waste time talking about the rest.'

She contrived to shudder, and hid her face against his coat, while he showered kisses on her neck and hair.

And the solemn pine trees watched them, the silvery moonlight fell on their faces, the scent of new-mown hay went floating past.

'I love you with my very soul,' he repeated with intense conviction. 'I'd do anything, give up anything, bear anything—just to give you a moment's happiness. I swear it—before God!'

There was a faint sound among the trees behind them, and the girl sat up, alert. She would have scrambled to her feet, but that he held her tight.

'What the devil's the matter with you to-night?' he asked in a different tone, his vexation plainly audible. 'You're as nervy as if *you* were being watched, instead of me.'

She paused before she answered, her finger on her lip. Then she spoke slowly, hushing her voice a little:

'Watched!' she repeated. 'That's exactly what I did feel. I've felt it ever since we came into the wood.'

'Nonsense, Hermione. It's too many cigarettes.' He drew her back into his arms, forcing her head up so that he could kiss her better.

'I suppose it is nonsense,' she said, smiling. 'It's gone now, anyhow.'

He began admiring her hair, her dress, her shoes, her pretty ankles, while she resisted in a way that proved her practice. 'It's not *me* you love,' she pouted, yet drinking in his praise. She listened to his repeated assurance that he loved her with his 'soul' and was prepared for any sacrifice.

'I feel so safe with you,' she murmured, knowing the moves in the game as well as he did. She looked up guiltily into his face, while he looked down with a passion that he thought perhaps was joy.

'You'll be married before the summer's out,' he said, 'and all the thrill and excitement will be over. Poor Hermione!' She lay back in his arms, drawing his face down with both hands, and kissing him on the lips. 'You'll have more of him than you can do with—eh? As much as you care about, anyhow.'

'I shall be much more free,' she whispered. 'Things will be easier. And I've got to marry someone——'

She broke off with another start. There was a sound again behind them. The man heard nothing. The blood in his temples pulsed too loudly, doubtless.

'Well, what is it this time?' he asked sharply.

She was peering into the wood, where the patches of dark shadow and moonlit spaces made odd, irregular patterns in the air. A low branch near them waved slightly in the wind.

'Did you hear?' she asked nervously.

'Wind,' he replied, annoyed that her change of mood disturbed his pleasure.

'But something moved——'

'Only a branch. We're quite alone, quite safe, I tell you,' and there was a rasping sound in his voice as he said it. 'Don't be so imaginative. I can take care of you.'

She sprang up. The moonlight caught her figure, revealing its exquisite young curves beneath the smother of the costly clothing. Her hair had dropped a little in the struggle. The man eyed her eagerly, making a quick, impatient gesture towards her, then stopped abruptly. He saw the terror in her eyes.

'Oh, hark! What's that?' she whispered in a startled voice. She put her finger up. 'Oh, let's go back. I don't like this wood. I'm frightened.'

'Rubbish,' he said, and tried to catch her by the waist.

'It's safer in the house—my room—or yours——' she broke off again. 'There it is—don't you hear? It's a footstep!' Her face was whiter than the moon.

'I tell you it's the wind in the branches,' he repeated gruffly. 'Oh, come on, *do*. We were just getting jolly together. There's nothing to be afraid of. Can't you believe me?' He tried to pull her down upon his knee again with force. His face wore an unpleasant expression that was half leer, half grin.

But the girl stood away from him. She continued to peer nervously about her. She listened intently.

'You give me the creeps,' he exclaimed crossly, clawing at her waist again with passionate eagerness that now betrayed exasperation. His disappointment turned him coarse.

The girl made a quick movement of escape, turning so as to look in every direction. She gave a little scream.

'That *was* a step. Oh, oh, it's close behind us. I heard it. We're being watched!' she cried in terror. She darted towards him, then shrank back. He did not try to touch her this time.

'Moonshine!' he growled. 'You've spoilt my—spoilt our chance with your silly nerves.'

But she did not hear him apparently. She stood there shivering as with sudden cold.

'There! I saw it again. I'm sure of it. Something went past me through the air.'

And the man, still thinking only of his own pleasure frustrated, got up heavily, something like anger in his eyes. 'All right,' he said testily; 'if you're going to make a fuss, we'd better go. The house *is* safer, possibly, as you say. You know my room. Come along!' Even that risk he would not take. He loved her with his 'soul'.

They crept stealthily out of the wood, the girl slightly in front of him, casting frightened backward glances. Afraid, guilty, ashamed, with an air as though they had been detected, they stole back towards the garden and the house, and disappeared from view.

And a wind rose suddenly with a rushing sound, poured through the wood as though to cleanse it, swept out the artificial scent and trace of shame, and brought back again the song, the laughter, and the happy revels. It roared across the park, it shook the windows of the house, then sank away as quickly as it came. The trees stood motionless again, guarding their secret in the clean, sweet moonlight that held the world in dream until the dawn stole up, and sunshine took the earth again with joy.

# ENTRANCE AND EXIT

These three—the old physicist, the girl, and the young Anglican parson who was engaged to her—stood by the window of the country house. The blinds were not yet drawn. They could see the dark clump of pines in the field, with crests silhouetted against the pale wintry sky of the February afternoon. Snow, freshly fallen, lay upon lawn and hill. A big moon was already lighting up.

'Yes, that's the wood,' the old man said, 'and it was this very day fifty years ago—February 13—the man disappeared from its shadows; swept in this extraordinary, incredible fashion into invisibility—into *some other place*. Can you wonder the grove is haunted?' A strange impressiveness of manner belied the laugh following the words.

'Oh, please tell us,' the girl whispered; 'we're all alone now.' Curiosity triumphed; yet a vague alarm betrayed itself in the questioning glance she cast for protection at her younger companion, whose fine face, on the other hand, wore an expression that was grave and singularly rapt. He was listening keenly.

'As though Nature,' the physicist went on, half to himself, 'here and there concealed vacuums, gaps, holes in space (his mind was always speculative; more than speculative, some said), in fact, at right angles to three known ones— "higher space", through which a man might drop invisibly—a new direction, as Boyle, Gauss, and Hinton might call it; and what you, with your mystical turn'—looking toward the young priest—'might consider a spiritual change of condition, into a region where space and time do not exist, and where all dimensions are possible—because they are *one*.'

'But, *please*, the story,' the girl begged, not understanding these dark sayings, 'although I'm not sure that Arthur ought to hear it. He's much too interested in such queer things as it is!'

Smiling, yet uneasy, she stood closer to his side, as though her body might protect his soul.

'Very briefly, then, you shall hear what I remember of this haunting, for I was barely ten years old at the time. It was evening—clear and cold like this, with snow and moonlight—when someone reported to my father that a peculiar sound, variously described as crying, wailing, was being heard in the grove. He paid no attention until my sister heard it too, and was frightened. Then he sent a groom to investigate. Though the night was brilliant the man took a lantern. We watched from this very window till we lost his figure against the trees, and the lantern stopped swinging suddenly, as if he had put it down. It remained motionless. We waited half an hour, and then my father, curiously excited, I remember, went out quickly, and I, utterly terrified, went after him. We followed his tracks, which came to an end beside the lantern, the last step being a stride almost impossible for a man to have made. All around the snow was unbroken by a single mark, but the man himself had vanished. Then we heard him calling for help—above, behind, beyond us; from all directions at once, yet from none, came the sound of his voice; but though we called back he made no answer, and gradually his cries grew fainter and fainter, as if going into tremendous distance, and at last died away altogether.'

'And the man himself?' asked both listeners.

'Never returned—from that day to this had never been seen... At intervals for weeks and months afterwards reports came in that he was still heard crying, always crying for help. With time, even these reports ceased—for most of us,' he added under his breath; 'and that is all I know. A mere outline, as you see.'

The girl did not quite like the story, for the old man's manner made it too convincing. She was half disappointed, half frightened.

'See! there are the others coming home,' she exclaimed, with a note of relief, pointing to a group of figures moving over the snow near the pine trees. 'Now we can think of tea!' She crossed the room to busy herself with the friendly tray as the servant approached to fasten the shutters. The young priest, however, deeply interested, talked on with their host, though in a voice almost too low for her to hear. Only the final sentences reached her, making her uneasy—absurdly so, she thought—till afterwards.

'——for matter, as we know, interpenetrates matter,' she heard, 'and two objects may conceivably occupy the same space. The odd thing really is that one should hear, but not see; that air-waves should bring the voice, yet ether-waves fail to bring the picture.'

And then the older man: '——as if certain places in Nature, yes, invited the change—places where these extraordinary forces stir from the earth as from the surface of a living Being with organs—places like islands, mountain-tops, pine-woods, especially pines isolated from their kind. You know the queer results of digging absolutely virgin soil, of course—and that theory of the earth's being *alive*——' The voice dropped again.

'States of mind also helping the forces of the place,' she caught the priest's reply in part; 'such as conditions induced by music, by intense listening, by certain moments in the Mass even—by ecstasy or——'

'I say, what *do* you think?' cried a girl's voice, as the others came in with welcome chatter and odours of tweeds and open fields. 'As we passed your old haunted pine-wood we heard *such* a queer noise. Like someone wailing or crying. Caesar howled and ran; and Harry refused to go in and investigate. He positively funked it!' They all laughed. 'More like a rabbit in a trap than a person crying,' explained Harry, a blush kindly concealing his startling pallor. 'I wanted my tea too much to bother about an old rabbit.'

It was some time after tea when the girl became aware that the priest had disappeared, and putting two and two together, ran in alarm to her host's study. Quite easily, from the hastily opened shutters, they saw his figure moving across the snow. The moon was very bright over the world, yet he carried a lantern that shone pale yellow against the white brilliance.

'Oh, for God's sake, quick!' she cried, pale with fear. 'Quick! or we're too late! Arthur's simply wild about such things. Oh, I might have known—I might have guessed. And this is the very night. I'm terrified!'

By the time he had found his overcoat and slipped round the house with her from the back door, the lantern, they saw, was already swinging close to the pine-wood. The night was still as ice, bitterly cold. Breathlessly they ran, following the tracks. Half-way his steps diverged, and were plainly visible in the virgin snow by themselves. They heard the whispering of the branches ahead of them, for pines cry even when no airs stir. 'Follow me close,' said the old man sternly. The lantern, he already saw, lay upon the ground unattended; no human figure was anywhere visible.

'See! The steps come to an end here,' he whispered, stooping down as soon as they reached the lantern. The tracks, hitherto so regular, showed an odd wavering—the snow curiously disturbed. Quite suddenly they stopped. The final step was a very long one—a stride, almost immense, 'as though he was pushed forward from behind,' muttered the old man, too low to be overheard, 'or sucked forward from in front—as in a fall.'

The girl would have dashed forward but for his strong restraining grasp. She clutched him, uttering a sudden dreadful cry. 'Hark! I hear his voice!' she almost sobbed. They stood still to listen. A mystery that was more than the mystery of night closed about their hearts—a mystery that is beyond life and death, that only great awe and terror can summon from the deeps of the soul. Out of the heart of the trees, fifty feet away, issued a crying voice, half wailing, half singing, very faint. 'Help! help!' it sounded through the still night; 'for the love of God, pray for me!'

The melancholy rustling of the pines followed; and then again the singular crying voice shot past above their heads, now in front of them, now once more behind. It sounded everywhere. It grew fainter and fainter, fading away, it seemed, into distance that somehow was appalling... The grove, however, was empty of all but the sighing wind; the snow unbroken by any tread. The moon threw inky shadows; the cold bit; it was a terror of ice and death and this awful singing cry...

'But why *pray*?' screamed the girl, distracted, frantic with her bewildered terror. 'Why *pray*? Let us *do* something to help—*do* something...!' She swung round in a circle, nearly falling to the ground. Suddenly she perceived that the old man had dropped to his knees in the snow beside her and was—praying.

'Because the forces of prayer, of thought, of the will to help, alone can reach and succour him where he now is,' was all the answer she got. And a moment later both figures were kneeling in the snow, praying, so to speak, their very heart's life out...

The search may be imagined—the steps taken by police, friends, newspapers, by the whole country in fact... But the most curious part of this queer 'Higher Space' adventure is the end of it—at least, the 'end' so far as at present known. For after three weeks, when the winds of March were a-roar about the land, there crept over the fields towards the house the small dark figure of a man. He was thin, pallid as a ghost, worn and fearfully emaciated, but upon his face and in his eyes were traces of an astonishing radiance—a glory unlike anything ever seen... It may, of course, have been deliberate, or it may have been a genuine loss of memory only; none could say—least of all the girl whom his return snatched from the gates of death; but, at any rate, what had come to pass during the interval of his amazing disappearance he has never yet been able to reveal.

'And you must never ask me,' he would say to her—and repeat even after his complete and speedy restoration to bodily health '—for I simply cannot tell. I know no language, you see, that could express it. I was near you all the time. But I was also—elsewhere and otherwise...'

## THE PIKESTAFFE CASE

### I

The vitality of old governesses deserves an explanatory memorandum by a good physiologist. It is remarkable. They tend to survive the grown-up married men and women they once taught as children. They hang on for ever, as a man might put it crudely, a man, that is, who, taught by one of them in his earliest schoolroom days, would answer enquiries fifty years later without enthusiasm: 'Oh, we keep her going, yes. She doesn't want for anything!'

Miss Helena Speke had taught the children of a distingushed family, and these distinguished children, with expensive progeny of their own now, still kept her going. They had clubbed together, seeing that Miss Speke retained her wonderful health, and had established her in a nice little house where she could take respectable lodgers—men for preference—giving them the three B's—bed, bath, and breakfast. Being a capable woman, Miss Speke more than made both ends meet. She wanted for nothing. She kept going.

Applicants for her rooms, especially for the first-floor suite, had to be recommended. She had a stern face for those who rang the bell without a letter in their pockets. She never advertised. Indeed, there was no need to do so. The two upper floors had been occupied by the same tenants for many years—a chief clerk in a branch bank and a retired clergyman respectively. It was only the best suite that sometimes 'happened to be vacant at the moment'. From two guineas inclusive before the war, her price for this had been raised, naturally, to four, the tenant paying his gas-stove, light, and bath extra. Breakfast—she prided herself legitimately on her good breakfast—was included.

For a long time now this first-floor suite had been unoccupied. The cost of living worried Miss Speke, as it worried most other people. Her servant was cheap but incompetent, and once she could let the suite she meant to engage a better one. The distinguished children were scattered out of reach about the world; the eldest had been killed in the war; a married one, a woman, lived in India; another married one was in the throes of divorce —an expensive business; and the fourth, the most generous and last, found himself in the Bankruptcy Court, and so was unable to help.

It was in these conditions that Miss Speke, her vitality impaired, decided to advertise. Although she inserted the words 'references essential,' she meant in her heart to use her own judgment, and if a likely gentleman presented himself and agreed to pay her price, she might accept him. The clergyman and the bank official upstairs were a protection, she felt. She invariably mentioned them to applicants: 'I have a clergyman of the Church of England on the top floor. He's been with me for eleven years. And a banker has the floor below. Mine is a very quiet house, you see.' These words formed part of the ritual she recited in the hall, facing her proposed tenants on the linoleum by the hat-rack; and it was these words she addressed to the tall, thin, pale-faced man with scanty hair and spotless linen, who informed her that he was a tutor, a teacher of higher mathematics to the sons of various families—he mentioned some first-class names where references could be obtained—a student besides and something of an author in his leisure hours. His pupils he taught, of course, in their respective houses, one being in Belgrave Square, another in The Albany; it was only after tea, or in the evenings, that he did his own work. All this he explained briefly, but with great courtesy of manner.

Mr. Thorley was well spoken, with a gentle voice, kind, far-seeing eyes, and an air of being lonely and uncared-for that touched some forgotten, dried-up spring in Miss Speke's otherwise rather cautious heart. He looked every inch a scholar—'and a gentleman', as she explained afterwards to everybody who was interested in him, these being numerous, of unexpected kinds and all very close, not to say unpleasantly close, questioners indeed. But what chiefly influenced her in his favour was the fact, elicited in conversation, that years ago he had been a caller at the house in Portman Square where she was governess to the distinguished family. She did not exactly remember him, but he had certainly known Lady Araminta, the mother of her charges.

Thus it was that Mr. Thorley—John Laking Thorley, M.A., of Jesus College, Cambridge—was accepted by Miss Speke as tenant of her best suite on the first floor at the price mentioned, breakfast included, winning her confidence so fully that she never went to the trouble even of taking up the references he gave her. She liked him, she felt safe with him, she pitied him. He had not bargained, nor tried to beat her down. He just reflected a moment, then agreed. He proved, indeed, an exemplary lodger, early to bed and not too early to rise, of regular habits, thoughtful of the expensive new servant, careful with towels, electric light, and inkstains, prompt in his payments, and never once troubling her with complaints or requests, as other lodgers did, not excepting the banker and the clergyman. Moreover, he was a tidy man, who never lost anything, because he invariably put everything in its proper place and thus knew exactly where to look for it. She noticed this tidiness at once.

Miss Speke, especially in the first days of his tenancy, studied him, as she studied all her lodgers. She studied his room when he was out 'of a morning'. At her leisure she did this, knowing he would never break in and disturb her unexpectedly. She was neither prying nor inquisitive, she assured herself, but she *was* curious. 'I have a right to know something about the gentlemen who sleep under my roof with me,' was the way she put it in her own mind. His clothes, she found, were ample, including evening dress, white gloves, and an opera hat. He had plenty of boots and shoes. His linen was good. His wardrobe, indeed, though a trifle uncared-for, especially his socks, was a gentleman's wardrobe. Only one thing puzzled her. The full-length mirror standing on mahogany legs—a present from the generous 'child', now in the Bankruptcy Court, and, a handsome thing, a special attraction in the best suite—this fine mirror Mr. Thorley evidently did not like. The second or third morning he was with her she went to his bedroom before the servant had done it up, and saw, to her surprise, that this full-length glass stood with its back to the room. It had been placed close against the wall in a corner, its unattractive back turned outward.

'It gave me quite a shock to see it,' as she said afterwards. 'And such a handsome piece, too!'

Her first thought, indeed, sent a cold chill down her energetic spine. 'He's cracked it!' But it was not cracked. She paused in some amazement, wondering why her new lodger had done this thing; then she turned the mirror again into its proper position, and left the room. Next morning she found it again with its face close against the wall. The following day it was the same—she turned it round, only to find it the next morning again with its back to the room.

She asked the servant, but the servant knew nothing about it.

'He likes it that way, I suppose, mum,' was all Sarah said. 'I never laid a 'and on it once.'

Miss Speke, after much puzzled consideration, decided it must be something to do with the light. Mr. Thorley, she remembered, wore horn-rimmed spectacles for reading. She scented a mystery. It caused her a slight—oh, a very slight—feeling of discomfort. Well, if he did not like the handsome mirror, she could perhaps use in it her own room. To see it neglected hurt her a little. Not many furnished rooms could boast a full-length glass, she reflected. A few days later, meeting Mr. Thorley on the linoleum before the hat-rack, she enquired if he was quite comfortable, and if the breakfast was to his liking. He was polite and even cordial. Everything was perfect, he assured her. He had never been so well looked after. And the house was so quiet.

'And the bed, Mr. Thorley? You sleep well, I hope.' She drew nearer to the subject of the mirror, but with caution. For some reason she found a difficulty in actually broaching it. It suddenly dawned upon her that there was something queer about his treatment of that full-length glass. She was by no means fanciful, Miss Speke, retired governess; only the faintest suspicion of something odd brushed her mind and vanished. But she did feel something. She found it impossible to mention the handsome thing outright.

'There's nothing you would like changed in the room, or altered?' she enquired with a smile, 'or—in any way put different—perhaps?'

Mr. Thorley hesitated for a moment. A curious expression, half sad, half yearning, she thought, lit on his thoughtful face for one second and was gone. The idea of moving anything seemed distasteful to him.

'Nothing, Miss Speke, I thank you,' he replied courteously, but without delay. 'Everything is really *just* as I like it.' Then, with a little bow, he asked: 'I trust my typewriter disturbs nobody. Please let me know if it does.'

Miss Speke assured him that nobody minded the typewriter in the least, nor even heard it, and, with another charming little bow and a smile, Mr. Thorley went out to give his lessons in the higher mathematics.

'There!' she reflected, 'and I never even asked him!' It had been impossible.

From the window she watched him going down the street, his head bent, evidently in deep thought, his books beneath his arm, looking, she thought, every inch the gentleman and the scholar that he undoubtedly was. His personality left a very strong impression on her mind. She found herself rather wondering about him. As he turned the corner Miss Speke owned to two things that rose simultaneously in her mind: first, the relief that the lodger was out for the day and could be counted upon not to return unexpectedly; secondly, that it would interest her to slip up and see what kind of books he read. A minute later she was in his sitting-room. It was already swept and dusted, the breakfast cleared away, and the books, she saw, lay partly on the table where he had just left them and partly on the broad mantelpiece he used as a shelf. She was alone, the servant was downstairs in the kitchen. She examined Mr. Thorley's books.

The examination left her bewildered and uninspired. 'I couldn't make them out at all,' she put it. But they were evidently what she called costly volumes, and that she liked. 'Something to do with his work, I suppose—mathematics, and all that,' she decided, after turning over pages covered with some kind of hieroglyphics, symbols being a word she did not know in that connection. There was no printing, there were no sentences, there was nothing she could lay hold of, and the diagrams she thought perhaps were Euclid, or possibly astronomical. Most of the names were odd and quite unknown to her. Gauss! Minowski! Lobatchewski! And it affronted her that some of these were German. A writer named Einstein was popular with her lodger, and that, she felt, was a pity, as well as a mistake in taste. It all alarmed her a little; or, rather she felt that touch of respect, almost of awe, pertaining to some world entirely beyond her ken. She was rather glad when the search—it was a duty—ended.

'There's nothing there,' she reflected, meaning there was nothing that explained his dislike of the full-length mirror. And disappointed, yet with a faint relief, she turned to his private papers. These, since he was a tidy man, were in a drawer. Mr. Thorley never left anything lying about. Now, a letter Miss Speke would not have thought of reading, but papers, especially learned papers, were another matter. Conscience, nevertheless, did prick her faintly as she cautiously turned over sheaf after sheaf of large white foolscap, covered with designs, and curves, and diagrams in ink, the ink he never spilt, and assuredly in his recent handwriting. And it was among these foolscap sheets that she suddenly came upon one sheet in particular that caught her attention and even startled her. In the centre, surrounded by scriggly hieroglyphics, numbers, curves and lines meaningless to her, she saw a drawing of the full-length mirror. Some of the curves ran into it and through it, emerging on the other side. She knew it was *the* mirror because its exact measurements were indicated in red ink.

This, as mentioned, startled her. What could it mean? She asked herself, staring intently at the curious sheet, as though it must somehow yield its secret to prolonged even if unintelligent enquiry. 'It looks like an experiment or something,' was the furthest her mind could probe into the mystery, though this, she admitted, was not very far. Holding the paper at various angles, even upside down, she examined it with puzzled curiosity, then slowly laid it down again in the exact place whence she had taken it. That faint breath of alarm had again suddenly brushed her soul, as though she approached a mystery she had better leave unsolved.

'It's very strange——' she began, carefully closing the drawer, but unable to complete the sentence even in her mind. 'I don't think I like it—quite,' and she turned to go out. It was just then that something touched her face, tickling one cheek, something fine as a cobweb, something in the air. She picked it away. It was a thread of silk, extremely fine, so fine, indeed, that it might almost have been a spider's web of gossamer such as one sees floating over the garden lawn on a sunny morning. Miss Speke brushed it away, giving it no further thought, and went about her usual daily duties.

## II

But in her mind was established now a vague uneasiness, though so vague that at first she did not recognise it. Her thought would suddenly pause. 'Now, what is it?' she would ask herself. 'Something's on my mind. What is it I've forgotten?' The picture of her first-floor lodger appeared, and she knew at once. 'Oh, yes, it's that mirror and the diagrams, of course.' Some taut wire of alarm was quivering at the back of her mind. It was akin to those childhood alarms that pertain to the big unexplained mysteries no parent can elucidate because no parent knows. 'Only God can tell that,' says the parent evading the insoluble problem. 'I'd better not think about it,' was the analogous conclusion reached by Miss Speke. Meanwhile the impression the new lodger's personality made upon her mind perceptibly deepened. He seemed to her full of power, above little things, a man of intense and mysterious mental life. He was constantly and somewhat possessingly in her thoughts. The mere thought of him, she found, stimulated her.

It was just before luncheon, as she returned from her morning marketing, that the servant drew her attention to certain marks upon the carpet of Mr. Thorley's sitting-room. She had discovered them as she handled the vacuum cleaner—faint, short lines drawn by dark chalk or crayons, in shape like the top or bottom right-angle of a square bracket, and sometimes with a tiny arrow shown as well. There were occasional other marks, too, that Miss Speke recognised as the hieroglyphics she called squiggles. Mistress and servant examined them together in a stooping position. They found others on the bedroom carpet, too, only these were not straight; they were small curved lines; and about the feet of the full-length mirror they clustered in a quantity, segments of circles, some large, some small. They looked as if someone had snipped off curly hair, or pared his finger-nails with sharp scissors, only considerably larger, and they were so faint that they were only visible when the sunlight fell upon them.

'I knew they was drawn on,' said Sarah, puzzled, yet proud that she had found them, 'because they didn't come up with the dust and fluff.'

'I'll—speak to Mr. Thorley,' was the only comment Miss Speke made. 'I'll tell him.' Her voice was not quite steady, but the girl apparently noticed nothing.

'There's all this too, please, mum.' She pointed to a number of fine silk threads she had collected upon a bit of newspaper, preparatory to the dust-bin. 'They was stuck on the cupboard door and the walls, stretched all across the room, but rather 'igh up. I only saw them by chance. One caught on my face.'

Miss Speke stared, touched, examined for some seconds without speaking. She remembered the thread that had tickled her own cheek. She looked enquiringly round the room, and the servant, following her suggestion, indicated where the threads had been attached to walls and furniture. No marks, however, were left, there was no damage done.

'I'll mention it to Mr. Thorley,' said her mistress briefly, unwilling to discuss the matter with the new servant, much less to admit that she was uncomfortably at sea. 'Mr. Thorley,' she added, as though there was nothing unusual, 'is a high mathematician. He makes—measurements and—calculations of that sort.' She had not sufficient control of her voice to be more explicit, and she went from the room aware that, unaccountably, she was trembling. She had first gathered up the threads, meaning to show them to her lodger when she demanded an explanation. But the explanation was delayed, for—to state it bluntly—she was afraid to ask him for it. She put it off till the following morning, then till the day after, and, finally, she decided to say nothing about the matter at all. 'I'd better leave it, perhaps, after all,' she persuaded herself. 'There's no damage done, anyhow. I'd better not enquire.' All the same she did not like it. By the end of the week, however, she was able to pride herself upon her restraint and tact; the marks on the carpet, rubbed out by the girl, were not renewed, and the fine threads of silk were never again found stretching through the air from wall to furniture. Mr. Thorley had evidently noticed their removal and had discontinued what he had observed was an undesirable performance. He was a scholar and a gentleman. But he was more. He was frank and straight-dealing. One morning he asked to see his landlady and told her all about it himself.

'Oh,' he said in his pleasantest, easiest manner when she came into the room, 'I wanted to tell you, Miss Speke—indeed, I meant to do so long before this—about the marks I made on your carpets'—he smiled apologetically—'and the silk threads I stretched. I use them for measurements—for problems I set my pupils, and one morning I left them by mistake. The marks easily rub out. But I will use scraps of paper instead another time. I can pin these on—if you will kindly tell your excellent servant not to touch them—er—they're rather important to me.' He smiled again charmingly, and his face wore the wistful, rather yearning expression that had already appealed to her. The eyes, it struck her, were very brilliant. 'Any damage,' he added—

'though, I assure you, none is possible really—I would, of course, make good to you, Miss Speke.'

'Thank you, Mr. Thorley,' was all Miss Speke could find to say, so confused was her mind by troubling thoughts and questions she dared not express. 'Of course—this *is* my best suite, you see.'

It was all most amicable and pleasant between them.

'I wonder—have my books come?' he asked, as he went out. 'Ah, there they are, I do believe!' he exclaimed, for through the open front door a van was seen discharging a very large packing-case.

'Your books, Mr. Thorley——?' Miss Speke murmured, noting the size of the package with dismay. 'But I'm afraid—you'll hardly find space to put them in,' she stammered. 'The rooms—er'—she did not wish to disparage them—'are so small, aren't they?'

Mr. Thorley smiled delightfully. 'Oh, please do not trouble on that account,' he said. 'I shall find space all right, I assure you. It's merely a question of knowing where and how to put them,' and he proceeded to give the man instructions.

A few days later a second case arrived.

'I'm expecting some instruments, too,' he mentioned casually, 'mathematical instruments,' and he again assured her with his confident smile that she need have no anxiety on the score of space. Nor would he dent the walls or scrape the furniture the least little bit. There was always room, he reminded her gently again, provided one knew how to stow things away. Both books and instruments were necessary to his work. Miss Speke need feel no anxiety at all.

But Miss Speke felt more than anxiety, she felt uneasiness, she felt a singular growing dread. There lay in her a seed of distress that began to sprout rapidly. Everything arrived as Mr. Thorley has announced, case upon case was unpacked in his room by his own hands. The straw and wood she used for firing purposes, there was no mess, no litter, no untidiness, nor were walls and furniture injured in any way. What caused her dread to deepen into something bordering upon actual alarm was the fact that, on searching Mr. Thorley's rooms when he was out, she could discover no trace of any of the things that had arrived. There was no sign of either books or instruments. Where had he stored them? Where could they lie concealed? She asked herself innumerable questions, but found no answer to them. These stores, enough to choke and block the room, had been brought in through the sitting-room door. They could not possibly have been taken out again. They had *not* been taken out. Yet no trace of them was anywhere to be seen. It was very strange, she thought; indeed, it was more than strange. She felt excited. She felt a touch of hysterical alarm.

Meanwhile, thin strips of white paper, straight, angled, curved, were pinned upon the carpet; threads of finest silk again stretched overhead connecting the top of the door lintel with the window, the high cupboard with the curtain rods—yet too high to be brushed away merely by the head of anyone moving in the room. And the full-length mirror still stood with its face close against the wall.

The mystery of these aerial entanglements increased Miss Speke's alarm considerably. What could their purpose be? 'Thank God,' she thought, 'this isn't war time!' She knew enough to realise their meaning was not 'wireless'. That they bore some relation to the lines on the carpet and to the diagrams and curves upon the paper, she grasped vaguely. But what it all meant baffled her and made her feel quite stupid. Where all the books and instruments had disappeared added to her bewilderment. She felt more and more perturbed. A vague, uncertain fear was worse than something definite she could face and deal with. Her fear increased. Then, suddenly, yet with a reasonable enough excuse, Sarah gave notice.

For some reason Miss Speke did not argue with the girl. She preferred to let the real meaning of her leaving remain unexpressed. She just let her go. But the fact disturbed her extraordinarily. Sarah had given every satisfaction, there had been no sign of a grievance, no complaint, the work was not hard, the pay was good. It was simply that the girl preferred to leave. Miss Speke attributed it to Mr. Thorley. She became more and more disturbed in mind. Also she found herself, more and more, avoiding her lodger, whose regular habits made such avoidance an easy matter. Knowing his hours of exit and entrance, she took care to be out of the way. At the mere sound of his step she flew to cover. The new servant, a stupid, yet not inefficient country girl, betrayed no reaction of any sort, no unfavourable reaction at any rate. Having received her instructions, Lizzie did her work without complaint from either side. She did not remove the paper and the thread, nor did she mention them. She seemed just the country clod she was. Miss Speke, however, began to have restless nights. She contracted an unpleasant habit: she lay awake—listening.

## III

As the result of one of these sleepless nights she came to the abrupt conclusion that she would be happier without Mr. Thorley in the house—only she had not the courage to ask him to leave. The truth was she had not the courage to speak to him at all, much less to give him notice, however nicely.

After much cogitation she hit upon a plan that promised well: she sent him a carefully worded letter explaining that, owing to increased cost of living, she found herself compelled to raise his terms. The 'raise' was more than considerable, it was unreasonable, but he paid what she demanded, sending down a cheque for three months in advance with his best compliments. The letter somehow made her tremble. It was at this stage she first became aware of the existence in her of other feelings than discomfort, uneasiness, and alarm. These other feelings, being in contradiction of her dread, were difficult to describe, but their result was plain—she did not really wish Mr. Thorley to go after all. His friendly 'compliments', his refusal of her hint, caused her a secret pleasure. It was not the cheque at the increased rate that pleased her—it was simply the fact that her lodger meant to stay.

It might be supposed that some delayed sense of romance had been stirred in her, but this really was not the case at all. Her pleasure was due to another source, but to a source uncommonly obscure and very strange. She feared him, feared his presence, above all, feared going into his room, while yet there was something about the mere idea of Mr. Thorley that entranced her. Another thing may as well be told at once—she herself faced it boldly—she would enter his dreaded room, when he was out, and would deliberately linger there. There was an odd feeling in the room that gave her pleasure, and more than pleasure—happiness. Surrounded by the enigmas of his personality, by the lines and curves of white paper pinned upon her carpet, by the tangle of silken threads above her head, by the mysterious books, the more than mysterious diagrams in his drawer—yet all these, even the dark perplexity of the rejected mirror and the vanished objects, were forgotten in the curious sense of happiness she derived from merely sitting in his room. Her fear contained this other remarkable ingredient—an uncommon sense of joy, of liberty, of freedom. She felt *exaltée.*

She could not explain it, she did not attempt to do so. She would go shaking and trembling into his room, and a few minutes later this sense of uncommon happiness—of release, almost of escape, she felt it—would steal over her as though in her dried-up frozen soul spring had burst upon midwinter, as though something that crawled had suddenly most gloriously found wings. An indescribable exhilaration caught her.

Under this influence the dingy street turned somehow radiant, and the front door of her poor lodging-house opened upon blue seas, yellow sands, and mountains carpeted with flowers. Her whole life, painfully repressed and crushed down in the dull service of conventional nonentities, flashed into colour, movement, and adventure. Nothing confined her. She was no longer limited. She knew advance in all possible directions. She knew the stars. She knew escape!

An attempt has been made to describe for her what she never could have described herself.

The reaction, upon coming out again, was painful. Her life in the past as a governess, little better than a servant; her life in the present as lodging-house keeper; her struggle with servants, with taxes, with daily expenses; her knowledge that no future but a mere 'living' lay in front of her until the grave was reached—these overwhelmed her with an intense depression that the contrast rendered almost insupportable. Whereas in *his* room she had perfume, freedom, liberty, and wonder—the wonder of some entirely new existence.

Thus, briefly, while Miss Speke longed for Mr. Thorley to leave her house, she became obsessed with the fear that one day he really *would* go. Her mind, it is seen, became uncommonly disturbed; her lodger's presence being undoubtedly the cause. Her nights were now more than restless, they were sleepless. Whence came, she asked herself repeatedly in the dark watches, her fear? Whence came, too, her strange enchantment?

It was at this juncture, then, that a further item of perplexity was added to her mind. Miss Speke, as has been seen, was honourably disposed; she respected the rights of others, their property as well. Yet, included in the odd mood of elation the room and its atmosphere caused her, was also a vagrant, elusive feeling that the intimate, the personal—above all, the personal—had lost their original rigidity. Small individual privacies, secrecy, no longer held their familiar meaning quite. The idea that most things in life were to be shared slipped into her. A 'secret', to this expensive mood, was a childish attitude.

At any rate, it was while lingering in her lodger's attractive room one day—a habit now—that she did something that caused her surprise, yet did not shock her. She saw an open letter lying on his table—and she read it.

Rather than an actual letter, however, it seemed a note, a memorandum. It began 'To J. L. T'.

In a boyish writing, the meaning of the language escaped her entirely. She understood the strange words as little as she understood the phases of the moon, while yet she derived from their perusal a feeling of mysterious beauty, similar to the emotions the changes of that lovely satellite stirred in her:

'To J. L. T.

'I followed your instructions, though with intense effort and difficulty. I woke at 4 o'clock. About ten minutes later, as you said might happen, I woke a *second time*. The change into the second state was as great as the change from sleeping to waking, in the ordinary meaning of these words. But I could not remain 'awake'. I fell asleep again in about a minute—back into the usual waking state, I mean. Description in words is impossible, as you know. What I felt was too terrific to feel for long. The new energy must presently have *burned me up*. It frightened me—as you warned me it would. And this fear, no doubt, was the cause of my 'falling asleep' again so quickly.

'Cannot we arrange a Call for Help for similar occasions in future?

G. P.'

Against this note Mr. Thorley had written various strangest 'squiggles'; higher mathematics, Miss Speke supposed. In the opposite margin, also in her lodger's writing, were these words:

'We must agree on a word to use when frightened. *Help*, or *Help me*, seems the best. To be uttered with the whole being.'

Mr. Thorley had added a few other notes. She read them without the faintest prick of conscience. Though she understood no single sentence, a thrill of deep delight ran through her:

'It amounts, of course, to a new direction; a direction at right angles to all we know, a new direction in oneself, a new direction—in living. But it can, perhaps, be translated into mathematical terms by the intellect. This, however, only a simile at best. Cannot be experienced that way. Actual experience possible only to *changed consciousness*. But good to become mathematically accustomed to it. The mathematical experiments are worth it. They induce the mind, at any rate, to dwell upon the new direction. This helps. ...'

Miss Speke laid down the letter exactly where she had found it. No shame was in her. 'G. P.' she knew, meant Gerald Pikestaffe; he was one of her lodger's best pupils, the one in Belgrave Square. Her feeling of mysterious elation, as already mentioned, seemed above all such matters as small secrecies or petty personal privacies. She had read a 'private' letter without remorse. One feeling only caused in her a certain commonplace emotion: the feeling that, while she read the letter, her lodger was present, watching her. He seemed close behind her, looking over her shoulder almost, observing her acts, her mood, her very thoughts —yet not objecting. He was aware, at any rate, of what she did...

It was under these circumstances that she bethought herself of her old tenant, the retired clergyman on the top floor, and sought his aid. The consolation of talking to another would be something, yet when the interview began all she could manage to say was that her mind was troubled and her heart not quite as it should be, and that she 'didn't know what to do about it all'. For the life of her she could not find more definite words. To mention Mr. Thorley she found suddenly utterly impossible.

'Prayer,' the old man interrupted her half-way, 'prayer, my dear lady. Prayer, I find,' he repeated smoothly, 'is always the best course in all one's troubles and perplexities. Leave it to God. He knows. And in His good time He will answer.' He advised her to read the Bible and Longfellow. She added Florence Barclay to the list and followed his advice. The books, however, comforted her very little.

After some hesitation she then tried her other tenant. But the 'banker' stopped her even sooner than the clergyman had done. MacPherson was very prompt:

'I can give you another ten shillings or maybe half a guinea,' he said briskly. 'Times are deeficult, I know. But I can't do more. If that's suffeecient I shall be delighted to stay on——' and, with a nod and a quick smile that settled the matter then and there, he was through the door and down the steps on the way to his office.

It was evident that Miss Speke must face her troubles alone, a fact, for the rest, life had already taught her. The loyal, courageous spirit in her accepted the situation. The alternate moods of happiness and depression, meanwhile, began to wear her out. 'If only Mr. Thorley would go! If only Mr. Thorley will not go!' For some weeks now she had successfully avoided him. He made no requests nor complaints. His habits were as regular as sunrise, his payments likewise. Not even the servant mentioned him. He became a shadow in the house.

Then, with the advent of summer-time, he came home, as it were, an hour earlier than usual. He invariably worked from 5.30 to 7.30, when he went out for his dinner. Tea he always had at a pupil's house. It was a light evening, caused by the advance of the clock, and Miss Speke, mending her underwear at the window, suddenly perceived his figure coming down the street.

She watched, fascinated. Of two instincts—to hide herself, or to wait there and catch his eye—she obeyed the latter. She had not seen him for several weeks, and a deep thrill of happiness ran through her. His walk was peculiar, she noticed at once; he did not walk in a straight line. His tall, thin outline flowed down the pavement in long, sweeping curves, yet quite steadily. He was not drunk. He came nearer; he was not twenty feet away; at ten feet she saw his face clearly, and received a shock. It was worn, and thin, and wasted, but a light of happiness, of something more than happiness indeed, shone in it. He reached the area railings. He looked up. His face seemed ablaze. Their eyes met, his with no start of recognition, hers with a steady stare of wonder. She ran into the passage, and before Mr. Thorley had time to use his latch-key she had opened the door for him herself. Little she knew, as she stood there trembling, that she stood also upon the threshold of an amazing adventure.

Face to face with him her presence of mind deserted her. She could only look up into that worn and wasted face, into those happy, severe, and brilliant eyes, where yet burned a strange expression of wistful yearning, of uncommon wonder, of something that seemed not of this world quite. Such an expression she had never seen before upon any human countenance. Its light dazzled her. There was uncommon fire in the eyes. It enthralled her. The same instant, as she stood there gazing at him without a single word, either of welcome or enquiry, it flashed across her that he needed something from her. He needed help, her help. It was a far-fetched notion, she was well aware, but it came to her irresistibly. The conviction was close to her, closer than her skin.

It was this knowledge, doubtless, that enabled her to hear without resentment the strange words he at once made use of:

'Ah, I thank you, Miss Spcke, I thank you,' the thin lips parting in a smile, the shining eyes lit with an emotion of more than ordinary welcome. 'You cannot know what a relief it is to me to see you. You are so sound, so wholesome, so ordinary, so—forgive me, I beg—so commonplace.'

He was gone past her and upstairs into his sitting-room. She heard the key turn softly. She was aware that she had not shut the front door. She did so, then went back, trembling, happy, frightened, into her own room. She had a curious, rushing feeling, both frightful and bewildering, that the room did not contain her. ... She was still sitting there two hours later, when she heard Mr. Thorley's step come down the stairs and leave the house. She was still sitting there when she heard him return, open the door with his key, and go up to his sitting-room. The interval might have been two minutes or two weeks, instead of two hours merely. And all this time she had the wondrous sensation that the room did not contain her. The walls and ceilings did not shut her in. She was out of the room. Escape had come very close to her. She was out of the house ... out of herself as well....

## IV

She went early to bed, taking this time the Bible with her. Her strange sensations had passed, they had left her gradually. She had made herself a cup of tea and had eaten a soft-boiled egg and some bread-and-butter. She felt more normal again, but her nerves were unusually sensitive. It was a comfort to know there were two men in the house with her, two worthy men, a clergyman and a banker. The Bible, the banker, the clergyman, with Mrs. Barclay and Longfellow not far from her bed, were certainly a source of comfort to her.

The traffic died away, the rumbling of the distant motor-buses ceased, and, with the passing of the hours, the night became intensely still.

It was April. Her window was opened at the top and she could smell the cool, damp air of coming spring. Soothed by the books she began to feel drowsy. She glanced at the clock—it was just on two—then blew out the candle and prepared to sleep. Her thoughts turned automatically to Mr. Thorley, lying asleep on the floor above, his threads and paper strips and mysterious diagrams all about him—when, suddenly, a voice broke through the silence with a cry for help. It was a man's voice, and it sounded a long way off. But she recognised it instantly, and she sprang out of bed without a trace of fear. It was Mr. Thorley calling, and in the voice was anguish.

'He's in trouble? In danger! He needs help? I knew it!' ran rapidly through her mind, as she lit the candle with fingers that did not tremble. The clock showed three. She had slept a full hour. She opened the door and peered into the passage, but saw no one there; the stairs, too, were empty. The call was not repeated.

'Mr. Thorley!' she cried aloud. 'Mr. Thorley! Do you want anything?' And by the sound of her voice she realised how distant and muffled his own had been. 'I'm coming!'

She stood there waiting, but no answer came. There was no sound. She realised the uncommon stillness of the night.

'Did you call me?' she tried again, but with less confidence. 'Can I do anything for you?'

Again there was no answer; nothing stirred; the house was silent as the grave. The linoleum felt cold against her bare feet, and she stole back to get her slippers and a dressing-gown, while a hundred possibilities flashed through her mind at once. Oddly enough, she never once thought of burglars, nor of fire, nor, indeed, of any ordinary situation that required ordinary help. Why this was so she could not say. No ordinary fear, at any rate, assailed her in that moment, nor did she feel the smallest touch of nervousness about her own safety.

'Was it—I wonder—a dream?' she asked herself as she pulled the dressing-gown about her. 'Did I dream that voice——?' when the thrilling cry broke forth again, startling her so that she nearly dropped the candle:

'Help! Help! Help me!'

Very distinct, yet muffled as by distance, it was beyond all question the voice of Mr. Thorley. What she had taken for anguish in it she now recognised was terror. It sounded on the floor above, it was the closed door doubtless that gave the muffled effect of distance.

Miss Speke ran along the passage instantly, and with extraordinary speed for an elderly woman; she was half-way up the stairs in a moment, when, just as she reached the first little landing by the bathroom and turned to begin the second flight, the voice came again: 'Help! Help' but this time with a difference that, truth to tell, did set her nerves unpleasantly aquiver. For there were two voices instead of one, and they were not upstairs at all. Both were below her in the passage she had just that moment left. Close they were behind her. One, moreover, was not the voice of Mr. Thorley. It was a boy's clear soprano. Both called for help together, and both held a note of terror that made her heart shake.

Under these conditions it may be forgiven to Miss Speke that she lost her balance and reeled against the wall, clutching the banisters for a moment's support. Yet her courage did not fail her. She turned instantly and quickly went downstairs again—to find the passage empty of any living figure. There was no one visible. There was only silence, a motionless hat-rack, the door of her own room slightly ajar, and shadows.

'Mr. Thorley!' she called. 'Mr. Thorley!' her voice not quite so loud and confident as before. It had a whisper in it. No answer came. She repeated the words, her tone with still less volume. Only faint echoes that seemed to linger unduly came in response. Peering into her own room she found it exactly as she had left it. The dining-room, facing it, was likewise empty. Yet a moment before she had plainly heard two voices calling for help within a few yards of where she stood. Two voices! What could it mean? She noticed now for the first time a peculiar freshness in the air, a sharpness, almost a perfume, as though all the windows were wide open and the air of coming spring was in the house.

Terror, though close, had not yet actually gripped her. That she had gone crazy occurred to her, but only to be dismissed. She was quite sane and self-possessed. The changing direction of the sounds lay beyond all explanation, but an explanation, she was positive, there must be. The odd freshness in the air was heartening, and seemed to brace her. No, terror had not yet really gripped her. Ideas of summoning the servant, the clergyman, the banker, these she equally dismissed. It was no ordinary help that was needed, not theirs at any rate. She went boldly upstairs again and knocked at Mr. Thorley's bedroom door. She knocked again and again, loud enough to waken him, if he had perchance called out in sleep, but not loud enough to disturb her other tenants. No answer came. There was no sound within. No light shone through the cracks. With his sitting-room the same conditions held.

It was the strangeness of the second voice that now stole over her with a deadly fear. She found herself cold and shivering. As she, at length, went slowly downstairs again the cries were suddenly audible once more. She heard both voices: 'Help! Help! Help me!' Then silence. They were fainter this time. Far away, they sounded, withdrawn curiously into some remote distance, yet ever with the same anguish, the same terror in them as before. The direction, however, this time she could not tell at all. In a sense they seemed both close and far, both above her and below; they seemed—it was the only way she could describe the astounding thing—in any direction, or in all directions.

Miss Speke was really terrified at last. The strange, full horror of it gripped her, turning her heart suddenly to ice. The two voices, the terror in them, the extraordinary impression that they had withdrawn further into some astounding distance—this overcame her. She became appalled. Staggering into her room, she reached the bed and fell upon it in a senseless heap. She had fainted.

## V

She slept late, owing probably to exhausted nerves. Though usually up and about by 7.30, it was after nine when the servant woke her. She sprawled half in the bed, half out; the candle, which luckily had extinguished itself in falling, lay upon the carpet. The events of the night came slowly back to her as she watched the servant's face. The girl was white and shaking.

'Are you ill, mum?' Lizzie asked anxiously in a whisper; then, without waiting for an answer, blurted out what she had really come in to say: 'Mr. Thorley, mum! I can't get into his room. There's no answer.' The girl was very frightened.

Mr. Thorley invariably had breakfast at 8 o'clock, and was out of the house punctually at 8.45.

'Was he ill in the night—perhaps—do you think?' Miss Speke said. It was the nearest she could get to asking if the girl had heard the voices. She had admirable control of herself by this time. She got up, still in her dressing-gown and slippers.

'Not that I know of, mum,' was the reply.

'Come,' said her mistress firmly. 'We'll go in.' And they went upstairs together.

The bedroom door, as the girl had said, was closed, but the sitting-room was open. Miss Speke led the way. The freshness of the night before lay still in the air, she noticed, though the windows were all closed tightly. There was an exhilarating sharpness, a delightful tang as of open space. She particularly mentions this. On the carpet, as usual, lay the strips of white paper, fastened with small pins, and the silk threads, also as usual, stretched across from lintel to cupboard, from window to bracket. Miss Speke brushed several of them from her face.

The door into the bedroom she opened, and went boldly in, followed more cautiously by the girl. 'There's nothing to be afraid of,' said her mistress firmly. The bed, she saw, had not been slept in. Everything was neat and tidy. The long mirror stood close against the wall, showing its ugly back as usual, while about its four feet clustered the curved strips of paper Miss Speke had grown accustomed to.

'Pull the blinds up, Lizzie,' she said in a quiet voice.

The light now enabled her to see everything quite clearly. There were silken threads, she noticed distinctly, stretching from bed to window, and though both windows were closed there was this strange sweetness in the air as of a flowering spring garden. She sniffed it with a curious feeling of pleasure, of freedom, of release, though Lizzie, apparently, noticed nothing of all this.

'There's his 'at and mackintosh,' the girl whispered in a frightened voice, pointing to the hooks on the door. 'And the umbrella in the corner. But I don't see 'is boots, mum. They weren't put out to be cleaned.'

Miss Speke turned and looked at her, voice and manner under full command. 'What do you mean?' she asked.

'Mr. Thorley ain't gone out, mum,' was the reply in a tremulous tone.

At that very moment a faint, distant cry was audible in a man's voice: 'Help! Help!' Immediately after it a soprano, fainter still, called from what seemed even greater distance: 'Help me!' The direction was not ascertainable. It seemed both in the room, yet far away outside in space above the roofs. A glance at the girl convinced Miss Speke that she had heard nothing.

'Mr. Thorley is not *here*,' whispered Miss Speke, one hand upon the brass bed-rail for support.

The room was undeniably empty.

'Leave everything exactly as it is,' ordered her mistress as they went out. Tears in her eyes, she lingered a moment on the threshold, but the sounds were not repeated. 'Exactly as it is,' she repeated, closing the bedroom and then the sitting-room door behind her. She locked the latter, putting the key in her pocket. Two days later, as Mr. Thorley had not returned, she informed the police. But Mr. Thorley never returned. He had disappeared completely. He left no trace. He was never heard of again, though—once—he was seen.

Yet, this is not entirely accurate perhaps, for he was seen twice, in the sense that he was seen by two persons, and though he was not 'heard of', he was certainly heard. Miss Speke heard his voice from time to time. She heard it in the daytime and at night; calling for help and always with the same words she had first heard: 'Help! Help! Help me!' It sounded very far away, withdrawn into immense distance, the distance ever increasing. Occasionally she heard the boy's voice with it; they called together sometimes; she never heard the soprano voice alone. But the anguish and terror she had first noticed were no longer present. Alarm had gone out of them. It was more like an echo that she heard. Through all the hubbub, confusion and distressing annoyance of the police search and enquiry, the voice and voices came to her, though she never mentioned them to a single living soul, not even to her old tenants, the clergyman and the banker. They kept their rooms on—which was about all she could have asked of them. The best suite was never let again. It was kept locked and empty. The dust accumulated. The mirror remained untouched, its face against the wall.

The voices, meanwhile, grew more and more faint; the distance seemed to increase; soon the voice of the boy was no longer heard at all, only the cry of Mr. Thorley, her mysterious but perfect lodger, sang distantly from time to time, both in the sunshine and in the still darkness of the night hours. The direction whence it came, too, remained, as before, undeterminable. It came from anywhere and everywhere—from above, below, on all sides. It had become, too, a pleasant, even a happy sound; no dread belonged to it any more. The intervals grew longer then; days first, then weeks passed without a sound; and invariably, after these increasing intervals, the voice had become fainter, weaker, withdrawn into ever greater and greater distance. With the coming of the warm spring days it grew almost inaudible. Finally, with the great summer heats, it died away completely.

## VI

The disappearance of Mr. Thorley, however, had caused no public disturbance on its own account, not until it was bracketed with another disappearance, that of one of his pupils, Sir Mark Pikestaffe's son. The Pikestaffe Case then became a daily mystery that filled the papers. Mr. Thorley was of no consequence, whereas Sir Mark was a figure in the public eye.

Mr. Thorley's life, as enquiry proved, held no mystery. He had left everything in order. He did not owe a penny. He owned, indeed, considerable property, both in land and securities, and teaching mathematics, especially to promising pupils, seemed to have been a hobby merely. A half-brother called eventually to take away his few possessions, but the books and instruments he had brought into the lodging-house were never traced. He was a scholar and a gentleman to the last, a man, too, it appeared, of immense attainments and uncommon ability, one of the greatest mathematical brains, if the modest obituaries were to be believed, the world has ever known. His name now passed into oblivion. He left no record of his researches or achievements. Out of some mysterious sense of loyalty and protection Miss Speke never mentioned his peculiar personal habits. The strips of paper, as the silken threads, she had carefully removed and destroyed long before the police came to make their search of his rooms...

But the disappearance of young Gerald Pikestaffe raised a tremendous hubbub. It was some days before the two disappearances were connected, both having occurred on the same night, it was then proved. The boy, a lad of great talent, promising a brilliant future, and the favourite pupil of the older man, his tutor, had not even left the house. His room was empty—and that was all. He left no clue, no trace. Terrible hints and suggestions were, of course, spread far and wide, but there was not a scrap of evidence forthcoming to support them. Gerald Pikestaffe and Mr. Thorley, at the same moment of the same night, vanished from the face of the earth and were no more seen. The matter ended there. The one link between them appeared to have been an amazing, an exceptional gift for higher mathematics. The Pikestaffe Case merely added one more to the insoluble mysteries with which commonplace daily life is sprinkled.

It was some six weeks to a month after the event that Miss Speke received a letter from one of her former charges, the most generous one, now satisfactorily finished with the Bankruptcy Court. He had honourably discharged his obligations; he was doing well; he wrote and asked Miss Speke to put him up for a week or two. 'And do *please* give me Mr. Thorley's room,' he asked. 'The case thrilled me, and I should like to sleep in that room. I always loved mysteries, you remember... There's something *very* mysterious about this thing. Besides, I knew the P. boy a little—an astounding genius, if ever there was one.'

Though it cost her much effort and still more hesitation, she consented finally. She prepared the rooms herself. There was a new servant, Lizzie having given notice the day after the disappearance, and the older woman who now waited upon the clergyman and the banker was not quite to be trusted with the delicate job. Miss Speke, entering the empty rooms on tiptoe, a strange trepidation in her heart, but that same heart firm with courage, drew up the blinds, swept the floors, dusted the furniture, and made the bed. All she did with her own hands. Only the full-length mirror she did not touch. What terror still was in her clung to that handsome piece. It was haunted by memories. For her it was still both wonderful and somehow awful. The ghost of her strange experience hid invisibly in its polished, if now unseen, depths. She dared not handle it, far less move it from the resting-place where it rested in peace. *His* hands had placed it there. To her it was sacred.

It had been given to her by Colonel Lyle, who would now occupy the room, stand on the wondrous carpet, move through the air where once the mysterious silks had floated, sleep in the very bed itself. All this he could do, but the mirror he must not touch.

'I'll explain to him a little. I'll beg him not to move it. He's very understanding,' she said to herself, as she went out to buy some flowers for the sitting-room. Colonel Lyle was expected that very afternoon. Lilac, she remembered, was what he always liked. It took her longer than she expected to find really fresh bunches, of the colour that he preferred, and when she got back it was time to be thinking about his tea. The sun's rays fell slanting down the dingy street, touching it with happy gold. This, with thoughts of the tea-kettle and what vase would suit the flowers best, filled her mind as she passed along the linoleum in the narrow hall—then noticed suddenly a new hat and coat hanging on the usually empty pegs. Colonel Lyle had arrived before his time.

'He's already come,' she said to herself with a little gasp. A heavy dread settled instantly on her spirit. She stood a moment motionless in the passage, the lilac blossoms in her hand. She was listening.

'The gentleman's come, mum,' she heard the servant say, and at the same moment saw her at the top of the kitchen stairs in the hall. 'He went up to his room, mum.'

Miss Speke held out the flowers. With an effort to make her voice sound ordinary she gave an order about them. 'Put them in water, Mary, please. The double vase will do.' She watched the woman take them slowly, oh, so slowly, from her. But her mind was elsewhere. It was still listening. And after the woman had gone down to the kitchen again slowly, oh, so slowly, she stood motionless for some minutes, listening, still intently listening. But no sound broke the quiet of the afternoon. She heard only the blundering noises made by the woman in the kitchen below. On the floor above was—silence.

Miss Speke then turned and went upstairs.

Now, Miss Speke admits frankly that she was 'in a state', meaning thereby, doubtless, that her nerves were tightly strung. Her heart was thumping, her ears and eyes strained to their utmost capacity; her hands, she remembers, felt a little cold, and her legs moved uncertainly. She denies, however, that her 'state', though it may be described as nervous, could have betrayed her into either invention or delusion. What she saw she saw, and nothing can shake her conviction. Colonel Lyle, besides, is there to support her in the main outline, and Colonel Lyle, when first he had entered the room, was certainly not 'in a state', whatever excuses he may have offered later to comfort her. Moreover, to counteract her trepidation, she says that, as she pushed the door wide open—it was already ajar—the original mood of elation met her in the face with its lift of wonder and release. This modified her dread. She declares that joy rushed upon her, and that her 'nerves' were on the instant entirely forgotten.

'What I saw, I saw,' remains her emphatic and unshakable verdict. 'I saw—everything.'

The first thing she saw admitted certainly of no doubt. Colonel Lyle lay huddled up against the further wall, half upon the carpet and half-leaning on the wainscoting. He was unconscious. One arm was stretched towards the mirror, the hand still clutching one of its mahogany feet. And the mirror had been moved. It turned now slightly more towards the room.

The picture, indeed, told its own story, a story Colonel Lyle himself repeated afterwards when he had recovered. He was surprised to find the mirror—his mirror—with its face to the wall; he went forward to put in it its proper position; in doing this he looked into it; he saw something, and—the next thing he knew—Miss Speke was bringing him round.

She explains, further, that her overmastering curiosity to look into the mirror, as Colonel Lyle had evidently looked himself, prevented her from immediately rendering first-aid to that gentleman, as she unquestionably should have done. Instead, she crossed the room, stepped over his huddled form, turned the mirror a little further round towards her, and looked straight into it.

The eye, apparently, takes in a great deal more than the mind is consciously aware of having 'seen' at the moment. Miss Speke saw everything, she claims. But details certainly came back to her later, details she had not been aware of at the time. At the moment, however, her impressions, though extremely vivid, were limited to certain outstanding items. These items were—that her own reflection was not visible, no picture of herself being there; that Mr. Thorley and a boy—she recognised the Pikestaffe lad from the newspaper photographs she had seen—were plainly there, and that books and instruments in great quantity filled all the nearer space, blocking up the foreground. Beyond, behind, stretching in all directions, she affirms, was empty space that produced upon her the effect of the infinite heavens as seen in a clear night sky. This space was prodigious, yet in some way not alarming. It did not terrify; rather it comforted, and, in a sense, uplifted. A diffused soft light pervaded the huge panorama. There were no shadows, there were no high lights.

Curiously enough, however, the absence of any reproduction of herself did not at first strike her as at all out of the way; she noticed the fact, no more than that; it was, perhaps, naturally, the deep shock of seeing Mr. Thorley and the boy that held her absolutely spell-bound, arresting her faculties as though they had been frozen.

Mr. Thorley was moving to and fro, his body bent, his hand thrown forward. He looked as natural as in life. He moved steadily, as with a purpose, now nearer, now further, but his figure always bent as though he were intent upon something in his hands. The boy moved, too, but with a more gentle, less vigorous, motion that suggested floating. He followed the larger figure, keeping close, his face raised from time to time as though his companion spoke to him. The expression that he wore was quiet, peaceful, happy, and intent. He was absorbed in what he was doing at the moment. Then, suddenly, Mr. Thorley straightened himself up. He turned. Miss Speke saw his face for the first time. He looked into her eyes. The face blazed with light. The gaze was straight, and full, and clear. It betrayed recognition. Mr. Thorley smiled at her.

In a very few seconds she was aware of all this, of its main outlines, at any rate. She saw the moving, living figures in the midst of this stupendous and amazing space. The overwhelming surprise it caused her prevented, apparently, the lesser emotion of personal alarm; fear she certainly did not feel at first. It was when Mr. Thorley looked at her with his brilliant eyes and blazing smile that her heart gave its violent jump, missed a beat or two, then began hammering against her ribs like released machinery that has gone beyond control. She was aware of the happy glory in the face, a face that was thin to emaciation, almost transparent, yet wearing an expression that was no longer earthly. Then, as he smiled, he came towards her; he beckoned; he stretched both hands out, while the boy looked up and watched.

Mr. Thorley's advance, however, had two distracting peculiarities—that as he drew nearer he moved not in a straight line, but in a curve. As a skater performing 'edges', though on both feet instead of on one, he swept gracefully and with incredible speed in her direction. The other peculiarity was that with each step nearer his figure grew smaller. It lessened in height. He seemed, indeed, to be moving in two directions at once. He became diminutive.

The sight ought by rights to have paralysed her, yet it produced again, instead of terror, an effect of exhilaration she could not possibly account for. There came once again that fine elation to her mind. Not only did all desire to resist die away almost before it was born, but more, she felt its opposite—an overpowering wish to join him. The tiny hands were still stretched out to greet her, to draw her in, to welcome her; the smile upon the diminutive face, as it came nearer and nearer, was enchanting. She heard his voice then:

'Come, come to us! Here reality is nearer, and there is liberty...!'

The voice was very close and loud as in life, but it was not in front. It was behind her. Against her very ear it sounded in the air behind her back. She moved one foot forward; she raised her arms. She felt herself being sucked in—into that glorious space. There was an indescribable change in her whole being.

The cumulative effect of so many amazing happenings, all of them contrary to nature, should have been destructive to her reason. Their combined shock should have dislocated her system somewhere and have laid her low. But with every individual, it seems, the breaking-point is different. Her system, indeed, was dislocated, and a moment later and she was certainly laid low, yet it was not the effect of the figure, the voice, the gliding approach of Mr. Thorley that produced this. It was the flaw of little human egoism that brought her down. For it was in this instant that she first *realised* the absence of her own reflection in the mirror. The fact, though noticed before, had not entered her consciousness as such. It now definitely did so. The arms she lifted in greeting had no reflected counterpart. Her figure, she realised with a shock of terror, was not there. She dropped, then, like a stricken animal, one outstretched hand clutching the frame of the mirror as she did so.

'Gracious God!' she heard herself scream as she collapsed. She heard, too, the crash of the falling mirror which she overturned and brought down with her.

Whether the noise brought Colonel Lyle round, or whether it was the combined weight of Miss Speke and the handsome piece upon his legs that roused him, is of no consequence. He stirred, opened his eyes, disentangled himself and proceeded, not without astonishment, to render first-aid to the unconscious lady.

The explanations that followed are, equally, of little consequence. His own attack, he considered, was chiefly due to fatigue, to violent indigestion, and to the after-effects of his protracted bankruptcy proceedings. Thus, at any rate, he assured Miss Speke. He added, however, that he had received rather a shock from the handsome piece, for, surprised at finding it turned to the wall, he had replaced it and looked into it, but had not seen himself reflected. This had amazed him a good deal, yet what amazed him still more was that he had seen something moving in the depths of the glass. 'I saw a face, and it was a face I knew. It was Gerald Pikestaffe. Behind him was another figure, the figure of a man, whose face I could not see.' A mist rose before his eyes, his head swam a bit, and he evidently swayed for some unaccountable reason. It was a blow received in falling that stunned him momentarily.

He stood over her, while he fanned her face; her swoon was of brief duration; she recovered quickly; she listened to his story with a quiet mind. The after-effect of too great wonder leaves no room for pettier emotions, and traces of the exhilaration she had experienced were still about her heart and soul.

'Is it smashed?' was the first thing she asked, to which Colonel Lyle made no answer at first, merely pointing to the carpet where the frame of the long mirror lay in broken fragments.

'There was no glass, you see,' he said presently. He, too, was quiet, his manner very earnest; his voice, though subdued as by a hint of awe, betrayed the glow of some intense inner excitement that lit fire in his eyes as well. 'He had cut it out long ago, of course. He used the empty framework, merely.'

'Eh?' said Miss Speke, looking down incredulously, but finding no sign of splinters on the floor.

Her companion smiled. 'We shall find it about somewhere if we look,' he said calmly, which, indeed, proved later true—lying flat beneath the carpet under the bed. 'His measurements and calculations led—probably by chance—towards the mirror'—he seemed speaking to himself more than to his bewildered listener—'perhaps by chance, perhaps by knowledge,' he continued, 'up to the mirror—and then *through* it.' He looked down at Miss Speke and laughed a little. 'So, like Alice, he went through it, too, taking his books and instruments, the boy as well, all with him. The boy, that is, had the knowledge too.'

'I only know one thing,' said Miss Speke, unable to follow

him or find meaning in his words, 'I shall never let these rooms again. I shall lock them up.'

Her companion collected the broken pieces and made a little heap of them.

'And I shall pray for him,' added Miss Speke, as he led her presently downstairs to her own quarters. 'I shall never cease to pray for him as long as I live.'

'He hardly needs that,' murmured Colonel Lyle, but to himself. 'The first terror has long since left him. He's found the new direction—and moved along it.'

# THE EMPTY SLEEVE

## I

The Gilmer brothers were a couple of fussy and pernickety old bachelors of a rather retiring, not to say timid, disposition. There was grey in the pointed beard of John, the elder, and if any hair had remained to William it would also certainly have been of the same shade. They had private means. Their main interest in life was the collection of violins, for which they had the instinctive *flair* of true connoisseurs. Neither John nor William, however, could play a single note. They could only pluck the open strings. The production of tone, so necessary before the purchase, was done vicariously for them by another.

The only objection they had to the big building in which they occupied the roomy top floor was that Morgan, liftman and caretaker, insisted on wearing a billycock with his uniform after six o'clock in the evening, with a result disastrous to the beauty of the universe. For 'Mr. Morgan', as they called him between themselves, had a round and pasty face on the top of a round and conical body. In view, however, of the man's other rare qualities—including his devotion to themselves—this objection was not serious.

He had another peculiarity that amused them. On being found fault with, he explained nothing, but merely repeated the words of the complaint.

'Water in the bath wasn't really hot this morning, Morgan!'

'Water in the bath reely 'ot, wasn't it, sir?'

Or, from William, who was something of a faddist:

'My jar of sour milk came up late yesterday, Morgan.'

'Your jar sour milk come up late, sir, yesterday?'

Since, however, the statement of a complaint invariably

resulted in its remedy, the brothers had learned to look for no further explanation. Next morning the bath *was* hot, the sour milk *was* 'brortup' punctually. The uniform and billycock hat, though, remained an eyesore and source of oppression.

On this particular night John Gilmer, the elder, returning from a Masonic rehearsal, stepped into the lift and found Mr. Morgan with his hand ready on the iron rope.

'Fog's very thick outside,' said Mr. John pleasantly; and the lift was a third of the way up before Morgan had completed his customary repetition: 'Fog very thick outside, yes, sir.' And Mr. Gilmer then asked casually if his brother were alone, and received the reply that Mr. Hyman had called and had not yet gone away.

Now this Mr. Hyman was a Hebrew, and, like themselves, a connoisseur in violins, but, unlike themselves, who only kept their specimens to look at, he was a skilful and exquisite player. He was the only person they ever permitted to handle their pedigree instruments, to take them from the glass cases where they reposed in silent splendour, and to draw the sound out of their wondrous painted hearts of golden varnish. The brothers loathed to see his fingers touch them, yet loved to hear their singing voices in the room, for the latter confirmed their sound judgment as collectors, and made them certain their money had been well spent. Hyman, however, made no attempt to conceal his contempt and hatred for the mere collector. The atmosphere of the room fairly pulsed with these opposing forces of silent emotion when Hyman played and the Gilmers, alternately writhing and admiring, listened. The occasions, however, were not frequent. The Hebrew only came by invitation, and both brothers made a point of being in. It was a very formal proceeding—something of a sacred rite almost.

John Gilmer, therefore, was considerably surprised by the information Morgan had supplied. For one thing, Hyman, he had understood, was away on the Continent.

'Still in there, you say?' he repeated, after a moment's reflection.

'Still in there, Mr. John, sir.' Then, concealing his surprise from the liftman, he fell back upon his usual mild habit of complaining about the billycock hat and the uniform.

'You really should try and remember, Morgan,' he said, though kindly. 'That hat does not go well with that uniform!'

Morgan's pasty countenance betrayed no vestige of expression.

''at don't go well with the yewniform, sir,' he repeated, hanging up the disreputable bowler and replacing it with a gold-braided cap from the peg. 'No, sir, it don't, do it?' he added cryptically, smiling at the transformation thus effected.

And the lift then halted with an abrupt jerk at the top floor. By somebody's carelessness the landing was in darkness, and, to make things worse, Morgan, clumsily pulling the iron rope, happened to knock the billycock from its peg so that his sleeve, as he stooped to catch it, struck the switch and plunged the scene in a moment's complete obscurity.

And it was then, in the act of stepping out before the light was turned on again, that John Gilmer stumbled against something that shot along the landing past the open door. First he thought it must be a child, then a man, then—an animal. Its movement was rapid yet stealthy. Starting backwards instinctively to allow it room to pass, Gilmer collided in the darkness with Morgan, and Morgan incontinently screamed. There was a moment of stupid confusion. The heavy framework of the lift shook a little, as though something had stepped into it and then as quickly jumped out again. A rushing sound followed that resembled footsteps, yet at the same time was more like gliding—someone in soft slippers or stockinged feet, greatly hurrying. Then came silence again. Morgan sprang to the landing and turned up the electric light. Mr. Gilmer, at the same moment, did likewise to the switch in the lift. Light flooded the scene. Nothing was visible.

'Dog or cat, or something, I suppose, wasn't it?' exclaimed Gilmer, following the man out and looking round with bewildered amazement upon a deserted landing. He knew quite well, even while he spoke, that the words were foolish.

'Dog or cat, yes, sir, or—something,' echoed Morgan, his eyes narrowed to pin-points, then growing large, but his face stolid.

'The light should have been on,' Mr. Gilmer spoke with a touch of severity. The little occurrence had curiously disturbed his equanimity. He felt annoyed, upset, uneasy.

For a perceptible pause the liftman made no reply, and his employer, looking up, saw that, besides being flustered, he was white about the jaws. His voice, when he spoke, was without its normal assurance. This time he did not merely repeat. He explained.

'The light *was* on, sir, when last *I* come up!' he said, with emphasis, obviously speaking the truth. 'Only a moment ago,' he added.

Mr. Gilmer, for some reason, felt disinclined to press for explanations. He decided to ignore the matter.

Then the lift plunged down again into the depths like a diving-bell into water; and John Gilmer, pausing a moment first to reflect, let himself in softly with his latchkey, and, after hanging up hat and coat in the hall, entered the big sitting-room he and his brother shared in common.

The December fog that covered London like a dirty blanket had penetrated, he saw, into the room. The objects in it were half shrouded in the familiar yellowish haze.

## II

In his dressing-gown and slippers, William Gilmer, almost invisible in his armchair by the gas-stove across the room, spoke at once. Through the thick atmosphere his face gleamed, showing an extinguished pipe hanging from his lips. His tone of voice conveyed emotion, an emotion he sought to suppress, of a quality, however, not easy to define.

'Hyman's been here,' he announced abruptly. 'You must have met him. He's this very instant gone out.'

It was quite easy to see that something had happened, for 'scenes' leave disturbance behind them in the atmosphere. But John made no immediate reference to this. He replied that he had seen no one—which was strictly true—and his brother thereupon, sitting bolt upright in the chair, turned quickly and faced him. His skin, in the foggy air, seemed paler than before.

'That's odd,' he said nervously.

'What's odd?' asked John.

'That you didn't see—anything. You ought to have run into one another on the doorstep.' His eyes went peering about the room. He was distinctly ill at ease. 'You're positive you saw no one? Did Morgan take him down before you came? Did Morgan see him?' He asked several questions at once.

'On the contrary, Morgan told me he was still here with you. Hyman probably walked down, and didn't take the lift at all,' he replied. 'That accounts for neither of us seeing him.' He decided to say nothing about the occurrence in the lift, for his brother's nerves, he saw plainly, were on edge.

William then stood up out of his chair, and the skin of his face changed its hue, for whereas a moment ago it was merely pale, it had now altered to a tint that lay somewhere between white and a livid grey. The man was fighting internal terror. For a moment these two brothers of middle age looked each other straight in the eye. Then John spoke:

'What's wrong, Billy?' he asked quietly. 'Something's upset you. What brought Hyman in this way—unexpectedly? I thought he was still in Germany.'

The brothers, affectionate and sympathetic, understood one another perfectly. They had no secrets. Yet for several minutes the younger one made no reply. It seemed difficult to choose his words apparently.

'Hyman played, I suppose—on the fiddles?' John helped him, wondering uneasily what was coming. He did not care much for the individual in question, though his talent was of such great use to them.

The other nodded in the affirmative, then plunged into rapid speech, talking under his breath as though he feared someone might overhear. Glancing over his shoulder down the foggy room, he drew his brother close.

'Hyman came,' he began, 'unexpectedly. He hadn't written, and I hadn't asked him. You hadn't either, I suppose?'

John shook his head.

'When I came in from the dining-room I found him in the passage. The servant was taking away the dishes, and he had let himself in while the front door was ajar. Pretty cool, wans't it?'

'He's an original,' said John, shrugging his shoulders. 'And you welcomed him?' he asked.

'I asked him in, of course. He explained he had something glorious for me to hear. Silenski had played it in the afternoon, and he had bought the music since. But Silenski's "Strad" hadn't the power—it's thin on the upper string, you remember, unequal, patchy—and he said no instrument in the world could do it justice but our "Joseph"—the small Guarnerius, you know, which he swears is the most perfect in the world.'

'And what was it? Did he play it?' asked John, growing more uneasy as he grew more interested. With relief he glanced round and saw the matchless little instrument lying there safe and sound in its glass case near the door.

'He played it—divinely: a Zigeuner Lullaby, a fine, passionate, rushing bit of inspiration, oddly misnamed "lullaby". And fancy, the fellow had memorised it already! He walked about the room on tiptoe while he played it, complaining of the light——'

'Complaining of the light?'

'Said the thing was crepuscular, and needed dusk for its full effect. I turned the lights out one by one, till finally there was only the glow of the gas logs. He insisted. You know that way he has with him? And then he got me in another matter: insisted on using some special strings he had brought with him, and put them on, too, himself—thicker than the A and E *we* use.'

For though neither Gilmer could produce a note, it was their pride that they kept their precious instruments in perfect condition for playing, choosing the exact thickness and quality of strings that suited the temperament of each violin; and the little Guarnerius in question always 'sang' best, they held, with thin strings.

'Infernal insolence,' exclaimed the listening brother, wondering what was coming next. 'Played it well, though, didn't he, this Lullaby thing?' he added, seeing that William hesitated. As he spoke he went nearer, sitting down close beside him in a leather chair.

'Magnificent! Pure fire of genius!' was the reply with enthusiasm, the voice at the same time dropping lower. 'Staccato like a silver hammer; harmonics like flutes, clear, soft, ringing; and the tone—well, the G string was a baritone, and the upper registers creamy and mellow as a boy's voice. John,' he added, 'that Guarnerius is the very pick of the period and'—again he hesitated—'Hyman loves it. He'd give his soul to have it.'

The more John heard, the more uncomfortable it made him. He had always disliked this gifted Hebrew, for in his secret heart he knew that he had always feared and distrusted him. Sometimes he had felt half afraid of him; the man's very forcible personality was too insistent to be pleasant. His type was of the dark and sinister kind, and he possessed a violent will that rarely failed of accomplishing its desire.

'Wish I'd heard the fellow play,' he said at length, ignoring his brother's last remark, and going on to speak of the most matter-of-fact details he could think of. 'Did he use the Dodd bow, or the Tourte? That Dodd I picked up last month, you know, is the most perfectly balanced I have ever——'

He stopped abruptly, for William had suddenly got upon his feet and was standing there, searching the room with his eyes. A chill ran down John's spine as he watched him.

'What is it, Billy?' he asked sharply. 'Hear anything?'

William continued to peer about him through the thick air.

'Oh, nothing, probably,' he said, an odd catch in his voice; 'only——I keep feeling as if there was somebody listening. Do you think, perhaps'—he glanced over his shoulder—'there is someone at the door? I wish—I wish you'd have a look, John.'

John obeyed, though without great eagerness. Crossing the room slowly, he opened the door, then switched on the light. The passage leading past the bathroom towards the bedrooms beyond was empty. The coats hung motionless from their pegs.

'No one, of course,' he said, as he closed the door and came back to the stove. He left the light burning in the passage. It was curious the way both brothers had this impression that they were not alone, though only one of them spoke of it.

'Used the Dodd or the Tourte, Bill—which?' continued John in the most natural voice he could assume.

But at that very same instant the water started to his eyes. His brother, he saw, was close upon the thing he really had to tell. But he had stuck fast.

## III

By a great effort John Gilmer composed himself and remained in his chair. With detailed elaboration he lit a cigarette, staring hard at his brother over the flaring match while he did so. There he sat in his dressing-gown and slippers by the fireplace, eyes downcast, fingers playing idly with the red tassel. The electric light cast heavy shadows across the face. In a flash then, since emotion may sometimes express itself in attitude even better then in speech, the elder brother understood that Billy was about to tell him an unutterable thing.

By instinct he moved over to his side so that the same view of the room confronted him.

'Out with it, old man,' he said, with an effort to be natural. 'Tell me what you saw.'

Billy shuffled slowly round and the two sat side by side, facing the fog-draped chamber.

'It was like this,' he began softly, 'only I was standing instead of sitting, looking over to that door as you and I do now. Hyman moved to and fro in the faint glow of the gas logs against the far wall, playing that "crepuscular" thing in his most inspired sort of way, so that the music seemed to issue from himself rather than from the shining bit of wood under his chin, when—I noticed something coming over me that was'—he hesitated, searching for words—'that wasn't *all* due to the music,' he finished abruptly.

'His personality put a bit of hypnotism on you, eh?'

William shrugged his shoulders.

'The air was thickish with fog and the light was dim, cast upwards upon him from the stove,' he continued. 'I admit all that. But there wasn't light enough to throw shadows, you see, and——

'Hyman looked queer?' the other helped him quickly.

Billy nodded his head without turning.

'Changed there before my very eyes—' he whispered it—'turned animal——'

'Animal?' John felt his hair rising.

'That's the only way I can put it. His face and hands and body turned otherwise than usual. I lost the sound of his feet. When the bow-hand or the fingers on the strings passed in to the light, they were'—he uttered a soft, shuddering little laugh—'furry, oddly divided, the fingers massed together. And he paced stealthily. I thought every instant the fiddle would drop with a crash and he would spring at me across the room.'

'My dear chap——'

'He moved with those big, lithe, striding steps one sees'—John held his breath in the little pause, listening keenly—'one sees those big brutes make in the cages when their desire is aflame for food or escape, or—or fierce passionate desire for anything they want with their whole nature——'

'The big felines!' John whistled softly.

'And every minute getting nearer and nearer to the door, as though he meant to make a sudden rush for it and get out.'

'With the violin! Of course you stopped him?'

'In the end. But for a long time, I swear to you, I found it difficult to know what to do, even to move. I couldn't get my voice for words of any kind; it was like a spell.'

'It *was* a spell,' suggested John firmly.

'Then, as he moved, still playing,' continued the other, 'he seemed to grow smaller; to shrink down below the line of the gas. I thought I should lose sight of him altogether. I turned the light up suddenly. There he was over by the door—crouching.'

'Playing on his knees, you mean?'

William closed his eyes in an effort to visualise it again.

'Crouching,' he repeated, at length, 'close to the floor. At least, I think so. It all happened so quickly, and I felt so bewildered, it was hard to see straight. But at first I could have sworn he was half his natural size. I called to him, I think I swore at him—I forget exactly, but I know he straightened up at once and stood before me down there in the light'—he pointed across the room to the door—'eyes gleaming, face white as chalk, perspiring like midsummer, and gradually filling out, straightening up, whatever you like to call it, to his natural size and appearance again. It was the most horrid thing I've ever seen.'

'As an—animal, you saw him still?'

'No; human again. Only much smaller.'

'What did he say?'

Billy reflected a moment.

'Nothing that I can remember,' he replied. 'You see, it was all over in a few seconds. In the full light, I felt so foolish, and nonplussed at first. To see him normal again baffled me. And, before I could collect myself, he had let himself out into the passage, and I heard the front door slam. A minute later—the same second almost, it seemed—you came in. I only remember grabbing the violin and getting it back safely under the glass case. The strings were still vibrating.'

The account was over. John asked no further questions. Nor did he say a single word about the lift, Morgan, or the extinguished light on the landing. There fell a longish silence between the two men; and then, while they helped themselves to a generous supply of whisky-and-soda before going to bed, John looked up and spoke:

'If you agree, Billy,' he said quietly, 'I think I might write and suggest to Hyman that we shall no longer have need for his services.'

And Billy, acquiescing, added a sentence that expressed something of the singular dread lying but half-concealed in the atmosphere of the room, if not in their minds as well:

'Putting it, however, in a way that need not offend him.'

'Of course. There's no need to be rude, is there?'

Accordingly, next morning the letter was written; and John, saying nothing to his brother, took it round himself by hand to the Hebrew's rooms near Euston. The answer he dreaded was forthcoming:

'Mr. Hyman's still away abroad,' he was told. 'But we're forwarding letters; yes. Or I can give you 'is address if you'll prefer it.' The letter went, therefore, to the number in Königstrasse, Munich, thus obtained.

Then, on his way back from the insurance company where he went to increase the sum that protected the small Guarnerius from loss by fire, accident, or theft, John Gilmer called at the offices of certain musical agents and ascertained that Silenski, the violinist, was performing at the time in Munich. It was only some days later, though, by diligent inquiry, he made certain that at a concert on a certain date the famous virtuoso had played a Zigeuner Lullaby of his own composition—the very date, it turned out, on which he himself had been to the Masonic rehearsal at Mark Masons' Hall.

John, however, said nothing of these discoveries to his brother William.

## IV

It was about a week later when a reply to the letter came from Munich—a letter couched in somewhat offensive terms, though it contained neither words nor phrases that could actually be found fault with. Isidore Hyman was hurt and angry. On his rerurn to London a month or so later, he proposed to call and talk the matter over. The offensive part of the letter, lay, perhaps, in his definite assumption that he could persuade the brothers to resume the old relations. John, however, wrote a brief reply to the effect that they had decided to buy no new fiddles; their collection being complete, there would be no occasion for them to invite his services as a performer. This was final. No answer came, and the matter seemed to drop. Never for one moment, though, did it leave the consciousness of John Gilmer. Hyman had said that he would come, and come assuredly he would. He secretly gave Morgan instructions that he and his brother for the future were always 'out' when the Hebrew presented himself.

'He must have gone back to Germany, you see, almost at once after his visit here that night,' observed William—John however, making no reply.

One night towards the middle of January the two brothers came home together from a concert in Queen's Hall, and sat up later than usual in their sitting-room discussing over their whisky and tobacco the merits of the pieces and performers. It must have been past one o'clock when they turned out the lights in the passage and retired to bed. The air was still and frosty; moonlight over the roofs—one of those sharp and dry winter nights that now seem to visit London rarely.

'Like the old-fashioned days when we were boys,' remarked William, pausing a moment by the passage window and looking out across the miles of silvery, sparkling roofs.

'Yes,' added John; 'the ponds freezing hard in the fields, rime on the nursery windows, and the sound of a horse's hoofs coming down the road in the distance, eh?' They smiled at the memory, then said good night, and separated. Their rooms were at opposite ends of the corridor; in between were the bathroom, dining-room, and sitting-room. It was a long, straggling flat. Half an hour later both brothers were sound alseep, the flat silent, only a dull murmur rising from the great city outside, and the moon sinking slowly to the level of the chimneys,

Perhaps two hours passed, perhaps three, when John Gilmer, sitting up in bed with a start, wide-awake and frightened, knew that someone was moving about in one of the three rooms that lay between him and his brother. He had absolutely no idea why he should have been frightened, for there was no dream or nightmare-memory that he brought over from unconsciousness, and yet he realised plainly that the fear he felt was by no means a foolish and unreasoning fear. It had a cause and a reason.

Also—which made it worse—it was fully warranted. Something in his sleep, forgotten in the instant of waking, had happened that set every nerve in his body on the watch. He was positive only of two things—first, that it was the entrance of this person, moving so quietly there in the flat, that sent chills down his spine; and, secondly, that this person was *not* his brother William.

John Gilmer was a timid man. The sight of a burglar, his eyes black-masked, suddenly confronting him in the passage, would most likely have deprived him of all power of decision—until the burglar had either shot him or escaped. But on this occasion some instinct told him that it was no burglar, and that the acute distress he experienced was not due to any message of ordinary physical fear. The thing that had gained access to his flat while he slept had first come—he felt sure of it—into his room, and had passed very close to his own bed, before going on. It had then doubtless gone to his brother's room, visiting them both stealthily to make sure they slept. And its mere passage through his room had been enough to wake him and set these drops of cold perspiration upon his skin. For it was—he felt it in every fibre of his body—something hostile.

The thought that it might at that very moment be in the room of his brother, however, brought him to his feet on the cold floor and set him moving with all the determination he could summon towards the door. He looked cautiously down an utterly dark passage; then crept on tiptoe along it. On the wall were old-fashioned weapons that had belonged to his father; and feeling a curved, sheathless sword that had come from some Turkish campaign of years gone by, his fingers closed tightly round it, and lifted it silently from the three hooks whereon it lay. He passed the doors of the bathroom and dining-room, making instinctively for the big sitting-room where the violins were kept in their glass cases. The cold nipped him. His eyes smarted with the effort to see in the darkness. Outside the closed door he hesitated.

Putting his ear to the crack, he listened. From within came a faint sound of someone moving. The same instant there rose the sharp, delicate 'ping' of a violin-string being plucked; and John Gilmer, with nerves that shook like the vibrations of that very string, opened the door wide with a fling and turned on the light at the same moment. The plucked string still echoed faintly in the air.

The sensation that met him on the threshold was the well-known one that things had been going on in the room which his unexpected arrival had that instant put a stop to. A second earlier and he would have discovered it all in the act. The atmosphere still held the feeling of rushing, silent movement with which the things had raced back to their normal, motionless positions. The immobility of the furniture was a mere attitude hurriedly assumed, and the moment his back was turned the whole business, whatever it might be, would begin again. With this presentment of the room—however—a purely imaginative one—came another, swiftly on its heels.

For one of the objects, less swift than the rest, had not quite regained its 'attitude' of repose. It still moved. Below the window curtains on the right, not far from the shelf that bore the violins in their glass cases, he made it out, slowly gliding along the floor. Then, even as his eye caught it, it came to rest.

And, while the cold perspiration broke out all over him afresh, he knew that this still moving item was the cause both of his waking and of his terror. This was the disturbance whose presence he had divined in the flat without actual hearing, and whose passage through his room, while he yet slept, had touched every nerve in his body as with ice. Clutching his Turkish sword tightly, he drew back with the utmost caution against the wall and watched, for the singular impression came to him that the movement was not that of a human being crouching, but rather of something that pertained to the animal world. He remembered, flash-like, the movements of reptiles, the stealth of the larger felines, the undulating glide of great snakes. For the moment, however, it did not move, and they faced one another.

The other side of the room was but dimly lighted, and the noise he made clicking up another electric lamp brought the thing flying forward again—towards himself. At such a moment it seemed absurd to think of so small a detail, but he remembered his bare feet, and, genuinely frightened, he leaped upon a chair and swished with his sword through the air about him. From this better point of view, with the increased light to aid him, he then saw two things—first, that the glass case usually covering the Guarnerius violin had been shifted; and, secondly, that the moving object was slowly elongating itself into an upright position. Semi-erect, yet most oddly, too, like a creature on its hind legs, it was coming swiftly towards him. It was making for the door—and escape.

The confusion of ghostly fear was somehow upon him so that he was too bewildered to see clearly, but he had sufficient control it seemed, to recover a certain power of action; for the moment the advancing figure was near enough for him to strike, that curved scimitar flashed and whirred about him, with such misdirected violence, however, that he not only failed to strike it even once, but at the same time lost his balance and fell forward from the chair whereon he perched—straight into it.

And then came the most curious thing of all, for as he dropped, the figure also dropped, stooped low down, crouched, dwindled amazingly in size, and rushed past him close to the ground like an animal on all fours. John Gilmer screamed, for he could no longer contain himself. Stumbling over the chair as he turned to follow, cutting and slashing wildly with his sword, he saw half-way down the darkened corridor beyond the scuttling outline of, apparently, an enormous—cat!

The door into the outer landing was somehow ajar, and the next second the beast was out, but not before the steel had fallen with a crashing blow upon the front disappearing leg, almost severing it from the body.

It was dreadful. Turning up the lights as he went, he ran after it to the outer landing. But the thing he followed was already well away, and he heard, on the floor below him, the same oddly gliding, slithering, stealthy sound, yet hurrying, that he heard weeks before when something had passed him in the lift, and Morgan, in his terror, had likewise cried aloud.

For a time he stood there on that dark landing, listening, thinking, trembling; then turned into the flat and shut the door. In the sitting-room he carefully replaced the glass case over the treasured violin, puzzled to the point of foolishness, and strangely routed in his mind. For the violin itself, he saw, had been dragged several inches from its cushioned bed of plush.

Next morning, however, he made no allusion to the occurrence of the night. His brother apparently had not been disturbed.

## V

The only thing that called for explanation—an explanation not fully forthcoming—was the curious aspect of Mr. Morgan's countenance. The fact that this individual gave notice to the owners of the building, and at the end of the month left for a new post, was, of course, known to both brothers; whereas the story he told in explanation of his face was known only to the one who questioned him about it—John. And John, for reasons best known to himself, did not pass it on to the other. Also, for reasons best known to himself, he did not cross-question the liftman about those singular marks, or report the matter to the police.

Mr. Morgan's pasty visage was badly scratched, and there were red lines running from the cheek into the neck that had the appearance of having been produced by sharp points viciously applied—claws. He had been disturbed by a noise in the hall, he said, about three in the morning. A scuffle had ensued in the darkness, but the intruder had got clear away. ...

'A cat, or something of the kind, no doubt,' suggested John Gilmer at the end of the brief recital. And Morgan replied in his usual way: 'A cat, or something of the kind, Mr. John, no doubt.'

All the same, he had not cared to risk a second encounter, but had departed to wear his billycock and uniform in a building less haunted.

Hyman, meanwhile, made no attempt to call and talk over his dismissal. The reason for this was only apparent, however, several months later when, quite by chance, coming along Piccadilly in an omnibus, the brothers found themselves seated opposite to a man with a thick black beard and blue glasses. William Gilmer hastily rang the bell and got out, saying something half intelligible about feeling faint. John followed him.

'Did you see who it was?' he whispered to his brother the moment they were safely on the pavement.

John nodded.

'Hyman, in spectacles. He's grown a beard, too.'

'Yes, but didn't you also notice——'

'What?'

'He had an empty sleeve.'

'An empty sleeve?'

'Yes,' said William; 'he's lost an arm.'

There was a long pause before John spoke. At the door of their club the elder brother added:

'Poor devil! He'll never again play on'—then, suddenly changing the preposition—'*with* a pedigree violin!'

And that night in the flat, after William had gone to bed, he looked up a curious old volume he had once picked up on a secondhand bookstall, and read therein quaint descriptions of how the 'desire-body of a violent man' may assume animal shape, operate on concrete matter even at a distance; and, further, how a wound inflicted thereon can reproduce itself upon its physical counterpart by means of the mysterious so-called phenomenon of 're-percussion.'

'But what seems so odd to me, so horribly pathetic, is that such people don't resist,' said Leidall, suddenly entering the conversation. The intensity of his tone startled everybody; it was so passionate, yet with a beseeching touch that made the women feel uncomfortable a little. 'As a rule, I'm told, they submit willingly, almost as though——'

He hesitated, grew confused, and dropped his glance to the floor; and a smartly dressed woman, eager to be heard, seized the opening. 'Oh, come now,' she laughed; 'one always hears of a man being *put* into a strait waistcoat. I'm sure he doesn't slip it on as if he were going to a dance!' And she looked flippantly at Leidall, whose casual manners she resented. 'People are *put* under restraint. It's not in human nature to accept it—healthy human nature, that is?' But for some reason no one took her question up. 'That is so, I believe, yes,' a polite voice murmured, while the group at tea in the Dover Street Club turned with one accord to Leidall as to one whose interesting sentence still remained unfinished. He had hardly spoken before, and a silent man is ever credited with wisdom.

'As though—you were just saying, Mr. Leidall?' a quiet little man in a dark corner helped him.

'As though, I meant, a man in that condition of mind is not insane—all though,' Leidall continued stammeringly; 'but that some wise portion of him watches the proceeding with gratitude, and welcomes the protection against himself. It seems awfully pathetic. Still,' again hesitating and fumbing in his speech— 'er—it seems queer to me that he should yield quietly to enforced restraint—the waistcoat, handcuffs, and the rest.' He looked round hurriedly, half suspiciously, at the faces in the circle, then dropped his eyes again to the floor. He sighed, leaning back in his chair. 'I cannot understand it,' he added, as no one spoke, but in a very low voice, and almost to himself. 'One would expect them to struggle furiously.'

Someone had mentioned that remarkable book, *The Mind that Found Itself,* and the conversation had slipped into this serious vein. The women did not like it. What kept it alive was the fact that the silent Leidall, with his handsome, melancholy face, had suddenly wakened into speech, and that the little man opposite to him, half invisible in his dark corner, was assistant to one of London's great hypnotic doctors, who could, an' he would, tell interesting and terrible things. No one cared to ask the direct question, but all hoped for revelations, possibly about people they actually knew. It was a very ordinary tea-party indeed. And this little man now spoke, though hardly in the desired vein. He addressed his remarks to Leidall across the disappointed lady.

'I think, probably, your explanation *is* the true one,' he said gently, 'for madness in its commoner forms is merely want of proportion; the mind gets out of right and proper relations with its environment. The majority of madmen are mad on one thing only, while the rest of them is as sane as myself—or you.'

The words fell into the silence. Leidall bowed his agreement, saying no actual word. The ladies fidgeted. Someone made a jocular remark to the effect that most of the world was mad anyhow, and the conversation shifted with relief into a lighter vein—the scandal in the family of a politician. Everybody talked at once. Cigarettes were lit. The corner soon became excited and even uproarious. The tea-party was a great success, and the offended lady, no longer ignored, led all the skirmishes—towards herself. She was in her element. Only Leidall and the little invisible man in the corner took small part in it; and presently, seizing the opportunity when some new arrivals joined the group, Leidall rose to say his adieux, and slipped away, his departure scarcely noticed. Dr. Hancock followed him a minute later. The two men met in the hall; Leidall already had his hat and coat on.

'I'm going West, Mr. Leidall. If that's your way too, and you feel inclined for the walk we might go together.' Leidall turned with a start. His glance took in the other with avidity—a keenly-searching, hungry glance. He hesitated for an imperceptible moment, then made a movement towards him, half inviting, while a curious shadow dropped across his face and vanished. It was both pathetic and terrible. The lips trembled. He seemed to say, 'God bless you; *do* come with me!' But no words were audible.

'It's a pleasant evening for a walk,' added Dr. Hancock gently; 'clean and dry under foot for a change. I'll get my hat and join you in a second.' And there was a hint, the merest flavour of authority in his voice.

That touch of authority was his mistake. Instantly Leidall's hesitation passed. 'I'm sorry,' he said abruptly, 'but I'm afraid I must take a taxi. I have an appointment at the Club and I'm late already.' 'Oh, I see,' the other replied, with a kindly smile; 'then I mustn't keep you. But if you ever have a free evening, won't you look me up, or come and dine? You'll find my telephone number in the book. I should like to talk with you about—those things we mentioned at tea.' Leidall thanked him politely and went out. The memory of the little man's kindly sympathy and understanding eyes went with him.

'Who was that man?' someone asked, the moment Leidall had left the tea-table. 'Surely he's not the Leidall who wrote that awful book some years ago?'

'Yes—the *Gulf of Darkness*. Did you read it?'

They discussed it and its author for five minutes, deciding by a large majority that it was the book of a madman. Silent, rude men like that always had a screw loose somewhere, they agreed. Silence was invariably morbid.

'And did you notice Dr. Hancock? He never took his eyes off him. That's why he followed him out like that. I wonder if *he* thought anything!'

'I know Hancock well,' said the lady of the wounded vanity. 'I'll ask him and find out.' They chattered on, somebody mentioned a *risqué* play, and talk switched into other fields, and in due course the tea-party came to an end.

And Leidall, meanwhile, made his way towards the Park on foot, for he had not taken a taxi after all. The suggestion of the other man, perhaps, had worked upon him. He was very open to suggestion. With hands deep in his overcoat pockets, and head sunk forward between his shoulders, he walked briskly, entering the Park at one of the smaller gates. He made his way across the wet turf, avoiding the paths and people. The February sky was shining in the west; beautiful clouds floated over the houses; they looked like the shore-line of some radiant strand his childhood once had known. He sighed; thought dived and searched within; self-analysis, that old, implacable demon, lifted its voice; introspection took the reins again as usual. There seemed a strain upon the mind he could not dispel. Thought circled poignantly. He knew it was unhealthy, morbid, a sign of these many years of difficulty and stress that had marked him so deeply, but for the life of him he could not escape from the hideous spell that held him. The same old thoughts bored their way into his mind like burning wires, tracing the same unanswerable questions. From this torture, waking or sleeping, there was no escape. Had a companion been with him it might have been different. If, for instance, Dr. Hancock——

He was angry with himself for having refused—furious; it was that vile, false pride his long loneliness had fostered. The man was sympathetic to him, friendly, marvellously understanding; he could have tallked freely with him, and found relief. His intuition had picked out the little doctor as a man in ten thousand. Why had he so curtly declined his gentle invitation? Dr. Hancock *knew*; he guessed his awful secret. But how? In what had he betrayed himself?

The weary self-questioning began again, till he sighed and groaned from sheer exhaustion. He *must* find people, companionship, someone to talk to. The Club—it crossed his tortured mind for a second—was impossible; there was a conspiracy among the members against him. He had left his usual haunts everywhere for the same reason—his restaurants, where he had his lonely meals; his music hall, where he tried sometimes to forget himself; his favourite walks, where the very policemen knew and eyed him. And, coming to the bridge across the Serpentine just then, he paused and leaned over the edge, watching a bubble rise to the surface. 'I suppose there *are* fish in the Serpentine?' he said to a man a few feet away.

They talked a moment—the other was evidently a clerk on his way home—and then the stranger edged off and continued his walk, looking back once or twice at the sad-faced man who had addressed him. 'It's ridiculous, that with all our science we can't live under water as the fish do,' reflected Leidall, and moved on round the other bank of the water, where he watched a flight of duck whirl down from the darkening air and settle with a long, mournful splash beside the bushy island. 'Or that, for all our pride of mechanism in a mechanical age, we cannot really fly.' But these attempts to escape from self were never very successful. Another part of him looked on and mocked. He returned ever to the endless introspection and self-analysis, and in the deepest moment of it—ran into a big, motionless figure that blocked his way. It was the Park policeman, the one who always eyed him. He sheered off suddenly towards the trees, while the man, recognising him, touched his cap respectfully. 'It's a pleasant evening, sir; turned quite mild again.' Leidall mumbled some reply or other, and hurried on to hide himself among the shadows of the trees. The policeman stood and watched him, till the darkness swallowed him. 'He knows too!' groaned the wretched man. And every bench was occupied; every face turned to watch him; there were even figures behind the trees. He dared not go into the street, for the very taxi-drivers were against him. If he gave an address, he would not be driven to it; the man would *know,* and take him elsewhere. And something in his heart, sick with anguish, weary with the endless battle, suddenly yielded.

'There *are* fish in the Serpentine,' he remembered the stranger had said. 'And,' he added to himself, with a wave of delicious comfort, 'they lead secret, hidden lives that no one can disturb.' His mind cleared surprisingly. In the water he could find peace and rest and healing. Good Lord! How easy it all was! Yet he had never thought of it before. He turned sharply to retrace his steps, but in that very second the clouds descended upon his thought again, his mind darkened, he hesitated. Could he get out again when he had had enough? Would he rise to the surface? A battle began over these questions. He ran quickly, then stood still again to think the matter out. Darkness shrouded him. He heard the wind rush laughing through the trees. The picture of the whirring duck flashed back a moment, and he decided that the best way was by air, and not by water. He would *fly* into the place of rest, not sink or merely float; and he remembered the view from his bedroom window, high over old smoky London town, with a drop of eighty feet on to the pavements. Yes, that was the best way. He waited a moment, trying to think it all out clearly, but one moment the fish had it, and the next the birds. It was really impossible to decide. Was there no one who could help him, no one in all this enormous town who was sufficiently on his side to advise him on the point? Some clear-headed, experienced, kindly man?

And the face of Dr. Hancock flashed before his vision. He saw the gentle eyes and sympathetic smile, remembered the soothing voice and the offer of companionship he had refused. Of course, there was one serious drawback: Hancock *knew*. But he was far too tactful, too sweet and good a man to let that influence his judgment, or to betray in any way at all that he did know.

Leidall found it in him to decide. Facing the entire hostile world, he hailed a taxi from the nearest gate upon the street, looked up the address in a chemist's telephone-book, and reached the door in a condition of delight and relief. Yes, Dr. Hancock was at home. Leidall sent his name in. A few minutes later the two men were chatting pleasantly together, almost like old friends, so keen was the little man's intuitive sympathy and tact. Only Hancock, patient listener though he proved himself to be, was uncommonly full of words. Leidall explained the matter very clearly. 'Now, what is your decision, Dr. Hancock? Is it to be the way of the fish or the way of the duck?' And, while Hancock began his answer with slow, well-chosen words, a new idea, better than either, leaped with a flash into his listener's mind. It was an inspiration. For where could he find a better hiding-place from all his troubles than—inside Hancock himself? The man was kindly; he surely would not object. Leidall this time did not hesitate a second. He was tall and broad; Hancock was small; yet he was sure there would be room. He sprang upon him like a wild animal. He felt the warm, thin throat yield and bend between his great hands... then darkness, peace and rest, a nothingness that surely was the oblivion he had so long prayed for. He had accomplished his desire. He had secreted himself for ever from persecution—inside the kindliest little man he had ever met—inside Hancock. ...

He opened his eyes and looked about him into a room he did not know. The walls were soft and dimly coloured. It was very silent. Cushions were everywhere. Peaceful it was, and out of the world. Overhead was a skylight, and one window, opposite the door, was heavily barred. Delicious! No one could get in. He was sitting in a deep comfortable chair. He felt rested and happy. There was a click, and he saw a tiny window in the door drop down, as though worked by a sliding panel. Then the door opened noiselessly, and in came a little man with smiling face and soft brown eyes—Dr. Hancock.

Leidall's first feeling was amazement. 'Then I didn't get into him properly after all! Or I've slipped out again, perhaps! The dear, good fellow!' And he rose to greet him. He put his hand out, and found that the other came with it in some inexplicable fashion. Movement was cramped. 'Ah, then I've had a stroke,' he thought, as Hancock pressed him, ever so gently, back into the big chair. 'Do not get up,' he said soothingly but with authority; 'sit where you are and rest. You must take it very easy for a bit; like all clever men who have overworked——'

'I'll get in the moment he turns,' thought Leidall. 'I did it badly before. It must be through the back of his head, ot course, where the spine runs up into the brain,' and he waited till Hancock should turn. But Hancock never turned. He kept his face towards him all the time, while he chatted, moving gradually nearer to the door. On Leidall's face was the smile of an innocent child, but there lay a hideous cunning behind that smile, and the eyes were terrible.

'Are those bars firm and strong,' asked Leidall, 'so that no one can get in?' He pointed craftily, and the doctor, caught for a second unawares, turned his head. That instant Leidall was upon him with a roar, then sank back powerless into the chair, unable to move his arms more than a few inches in any direction. Hancock stepped up quietly and made him comfortable again with cushions.

And something in Leidall's soul turned round and looked another way. His mind became clear as daylight for a moment. The effort perhaps had caused the sudden change from darkness to great light. A memory rushed over him. 'Good God!' he cried. 'I am violent. I was going do you an injury—you, who are so sweet and good to me!' He trembled dreadfully, and burst into tears. 'For the sake of Heaven,' he implored, looking up, ashamed and keenly penitent, 'put me under restraint. Fasten my hands before I try it again.' He held both hands out willingly, beseechingly, then looked down, following the direction of the other's kind brown eyes. His wrists, he saw, already wore steel handcuffs, and a strait waistcoat was across his chest and arms and shoulders.

## THE LOST VALLEY

### I

Mark and Stephen, twins, were remarkable even of their kind: they were not so much one soul split in twain, as two souls fashioned in precisely the same mould. Their characters were almost identical—tastes, hopes, fears, desires, everything. They even liked the same food, wore the same kind of hats, ties, suits; and, strongest link of all, of course disliked the same things too. At the age of thirty-five neither had married, for they invariably liked the same woman; and when a certain type of girl appeared upon their horizon they talked it over frankly, agreed it was impossible to separate, and together turned their backs upon her for a change of scene before she could endanger their peace.

For their love for one another was unbounded—irresistible as a force of nature, tender beyond words—and their one keen terror was that they might one day be separated.

To look at, even for twins, they were uncommonly alike. Even their eyes were similar: that grey-green of the sea that sometimes changes to blue, and at night becomes charged with shadows. And both faces were of the same strong type with aquiline noses, stern-lipped mouths, and jaws well marked. They possessed imagination, real imagination of the winged kind, and at the same time the fine controlling will without which such a gift is apt to prove a source of weakness. Their emotions, too, were real and living: not the sort that merely tickle the surface of the heart, but the sort that plough.

Both had private means, yet both had studied medicine because it interested them, Mark specialising in diseases of eye and ear, Stephen in mental and nervous cases; and they carried on a select, even a distinguished, practice in the same house in Wimpole Street with their names on the brass plate thus: Dr. Mark Winters, Dr. Stephen Winters.

In the summer of 1900 they went abroad together as usual for the months of July and August. It was their custom to explore successive ranges of mountains, collecting the folklore, and natural history of the region into small volumes, neatly illustrated with Stephen's photographs. And this particular year they chose the Jura, that portion of it, rather, that lies between the Lac de Joux, Baulmes and Fleurier. For, obviously, they could not exhaust a whole range in a single brief holiday. They explored it in sections, year by year. And they invariably chose for their head-quarters quiet, unfashionable places where there was less danger of meeting attractive people who might break in upon the happiness of their profound brotherly devotion—the incalculable, mystical devotion of twins.

'For abroad, you know,' Mark would say, 'people have an insinuating way with them that is often hard to withstand. The chilly English reserve disappears. Acquaintanceship becomes intimacy before one has time to weigh it.'

'Exactly,' Stephen added. 'The conventions that protect one at home suddenly wear thin, don't they? And one becomes soft and open to attack—unexpected attack.'

They looked up and laughed, reading each other's thoughts like trained telepathists. What each meant was the dread that one should, after all, be taken and the other left—by a woman.

'Though at your age, you know, one is almost immune,' Mark observed; while Stephen smiling agreed philosophically——

'Or *ought* to be.'

'*Is*,' quoth Mark decisively. For by common consent Mark played the *rôle* of the elder brother. His character, if anything, was a shade more practical. He was slightly more critical of life, perhaps, Stephen being ever more apt to accept without analysis, even without reflection. But Stephen had that richer heritage of dreams which comes from an imagination loved for its own sake.

## II

In the peasant's chalet, where they had a sitting-room and two bedrooms, they were very comfortable. It stood on the edge of the forests that run along the slopes of Chasseront, on the side of Les Rasses farthest from Ste Croix. Marie Petavel provided them with the simple cooking they liked; and they spent their days walking, climbing, exploring, Mark collecting legend and folklore, Stephen making his natural history studies, with the little maps and surveys he drew so cleverly. Even this was only a division of labour, for each was equally interested in the occupation of the other; and they shared results in the long evenings, when expeditions brought them back in time, smoking on the rickety wooden balcony, comparing notes, shaping chapters, happy as two children. They brought the enthusiasm of boys to all they did, and they enjoyed the days apart almost as much as those they spent together. After separate expeditions each invariably returned with surprises which awakened the other's interest—even amazement.

Thus, the life of the foreign element in the hotels—unpicturesque in the daytime, noisy and overdressed at night—passed them by. The glimpses they caught as they passed these caravanserais, when gaieties were the order of the evening, made them value their peaceful retreat among the skirts of the forest. They brought no evening dress with them, not even 'le smoking'.

'The atmosphere of these huge hotels simply poisons the mountains,' quoth Stephen. 'All that "haunted" feeling goes.'

'Those people,' agreed Mark, with scorn in his eyes, 'would be far happier at Trouville or Dieppe, gambling, flirting, and the rest.'

Feeling, thus, secure from that jealousy which lies so terribly close to the surface of all giant devotions where the entire life depends upon exclusive possession, the brothers regarded with indifference the signs of this gayer world about them. In that throng there was no one who could introduce an element of danger into their lives—no woman, at least, either of them could like would be found *there*!

For this thought must be emphasised, though not exaggerated. Certain incidents in the past, from which only their strength of will had made escape possible, proved the danger to be a real one. (Usually, too, it was some un-English woman: to wit, the Budapest adventure, or the incident in London with the Greek girl who was first Mark's patient and then Stephen's.) Neither of them made definite reference to the danger, though undoubtedly it was present in their minds more or less vividly whenever they came to a new place: this singular dream that one day a woman would carry off one, and leave the other lonely. It was instinctive, probably, just as the dread of the wolf is instinctive in the deer. The curious fact, though natural enough, was that each brother feared for the other and not for himself. Had any one told Mark that some day he would marry, Mark would have shrugged his shoulders with a smile, and replied, 'No; but I'm awfully afraid Stephen may!' And *vice versa*.

## III

Then out of a clear sky the bolt fell—upon Stephen. Catching him utterly unawares it sent him fairly reeling. For Stephen, even more than his brother, possessed that glorious yet fatal gift, common to poets and children, by which out of a few insignificant details the soul builds for itself a whole sweet heaven to dwell in.

It was at the end of their first month, a month of unclouded happiness together. Since their exploration of the Abruzzi, two years before, they had never enjoyed anything so much. And not a soul had come to disturb their privacy. Plans were being mooted for moving their head-quarters some miles farther towards the Val de Travers and the Creux du Van; only the day of departure, indeed, remained to be fixed, when Stephen, coming home from an afternoon of photography alone, saw, with bewildering and arresting suddenness—a Face. And with the effect of a blow full upon the heart it literally struck him.

How such a thing can come upon a strong man, a man of balanced mind, healthy in nerves and spirit, and in a single moment change serenity into a state of feverish and passionate desire for possession, is a mystery that lies too deep for philosophy or science to explain. It turned him dizzy with a sudden and tempestuous delight—a veritable sickness of the soul, wondrous sweet as it was deadly. Rare enough, of course, such instances may be, but that they happen is undeniable.

He was making his way home in the dusk somewhat wearily. The sun had already dipped below the horizon of France behind him. Across the open country that stretched away to the distant mountains of the Rhone Valley, the moonlight climbed with wings of ghostly radiance that fanned their way into the clefts and pinewoods of the Jura all about him. Cool airs of night stirred and whispered; lights twinkled through the openings among the trees, and all was scented like a garden.

He must have strayed considerably from the right trail—path there was none—for instead of striking the mountain road that led straight to his chalet, he suddenly emerged into a pool of electric light that shone round one of the smaller wooden hotels by the borders of the forest. He recognised it at once, because he and his brother always avoided it deliberately. Not so gay or crowded as the larger caravanserais, it was nevertheless full of people of the kind they did not care about. Stephen was a good half-mile out of his way.

When the mind is empty and the body tired it would seem that the system is sensitive to impressions with an acuteness impossible when these are vigorously employed. The face of this girl, framed against the glass of the hotel verandah, rushed out towards him with a sudden invading glory, and took the most complete imaginable possession of this temporary unemployment of his spirit. Before he could think or act, accept or reject, it had lodged itself eternally at the very centre of his being. He stopped, as before an unexpected flash of lightning, caught his breath—and stared.

A little apart from the throng of 'dressy' folk who sat there in the glitter of the electric light, this face of melancholy dark splendour rose close before his eyes, all soft and wondrous as though the beauty of the night—of forest, stars and moon-rise—had dropped down and focussed itself within the compass of a single human countenance. Framed within a corner pane of the big windows, peering sideways into the darkness, the vision of this girl, not twenty feet from where he stood, produced upon him a shock of the most convincing delight he had ever known. It was almost as though he saw some one who had dropped down among all these hotel people from another world. And from another world, in a sense, she undoubtedly, was; for her face held in it nothing that belonged to the European countries he knew. She was of the East. The magic of other suns swept into his soul with the vision; the pageantry of other skies flashed brilliantly and was gone. Torches flamed in recesses of his being hitherto dark.

The incongruous surroundings unquestionably deepened the contrast to her advantage, but what made this first sight of her so extraordinarily arresting was the curious chance that where she sat the glare of the electric light did not touch her. She was in shadow from the shoulders downwards. Only, as she leaned backwards against the window, the face and neck turned slightly, there fell upon her exquisite Eastern features the soft glory of the rising moon. And comely she was in Stephen's eyes as nothing in his life had hitherto seemed comely. Apart from the vulgar throng as an exotic is apart from the weeds that choke its growth, this face seemed to swim towards him along the pathway of the slanting moonbeams. And, with it, came literally herself. Some released projection of his consciousness flew forth to meet her. The sense of nearness took his breath away with the faintness of too great happiness. She was in his arms, and his lips were buried in her scented hair. The sensation was vivid with pain and joy, as an ecstasy. And of the nature of true ecstasy, perhaps, it was: for he stood, it seemed, *outside himself*.

He remained there rivetted in the patch of moonlight at the forest edge, for perhaps a whole minute, perhaps two, before he realised what had happened. Then came a second shock, that was even more conquering than the first, for the girl, he saw, was not only gazing into his very face, she was also rising, as with an incipient gesture of recognition. As though she knew him, the little head bent itself forward gently, gracefully, and the dear eyes positively smiled.

The impetuous yearning that leaped full-fledged into his blood taught him in that instant the spiritual secret that pain and pleasure are fundamentally the same force. His attempt at self-control, made instinctively, was utterly overwhelmed. Something flashed to him from her eyes that melted the very roots of resolve; he staggered backwards, catching at the nearest tree for support, and in so doing left the patch of moonlight and stood concealed from view within the deep shadows behind.

Incredible as it must seem in these days of starved romance, this man of strength and firm character, who had hitherto known of such attacks only vicariously from the description of others, now reeled back against the trunk of a pine-tree, knowing all the sweet faintness of an overpowering love at first sight.

'For that, by God, I'd let myself waste utterly to death! To bring her an instant's happiness I'd suffer torture for a century——!'

For the words, with their clumsy, concentrated passion, were out before he realised what he was saying, what he was doing; but, at once out, he knew how pitifully inadequate they were to express a tithe of what was in him a rising storm. All words dropped away from him; the breath that came and went so quickly clothed no further speech.

With his retreat into the shadows the girl had sat down again, but she still gazed steadily at the place where he had stood. Stephen, who had lost the power of further movement, also stood and stared. The picture, meanwhile, was being traced with hot iron upon plastic deep in his soul of which he had never before divined the existence. And, again, with the magic of this master-yearning, it seemed that he drew her out from that horde of hotel guests till she stood close before his eyes, warm, perfumed, caressing. The delicate, sharp splendour of her face, already dear beyond all else in life, flamed there within actual touch of his lips. He turned giddy with the joy, wonder and mystery of it all. The frontiers of his being melted—then extended to include her.

From the words a lover fights among to describe the face he worships one divines only a little of the picture; these dimly-coloured symbols conceal more beauty than they reveal. And of this dark, young oval face, first seen sideways in the moon-light, with drooping lids over the almond-shaped eyes, soft cloudy hair, all enwrapped with the haunting and penetrating mystery of love, Stephen never attempted to analyse the in-effable secret. He just accepted it with a plunge of utter self-abandonment. He only realised vaguely by way of detail that the little nose, without being Jewish, curved singularly down towards a chin daintily chiselled in firmness; that the mouth held in its lips the invitation of all womankind as expressed in another race, a race alien to his own—an Eastern race; and that something untamed, almost savage, in the face was corrected by the exquisite tenderness of the large dreamy, brown eyes. The mighty revolution of love spread its soft tide into every corner of his being.

Moreover, that gesture of welcome, so utterly unexpected yet so spontaneous (so natural, it seemed to him now!), the smile of recognition that had so deliciously perplexed him, he accepted in the same way. The girl had felt what he had felt, and had betrayed herself even as he had done by a sudden, uncontrollable movement of revelation and delight; and to explain it otherwise by any vulgar standard of worldly wisdom, would be to rob it of all its dear modesty, truth and wonder. She yearned to know him, even as he yearned to know her.

And all this in the little space, as men count time, of two minutes, even less.

How he was able at the moment to restrain all precipitate and impulsive action, Stephen has never properly understood. There was a fight, and it was short, painful and confused. But it ended on a note of triumphant joy—the rapture of happiness to come...

With a great effort he remembers that he found the use of his feet and continued his journey homewards, passing out once more into the moonlight. The girl in the verandah followed his disappearing figure with her turning head; she craned her neck to watch till he disappeared beyond the angle of vision; she even waved her little dark hand.

'I shall be late,' ran the thought sharply through Stephen's mind. It was cold; vivid with keen pain. 'Mark will wonder what in the world has become of me——!'

For, with swift and terrible reaction, the meaning of it all—the possible consequences of The Face—swept over his heart and drowned it in a flood of icy water. In estimating his brotherly love, even the love of the twin, he had never conceived such a thing as this—had never reckoned with the possibility of a force that could make all else in the world seem so trivial. ...

Mark, had he been there, with his more critical attitude to life, might have analysed something of it away. But Mark was not there. And Stephen had—*seen*.

Those mighty strings of life upon which, as upon an instrument, the heart of man lies stretched, had been set powerfully a-quiver. The new vibrations poured and beat through him. Something within him swiftly disintegrated; in its place something else grew marvellously. The Face had established dominion over the secret places of his soul; thenceforward the process was automatic and inevitable.

## IV

Then, spectre-like and cold, the image of his brother rose before his inner vision. The profound brotherly love of the twin confronted him in the path.

He stumbled among the roots and stones, searching for the

means of self-control, but finding them with difficulty. Windows had opened everywhere in his soul; he looked out through them upon a new world, immense and gloriously coloured. Behind him in the shadows, as his vision searched and his heart sang, reared the single thought that hitherto had dominated his life: his love for Mark. It had already grown indisputably dim.

For both passions were genuine and commanding, the one built up through thirty-five years of devotion cemented by ten thousand associations and sacrifices, the other dropping out of heaven upon him with a suddenness simply appalling. And from the very first instant he understood that both could not live. One must die to feed the other...

On the staircase was the perfume of a strange tobacco, and, to his surprise and intense relief, when he entered the chalet he found that his brother for the first time was not alone. A small, dark man stood talking earnestly with him by the open window—the window where Mark had obviously been watching with anxiety for his arrival. Before introducing him to the stranger, Mark at once gave expression to his relief.

'I was beginning to be afraid something had happened to you,' he said quietly enough, but in a way that the other understood. And after a moment's pause, in which he searched Stephen's face keenly, he added, 'but we didn't wait supper as you see, and old Petavel has kept yours all hot and ready for you in the kitchen.'

'I—er—lost my way,' Stephen said quickly, glancing from Mark to the stranger, wondering vaguely who he was. 'I got confused somehow in the dusk——'

Mark, remembering his manners now that his anxiety was set at rest, hastened to introduce him—a Professor in a Russian University, interested in folklore and legend, who had read the book on the Abruzzi and discovered quite by chance that they were neighbours here in the forest. He was staying in a little hotel at Les Rasses, and had ventured to come up and introduce himself. Stephen was far too occupied trying to conceal his new battling emotions to notice that Mark and the stranger seemed on quite familiar terms. He was so fearful lest the perturbations of his own heart should betray him that he had no power to detect anything subtle or unusual in anybody else.

'Professor Samarianz comes originally from Tiflis,' Mark was explaining, 'and has been telling me the most fascinating things about the legends and folklore of the Caucasus. We really must go there another year, Stephen... Mr. Samarianz most kindly has promised me letters to helpful people... He tells me, too, of a charming and exquisite legend of a "Lost Valley" that exists hereabouts, where the spirits of all who die by their own hands, or otherwise suffer violent deaths, find perpetual peace—the peace denied them by all the religions, that is...'

Mark went on talking for some minutes while Stephen took off his knapsack and exchanged a few words with their visitor, who spoke excellent English. He was not quite sure what he said, but hoped he talked quietly and sensibly enough, in spite of the passions that waged war so terrifically in his breast. He noticed, however, that the man's face held an unusual charm, though he could not detect wherein its secret specifically lay. Presently, with excuses of hunger, he went into the kitchen for his supper, hugely relieved to find the opportunity to collect his thoughts a little; and when he returned twenty minutes later he found that his brother was alone. Professor Samarianz had taken his leave. In the room still lingered the perfume of his peculiarly flavoured cigarettes.

Mark, after listening with half an ear to his brother's description of the day, began pouring out his new interest; he was full of the Caucasus, and its folklore, and of the fortunate chance that had brought the stranger their way. The legend of the 'Lost Valley' in the Jura, too, particularly interested him, and he spoke of his astonishment that he had hitherto come across no trace anywhere of the story.

'And fancy,' he exclaimed, after a recital that lasted half-an-hour, 'the man came up from one of those little hotels on the edge of the forest—that noisy one we have always been so careful to avoid. You never know where your luck hides, do you?' he added, with a laugh.

You never do, indeed,' replied Stephen quietly, now wholly master of himself, or, at least, of his voice and eyes.

And, to his secret satisfaction and delight, it was Mark who provided the excuses for staying on in the chalet, instead of moving further down the valley as they had intended. Besides, it would have been unnatural and absurd to leave without investigating so picturesque a legend as the 'Lost Valley'.

'We're uncommonly happy here,' Mark added quietly; 'why not stay on a bit?'

'Why, not, indeed?' answered Stephen, trusting that the fearful inner storm instantly roused again by the prospect did not betray itself.

'You're not very keen, perhaps, old fellow?' suggested Mark gently.

'On the contrary—I am, *very*,' was the reply.

'Good. Then we'll stay.'

The words were spoken after a pause of some seconds. Stephen, who was down at the end of the room sorting his specimens by the lamp, looked up sharply. Mark's face, where he sat on the window-ledge in the dusk, was hardly visible. It must have been something in his voice that had shot into Stephen's heart with a flash of sudden warning.

A sensation of cold passed swiftly over him and was gone. Had he already betrayed himself? Was the subtle, almost telepathic sympathy between the twins developed to such a point that emotions could be thus transferred with the minumum of word or gesture, within the very shades of their silence even? And another thought: Was there something different in Mark too—something in him also that had changed? Or was it merely his own raging, heaving passion, though so sternly repressed, that distorted his judgment and made him imaginative?

What stood so darkly in the room—between them?

A sudden and fearful pain seared him inwardly as he realised, practically, and with cruelly acute comprehension, that one of these two loves in his heart must inevitably die to feed the other; and that it might have to be—Mark. The complete meaning of it came home to him. And at the thought all his deep love of thirty years rose in a tide within him, flooding through the gates of life, seeking to overwhelm and merge in itself all obstacles that threatened to turn it aside. Unshed tears burned behind his eyes. He ached with a degree of actual, physical pain.

After a moment of savage self-control he turned and crossed the room: but before he had covered half the distance that separated him from the window where his brother sat smoking, the rush of burning words—were they to have been of confession, of self reproach, or of renewed devotion?—swept away from him, so that he wholly forgot them. In their place came the ordinary dead phrases of convention. He hardly heard them himself, though his lips uttered them.

'Come along, Mark, old chap,' he said, conscious that his voice trembled, and that another face slipped imperiously in front of the one his eyes looked upon; 'it's time to go to bed. I'm dead tired like yourself.'

'You are right,' Mark replied, looking at him steadily as he turned towards the lamplight. 'Besides, the night air's getting chilly—and we've been sitting in a draught, you know, all along.'

For the first time in their lives the eyes of the two brothers could not quite find each other. Neither gaze hit precisely the middle of the other. It was as though a veil hung down between them and a deliberate act of focus was necessary. They looked one another straight in the face as usual, but with an effort—with momentary difficulty. The room, too, as Mark had said, was cold, and the lamp, exhausted of its oil, was beginning to smell. Both light and heat were going. It was certainly time for bed.

The brothers went out together, arm in arm, and the long shadows of the pines, thrown by the rising moon through the window, fell across the floor like arms that waved. And from the black branches outside, the wind caught up a shower of sighs and dropped them about the roofs and walls as they made their way to their bedrooms on opposite sides of the little corridor.

## V

Four hours later, when the moon was high overhead and the room held but a single big shadow, the door opened softly and in came—Stephen. He was dressed. He crossed the floor stealthily, unfastened the windows, and let himself out upon the balcony. A minute afterwards he had disappeared into the forest beyond the strip of vegetable garden at the back of the chalet.

It was two o'clock in the morning, and no sleep had touched his eyes. For his heart burned, ached, and fought within him, and he felt the need of open spaces and the great forces of the night and mountains. No such battle had he ever known before. He remembered his brother saying years ago, with a laugh half serious, half playful, '...for if ever one of us comes a cropper in love, old fellow, it will be time for the other to—go!' And by 'go' they both understood the ultimate meaning of the word.

Through the glades of forest, sweet-scented by the night, he made his way till he reached the spot where that Face of soft splendour had first blessed his soul with its mysterious glory. There he sat down and, with his back against the very tree that had supported him a few hours ago, he drove his thoughts forward into battle with the whole strength of his will and character behind him. Very quietly, and with all the care, precision and steadiness of mind that he would have brought to bear upon a difficult 'case' at Wimpole Street, he faced the situation and wrestled with it. The emotions during four hours, tossing upon a sleepless bed, had worn themselves out a little. He was, in one sense of the word, calm, master of himself. The facts, with the huge issue that lay in their hands, he saw naked. And, as he thus saw them, he discerned how very, very far he had already travelled down the sweet path that led him towards the girl—and away from his brother.

Details about her, of course, he knew none; whether she was free even; for he only knew that he loved, and that his entire life was already breaking with the yearning to sacrifice itself for that love. That was the naked fact. The problem bludgeoned him. Could he do anything to hold back the flood still rising, to arrest its terrific flow? Could he divert its torrent, and take it, girl and all, to offer upon the altar of that other love—the devotion of the twin for its twin, the mysterious affinity that hitherto had ruled and directed all the currents of his soul?

There was no question of undoing what had already been done. Even if he never saw that face again, or heard the accents of those beloved lips; if he never was to know the magic of touch, the perfume of close thought, or the strange blessedness of telling her his burning message and hearing the murmur of her own—the fact of love was already accomplished between them. That was ineradicable. He had seen. The sensitive plate had received its undying picture.

For this was no foolish passion arising from the mere propinquity that causes so many of the world's misfit marriages. It was a profound and mystical union already accomplished, psychical in the utter sense, inevitable as the marriage of wind and fire. He almost heard his soul laugh as he thought of the revolution effected in an instant of time by the message of a single glance. What had science, or his own special department of science, to say to this tempest of force that invaded him, and swept with its beautiful terrors of wind and lightning the furthest recesses of his being? This whirlwind that so shook him, that so deliciously wounded him, that already made the thought of sacrificing his brother seem sweet—what was there to say to it, or do with it, or think of it?

Nothing, nothing, nothing!... He could only lie in its arms and rest, with that peace, deeper than all else in life, which the mystic knows when he is conscious that the everlasting arms are about him and that his union with the greatest force of the world is accomplished.

Yet Stephen struggled like a lion. His will rose up and opposed itself to the whole invasion... and in the end his will of steel, trained as all men of character train their wills against the difficulties of life, did actually produce a certain, definite result. This result was almost a *tour de force,* perhaps, yet it seemed valid. By its aid Stephen forced himself into a position he felt intuitively was an impossible one, but in which nevertheless he determined, by a deliberate act of almost incredible volition, that he would remain fixed. He decided to conquer his obsession, and to remain true to Mark. ...

The distant ridges of the dim blue Jura were tipped with the splendours of the coming dawn when at length he rose, chilly and exhausted, to retrace his steps to the chalet.

He realised fully the meaning of the resolve he had come to. And the knowledge of it froze something within him into a stiffness that was like the stiffness of death. The pain in his heart battling against the resolution was atrocious. He had estimated, or thought so, at least, the meaning of his sacrifice. As a matter of fact his decision was entirely artificial, of course, and his resolve dictated by a moral code rather than by the living forces that direct life and can alone make its changes permanent. Stephen had in him the stuff of the hero; and, having said that, one has said all that language can say.

On the way home in the cool white dawn, as he crossed the open spaces of meadow where the mist rose and the dew lay like rain, he suddenly thought of her lying dead—dead, that is, as he had thus decided she was to be dead—for him. And instantly, as by a word of command, the entire light went out of the landscape and out of the world. His soul turned wintry, and all the sweetness of his life went bleak. For it was the ancient soul in him that loved, and to deny it was to deny life itself. He had pronounced upon himself a sentence of death by starvation—a lingering and prolonged death accompanied by tortures of the most exquisite description. And along this path he really believed at the moment his little human will could hold him firm.

He made his way through the dew-drenched grass with the elation caused by so vast a sacrifice singing curiously in his blood. The splendour of the mountain sunrise and all the vital freshness of the dawn was in his heart. He was upon the chalet almost before he knew it, and there on the balcony, waiting to receive him, his grey dressing-gown wrapped about his ears in the sharp air, stood—Mark!

And, somehow or other, at the sight, all this false elation passed and dropped. Stephen looked up at him, standing suddenly still there in his tracks, as he might have looked up at his executioner. The picture had restored him most abruptly, with sharpest pain, to reality again.

'Like me, you couldn't sleep, eh?' Mark called softly, so as not to waken the peasants who slept on the ground floor.

'Have *you* been lying awake, too?' Stephen replied.

'All night. I haven't closed an eye.' Then Mark added, as his brother came up the wooden steps towards him, 'I knew you were awake. I felt it. I knew, too—you had gone out.'

A silence passed between them. Both had spoken quietly, naturally, neither expressing surprise.

'Yes,' Stephen said slowly at length; 'we always reflect each other's pain—each other's moods——' He stopped abruptly, leaving the sentence unfinished.

Their eyes met as of old. Stephen knew an instant of quite freezing terror in which he felt that his brother had divined the truth. Then Mark took his arm and led the way indoors on tiptoe.

'Look here, Stevie, old fellow,' he said, with extraordinary tenderness, 'there's no good saying anything, but I know perfectly well that you're unhappy about something; and so, of course, I am unhappy too.' He paused, as though searching for words. Under ordinary circumstances Stephen would have caught his precise thought, but now the tumult of suppressed emotion in him clouded his divining power. He felt his arm clutched in a sudden vice. They drew closer to one another. Neither spoke. Then Mark, low and hurriedly, said—he almost mumbled it—'It's all my fault *really,* all my fault—dear old boy!'

Stephen turned in amazement and stared. What in the world did his brother mean? What was he talking about? Before he could find speech, however, Mark continued, speaking distinctly now, and with evidences of strong emotion in his voice—

'I'll tell you what we'll do,' he exclaimed, with sudden decision; 'we'll go away; we'll leave! We've stayed here a bit too long, perhaps. Eh? What d'you say to that?'

Stephen did not notice how sharply Mark searched his face. At the thought of separation all his mighty resolution dropped like a house of cards. His entire life seemed to melt away and run in a stream of impetuous yearning towards the Face.

But he answered quietly, sustaining his purpose artificially by a force of will that seemed to break and twist his life at the source with extraordinary pain. He could not have endured the strain for more than a few seconds. His voice sounded strange and distant.

'All right; at the end of the week,' he said—the faintness in him was dreadful, filling him with cold—'and that'll give us just three days to make our plans, won't it?'

Mark nodded his head. Both faces were lined and drawn like the faces of old men; only there was no one there to remark upon it—nor upon the fixed sternness that had dropped so suddenly upon their eyes and lips.

Arm in arm they entered the chalet and went to their bedrooms without another word. The sun, as they went, rose close over the tree-tops and dropped its first rays upon the spot where they had just stood.

## VI

They came down in dressing-gowns to a very late breakfast. They were quiet, grave and slightly preoccupied. Neither made the least reference to their meeting at sunrise. New lines had graved themselves upon their faces, identical lines it seemed, drawing the mouth down at the corners with a touch of grimness where hitherto had been merely firmness.

And the eyes of both saw new things, new distances, new terrors. Something, feared till now only as a possibility, had come close, and stood at their elbows for the first time as an actuality. Sleep, in which changes offered to the soul during the day are confirmed and ratified, had established this new element in their personal equation. They had changed—if not towards one another, then towards something else.

But Stephen saw the matter only from his own point of view. For the first time in his memory he seemed to have lost the intuitive sympathy which enabled him to see things from his brother's point of view as well. The change, he felt positive, was in himself, not in Mark.

'He knows—he feels—something in me has altered dreadfully, but he doesn't yet understand what,' his thoughts ran. 'Pray to God he need never know—at least until I have utterly conquered it!'

For he still held with all the native tenacity of his strong will to the course he had so heroically chosen. The degree of self-deception his imagination brought into the contest seemed incredible when his mind looked back upon it all from the calmness of the end. But at the time he genuinely hoped, wished, intended to conquer, even *believed* that he would conquer.

Mark, he noticed, reacted in little ways that curiously betrayed his mental perturbation, and at any other time might have roused his brother's suspicions. He put sugar in Stephen's coffee, for instance; he forgot to bring him a cigarette when he went to the cupboard to get one for himself; he said and did numerous little things that were contrary to his habits, or to the habits of his twin.

In all of which, however, Stephen saw only the brotherly reaction to the change he was conscious of in himself. Nothing happened to convince him that anything in Mark had suffered revolution. With the mystical devotion peculiar to the twin he was too keenly aware of his own falling away to imagine the falling away of the other. He, Stephen, was the guilty one, and he suffered atrociously. Moreover, the pain of his renunciation was heightened by the sense that his ideal love for Mark had undergone a change—that he was making this fatal sacrifice, therefore, for something that perhaps no longer existed. This, however, he did not realise yet as an accomplished fact. Even if it were true, the resolution he had come to, acted by way of hypnotic suggestion to conceal it. At the same time it added enormously to the confusion and perplexity of his mind.

That day for the brothers was practically a *dies non*. They spent what was left of the morning over many aimless and unnecessary little duties, somewhat after the way of women. Although neither referred to the decision to leave at the end of the week, both acted upon it in desultory fashion, almost as though they wished to make a point of proving to one another that it was *not* forgotten—not wholly forgotten, at any rate. They made a brave pretence of collecting various things with a view to ultimate packing. No word was spoken, however, that bore more closely upon it than occasional phrases such as, 'When the time comes to go'—'when we leave'—'better put *that* out, or it will be forgotten, you know.'

The sentences dropped from their mouths alternately at long intervals, the only one deceived being the utterer. It was not unlike the pretence of schoolboys, only more elaborate and infinitely more clumsy and ill-done. Stephen, at any other time, would probably have laughed aloud. Yet the curious thing was that he noticed the pretence only in his own case. Mark, he thought, was genuine, though perhaps not too eager. 'He's agreed to leave, the dear old chap, because he thinks I want it, and not for himself,' he said. And the idea of the small brotherly sacrifice pleased, yet pained him horribly at the same time. For it tended to rehabilitate the old love which stood in the way of the new one.

He began, however, to take less trouble to sort and find his things for packing; he wrote letters, put out photographs to print in the sun, even studied his maps for expeditions, making occasional remarks thereon aloud which Mark did not negative. Presently, he forgot altogether about packing. Mark said nothing. Mark followed his example, however.

During the afternoon both lay down and slept, meeting again for tea at five. It was rare that they found themselves in for tea. Mark to-day made a special little ritual of it; he made it over their own spirit-lamp—almost tenderly, looking after his brother's wants like a woman. And the little meal was hardly over when a boy in hotel livery arrived with a note—an invitation from Professor Samarianz.

'He has looked up a lot of his papers,' observed Mark carelessly as he tossed the note down, 'and suggests my coming in for dinner, so that he can show me everything afterwards without hurry.'

'I should accept,' said Stephen. 'It might be valuable for us if we go to the Caucasus later.'

Mark hesitated a minute or two, telling the boy to wait in the kitchen. 'I think I'll go in *after* dinner instead,' he decided presently. There was a trace of eagerness in his manner which Stephen, however, did not notice.

'Take your note-book and pump the old boy dry,' Stephen added, with a slight laugh. 'I shall go to bed early myself probably.' And Mark, stuffing the note into his pocket, laughed back and consented, to the other's great relief.

It was very late when Mark returned from the visit, but his brother did not hear him come, having taken a draught to ensure sleeping. And next morning Mark was so full of the interesting information he had collected, and would continue to collect, that the question of leaving at the end of the week dropped of its own accord without further ado. Neither of the brothers made the least pretence of packing. Both wished and intended to stay on where they were.

'I shall look up Samarianz again this afternoon,' Mark said casually during the morning, 'and—if you've no objection—I might bring him back to supper. He's the most obliging fellow I've ever met, and crammed with information.'

Stephen, signifying his agreement, took his camera, his specimen-tin and his geological hammer and went out with bread and chocolate in his knapsack for the rest of the afternoon by himself.

## VII

Moreover, he not only set out bravely, but for many hours held true, keeping so rigid a control over his feelings that it seemed literally to cost him blood. All the time, however, a passionate yearning most craftily attacked him, and the very memory he strove to smother rose with a persistence that ridiculed repression. Like snowflakes, whose individual weight is inappreciable but their cumulative burden irresistible, the thoughts of *her* gathered behind his spirit, ready at a given moment to overwhelm; and it was on the way home again in the evening that the temptation came upon him like a tidal wave that made the mere idea of resistance seem utterly absurd.

He remembered wondering with a kind of wild delight whether it could be possible for any human will to withstand such a tempest of pressure as that which took him by the shoulders and literally pushed him out of his course towards the little hotel on the edge of the forest.

It was utterly inconsistent, of course, and he made no pretence of argument or excuse. He hardly knew, indeed, what he expected to see or do; his mind, at least, framed no definite idea. But far within him that deep heart which refused to be stifled cried out for a drop of the living water that was now its very life. And, chiefly, he wanted to *see*. If only he could see her once again—even from a distance—the merest glimpse——! With one more sight of her that should charge his memory to the brim for life he might face the future with more courage perhaps. Ah! that *perhaps*!... For she was drawing him with those million invisible cords of love that persuade a man he is acting of his own volition when actually he is but obeying the inevitable forces that bind the planets and the suns.

And this time there was no hurry; there was a good hour before Mark would expect him home for supper; he could sit among the shadows of the wood, and wait.

In his pocket were the field-glasses, and he realised with a sudden secret shame that it was not by accident that they were there. He stumbled, even before he got within a quarter of a mile of the place, for the idea that perhaps he would see her again made him ridiculously happy, and like a schoolboy he positively trembled, tripping over roots and misjudging the distance of his steps. It was all part of a great whirling dream in which his soul sang and shouted the first delirious nonsense that came into his head. The possibility of his eyes again meeting hers produced a sensation of triumph and exultation that only one word describes—intoxication.

As he approached the opening in the trees whence the hotel was so easily visible, he went more slowly, moving even on tiptoe. It was instinctive; for he was nearing a place made holy by his love. Picking his way almost stealthily, he found the very tree; then leaned against it while his eyes searched eagerly for a sign of her in the glass verandah. The swiftness and accuracy of sight at such a time may be cause for wonder, but it is beyond question that in less than a single second he knew that the throng of moving figures did not contain the one he sought. She was not among them.

And he was just preparing to make himself comfortable for an extended watch when a sound or movement, perhaps both, somewhere among the trees on his right attracted his attention. There was a faint rustling; a twig snapped.

Stephen turned sharply. Under a big spruce, not half-a-dozen yards away, something moved—then rose up. At first, owing to the gloom, he took it for an animal of some kind, but the same second saw that it was a human figure. It was *two* human figures, standing close together. Then one moved apart from the other; he saw the outline of a man against a space of sky between the trees. And a voice spoke—a voice charged with great tenderness yet driven by high passion——

'But it's nothing, nothing! I shall not be gone two minutes. And to save you an instant's discomfort you know that I would run the whole circle of the earth! Wait here for me——!'

That was all; but the voice and figure caused Stephen's heart to stop beating as though it had been suddenly plunged into ice, for they were the voice and the figure of his brother Mark.

Quickly running down the slope towards the hotel, Mark disappeared.

The other figure, leaning against the tree, was the figure of a girl; and Stephen, even in that first instant of fearful bewilderment, understood why it was that the face of the man Samarianz had so charmed him. For this, of course, was his daughter. And then the whole thing flashed mercilessly clear upon his inner vision, and he knew that Mark, too, had been swept from his feet, and was undergoing the same fierce tortures, and fighting the same dread battle, as himself. ....

There seemed to be no conscious act of recognition. The fire that flamed through him and set his frozen heart so fearfully beating again, hammering against his ribs, left him apparently without volition or any power of cerebral action at all. *She* stood there, not half-a-dozen yards away from where he sat all huddled upon the ground, stood there in all her beauty, her mystery, her wonder, near enough for him to have taken her almost with a single leap into his arms;—stood there, veiled a little by the shadows of the dusk—waiting for the return of—Mark!

He remembers what happened with the blurred indistinctness common to moments of overwhelming passion. For in the next few seconds, that mocked all scale of time, he lived through a series of concentrated emotions that burned his brain too vividly for precise recollection. He rose to his feet unsteadily, his hand upon the rough bark of the tree. Absurd details only seem to remain of these few moments: that a foot was 'asleep' with pins and needles up to the knee, and that his slouch hat fell from his head, filling him with fury because it hid her from him for the fraction of a second. These odd details he remembers.

And then, as though the driving-power of the universe had deliberately pushed him from behind, he was advancing slowly, with short, broken steps, towards the tree where the girl stood with her back half turned against him.

He did not know her name, had never heard her voice, had

never even stood close enough to 'feel' her atmosphere; yet, so deeply had his love and imagination already prepared the little paths of intimacy within him, that he felt he was moving towards some one whom he had known ever since he could remember, and who belonged to him as utterly as if from the beginning of time his possession of her had been absolute. Had they shared together a whole series of previous lives, the sensation could not have been more convincing and complete.

And out of all this whirlwind and tumult two small actions, he remembers, were delivered: a confused cry that was no definite word came from his lips, and—he opened his arms to take her to his heart. Whereupon, of course, she turned with a quick start, and became for the first time aware of his near presence.

'Oh, oh! But how so softly quick you return!' she cried falteringly, looking into his eyes with a smile both of welcome and alarm. 'You a little frightened me, I tell you.'

It was just the voice he had known would come, with the curiously slow, dragging tone of its broken English, the words lingering against the lips as if loath to leave, the soft warmth of their sound in the throat like a caress. The next instant he held her smothered in his arms, his face buried in the scented hair about her neck.

There was an unbelievable time of forgetfulness in which touch, perfume, and a healing power that emanated from her blessed the depths of his soul with a peace that calmed all pain, stilled all tumult—a moment in which Time itself for once stopped its remorseless journey, and the very processes of life stood still to watch. Then there was a frightened cry, and she had pushed him from her. She stood there, her soft eyes puzzled and surprised, looking hard at him; panting a little, her breast heaving.

And Stephen understood then, if he had not already understood before. The gesture of recognition in the hotel verandah two days ago, and this glorious realisation of it that now seemed to have happened a century ago, shared a common origin. They were intended for another, and on both occasions the girl had taken him for his brother Mark.

And, turning sharply, almost falling with the abruptness of it all, as the girl's lips uttered that sudden cry, he saw close beside them the very person for whom they were intended. Mark had come up the slope behind them unobserved, carrying upon his arm the little red cloak he had been to fetch.

It was as though a wind of ice had struck him in the face. The revulsion of feeling with which Stephen saw the return of his brother passed rapidly into a state of numbness where all emotion whatsoever ebbed like the tides of death. He lost momentarily the power of realisation. He forgot who he was, what he was doing there. He was dazed by the fact that Mark had so completely forestalled him. His life shook and tottered upon its foundations...

Then the face and figure of his brother swayed before his eyes like the branch of a tree, as an attack of passing dizziness seized him. It may have been a mere hazard that led his fingers to close, moist and clammy, upon the geological hammer at his belt. Certainly, he let it go again almost at once. ... And, when the tide of emotion returned upon him with the dreadful momentum it had gathered during the interval, the possibility of his yielding to wild impulse and doing something mad or criminal, was obviated by the swift enactment of an exceedingly poignant little drama that made both brothers forget themselves in their desire to save the girl.

In sweetest bewilderment, like a frightened little child or animal, the girl looked from one brother to the other. Her eyes shone in the dusk. Strangely appealing her loveliness was in that moment of seeking some explanation of the double vision. She made a movement first towards Mark—turned halfway in her steps, and ran, startled, upon Stephen—then, with a sharp scream of fear, dropped in a heap to the ground midway between the two.

Her indecision of half-a-second, however, seemed to Stephen to have lasted many minutes. Had she fallen finally into the arms of his brother, he felt nothing on earth could have prevented his leaping upon him with the hands of a murderer. As it was—mercifully—the singular beauty of her little Eastern face, touched as it was by the white terror of her soul, momentarily arrested all other feeling in him. A shudder of fearful admiration passed through him as he saw her sway and fall. Thus might have dropped some soft angel from the skies. …

It was Mark, however, with his usual decision, who brought some possibility of focus back to his mind; and he did it with an action and a sentence so utterly unexpected, so incongruous amid this whirlwind of passion, that had he seen it on the stage or read it in a novel, he must surely have burst out laughing. For, in that very second after the dear form swayed and fell, while the eyes of the brothers met across her in one swift look that held the possibilities of the direst results, Mark, his face abruptly clearing to calmness, stooped down beside the prostrate girl, and, looking up at Stephen steadily, said in a gentle voice, but with his most deliberate professional manner—

'Stephen, old fellow, this is—*my* patient. One of us, perhaps, had better—go.'

He bent down to loosen the dress at the throat and chafe the cold hands, and Stephen, uncertain exactly what he did, and trembling like a child, turned and disappeared among the thick trees in the direction of their little house. For he understood only one thing clearly in that awful moment: that he must either kill—or not see. And his will, well-nigh breaking beneath the pressure, was just able to take the latter course.

'*Go!*' it said peremptorily.

And the little word sounded through the depths of his soul like the tolling of a last bell.

## VIII

'*This is my patient!*' The dreadful comedy of the phrase, the grim mockery of the professional manner, the contrast between the words that some one *ought* to have uttered and the words Mark actually *had* uttered—all this had the effect of restoring Stephen to some measure of sanity. No one but his brother, he felt, could have said the thing so exactly calculated to relieve the choking passion of the situation. It was an inspiration—yet horrible in its bizarre mingling of true and false.

'But it's all like a thing in a dream,' he heard an inner voice murmur as he stumbled homewards without once looking back; 'the kind of thing people say and do in the rooms of strange sleep-houses. We are all surely in a dream, and presently I shall wake up——!'

The voice continued talking, but he did not listen. A web of confusion began to spin itself about his thoughts, and there stole over him an odd sensation of remoteness from the actual things of life. It was surely one of those vivid, haunting dreams he sometimes had when his spirit seemed to take part in real scenes, with real people only far, far away, and on quite another scale of time and values.

'I shall find myself in my bed at Wimpole Street!' he exclaimed. He even tried to escape from the pain closing about him like a vice—tried to escape by waking up, only to find, of course, that the effort drove him more closely to the reality of his position.

Yet the texture of a dream certainly ran through the whole thing; the outlandish proportions of dream-events showed themselves everywhere; the tiny causes and prodigious effects: the terrific power of the Face upon his soul; the uncanny semi-quenching of his love for Mark; the ridiculous way he had come upon these two in the forest, with the nightmare discovery that they had known one another for days; and then the sight of that dear, magical face dropping through the dusky forest air between the two of them. Moreover—just when the dream ought to have ended with his sudden awakening, it had taken this abrupt and inconsequent turn, and Mark had uttered the language of—well, the impossible and rather horrible language of the nightmare world——

'*This is my patient. ...*'

Moreover, his face of ice as he said it; yet, at the same time, the wisdom, the gentleness of the decision that lay behind the words: the desire to relieve an impossibly painful situation. And then—the other words, meant kindly, even meant nobly, but charged for all that with the naked cruelty of life—

*'One of us, perhaps, had better—go.'*

And he had gone—fortunately, he had gone. .....

Yet an hour later, after lying motionless upon his bed seeking with all his power for a course of action his will could follow and his mind approve, it was no dream-voice that called softly to him through the keyhole—

'Stevie, old fellow ... she is well ... she is all right now. She leaves in the morning with her father... the first thing... very early. ...'

And then, after a pause in which Stephen said nothing lest he should at the same time say all—

'...and it is best, perhaps...we should not see one another ...you and I...for a bit. Let us go our ways...till to-morrow night. Then we shall be...alone together again... you and I...as of old. ...'

The voice of Mark did not tremble; but it sounded far away and unreal, almost like wind in the keyhole, thin, reedy, sighing; oddly broken and interrupted.

'...I'm yours Stevie, old fellow, always yours,' it added far down the corridor, more like the voice of dream again than ever.

But, though he made no reply at the moment, Stephen welcomed and approved both the proposal and the spirit in which it was made; and next day, soon after sunrise, he left the chalet very quietly and went off alone into the mountains with his thoughts, and with the pain that all night long had simply been eating him alive.

## IX

It is impossible to know precisely what he felt all that morning in the mountains. His emotions charged like wild bulls to and fro. He seemed conscious only of two master-feelings: first that his life now belonged beyond possibility of change or control—to another; yet, secondly, that his will, tried and tempered weapon of steel that it was, held firm.

Thus his powerful feelings flung him from one wall of his dreadful prison to another without possible means of escape. For his position involved a fundamental contradiction: the new love owned him, yet his will cried, 'I love Mark; I hold true to that; in the end I shall conquer!' He refused, that is, to capitulate, or rather to acknowledge that he had capitulated. And meanwhile, even while he cried, his inmost soul listened, watched, and laughed, well content to abide the issue.

But if his feelings were in too great commotion for clear analysis, his thoughts, on the other hand, were painfully definite—some of them, at least; and, as the physical exercise lessens the assaults of emotion, these stood forth in sharp relief against the confusion of his inner world. It was now clear as the day, for instance, that Mark had been through a battle similar to his own. The chance meeting with the Professor had led to the acquaintance with his daughter. Then, swiftly and inevitably, just as it would have happened to Stephen in his place, love had accomplished its full magic. And Mark had been afraid to tell him. The twins had travelled the same path, only personal feeling having clouded their usual intuition, neither had divined the truth.

Stephen saw it now with pitiless clarity: his brother's frequent visits to the hotel, omitting to mention that the notes of invitation probably also included himself; the desire, nay, the intention to stay on; the delay in packing—and a dozen other details stood out clearly. He remembered, too, with a pang how Mark had not slept that memorable night; he recalled their enigmatical conversation on the balcony as the sun rose... and all the rest of the miserable puzzle.

And, as he realised from his own torments what Mark must also have suffered—be suffering now—he was conscious of a strengthening of his will to conquer. The thought linked him fiercely again to his twin; for nothing in their lives had yet been separate, and the chain of their spiritual intimacy was of incalculably vast strength. They would win—win back to one another's side again. Mark would conquer her. He, Stephen, would also in the end conquer... her... !

But with the thought of her lying thus dead to him, and his life cold and empty without her, came the inevitable revulsion of feeling. It was the anarchy of love. The Face, the perfume, the rushing power of her melancholy dear eyes, with their singular touch of proud languor—in a word, all the amazing magic that had swept himself and Mark from their feet, tore back upon him with such an invasion of entreaty and command, that he sat down upon the very rock where he was and buried his face in his hands, literally groaning with the pain of it. For the thought lacerated within. To give her up was a sheer impossibility;... to give up his brother was equally inconceivable. The weight of thirty-five years' love and associations thus gave battle against the telling blow of a single moment. Behind the first lay all that life had built into the woof of his personality hitherto, but *beyond* the second lay the potent magic, the huge seductive invitation of what he might become in the future—with her.

The contest, in the nature of the forces engaged, was an unequal one. Yet all that morning as he wandered aimlessly over ridge and summit, and across the high Jura pastures above the forests, meeting no single human being, he fought with himself as only men with innate energy of soul know how to fight—bitterly, savagely, blindly. He did not stop to realise that he was somewhat in the position of a fly that strives to push from its appointed course the planet on which it rides through space. For the tides of life itself bore him upon their crest, and at thirty-five these tides are at the full.

Thus, gradually it was, then, as the hopelessness of the struggle became more and more apparent, that the door of the only alternative opened slightly and let him peer through. Once ajar, however, it seemed the same second wide open: he was through; and it was closed—behind him.

For a different nature the alternative might have taken a different form. As has been seen, he was too strong a man to drift merely; a definite way out that could commend itself to a man of action had to be found; and, though the raw material of heroism may have been in him, he made no claim to a martyrdom that should last as long as life itself. And this alternative dawned upon him now as the grey light of a last morning must dawn upon the condemned prisoner: given Stephen, and given this particular problem, it was the only way out.

He envisaged it thus suddenly with a kind of ultimate calmness and determination that was characteristic of the man. And in every way it *was* characteristic of the man, for it involved the precise combination of courage and cowardice, weakness and strength, selfishness and sacrifice, that expressed the true resultant of all the forces at work in his soul. To him, at the moment of his rapid decision, however, it seemed that the dominant motive was the sacrifice to be offered upon the altar of his love for Mark. The twisted notion possessed him that in this way he might atone in some measure for the waning of his brotherly devotion. His love for the girl, her possible love for him—both were to be sacrificed to obtain the happiness—the eventual happiness—of these other two. Long ago Mark had himself said that under such circumstances one or other of them would have to—*go*. And the decision Stephen had come to was that the one to 'go' was—himself.

This day among the woods and mountains should be his last on earth. By the evening of the following day Mark should be free.

'I'll give my life for him.'

His face was grey set as he said it. He stood on the high ridge, bathed by sun and wind. He looked over the fair world of wooded vales and mountains at his feet, but his eyes, turned inwards, saw only his brother—and that sweet Eastern face—then darkness.

'He will understand—and perforce accept it—and with time, yes, with time, the new happiness shall fill his soul utterly—and hers. It is for her, too, that I give it. It *must*—under these unparalleled circumstances be right ... !'

And although there was no single cloud in the sky, the landscape at his feet suddenly went dark and sunless from one horizon to the other.

## X

Then, having come into the gloom of this terrible decision, his imaginative nature at once bounded to the opposite extreme, and a kind of exaltation possessed him. The stereotyped verdict of a coroner's jury might in this instance have been true. The prolonged stress of emotion under which he had so long been labouring had at last produced a condition of mind that could only be considered—unsound.

A cool wind swept his face as he let his tired eyes wander over the leagues of silent forest below. The blue Jura with its myriad folded valleys lay about him like waves of a giant sea ready to swallow up the little atom of his life within its deep heart of forgetfulness. Clear away into France he saw on the one side where, beyond the fortress of Pontarlier, white clouds sailed the horizon before a westerly wind; and, on the other, towards the white-robed Alps rising mistily through the haze of the autumn sunshine. Between these extreme distances lay all that world of a hundred intricate valleys, curiously winding, deeply wooded, little inhabited, a region of soft, confusing loveliness where a traveller might well lose himself for days together before he discovered a way out of so vast a maze.

And, as he gazed, there passed across his mind, like the dim memory of something heard in childhood, that legend of the 'Lost Valley' in which the souls of the unhappy dead find the deep peace that is denied to them by all the religions—and to which hundreds, who have not yet the sad right of entry, seek to find the mournful forest gates. The memory was vivid, but swiftly engulfed by others and forgotten. They chased each other in rapid succession across his mind, as clouds at sunset pass before a high wind, merging on the horizon in a common mass.

Then, slowly, at length, he turned and made his way down the mountain-side in the direction of the French frontier for a last journey upon the sweet surface of the world he loved. In his soul was the one dominant feeling: this singular exaltation arising from the knowledge that in the long run his great sacrifice must ensure the happiness of the two beings he loved more than all else in life.

At the solitary farm where an hour later he had his lunch of bread and cheese and milk, he learned that he had wandered many miles out of the routes with which he was more or less familiar. He had been walking faster than he knew all these hours of battle. A physical weariness came upon him that made him conscious of every muscle in his body as he realised what a long road over mountain and valley he had to retrace. But, with the heaviness of fatigue, ran still the sense of interior spiritual exaltation. Something in him walked on air with springs of steel—something that was independent of the dragging limbs and the aching back. For the rest, his sensation seemed numb. His great Decision stood black before him, blocking the way. Thoughts and feelings forsook him as rats leave a sinking ship. The time for these was past. Two overmastering desires, however, clung fast: one, to see Mark again, and be with him; the other, to be once more—with her. These two desires left no room for others. With the former, indeed, it was almost as though Mark had called aloud to him by name.

He stood a moment where the depth of the valley he had to thread lay like a twisting shadow at his feet; it ran, soft and dim, through the slanting sunshine. From the whole surface of the woods rose a single murmur; like the whirring of voices heard in a dream, he thought. The individual purring of separate trees was merged. Peace, most ancient and profound, lay in it, and its hushed whisper soothed his spirit.

He hurried his pace a little. The cool wind that had swept his face on the heights earlier in the afternoon followed him down, urging him forwards with deliberate pressure, as though a thousand soft hands were laid upon his back. And there were spirits in the wind that day. He heard their voices; and far below he traced by the motion of the tree-tops, where they coiled upwards to him through miles of forest. His way, meanwhile, dived down through dense growths of spruce and pine into a region unfamiliar. There was an aspect of the scenery that almost suggested it was unknown—an undiscovered corner of the world. The countless signs that mark the passage of humanity were absent, or at least did not obtrude themselves upon him. Something remote from life, alien, at any rate, to the normal life he had hitherto known, began to steal gently over his burdened soul. ...

In this way, perhaps, the effect of his dreadful Decision already showed its influence upon his mind and senses. So very soon now he would be—*going*!

The sadness of autumn lay all about him, and the loneliness of this secluded vale spoke to him of the melancholy of things that die—of vanished springs, of summers unfulfilled, of things for ever incomplete and unsatisfying. Human effort, he felt, this valley had never known. No hoofs had ever pressed the mossy turf of these forest clearings; no traffic of peasants or woodsmen won echoes from these limestone cliffs. All was hushed, lonely, deserted.

And yet——? The depths to which it apparently plunged astonished him more and more. Nowhere more than a half-mile across, each turn of the shadowy trail revealed new distances below. With spots of a haunting, fairy loveliness too: for here and there, on isolated patches of lawn-like grass, stood wild lilac bushes, rounded by the wind; willows from the swampy banks of the stream waved pale hands; firs, dark and erect, guarded their eternal secrets on the heights. In one little opening, standing all by itself, he found a lime-tree; while beyond it, shining among the pines, was a group of shimmering beeches. And, although there was no wild life, there were flowers; he saw clumps of them—tall, graceful, blue flowers whose name he did not know, nodding in dream across the foaming water of the little torrent.

And his thoughts ran incessantly to Mark. Never before had he been conscious of so imperious a desire to see him, to hear his voice, to stand at his side. At moments it almost obliterated that other great desire. ... Again he increased his pace. And the path plunged more and more deeply into the heart of the mountains, sinking ever into deeper silence, ever into an atmosphere of deeper peace. For no sound could reach him here without first passing along great distances that were cushioned with soft wind, and padded, as it were, with a million feathery pine-tops. A sense of peace that was beyond reach of all possible disturbance began to cover his breaking life with a garment as of softest shadows. Never before had he experienced anything approaching the wonder and completeness of it. It was a peace, still as the depths of the sea which are motionless because they *cannot* move—cannot even tremble. It was a peace unchangeable —what some have called, perhaps, the Peace of God. ...

'Soon the turn *must* come,' he thought, yet without a trace of impatience or alarm, 'and the road wind upwards again to cross the last ridge!' But he cared little enough; for this enveloping peace drowned him, hiding even the fear of death.

And still the road sank downwards into the sleep-laden atmosphere of the crowding trees, and with it his thoughts, oddly enough, sank deeper and deeper into dim recesses of his own being. As though a secret sympathy lay between the path that dived and the thoughts that plunged. Only, from time to time, the thought of his brother Mark brought him back to the surface with a violent rush. Dreadfully, in those moments, he wanted him—to feel his warm, strong hand within his own—to ask his forgiveness—perhaps, too, to grant his own... he hardly knew.

'But is there no end to this delicious valley?' he wondered, with something between vagueness and confusion in his mind. 'Does it never stop, and the path climb again to the mountains beyond?' Drowsily, divorced from any positive interest, the question passed through his thoughts. Underfoot the grass already grew thickly enough to muffle the sound of his footsteps. The trail even had vanished, swallowed by moss. His feet sank in.

'I wish Mark were with me now—to see and feel all this——'

He stopped short and looked keenly about him for a moment, leaving the thought incomplete. A deep sighing, instantly caught by the wind and merged in the soughing of the trees, had sounded close beside him. Was it perhaps himself that sighed—unconsciously? His heart was surely charged enough!...

A faint smile played over his lips—instantly frozen, however, as another sigh, more distinct than the first, and quite obviously external to himself, passed him closely in the darkening air. More like deep breathing, though, it was, than sighing. ... It was nothing but the wind, of course. Stephen hurried on again, not surprised that he had been so easily deceived, for this valley was full of sighings and breathings—of trees and wind. It ventured upon no louder noise. Noise of any kind, indeed, seemed impossible and forbidden in this muted vale. And so deeply had he descended now, that the sunshine, silver rather than golden, already streamed past far over his head along the ridges, and no gleam found its way to where he was. The shadows, too, no longer blue and purple, had changed to black, as though woven of some delicate substance that had definite thickness, like a veil. Across the opposite slope, one of the mountain summits in the western sky already dropped its monstrous shadow fringed with pines. The day was rapidly drawing in.

## XI

And here, very gradually, there began to dawn upon his overwrought mind certain curious things. They pierced clean though the mingled gloom and exaltation that characterised his mood. And they made the skin upon his back a little to—stir and crawl.

For he now became distinctly aware that the emptiness of this lonely valley was only apparent. It is impossible to say through what sense, or combination of senses, this singular certainty was brought to him that the valley was not really as forsaken and deserted as it seemed—that, on the contrary, it was the very reverse. It came to him suddenly—as a certainty. The valley as a matter of fact was—full. Packed, thronged and crowded it was to the very brim of its mighty wooded walls—with life. It was now borne in upon him, with an inner conviction that left no room for doubt, that on all sides living things—persons—were jostling him, rubbing elbows, watching all his movements, and only waiting till the darkness came to reveal themselves.

Moreover, with this eerie discovery came also the further knowledge that a vast multitude of others, again, with pallid faces and yearning eyes, with arms outstretched and groping feet, were searching everywhere for the way of entrance that he himself had found so easily. All about him, he felt, were people by the hundred, by the thousand, seeking with a kind of restless fever for the narrow trail that led down into the valley, longing with an intensity that beat upon his soul in a million waves, for the rest, the calm silence of the place—but most of all for its strange, deep, and unalterable peace.

He, alone of all these, had found the Entrance; he, *and one other.*

For out of his singular conviction grew another even more singular: his brother Mark was also somewhere in this valley with him. Mark, too, was wandering like himself in and out among its intricate dim turns. He had said but a short time ago, 'I wish Mark were here!' Mark *was* here. And it was precisely then—while he stood still a moment, trying to face these overwhelming obsessions and deal with them—that the figure of a man, moving swiftly through the trees, passed him with a great gliding stride, and with averted face. Stephen started horribly, catching his breath. In an instant the man was gone again, swallowed up by the crowding pines.

With a quick movement of pursuit and a cry that should make the man turn, he sprang forward—but stopped again almost the same moment, realising that the extraordinary speed at which the man had shot past him rendered pursuit out of the question. He had been going downhill into the valley; by this time he was already far, far ahead. But in that momentary glimpse of him he had seen enough to know. The face was turned away, and the shadows under the trees were heavy, but the figure was beyond question the figure of—his brother Mark.

It was his brother, yet not his brother. It was Mark—but Mark altered. And the alteration was in some way—awful; just as the silent speed at which he had moved—the impossible speed in so dense a forest—was likewise awful. Then, still shaking inwardly with the suddenness of it all, Stephen realised that when he called aloud he had uttered certain definite words. And these words now came back to him—

'Mark. Mark! Don't go yet! Don't go—without me!'

Before, however, he could act, a most curious and unaccountable sensation of deadly faintness and pain came upon him, without cause, without explanation, so that he dropped backwards in momentary collapse, and but for the closeness of the tree stems would have fallen full length to the ground. From the centre of the heart it came, spreading thence throughout his whole being like a swift and dreadful fever. All the muscles of his body relaxed; icy perspiration burst forth upon his skin; the pulses of life seemed suddenly reduced to the threshold beyond which they stop. There was a thick, rushing sound in his ears and his mind went utterly blank.

These were the sensations of death by suffocation. He knew this as certainly as though another doctor stood by his side and labelled each spasm, explained each successive sinking of the vital flame. He was passing through the last throes of a dying man. And then into his mind, thus deliberately left blank, rushed at lightning speed a whole series of the pictures of his past life. Even while his breath failed, he saw his thirty-five years pictorially, successively, yet in some queer fashion *at once*, pass through the lighted chambers of his brain. In this way, it is said, they pass through the brain of a drowning man during the last second before death.

Childhood rose about him with its scenes, figures, voices; the

Kentish lawns where he had played with Mark in stained overalls, the summer-house where they had tea, the hay-fields where they romped. The scent of lime and walnut, of garden pinks and roses by the tumbled rockery came back to his nostrils... He heard the voices of grown-ups in the distance... faint barking of dogs... the carriage wheels upon the gravel drive... and then the sharp summons from the opened window—'Time to come in now! Time to come in!' ...

*Time to come in now*. It all drove before him as of yesterday on the scented winds of childhood's summer days... He heard his brother's voice—dreadfully faint and far away—calling him by name in the shrill accents of the boy: 'Stevie—I say, you *might* shut up... and play properly...

And then followed the panorama of the thirty years, all the chief events drawn in steel-like lines of white and black, vivid in sunshine, alive—right down to the present moment with the portentous dark shadow of his terrible Decision closing the series like a cloud.

Yes, like a smothering black cloud that blocked the way. There was nothing visible beyond it. There, for him, life ceased——

Only, as he gazed with inward-turned eyes that could not close even if they would, he saw to his amazement that the black cloud suddenly opened, and into a space of clear light there swam the vision, radiant as morning, of that dark young Eastern face—the face that held for him all the beauty in the world. The eyes instantly found his own, and smiled. Behind her, moreover, and beyond, before the moving vapours closed upon it, he saw a long vista of brilliance, crowded with pictures he could but half discern—as though, in spite of himself and his Decision, life continued—as though, too, it *continued with her*.

And instantly, with the sight and thought of her, the consuming faintness passed; strength returned to his body with the glow of life; the pain went; the pictures vanished; the cloud was no more. In his blood the pulses of life once again beat strong, and the blackness left his soul. The smile of those beloved eyes had been charged with the invitation to live. Although his determination remained unshaken, there shone behind it the joy of this potent magic: life with her...

With a strong effort, at length he recovered himself and continued on his way. More or less familiar, of course, with the psychology of vision, he dimly understood that his experiences had been in some measure subjective—within himself. To find the line of demarcation, however, was beyond him. That Mark had wandered out to fight his own battle upon the mountains, and so come into this same valley, was well within the bounds of coincidence. But the nameless and dreadful alteration discerned in that swift moment of his passing—that remained inexplicable. Only he no longer thought about it. The glory of that sweet vision had bewildered him beyond any possibility of reason or analysis.

His watch told him that the hour was past five o'clock—ten minutes past, to be exact. He still had several hours before reaching the country he was familiar with nearer home. Following the trail at an increased pace, he presently saw patches of meadow glimmering between the thinning trees, and knew that the bottom of the valley was at last in sight.

'And Mark, God bless him, is down there too—somewhere!' he exclaimed aloud. 'I shall surely find him.' For, strange to say, nothing could have persuaded him that his twin was not wandering among the shadows of this peaceful and haunted valley with himself, and—that he would shortly find him.

## XII

And a few minutes later he passed from the forest as through an open door and found himself before a farmhouse standing in a patch of bright green meadow against the mountain-side. He was in need both of food and information.

The chalet, less lumbering and picturesque than those found in the Alps, had, nevertheless, the appearance of being exceedingly ancient. It was not toy-like—as the Jura chalets sometimes are.

Solidly built, its balcony and overhanging roof supported by immense beams of deeply stained wood, it stood so that the back walls merged into the mountain slope behind, and the arms of pine, spruce and fir seemed stretched out to include it among their shadows. A last ray of sunshine, dipping between two far summits overhead, touched it with pale gold, bringing out the rich beauty of the heavily-dyed beams. Though no one was visible at the moment, and no smoke rose from the shingled chimney, it had the appearance of being occupied, and Stephen approached it with the caution due to the first evidence of humanity he had come across since he entered the valley.

Under the shadow of the broad balcony roof he noticed that the door, like that of a stable, was in two parts, and, wondering rather to find it closed, he knocked firmly upon the upper half. Under the pressure of a second knock this upper half yielded slightly, though without opening. The lower half, however, evidently barred and bolted, remained unmoved.

The third time he knocked with more force than he intended, and the knock sounded loud and clamorous as a summons. From within, as though great spaces stretched beyond, came a murmur of voices, faint and muffled, and then almost immediately—the footsteps of some one coming softly up to open.

But, instead of the heavy brown door opening, there came a voice. He heard it, petrified with amazement. For it was a voice he knew—hushed, soft, lingering. His heart, hammering atrociously, seemed to leave its place, and cut his breath away.

'Stephen!' it murmured, calling him by name, 'what are *you* doing here so soon? And what is it that you want?'

The knowledge that only this dark door separated him from her, at first bereft him of all power of speech or movement; and the possible significance of her words escaped him. Through the sweet confusion that turned his spirit faint he only remembered, flash-like, that she and her father were indeed to have left the hotel that very morning. After that his thought stopped dead.

Then, also flash-like, swept back upon him the memory of the figure that had passed him with averted face—and, with it, the clear conviction that at this moment Mark, too, was somewhere in this very valley, even close beside him. More: Mark was in this chalet—with her.

The torrent of speech that instantly crowded to his lips was almost too thick for utterance.

'Open, open, open!' was all he heard intelligibly from the throng of words that poured out. He raised his hands to push and force; but her reply again stopped him.

'Even if I open—you may not enter yet,' came the whisper through the door. And this time he could almost have sworn that it sounded within himself rather than without.

'I must enter,' he cried. 'Open to me, I say!'

'But you are trembling——'

'Open to me, O my life! Open to me!'

'But your heart—it is shaking.'

'Because you—you are so near,' came in passionate, stammering tones. 'Because you stand there beside me!' And then, before she could answer, or his will control the words, he had added: 'And because Mark—my brother—is in there—with you——'

'Hush, hush!' came the soft, astonishing reply. 'He is in here, true; but he is not with me. And it is for my sake that he has come—for my sake and for yours. My soul, alas! has led him to the gates...'

But Stephen's emotions had reached the breaking-point, and the necessity for action was upon him like a storm. He drew back a pace so as to fling himself better against the closed door, when to his utter surprise, it moved. The upper half swung slowly outwards, and he—saw.

He was aware of a vast room, with closely shuttered windows, that seemed to stretch beyond the walls into the wooded mountainside, thronged with moving figures, like forms of life gently gliding to and fro in some huge darkened tank; and there, framed against this opening—the girl herself. She stood, visible to the waist, radiant in the solitary beam of sunshine that reached the chalet, smiling down wondrously into his face with the same exquisite beauty in her eyes that he had seen before in the vision of the cloud: with, too, that supreme invitation in them—the invitation to live.

The loveliness blinded him. He could see the down upon her little dark cheeks where the sunlight kissed them; there was the cloud of hair upon her neck where his lips had lain; there, too, the dear, slight breast that not twenty-four hours ago had known the pressure of his arms. And, once again, driven forward by the love that triumphed over all obstacles, real or artificial, he advanced headlong with outstretched arms to take her.

'Katýa!' he cried, never thinking how passing strange it was that he knew her name at all, much more the endearing and shortened form of it. 'Katýa!'

But the young girl held up her little brown hand against him with a gesture that was more strong to restrain than any number of bolted doors.

'Not here,' she murmured, with her grave smile, while behind the words he caught in that darkened room the alternate hush and sighing as of a thousand sleepers. 'Not here! You cannot see him now; for these are the Reception Halls of Death and here I stand in the Vestibule of the Beyond. Our way... your way and mine... lies farther yet... traced there since the beginning of the world... together...'

In quaintly broken English it was spoken, but his mind remembers the singular words in their more perfect form. Even this, however, came later. At the moment he only felt the twofold wave of love surge through him with a tide of power that threatened to break him asunder: he *must* hold her to his heart; he *must* come instantly to his brother's side, meet his eyes, have speech with him. The desire to enter that great darkened room and force a path through the dimly gliding forms to his brother became irresistible, while tearing upon its heels came like a fever of joy the meaning of the words she had just uttered, and especially of that last word: '*Together!*'

Then, for an instant, all the forces in his being turned negative so that his will refused to act. The excess of feeling numbed him.

A flying interval of knowledge, calm and certain, came to him. The exaltation of spirit which produced the picture of all this spiritual clairvoyance moved a stage higher, and he realised that he witnessed an order of things pertaining to the world of eternal causes rather than of temporary effects. Some one had lifted the Veil.

With a feeling that he could only wait and let things take their extraordinary course, he stood still. For an instant, even less, he must have hidden his eyes in his hand, for when, a moment later, he again looked up, he saw that the half of the swinging door which had been open, was now closed. He stood alone upon the balcony. And the sunshine had faded entirely from the scene.

It was here, it seems, that the last vestige of self-control disappeared. He flung himself against the door; and the door met his assault like a wall of solid rock. Crying aloud alternately the names of his two loved ones, he turned, scarcely knowing what he did, and ran into the meadow. Dusk was about the chalet, drawing the encircling forests closer. Soon the true darkness would stalk down the slopes. The walls of the valley reached, it seemed, up to heaven.

Still calling, he ran about the walls, searching wildly for a way of entrance, his mind charged with bewildering fragments of what he had heard: 'The Reception Halls of Death'—'The Vestibule of the Beyond'—'You cannot see him now'—'Our way lies farther—*and together*!'

And, on the far side of the chalet, by the corner that touched the trees, he suddenly stopped, feeling his gaze drawn upwards, and there, pressed close against the window-pane of an upper room, saw that some one was peering down upon him.

With a sensation of freezing terror he realised that he was staring straight into the eyes of his brother Mark. Bent a little forward with the effort to look down, the face, pale and motionless, gazed into his own, but without the least sign of recognition. Not a feature moved: and although but a few feet separated the brothers, the face wore the dim, misty appearance of great distance. It was like the face of a man called suddenly from deep sleep—dazed, perplexed; nay, more—frightened and horribly distraught.

What Stephen read upon it, however, in that first moment of sight, was the signature of the great, eternal question men have asked since the beginning of time, yet never heard the answer. And into the heart of the twin the pain of it plunged like a sword.

'Mark!' he stammered, in that low voice the valley seemed to exact; 'Mark! Is that really *you*?' Tears swam already in his eyes, and yearning in a flood choked his utterance.

And Mark, with a dreadful, steady stare that still held no touch of recognition, gazed down upon him from the closed window of that upper chamber, motionless, unblinking as an image of stone. It was almost like an imitation figure of himself—only with the effect of some added alteration. For alteration certainly there was—awful and unknown alteration—though Stephen was utterly unable to detect wherein it lay. And he remembered how the figure had passed him in the woods with averted face.

He made then, it seems, some violent sign or other, in response to which his brother at last moved—slowly opening the window. He leaned forward, stooping with lowered head and shoulders over the sill, while Stephen ran up against the wall beneath and craned up towards him. The two faces drew close; their eyes met clean and straight. Then the lips of Mark moved, and the distraught look half vanished within the borders of a little smile of puzzled and affectionate wonder.

'Stevie, old fellow,' issued a tiny, far-away voice; 'but where are you? I see you—so dimly!'

It was like a voice crying faintly down half-a-mile of distance. He shuddered to hear it.

'I'm here, Mark—close to you,' he whispered.

'I hear your voice, I feel your presence,' came the reply like a man talking in his sleep, 'but I see you—as through a glass darkly. And I want to see you all clear, and close——'

'But *you*! Where are *you*?' interrupted Stephen, with anguish.

'Alone; quite alone—over here. And it's cold, oh, so cold! The words came gently, half veiling a complaint. The wind caught them and ran round the walls towards the forest, wailing as it went.

'But how did you come, how did you come?' Stephen raised himself on tiptoe to catch the answer. But there was no answer. The face receded a little, and as it did so the wind, passing up the walls again, stirred the hair on the forehead. Stephen saw it move. He thought, too, the head moved with it, shaking slightly to and fro.

'Oh, but tell me, my dear, dear brother! Tell me——!' he cried, sweating horribly, his limbs shaking.

Mark made a curious gesture, withdrawing at the same time a little farther into the room behind, so that he now stood upright, half shadow by the window. The alteration in him proclaimed itself more plainly, though still without betraying its exact nature. There was something about him that was terrible. And the air that came from the open window upon Stephen was so freezing that it seemed to turn the perspiration on his face into ice.

'I do not know; I do not remember,' he heard the tiny voice inside the room, ever withdrawing. 'Besides—I may not speak with you—yet; it is so difficult—and it hurts.'

Stephen stretched out his body, the arms scraping the wooden walls above his head, trying to climb the smooth and slippery surface.

'For the love of God!' he cried with passion, 'tell me what it all means and what you are doing here—you and—and—oh, and *all three of us*?' The words rang out through the silent valley.

But the other stood there motionless again by the window, his face distraught and dazed as though the effort of speech had already been too much for him. His image had begun to fade a little. He seemed, without moving, yet to be retreating into some sort of interior distance. Presently, it seemed, he would disappear altogether.

'I don't know,' came the voice at length, fainter than before, half muffled. 'I have been asleep, I think. I have just waked up, and come across from somewhere else—where we were all together, you and I and—and——'

Like his brother, he was unable to speak the name. He ended the sentence a moment later in a whisper that was only just audible. 'But I cannot tell you *how* I came,' he said, 'for I do not know the words.'

Stephen, then, with a violent leap tried to reach the window-sill and pull himself up. The distance was too great, however, and he fell back upon the grass, only just keeping his feet.

'I'm coming in to you,' he cried out very loud. 'Wait there for me! For the love of heaven, wait till I come to you. I'll break the doors in——!

Once again Mark made that singular gesture; again he seemed to recede a little farther into a kind of veiled perspective that caused his appearance to fade still more; and, from an incredible distance—a distance that somehow conveyed an idea of appalling height—his thin, tiny voice floated down upon his brother from the fading lips of shadow.

'Old fellow, don't you come! You are not ready—and it is too cold here. I shall wait, Stevie, I shall wait for you. Later—I mean farther from here—we shall one day all three be together. ... Only you cannot understand now. I am here for your sake, old fellow, and for hers. She loves us both, but... it is... you ... she loves... the best...'

The whispering voice rose suddenly on these last words into a long high cry that the wind instantly caught away and buried far in the smothering silences of the woods. For, at the same moment, Mark had come with a swift rush back to the window, had leaned out and stretched both hands towards his brother underneath. And his face had cleared and smiled. Caught within that smile, the awful change in him had vanished.

Stephen turned and made a mad rush round the chalet to find the door he would batter in with his hands and feet and body. He searched in vain, however, for in the shadows the supporting beams of the building were indistinguishable from the stems of the trees behind; the roof sank away, blotted out by the gloom of the branches, and the darkness now wove forest, sky and mountain into a uniform black sheet against which no item was separately visible.

There was no chalet any longer. He was simply battering with bruised hands and feet upon the solid trunks of pines and spruces in his path; which he continued to do, calling ever aloud for Mark, until finally he grew dizzy with exhaustion and fell to the ground in a state of semi-consciousness.

And for the best part of half-an-hour he lay there motionless upon the moss, while the vast hands of Night drew the cloak of her softest darkness over valley and mountain, covering his small body with as much care as she covered the sky, the hemisphere, and all those leagues of velvet forest.

## XIII

It was long before he came to himself again—shivering with cold, for the perspiration had dried upon him where he lay. He got up and ran. The night was now fairly down, and the keen air stung his cheeks. But, with a sure instinct not to be denied, he took the direction of home.

He travelled at an extraordinary pace, considering the thickness of the trees and the darkness. How he got out of the valley he does not remember; nor how he found his way over the intervening ridges that lay between him and the country he knew. At the back of his mind crashed and tumbled the loose fragments of all he had seen and heard, forming as yet no coherent pattern. For himself, indeed, the details were of small interest. He was a man under sentence of death. His determination, in spite of everything, remained unshaken. In a few short hours he would be gone.

Yet, with the habit of the professional mind, he tried a little to sort out things. During that state of singular exaltation, for instance, he understood vaguely that his deep longings had somehow translated themselves into act and scene. For these longings were life; his decision negatived them; hence, they dramatised themselves pictorially with what vividness his imagination allowed.

They were dramatised inventions, singularly elaborate, of the emotions that burned so fiercely within. All were projections of his consciousness, maimed and incomplete, masquerading as persons before his inner vision. It began with the singular sensations of death by drowning he had experienced. From that moment the other forces at work in the problem had taken their cue and played their part more or less convincingly, according to their strength...

He thought and argued a great deal as he hurried homewards through the night. But all the time he knew that it was untrue. He had no real explanation at al!

From the high ridges, cold and bleak under the stars, swept by the free wind of night, he ran almost the entire way. It was downhill. And during that violet descent of nearly an hour the details of his 'going' shaped themselves. Until then he had formed no definite plans. Now he settled everything. He chose the very pool where the water coiled and bubbled as in a cauldron just where the little torrent made a turn above their house; he decided upon the very terms of the letter he would leave behind. He would put it on the kitchen table so that they should know where to find him.

He urged his pace tremendously, for the idea that his brother would have left—that he would find him gone—haunted him. It grew, doubtless, out of that singular, detailed vision that had come upon him in his great weakness in the valley. He was terrified that he would not see his brother again—that he had already gone deliberately—after her...

'I *must* see Mark once more. I *must* get home before he leaves!' flashed the strong thought continually in his mind, making him run like a deer down the winding trail.

It was after ten o'clock when he reached the little clearing behind the chalet, panting with exhaustion, blinded with perspiration. There was no light visible; all the windows were dark; but presently he made out a figure moving to and fro below the balcony. It was *not* Mark—he saw that in a flash. It moved oddly. A sound of moaning reached him at the same time. And then he saw that it was the figure of the peasant woman who cooked for them, Marie Petavel.

And the instant he saw who it was, and heard her moaning, he knew what had happened. Mark had left a letter to explain—and gone: gone after the girl. His heart sank into death.

The woman came forward heavily through the darkness, the dew-drenched grass swishing audibly against her skirts. And the words he heard were precisely what he had expected to hear, though patois and excitement rendered them difficult—

'Your brother—oh, your poor brother, Monsieur le Docteur—he—has gone!'

And then he saw the piece of white paper glimmering in her hands as she stood quite close. He took it mechanically from her. It was the letter Mark had left behind to explain.

But before Stephen had time to read it, a man with a lantern came out of the barn that stood behind the house. It was her husband. He came slowly towards them.

'We searched for you, oh, we searched,' he said in a thick voice, 'my son went as far as Buttes even, and hasn't come back yet. You've been long, too long away——'

He stopped short and glanced down at his wife, telling her roughly to cease her stupid weeping. Stephen, shaking inwardly, with an icy terror in his blood, began to feel that things were not precisely as he had anticipated. Something else was the matter. The expression in the face of the peasant as the lantern's glare fell upon it came to him suddenly with the shock of a revelation.

'You have told monsieur—all?' the man whispered, stooping to his wife. She shook her head; and her husband led the way without another word. The interval of a few seconds seemed endless to Stephen; he was trembling all over like a man with the ague. Behind them the old woman floundered through the wet grass, moaning to herself.

'No one would have believed it could have happened—anythingof *that* sort,' the man mumbled. The lantern was unsteady in his hand. The next minute the barn, like some monstrous animal, rose against the stars, and the huge wooden doors gaped wide before them.

The peasant, uncovering his head, went first, and Stephen, following with stumbling footsteps, saw the shadows of the beams and posts shift across the boarded floor. Against the wall, whither the man led, was a small littered heap of hay, and upon this, covered by a white sheet, was stretched a human body. The peasant drew back the sheet gently with his heavy brown hand, stooping close over it so that the lantern threw its light full upon the act.

And Stephen, stumbling forward, scarcely knowing what he did, without further warning or preparation, looked down upon the face of his brother Mark. The eyes stared fixedly into nothing; the features wore the distraught expression he had seen upon them a few hours before through the window-pane of that upper chamber.

'We found him in that deep pool just where the stream makes the quick turn above the house,' the peasant whispered. 'He left a bit of paper on the kitchen table to say where he would be. It was after dark when we got there. His watch had stopped though, long before——' He muttered on unintelligibly.

Stephen looked up at the man, unable to utter a word, and the man replied to the unspoken question—

'At ten minutes past five the watch had stopped,' he said. 'That was when the water reached it.'

By the flicker of the lantern, then, sitting beside that still figure covered with the sheet, Stephen read the letter Mark had left for him—

> 'Stevie, old fellow, one of us, you know, has got to—go; and it is better, I think, that it should not be you. I know all you have been through, for I have fought and suffered every step with you. I have been along the same path, loving her too much for you, and you too much for her. And I leave her to you, boy, because I am convinced she now loves you even as she first believed she loved me. But all that

evening she cried incessantly for you. More I cannot explain to you now; she will do that. And she need never know more than that I have withdrawn in your favour: she need never know *how*. Perhaps, one day, when there is no marriage or giving in marriage, we may all three be together, and happy. I have often wondered, as you know...'

The remainder of the sentence was scratched out and illegible.

'...And, if it be possible, old fellow, of course *I shall wait*.'

Then came more words blackened out.

'...I am now going, within a few minutes of writing this last word to you of blessing and forgiveness (for I know you will want that, although there is nothing, *nothing* to forgive!)—going down into that Lost Valley her father told us about—the Valley hidden among these mountains we love—the Lost Valley where even the unhappy dead find peace. There I shall wait for you both.—Mark.'

* * * *

Several weeks later, before he took the train eastwards, Stephen retraced his steps to the farmhouse where he had bought milk and asked for directions. Thence for some distance he followed the path he well remembered. At a point, however, the confusion of the woods grew strangely upon him. The mountains, true to the map, were not true to his recollections. The trail stopped; high, unknown ridges intervened; and no such deep and winding valley as he had travelled that afternoon for so many hours was anywhere to be found. The map, the peasants, the very configuration of the landscape even, denied its existence.